Wise Monkeys

By Rhoda Chaalan

ISBN: 978-0-6450917-0-0 (Hardback)
ISBN: 978-0-6450917-1-7 (Paperback)
ISBN: 978-0-6450917-2-4 (ebook)

For AJ & Adam

My World

~

Life is my one big circus

You are my monkeys

Both, ever so wise

~

CONTENTS

WISE MONKEYS

三猿

*"Cover thy eye and look not at what is evil;
Cover thy ear and listen not to what is evil; Cover thy
mouth and speak not what is evil; Cover thy bodily
movement to encounter no act of evil"*

How is it the monkeys embody the proverbial principle to *'see no evil, hear no evil, speak no evil and do no evil?'*

Many people have taken on board these ancient traditional beliefs that manifested in BC. The first of the monkeys is that of *Mizaru*, covering his eyes, who sees no evil; then there is *Kikazaru*, covering his ears, who hears no evil, and *Iwazaru*, covering his mouth, who speaks no evil. The last Monkey, *Shizaru*, symbolizes the principle of 'do no evil,' covering his private parts.

The Four Wise Monkeys are the most likely known symbols of the Kōshin faith, a Japanese folk religion with Chinese Taoism origins and ancient Shinto influence. According to this faith, it is said that the Sanshi spirit is three worms living in every human body. Keeping track of the good deeds and particularly the bad deeds of the person they inhabit. Every sixty days, on the night called Kōshin-Machi, when the human is asleep, the spirit will leave the body and go to Ten-Tei, the *'Heavenly God'* to report about the deeds of that person. Ten-Tei will then decide the fate of people who have done bad deeds by punishing them accordingly.

Those believers of Kōshin who have reason to fear will try to stay awake during Kōshin nights. This is the only way to prevent the spirit from leaving their body and reporting to Ten-Tei.

The Wise Monkeys symbolize the Kōshin faith and were manifested to save people from the Ten-Tei; hear, see, speak, and do no evil.

CHAPTER 1

*'To act as if the past did not take place is
momentarily just an escape!'*

The Californian sun peeks through the slight gap in the curtains. Seconds later the alarm clock speaks *'Greetings loved ones, let's take a journey.'* Snoop Dog and Katy Perry's song *'California Girls'* is playing. Just a perfect start to a perfect day in California.

With a quick stretch, Shana jumps out of her bed, dressed in her black singlet top and matching French panties, leans over, and turns the volume up. She dances across the room grooving from side to side, smiling, forgetting her age and maturity for that little time she has to herself. Shana picks up her phone, at the same instant a calendar alert pops up on her phone. *Portia's birthday,* and with that, she makes the call.

Portia answers the call with, "You better not be calling to remind me of my age."

Shana laughs, "Now, why would I do a thing like that" Shana loves teasing her, after all, she was a few years younger. But Shana holds back, she knows Portia is not one to celebrate birthdays.

Now both are laughing, "Let me finish getting dressed and give you a call when I am in the car." Portia responds, not worried if she is late to work or not, but today she wants to be out of the house. With that, they both hang up and continue getting dressed.

These days, Shana dresses for comfort, in her straight-legged jeans, just tight enough to show her curves and a flowing top, teasing just a flash of skin above her jeans. She loves her TOM'S shoes; not only because they give back to needy children, but also, they were the only shoes comfortable enough for her line of work. Shana loves giving back to the community any way she knows how.

Shana gently brushes her dark brown shoulder-length hair with caramel highlights, and then simply clips the front back, keeping it out of her face. She applies light makeup, and finally her last essential, the lip gloss.

***

When it comes to work attire, Portia has an entirely different sense of style. She sticks to typical office wear, in a pencil skirt with a cream shirt tucked in and baby pink stilettos. Her jewelry is simple with pink crystal earrings and a matching bracelet. She is a natural beauty so there's no need to pile on the makeup, but she is known to be a bit excessive with her lipstick.

Portia has long sleek, chocolate hair she curls into voluminous waves, with a side-swept bang that frames her face. She piles her hair into a messy bun, ready for release the minute she walks into work.

Portia gets into her mini coupe, placing her Mont Blanc briefcase on the passenger seat. She turns on the ignition and the car radio came on, summer hits. She takes a deep breath as she prepares herself for the chaotic Californian traffic, but nothing will get in the way of a good-felt Monday. The rule is to block out the negativity and look at everything positively or at least try to do so. Portia may be in a traffic jam on her way to work, but she takes her thoughts to where she is now in her life, a well-respected clinical psychologist working in one of the most prestigious hospitals. Her *'grade A'* reputation means the hospital needs her more than she needs them. She can get any job she wanted; other hospitals are always approaching Portia. She takes advantage of that reputation in three ways; coming in *slightly* late to work, having a *slightly* longer lunch break, and leaving *slightly* early from work. It was perfect.

As she merges into bumper-to-bumper traffic, she smiles and thinks *I have some time to apply more lipstick.*

Using one hand to fish through her purse, she looks for her exotic MAC rose lipstick, the other hand on the steering wheel as she moves her head from side to side in beat with the music. Her phone rings. It's Shana.

***

Shana lives close to Venice beach. As she opens the door of her house, she walks past her little weed-infested front garden to her small standing gate, slides it open, and strolls for a few blocks before she reaches her store. It's located close to the beach with partial views of the water and a brilliant coffee shop next door. She has her morning coffee in one hand and the keys to the store in the other. She opens her rolling door then the second door before turning the closed sign around and making her way inside. The name of the store is *'Phun Photos'* with a white banner under it letting people know that it is under new management.

She has had the store for five months and they have been the best five months of her life. Locals and tourists alike use her store constantly. Some come in to print out their photos, others come in to save photos, or just use the internet. Shana grabs her little dust feather, and goes to the packed shelves, holding various cameras, USB sticks, basically all the necessities one needs to capture the most important moments life has to offer. She picks up the phone and calls Portia.

"Have you found your lipstick yet?" Shana knows Portia all too well,

Portia turns the volume down on her car radio. "Ha-ha very funny, and yes I did"

"Put your hands-free on, before they put you in a mental institute," Shana is known for her sarcasm.

"Ok Miss entrepreneur, I swear the air in Venice beach is getting to you, inhaling all that marijuana, while walking to work." She laughs at her joke "When are you going to come to live with me?"

"Oh, stop worrying! I'm enjoying this, no stress, no shift work, no headaches, and it's close to Dad, you know he needs me."

"Isn't it enough that you did what he wanted for 30 years? He basically chose your career path, and look where that has gotten you, Sh…" but before Portia could finish, Shana cuts in.

"And what career path is that?" With a smile on her face, knowing Portia is coming from a good place. "I currently am in a completely different career, and if I remember correctly, I made that choice. It took Dad not speaking to me for a couple of months, but I'm here, so it's all about baby steps, my dear Portia."

"Just saying Santa Monica is not that far." Portia then changes the subject "in any case don't forget Friday."

Shana replies, "I won't. So that will be a bottle of red wine, I assume?"

"I need to find a good red wine, Patrick said that I need to have a glass a day, the good old protective oxygen, or something like that. I have found a way I can reduce my risk of illness." Shana rolls her eyes; her thoughts of how Portia admires this Patrick guy she works with is not pleasant. Patrick is married and indefinitely flirts with Portia, and not to mention with Shana when he gets the chance. A horny prick of a man that Shana has no respect for.

Shana goes on to correct what Portia is saying "It's antioxidants, you need to find a wine that has a good amount of Resveratrol with focus on the color pigment of the developing grapes and this will give you an increase of antioxidants, basically the stronger the grapes is the higher amount of Resveratrol and antioxidant benefit you will......" Shana stopped herself, noticing her getting too scientific. Both pause for a little, before Shana continues "Look forget it. Let me pick out the wine." She stops herself from talking, she feels herself step backward, back into old Shana. She doesn't want to go there. Shana could have gone on, she could have named all the ingredients, what was involved in making the wine, also explain in-depth what wine can do for the body but she needs to stop.

"Ok, take a breather, and listen to me Shana. t's all good, go look out through the left-hand corner of your window to what you call your ocean views." Shana laughs, it is beautiful to look at.

"Yes, I see it; I truly hope this isn't coming from a jealous place?"

"You get to see that every day for the rest of your life, I am stuck with mentally ill patients all day, with some extreme cases of harm they cause to others. Sometimes I think I'm the insane one and they are sane. Last night, one patient was telling me of a dream that he once had, all I kept thinking was how did he get into my dream." they both laugh hysterically.

"You seriously need a psychologist."

"Nah I have a friend." She, of course, was referring to Shana. "Friday is wine and pasta ok? I'm here if you need me. Adios Bella." trying out her Italian accent this time.

"Oh, now your Italian? Adios, crazy girl," they both hang up.

A slight reminder of her past nearly resurfaced, but it did not get to that point. It was a wonderful Monday morning, and nothing is going to ruin it. She is looking forward to her weekly meeting with Portia, a lot of gossip laughs, and fun. Having these types of traditions between friends was important. Even though they have only been in place for five months, she wished they would have been in place many years ago, but circumstances didn't allow it back then. Life experience was their wake-up call.

Shana and Portia are both only children. Losing their mothers at an early age drew them closer together. Portia lost her mother at two years old and Shana at three years old. They both were also raised by single working fathers. Shana's father was a Chief and head of the LA District Police Force and Portia's father was a renowned plastic surgeon. They didn't get along with each other, but their daughters didn't seem to care. They weren't just friends they were family, it was perfect, and it was their mothers up above looking out for them.

Shana thinks today is going to be a great day.

She thought wrong.

***

CHAPTER 2

'An untreated wound will never properly heal'

Shana looks around her store. From where she was located through the slight corner of her window, she can get a glimpse of the beautiful ocean. She sips her coffee and looks at her watch.

Right on time she thinks to herself as she sees her boyfriend walking toward her, his police car parked right outside the front. He makes his way to the store, lifting Shana in the air, and greets her with a passionate kiss.

Shana and Ryan have been dating for a while, they both worked together in the same police station, and you could say it was love at first sight - for Ryan that is. Shana was too focused on her work. But when he finally made his move, Shana could not resist. He was her breath of fresh air. She is herself with him, and with him, she loves who she is.

Ryan is a tall tanned handsome man; whose dimples make Shana melt, and his jawline entices her. She has no sense of responsibility in his presence. She feels free and at ease with Ryan. Shana is a girl in love and always feels protected when he is around.

He pulls her in closer and she can feel his police belt, running her hand slowly all over the instruments on his belt. She slowly places her hand around Ryan, moving him closer towards her. She leans in, nibbling the edge of his ear ever so gently. Suddenly, Shana grabs his gun from his side belt and pulls back.

Pointing the gun at him with the safety intact she shouts, "Take your shirt off!" trying to be firm in her voice and not smile, proud that she has once again able to get the gun from his belt without him realizing. It is a game the two of them played when Shana was on the force.

He smiles "Cheater! You did that ear thing, you seriously still playing this game?"

"Yes, and it still counts my dear," She laughs and hands his gun back while walking back into the store "that's seven to three, my way. Such a shame Ryan. I thought your reflexes would have been better!" she sarcastically shakes her head.

"Hold on, my dear." he replies with his charming smirk, "You're no longer on the force, so this game was supposed to be over months ago."

She leans over close to him again, aiming for his ear, and whispers "Not until I get to ten points."

He pulls her away. "Well, you're not going to get an extra point today," Ryan leans against the bench.

"Tim, Louise, and Catherine were asking about you this morning when we had a briefing. Everyone has been missing you, I'm missing you, Shana." He reaches over, stroking her hand "Are you sure this is what you want to do? The Chief said you're welcome back any time. Your dad would want you to come back…"

"This has nothing to do with my dad, or with them, and did the Chief forget the exchange of words we had when I left? He just wanted Dad's job so bad. Chief my arse!" she says, defensively. "Ryan you know that I can't go back. I don't want to go back."

At that moment, Ryan realizes his mistake of bringing this topic up - it is still too early.

"Baby, I'm sorry. You don't have to go back, just with your dad retiring, and you have left the force it can kind of gets lonely." His dimples enhance as his cheeky smile appears. Those dimples are her weakness, Ryan knows this all too well.

Her inner sadness automatically vanishes.

"Ok sweetness, I better get back to work. Pick you up at seven pm?" she nods and smiles. He places his arm around her and brings her in toward him until their lips touch. Ryan then makes his way out, Shana leans on the open door as his car pulls away.

Shana looks up at the wall full of photos, coming into focus on one photo. It was her father's retirement dinner; he didn't want a party and with what had happened who could blame him? Shana looked closely at the photo, her father standing tall, with a cigar in his hand, a straight face.

She then looked over to the other people in the photo. Ryan, slightly pale with nerves, trying to smile, and the senior sergeant at the time, who now was '*the Chief,*' smiling from ear to ear. She didn't need to look at herself in that photo. She was not even looking at the camera, lost in her thoughts. That photo is placed in her store for her to be constantly reminded that she couldn't go back.

The rest of the morning flew by with customers entering her store. She loves her job, developing endless memories, catching moments of beauty- whether it's scenic, family, or a night out. All the photos represented the diversity of beauty, enticed in colors, and abstract. A photo captures the moment of happiness that we want to share, we want to treasure, and we want to be remembered *forever*.

Shana is digging into her turkey sandwich for lunch when a young boy makes his way in. Shana smiles and puts her sandwich down. He is an adorable boy with scruffy hair, blue crystal eyes, blue shorts, and a white shirt with a few brown-like stains on it. *Probably ice-cream.* She looks at his hand and there he has a watch, large enough to fit around a grown man's wrist and his other hand tucked nervously behind his back.

Shana bends down to be on the same level as him "How can I help you, little man?"

His eyes flickered, he then swings over his arm from behind his back and hands over a film to Shana.

Shana's gut was saying something was not right, "Are you saying you want me to develop this film for you?"

He nods.

"Ok little man, it will take up to twenty minutes. Where is your mommy or daddy? Do you want to wait or come back?" It had been a while since she received a roll of film to develop since things went digital.

He looks at his watch, and shakes his head, frowning and his eyes slightly watering.

His watch then beeps and the little boy jumps. He looks at Shana as if he were about to say something, but then must have changed his mind. He turns around and runs out of the store.

Shana puts the film down and ran out to see where he went, but just like that – *he had vanished.*

Shana is puzzled but did not think too much of it. She bases it on her being suspicious, reminding herself, that in California you can get a huge number of different kinds of interesting people. She has experienced this with her time in the force. She does not want her investigating nature to get the best of her, but she couldn't help herself and is eager to develop the film. She places the film in the machine, waiting for development.

She leaves it to run; finishing off her turkey sandwich and keeping herself busy as she reshuffled things around the store.

All photos are now spitting out of the machine, facing downwards. Shana picks up the warm photos, sits up on her stool, and turns them around.

With a crash, she falls off the stool, with the photos all flying out of her hand and falling all around her.

The unsolved crime scene, the reason for her departure from the forensic team within the police force. The detailed photos that were not taken by her team were laying in front of her.

Her hands are shaking, eyes watering. She is trying to take hold of herself. Shana picks up the photos one after the other critically analyzing them. These photos are detailed. She sighs and her stomach turns, as she looks at the last photo of the little boy holding his tongue which was cut off and made to pose for the camera. *Good God, what has he done?* That's why the little boy didn't speak. *Oh, God!* She feels sick in the stomach.

Shaken up, Shana stares at the photos. *What unfinished business does he have? What more can he take away?* That little boy is going to die. She knows who did this, and she knows that he isn't going to keep that boy alive. No one knows this better than Shana.

Shana collects all the photos while trying to get herself together, locks the door, and heads straight to her phone.

She calls the first person she could think of someone who knew this case all too well.

Shana calls her dad.

**

CHAPTER 3

"A collection of mental pictures can be confused with the authenticity of current thought" R. Chaalan

"Hello?" Her father is quick to answer.

"Dad!" her voice trembling, flashbacks from her past case are resurfacing. "Oh God, Dad!" She has no idea how to start the conversation.

"Shana? What is it?" Noticing her worried voice, he tries to calm her down "Take a big breath in. Now relax! Are you ok? Shall I come? Where are you?" George is always worried about his little girl. Regardless, if she is in her thirties, she will always be his little girl.

"Dad..." she swallows, then breathes taking her father's advice "Dad! The criminal... the Wise Monkey's Case... the photos, he's here, he's back! He's in California, he's in LA... Oh dear God!"

He cuts her off, confusion clear in his voice "What are you saying? Shana, get a hold of yourself, you're not making any sense."

She takes a big breath and calms herself down. "Dad... the criminal... the reason I left the force." She pauses and tries to get a hold of herself. "A little kid came in with a film for me to develop. He had no tongue; I found this out later when I developed the photos. The photos are of the crime scene..." she rubs her head and takes another shuddering breath "Dad, they are photos he took of the crime scene. They are much more detailed. There are photos where his hand is present as if he is pointing to his artwork, he took the photos while dismantling the bodies. I need to call Ryan... I need to notify everyone, we, I mean, they..." she is muddling up her words, "I mean I need to help. I..." she pauses, all over the place and losing all concentration. Then she stops, her dad staying quiet as he was taking in all the information.

"Dad he sent these to me, he wants me!"

"Shana, listen to me don't call anyone, not Ryan, not anyone, not yet we can't trust anyone." His voice shows how agitated he was.

"But Dad, he is here! This new evidence can bring us closer to finding him, and are you forgetting that poor little boy?"

"Listen to me." His voice went from angry to firm, "Close the store and come here. Bring the photos! I'm waiting, we'll discuss it when you get here."

Shana knows that voice too well. Even though she is confused, she nods, and then verbally agrees. She hangs up and places the photos in an envelope, closes and locks the store, and heads out to see her father.

Shana is now more cautious. Everyone is a suspect - the case had too many loose ends. While walking back to her place, she keeps looking around, for the first time in just over Six months did she once again experience the feeling of paranoia and stress, it was overwhelming. Shana has gone into the investigator mode. Everyone seems suspicious right now.

Shana can't believe her eyes. She sees the kid that had come into her store, running across the road, just missing oncoming traffic. She runs after him, barely missing oncoming traffic herself. He was now a step-in front of her. Without thinking she grabs the boy, only to notice he is not the boy and quickly puts him down while he kicks and screams. Shana stands still for a second, reality kicking in before she starts to run the rest of the way to her house, jumps into her car and heads toward her father's place.

She enters her father's street and can see her father outside the house pacing. She parks the car, and her father is beside the window before she has a chance to turn the car off. "Are these the photos?" he asks, pointing to the passenger seat where the envelope lay. She picks them up and hands them to him. He snatches it out of her hand and moves toward the house, making his way in.

Shana quickly gets out of the car, following her dad.

"Dad! Why is the fireplace on?" she points in the direction of the fireplace. It was 107 Fahrenheit outside! He doesn't bother answering as he opens the envelope. Swearing at the photos, he launches them in the fireplace.

"What are you doing? Have you gone mad?" she screams while trying to lean into the fireplace to rescue the photos, but he holds her back.

"Listen to me. Listen to me!" he shakes her to get her attention. "You don't want anything to do with this. Everyone who made it their life commitment to finding this guy died. I won't let that happen to you."

"But why did he send these photos to me? I need to find that boy, that boy was so scared," she breaks down falling to the floor and crying in her father's arms, "I need to find this guy, what have you done? What the fuck have you done?!"

George waits until the photos are burned before he lets her go. He heads over to the corner bar and pours himself a scotch. "It's just me and you little girl, I'm not ready to lose you. I'll take care of this. Take some time off work and go spend a week with Portia."

"Taking time off won't fix anything, I'm not running anymore! That boy is going to die because of you!" she tries to get some sense across to her dad. She also needs empathy. "I haven't been the same since this case, let me close this!"

He drinks the whole glass and turns to his daughter, "You listen to me! I'm not going to be called on one day to find you cut up into pieces!" he pauses, "He will cut you while you're alive, feeling every ounce of pain and not being able to scream for help!" She knows he is right, and the thought freaks her out "Not in this lifetime, so please just do what I'm asking. Pack and head to Portia's for the week," he takes a deep breath, calming himself down while pacing. "Leave it with me. I'll make a few calls and figure out what to do. As for the little boy, he's probably already dead. He was just a prop! You know it, I know it."

She doesn't have much of a choice. She doesn't even bother saying goodbye to her father. She leaves the house and gets in her car, heading home.

While driving home, the images were flashing through her mind. Shana was well-known for her photographic memory.

One photo after the other, as if a slide show was taking place in her head. She then paused and parked on the side of the road.

One photo stands out the most. It has a shadow or something coming from the closest. *'There has to be a witness'* she gasped. *'How could I have missed this?'* She was genuinely disappointed in herself.

She closes her eyes, focusing on the photo that had the serial killer's hand over the father's face. He was lying on the floor with his hands tied to the bed leg above his head Shana remembers that case as if it were yesterday. The autopsy report said he was conscious when he had his genitals cut out. All too disturbing. But the lamp that was on in the bedroom at the time, showed a slither of light that someone was standing behind the closet. *Whoever was behind that door saw everything.* The serial killer missed one family member. Shana then accelerates, taking an illegal U-turn *'the daughter'* she thought. It had to be. Shana was heading back to the store. She hadn't given her dad the negatives. Shana needs to see those photos. She needs to make sure. She is merging in and out of traffic, taking back streets to get to the store as fast as she can. She parks the car, not even having time to lock it, and runs to her store. She closes the door behind her and places the negatives through the machine.

She picks up the phone, dialing Ryan's number. She puts the phone to her ear, but just before it rings, she hangs up. She will see him tonight; she will explain to his face to face. He will get all the files she needs. She dials another number.

It answers after two rings. "Portia, thank God you answered. When can you get off work? I'm heading to your place tonight after I meet Ryan." Shana using her time wisely.

"What's going on? You're freaking me out." Portia was worried.

"The Wise Monkeys case, Portia. He knows where I work. He sent me photos of his first crime scene, except these images, were ones he took." Shana pauses as she was looking at the photography machine. "I am dead now anyway; you know how this works. If I run, he will find me, he sent these to me for a reason." She is trying to convince herself more so than Portia.

"Have you spoken to Ryan?" Portia asks,

"No, I was going to see him tonight. I called Dad, he was so worried and scared for me that he burned the photos." She switches to one hand holding the phone to her ear, the other putting the negatives through. "But he didn't know I had the negatives. I am back at the store printing out new copies. I'll do what I need to do and head to your place."

"Ok Shana, you do what you need to do. Call me twenty minutes before you head out my way, I'll be there waiting for you." Portia pauses, "I love you." She sounds scared now.

"I love you too." Shana responds. Shana hears the fear in Portia's voice, and she had seen it in her dad's eyes. They had every reason to be scared. She is not dealing with someone she can negotiate with; she knows this very well. One wrong move and she will be dead. She has to go in with a new game plan.

She closes her eyes, the same way she had always done before she entered a crime scene. She took a deep breath and then goes back in time to the image of her mother standing in the front yard.

Shana's mother Cherie was what some would call a free spirit and others would call a hippie. She had a love for life, a carefree spirit that found its way into everyone's heart. That's what drew George, her dad, to her; she was the rain to his drought. Like rain, she supported his growth with his line of work and angelically made all muddy situations appear beautiful. She flooded his life with positive energy. He needed someone who saw the world as beautiful, to be an escape from his reality of crime at work, a delightful illusion. Cherie was truly mystical and magical. Her smile never left her face, and she only ever saw the good in all situations. She lived to love.

***

Shana closes her eyes, as she is taking a trip back into a favorite pastime. Lionel Hampton's album '*Flying Home*,' was playing the album that Cherie loved and listened to as she cleaned around the house, made breakfast, lunch and dinner. Cherie was a true jazz classic lover.

The final images she had of her mother were simple. Shana's mother was wearing a long white summer dress, her long brown wavy hair slightly moving with the simple spring breeze, her smile showing off her white glowing teeth, her hazel eyes sparkling and her skin so soft and smooth. Her mother was running to her with her arms wide open. Shana would then pull her hands out as if her mother were right in front of her, inviting her in. Three-year-old Shana was picked up and swung around by her mother; they both laugh and stare into each other's eyes. Shana can hear the sprinkler going in the background feeding the freshly cut grass and her mother's favorite music playing through the house and making its way to the front of the yard.

Shana was swinging in her mother's arms, the melody reaches the point where the saxophone is taking over, both interlocking their hands, Shana not wanting to let go. Then she opens her eyes. She takes a long breath in and exhales before looks at the photos in front of her. She knows now what she must do. A deep dive into her past and these photos, were her secret weapon of seeing the present clearer. She couldn't explain it and didn't feel the need to. *It just worked for her.*

***

CHAPTER 4

"Awaiting approval can be haunting, especially from those that were once dear."

TWELVE MONTHS AGO

Albert kept his eyes closed and tried to block out what was taking place, he needed to cum! If he did then maybe just maybe this psycho will let them both go!

He tried, he cried and pushed, angry at his dick for not staying up.

The Widow Hunter leaned over, pulling the prostitute's nipple with one hand, and slicing it off with the other. The prostitute could not stop him, her hands were tied. She screamed and swooned in pain covered in her blood. She looked at Albert screaming.

"God please, just fuck me, please!" Albert was shaking and in shock as to what the Widow Hunter just did. He looked at the hooker

"I'm so sorry" he mumbled, knowing that an apology would not solve anything. She was crying in pain; her cheap mascara was running everywhere. Albert turned to the Hunter, begging, and pleading for their lives. The Widow Hunter lashed out and kicked Albert until Albert could take no more, "OK, OK." he yelled out, knowing he had no choice.

Albert closed his eyes - he needed to make this work. *How was he supposed to get erect in a situation like this?* He took a deep breath in and drifted his thinking to his wife. Just one night ago, they had been lying in the bed making love. He grabbed the prostitute and with his eyes closed he whispered the name "Jane." The prostitute knew exactly what he was doing. He was a man who was in love with his wife, and she understood, she didn't care what name he gave her or pretending that she was another woman, she was used to that. She just wanted to live, this freak wanted to watch two strangers fuck, then so be it. They both just wanted to go home and pretend this never happened.

With his eyes closed, he could no longer see the blood that was pouring out of the prostitute's chest. All he could feel was a woman's touch, his wife's body. His dick slowly rose. He reached out and grabbed the prostitute's breast, kissing her cheek and making his way to her neck, his dick reaching its full length. The prostitute clenching her eyes to shut out the pain. Albert had forgotten her freshly cut breast, but the prostitute didn't want to distract his concentration. She bit on her lips wanting so badly to scream, but to Albert, it sounded like his wife moaning with excitement.

He was ready to enter her, *"I love you"* he whispered in what he thought was Jane's ear, his penis ready and the prostitute's legs were already spread. He guided the head of his penis to the tip of her vagina; he pushed his body closer until his penis was in. Albert let out a sigh.

His eyes still closed, Albert placed his hand on her face, then gently moving her hair out of her face while kissing Jane.

Albert was moving in a gentle motion back and forth with each movement he was pushing in deeper and deeper into her vagina.

The Hunter stood in silence over them, he was completely aroused. He touched himself on the outside of his jeans, he was as hard as a rock. He was enjoying his work. He didn't want it to stop. The Hunter was moving around, he was sexually hyper.

Albert was sweating and speeding up, to the point where she could not only feel the testis slapping against her but hear them. He grabbed her and leaned up, pushing with all his might inside her, he let out a sigh as he came.

He fell on top of the prostitute, tired, and then slowly opened his eyes to see the reality that was taking place. Albert was dizzy and angry, his subconscious mind going a thousand miles an hour, He removed his penis and fell to the floor next to the prostitute. He looked at her as if shocked that it was not Jane. Albert started to smack himself in a rage, pulling his hair while crying in disgust of himself, this situation, his act. His hands and body were all covered in her blood. He looked around the room, the prostitute was crying helplessly on the floor, and The Widow Hunter looked down at them in rage.

"Why? Why?" Albert pleaded, "I have done what you wanted, you promised we can go you sick fuck!"

The Hunter shot Albert straight in the head with a silencer, pacing up and down, while the prostitute was trying to wiggle her way out of the ropes, screaming, knowing what was coming. The Hunter turned around to the loud prostitute and pulled the trigger. His penis lost its erection, and his mind returned to him. It was time to mind-fuck the crime scene before he left.

He took Albert's wallet, in the aim of making it look like it was a normal hotel robbery. Even the detectives who were called to the scene wanted to close the case and call it a *robbery-homicide*. A man having an affair, in a dirt-cheap motel with a prostitute and then robbed. That was until Shana and her investigation team intervened.

* * *

Shana started as a forensic scientist. She was the youngest among the small specialty team, focusing on field investigation. Shana was extremely gifted, with her photographic memory and a love of riddles, she could have had any career path she wanted, from being a heart surgeon to a professor of some sort, or even an astronaut. She chose the path closest to that of her father's. She graduated first in her class and solved all cases she was on accordingly.

Shana was only in the forensic department working under the coroner for two years, he saw that she was not just scientific. Shana was not someone you could just close off in a lab, especially since she was easily doing four people's jobs. A new role was put in place to test her within the forensic and police departments, which promoted her to team leader. After achieving all expectations and more, she became a head investigator, and shortly after, she was the *'Chief forensic field investigator,'* in charge of her team. The youngest ever to oversee such a team.

Shana already held a high reputation in her line of work, but her reputation grew when she worked on the Widow Hunter case.

The Widow Hunter would target women who had lost their husbands. In some cases, he would kill the husband, give the woman time to mourn, and then come back and kill her. During the waiting process of mourning, he would kill other victims. The killer aimed to outdo himself each time. In some cases, he

26

would make the killing of the men look as if it were accidental, suicidal, or just make them simply disappear.

On the contrary, for the victim Jane, he had the worst plan possible. The Widow Hunter seemed to want to see how much he could break Jane. Jane's husband Albert died in a dirty cheap motel with a hooker. The hooker was also killed and placed on top of him. It felt as if he almost wanted to confuse the investigation process.

Shana's gut said it wasn't the case. She knew better.

There was a pattern of killings that were taking place in the United States, starting in Redding. Albert and the prostitute would later be known to be a part of The Widow Hunter's longline of murder victims.

The case was handed to Shana only weeks ago.

Shana was well aware of this case, but sixteen of the killings were out of her jurisdiction and she couldn't do anything. But now that The Widow Hunter had made his way to Los Angeles; it was officially Shana's case. She was now in charge.

Shana made her way into the cheap motel. "Do you think it's The Widow Hunter?" One officer asks Shana as she and her team are making their way up to the crime scene. The others were lined up on the stairway, listening for her answer.

Another officer standing near him didn't give Shana a chance to talk, quickly answering the rookie's question. "Yeah, as if The Widow Hunter is going to kill a man and a hooker! I don't think so. It's an open shut case. Hooker and businessman fucking in motel, thug come in robs them, they try to defend themselves and he shoots them." Shana shrugged and shook her head in disappointment at the ignorant officer. Without any crime scene analysis, who was he to make a judgment? She didn't bother much with people like that. She continued to make her way up the stairs.

The first thing she noticed as she walked into the crime scene was a well-dressed businessman. She knew that the motel was not under his name, nor under that of the prostitute. *What was he doing in this neighborhood?* She looked around the room. Some police officers and detectives were around her crime scene one looking around and the other on his phone. One of them was Ryan's best friend John. There was also a journalist in the stairway near the door, trying to get a glimpse of the scene with her cameraman.

"John, get rid of the journalist for me. They should have been stopped downstairs! What are the other officers doing letting them in?" she looked at the officers that were in the room "Everyone else out of my crime scene." As everyone made their way out, one officer was about to pick something up off the floor.

"Don't even THINK of touching that!" Shana was quick to respond. The officer quickly got up, keeping his hands in the air sarcastically, and made his way out. Why couldn't people respect her crime scene?

Her team was just outside the door, waiting for orders to come in. They knew the drill all too well.

Shana took a deep breath in; closed her eyes and she went to her place of comfort. There was pure silence. Minutes later, Shana opened her eyes, returning to the ugly reality of a cheap hotel and a noisy crime scene. She was in the perfect mind frame for work.

She looked over the two bodies. The prostitute's body lay on top of the man. Her head and shoulder slightly covering his face, her hand-tied up, similar to that of a person about to dive. Shana stared for a while at her tied hands. The bullet wound was located toward the middle of her forehead, and with bruising located on her back was a clear indication that the bodies had been moved after they were shot.

Shana grabbed a pen from her front pocket. She used the point of the pen to move the prostitute's hair out of the way revealing Albert's face. There was a dry, white patch coming from his eye. Like the way one's skin looks after swimming in the salty beaches and then drying in the sand. She shook her head. This man was in fear of his life, he was crying. *They were dry patches of tears.*

She wanted to quickly remove the body to see if there was a signature that The Widow Hunter left behind. Shana called her team in. The noise was increasing from the hallway and the stairway as she could hear Detective Grant's and Ryan's voice making their way up the stairs, she was happy they were finally here.

"I need you to take photos of these bodies. Let me know when you're done." She spoke to one of her trusted team members, Phil Wong. Wong had the experience to be told once and have it done perfectly, assigning work to him made life easier for Shana.

Shana already had her thoughts, "Monica, I need all the officers out of here." Monica nodded and made her way down the stairs to speak directly to the sergeant.

She walks over to John and Detective Grant; Shana's mind was already critically analyzing the room. "This was a double murder, and this was executed by a professional killer." They both looked puzzled.

"This man was led here, and this prostitute thought she was meeting a client, there is no way this man was here to meet a prostitute. He was not cheating on his wife. Not with a prostitute anyway."

John looked up at Shana "How do you know this?" he was intrigued by her intelligence but also questioning her thoughts. John was a little jealous of his best friend. He had liked Shana for a while, but his shy, reserved character didn't help him much. He also was the type of person who kept his emotions to himself. He couldn't fault Ryan though. After three years of being together, even he had to admit they made the perfect couple.

Shana guided them in and the three of them stood over the corpse. She pointed to the rope that still had the prostitute's hands tied. "I have seen this specific type of knot before. I remember looking over some of the images in The Widow Hunter cases. This is his knot. The Hunter has made his way down here and will continue to kill until he reaches his destination. I don't know exactly where that is… yet. Also, when Wong finishes taking photos, I am almost certain there will be a nipple missing, that's his signature, he can't help but take that piece of the woman with him."

The team had finished the digital forensic photography of the bodies a little while later.

"Okay, slowly." Wong and John crouched near the bodies, both wearing gloves, "On three, one… two… three" they both lifted the prostitute's body and placed it gently in line with the man, leaving enough space for Shana to walk between the two. As they did this, a squishy sound was made. Everyone stopped and turned around, even Shana. As the bodies lay side-by-side, their private parts now visual to the public, the noise was that of the vagina releasing some fluids.

"Well, at least he died a happy man." One of the cocky officers outside the door commented, sarcastically. Shana gave them a look that efficiently implied she was not impressed, and they knew it was time for them to leave.

Nobody wanted to mess with the Chief's daughter.

"Shit! You're right!" Detective Grant was quick to notice the nipple missing. John went pale and excused himself from the room. She didn't blame him. Shana knew she was on the right track. Detective Grant and Wong also headed out knowing this was *'alone time'* for Shana. Shana then closed the door. She took out some eucalyptus oil from her pocket and placed a few drops under her nose intending to block out the postmortem smell.

Walking back over to the bodies, she noticed the prostitute's face was also sliced as if to punish her, or to terrify the male victim.

This killer was perverted. He came in wanting to watch a gruesome sex show. She looked at her face, closely; and noticed bruising on the face. Like those also located on her arms, she was using her face and her tied up hands to defend herself.

The nipple was a clean-cut, most probably done with a surgical knife, like the victims before her. Shana pulled out her tape recorder and pushed the red record button.

"The first body is that of a normal developed white female, estimated age early thirties, ligature mark found on the face." She paused "Odor is that of cheap perfume, trying to cover the smell of a strong smoker. Ripped knee-high stockings, plastic bracelets, and a belly button ring are the only types of clothing and jewelry located on the body. Clothing of the girl found two feet from the female body, is that of a short skirt and a top."

She paused and looked above the prostitute's head. "Her hands are tied above her head, with a specialty knot, similar to that done on the previous victims of The Widow Hunter. Fingernails medium length. Acrylic nails, unable to see the fingernail beds. The middle finger is missing. A clean-cut, like that used by surgical equipment. No residual scares or markings located on the hands." She put the hand down gently and continued to walk around the body.

"Bruise-like marking, weapon probably used is the criminal's gun. This bruising is located on the forearms, same marks are also found on the left cheek, lower chin and forehead." Shana took it all in. "Nipple removed, slight blood splatters, reaching female victim's neck and abdominal area, dried up blood located under the breast. From the look of things, the same instrument used to remove the finger was used to remove the nipple. There are multiple crisscross lacerations located on the face. The tip of a gun was first pressed on the forehead, leaving a blotch round bruising tattoo like where she was shot. The victim must have moved. Gunshot wound has gone through the chin; with a severe fracture to the mandible and teeth. The gunshot exit wound is on the left side of the back of the head. Injury to the skull and lower brain." She moved to the other side of the prostitute's head "Blood splatter on the face and caked out on the back of the carpet, initiating that she was shot near the left leg of the end of the bed and then later moved. Blood smearing from the right ear and left nostril. Dried blood clots are presented on the back of the head. The vagina shows no evidence of injury but was involved in sexual activity before death. Semen located on the tip of the vagina and lower pelvic region. Upon moving the female victim off of the male victim, the penis was slightly intact within the vagina."

She stood up and paused for a second, then continued. "This psycho must have then placed the penis slightly back into the vagina after killing both victims." Shana leaned over and placed the thermometer on the body. She looked closely at the body's coloring, its temperature, and the smell, all helped in indicating a rough estimation of the time. "Body temperature, rigor and livor mortis, indicates a time of death between 8:30 pm and 11:30 pm Thursday - *Last night*"

She pressed pause again and went over to the man. She stood over him, for a second, before walking around him, pressing record "No identification located on the scene of both male and female bodies. No belongings other than the clothing and jewelry worn by victims."

"The male victim was shot at point-blank, most probably with a silencer gun. It has also been placed firmly on the forehead, located in the middle; injuries caused by hot residue from the gun are visible. Slight burn and rash-like marks are visible at the entrance wound. The barrel was pressed firmly against the forehead around causing it to balloon out; the star-like tearing wound is also visible around the entrance wound, indicating the point-blank shot." She moved away from the man's head to his clothes, he had all his clothing on him, his belt undone, and his pants and underwear were pulled down. "His dress sense is that of a businessman, looks like…." She got closer to the fabric touching it and pulling it back to see the stitching. "Hugo Boss, if I am not mistaken the signature style." She moved the jacket to one side and smiled at herself for being correct. There it was *HUGO BOSS* sewn-in label on the inside. She was all too familiar with suits and the men wearing them, the white-collar crimes, especially in her money laundering case, "A tailored modern fit sharp suit, with Chesterfield slip-on shoes, this man sure favored this designer label." Shana then pulled his jacket to reveal his wrist, the bloody shirt also the same brand and the cuff links most probably purchased from Hugo Boss.

Shana was intrigued, she leaned over to the handsome victim's neck, moved his head back, and smelled his neck, she wanted to see if this person was obsessed with *Hugo Boss*. Even with eucalyptus under her nose and the smell of a corpse, Shana could slightly smell the man's cologne taking a deep breath in and thinking, she leaned back a second time took another sniff to confirm. She knew exactly what it was. The fragrance that consisted of an entrance of Lebanese cedar trees then invites patchouli and partners with slight musk, then ends with a touch of basil and sweetened with mint, the *Hugo XY* cologne. It was the same cologne she bought for Ryan recently. She continued to record what she found on the bodies. She then stopped, turned her recorder off and stood in the corner of the room, speaking to herself. *'Now, what is it that you have left for me?'*

Every criminal is said to leave something behind, and often enough also takes something from the scene. Shana was pacing around thoughts going through her head, of where did he walk, what was it that he had touched, why was he here, did he take something. Thought after thought, each one had to have an answer, if not now, then definitely later.

As a student, the first introduction to forensics was through the teachings of Dr. Edmond Locard. He was a pioneer of forensic science and to Shana, a God. The two had a lot in common.

Dr. Locard had formulated a principle that stated that every contact that one makes they will leave some sort of trace. This was referred to as *'Locard's Exchange Principle.'* Simply put, every contact you make with another person, place, or object *will* definitely without fail result in an exchange of some sort of physical material. It was one of the first things they checked at a crime scene.

Shana needed to be precise in her collection. There was no room for error. One had to take note of everything, test everything three times over, and confirm all findings. She minimized human error as much as possible to ensure that valuable evidence is not contaminated, tampered with, or destroyed. Shana's team establishes a chain of custody. Each forensic investigator or technician in her team makes a record whenever a piece of evidence comes into their custody during crime scene analysis and throughout the length of the investigation.

The corpses that Shana saw daily in her line of work could not physically talk to her, but by examining them, understanding them, and investigating them both scientifically and physically, she was able to communicate on their behalf and more importantly, allowing their souls to rest and their loves ones to get closure.

She walked around the room in a spiral-like movement to make sure she did not miss a thing, observing only, while recording her findings as she went along.

Upon completing this, she stood back over the bodies. She looked at where would be the best place to stand if she were the criminal. "If I were the criminal and I had a gun in my hand, held at two people while forcing them to engage in sex, where would I stand? Where is the best place for observation?" Shana thought out loud.

She walked around and then found the perfect location. "Let's say he was right here," talking to herself again, she held out her righthand improvising holding a gun, pointing it over where the bodies lay. She knew from conversations with the criminologist that The Widow Hunter was most probably getting off and sexually enticed with his crimes. "My other hand is free, I am sweating, I need to keep the gun focused. I am wiping my forehead, I am pacing, I'm touching myself." While Shana was pacing, she walked past a table near the head of the bed, it was covered in dust, a large motel phone was located on it. It was not touched, and the dust was intact.

She shook her head, "Fine. Let's say I am a left-hander." She then held the gun in her left-hand pacing in the opposite direction she saw a shelf hanging from the wall with a plastic dusted old pot plant on it. The dust on the wood was present, except for a small patch the size of a partial small fingerprint. Shana looked closer at it. *Got you!* She was proud of herself. The introduction of DNA technology was truly the greatest advancements in forensic science. Being able to obtain genetic information from biological material left behind at a crime scene and being able to then compare that to the victim, suspects, witnesses, and then being able to filter out who may have committed the crime and in turn exonerate those who didn't.

She called her team, plus Detective Grant. "Finish the photography then remove the bodies; get them down to the morgue. Get Dr. Muller to start on them the second they come in. The Widow Hunter would be planning his next target attack, so we need the evidence now!"

"Make sure to photograph before evidence collecting." Her team already knew this, but she always reminded them. She called one of the members of the forensic team over with a flick of her wrist.

"Jake, collect this and get me the DNA. Make this a priority. This is our man." She pointed to the shelf.

She turned to Monica "I need all the previous cases concerning The Widow Hunter on my desk before I get to the office. You have half an hour." Monica was out the door the second Shana finished talking.

"Get the fingerprints of the girl before getting the body out. We need to notify her family."

While dictating to her team, she took a photo of the dead man's face and sent it to the detective's phone. She had a gut feeling that The Widow Hunter's fingerprints would not be in the system. This was not his first case, and it had bypassed ten cases. He was a step ahead. By the time they got one step ahead, The Widow Hunter would have attacked again.

"Shana, what about the fingerprints and identification of the man?" The detective had a confused look on his face.

"I know it's not the best picture, but I just sent you a picture of his face. I recommend that you go to all the Hugo Boss stores in LA, and I can assure you that one of the stores will identify the victim."

"They are probably hundreds of these stores." The detective's phone beeped indicating he received the picture message.

Shana looked up the Hugo Boss stores on her phone and showed the detective. "There are actually around ten, however only six within a close radius of where I feel the victim is most likely to have shopped. Start at Beverly Hills' Rodeo Drive, then try Sunset Boulevard, go to Century, and then hit Santa Monica." She then put her phone down intending to capture his full attention "Detective, finding who this man is... is crucial. Without knowing who he is, we can't save his wife."

He nodded, "Consider it done." Instead of just heading out on his own, he called out to Detective Roger, who was at the bottom of the motel stairway. He was also standing with two other officers including Detective Grant. He gave them each a location to go to and sent the photos to their phones.

Shana could hear him delegate the workload; she was at ease that they were cooperating. This was one of the main reasons for their success.

Shana headed out of the motel and left her team to do the work that needed to be done. She removed her gloves and the protective bags that were on her shoes and opened the top of her overalls to get some air in, and slowly rotated her head to gently relax her neck. Shana took a few deep breaths, inhaling and exhaling slowly.

She got in her car; she needed to get to her office. While passing traffic, her phone rang. "Figures! The day that I am off, a serial killer decided to visit LA," she shook her head and smiled.

"Seems John was quick to call and inform you," Shana assumed it had to be John who had told him, seeing as she had seen and spoken to him at the scene.

"No, your dad called me, I think he was calling to make sure I don't distract you today……opps, does that mean I was not supposed to call you?"

Shana was rolling her eyes; she knew how protective her father was.

Even though a little irritated that her father had called Ryan she was also flattered, that he in a way has come to terms that his little girl was growing up and had somewhat accepted that she was in a relationship.

"Speaking of which, my dad's on the other line," she joked,

"Don't tell him I, um, I called." Shana burst out laughing, as she parked her car right in front of the entrance to the police station.

"Seriously, Shana, seriously?" Ryan groaned, trying to sound like it didn't affect him.

"Does my daddy scare you that much?" she laughed.

"No, I'm not scared of your dad. I'll get you back woman, but seriously I never called…. Do you think he taps your phone?" he is asking jokingly. Shana continued to laugh; this time Ryan joined in.

"Ryan, I just arrived back at the station, I'll talk to you later." She headed into the office expecting to find all The Widow Hunter case files on her desk.

"Take care" Ryan replied.

Shana responded confidently "Always." She made her way down the hallway, relieved that the elevator was open, and went down one level to her floor. She walked straight to her office and right on her desk and as expected, there were all the previous cases ready for her. Monica even researched some other cases which she felt would be relevant but was not placed in The Widow Hunter files. She called out for Monica and Tim, got them to take the boxes filled with the case files to the board room. A large whiteboard was located on the wall and folding tables. This was normally the field officer's training and meeting room. Today, however, this was Shana's room.

***

CHAPTER 5

"Give me a clear picture, with detailed surroundings, a thorough examination and its history and in turn, I will give you an ultra-precise answer"

A forensic team's job is to search for evidence that points to how a crime was committed to figure out who may have been responsible. Shana worked hard at establishing the best forensic team possible. A team that not only points to how the crime was committed and who may be responsible for evidence collection but a team willing to go that extra mile if need be.

The team stressed a *'one team'* mentality with a strong work ethic. Learning respect for dissenting opinions and continuously acquiring knowledge and skill is crucial to effective participation in Shana's team. They never stopped learning, they never stopped implementing and most importantly, they never stop growing.

Shana walked past her staff members watching them all enter the training room, calming herself that with her team this case should be solved sooner than expected.

Shana was waiting for a chance to look over the bodies in the morgue. She would later go down and communicate her routine conversation with the deceased.

Criminal investigators need a clear picture of the details surrounding a victim's death, not just an examination of the body, known as an autopsy, but where the body was found, and its surroundings are all contributing factors to finding any answers.

The first thing one would want to know from an autopsy is whether the death was natural, accidental, criminal, or self-inflicted. The simple and most essential findings start with identifying who the victim is, getting the accurate time of death and what had caused the person to die.

However, now it was time to focus on the case at hand. Monica, Jake, Wong, and Tim were in the room, *"Where is Louise?"* Shana did not want to have to repeat herself when she briefed them.

Jake was her first team member. Shana extracted him from New York where LA became his new home. Jake was efficient and an all-rounder, he had the most experience under his belt.

She brought Tim over from Germany, who was a true genius concerning Information Technology, DNA analysis, and making things happen. Monica was excellent in chromatography, digital photography, and a medical devices expert. She was a quiet girl, yet enthusiastic. She had a sharp eye, and her mind was constantly working. Wong was a specialist of all sorts. Shana was not sure about him at the beginning, but his persistence and determination made her take him on board. Given that he proved to be a hard worker, perfect and precise in all areas. Wong's specialty was digital photography, crime scene collection and analysis, gun residue, toxicology, and a weapons specialist. Overall, Shana was grateful to have taken him in and could not believe that she had questioned taking him on board. He was an asset to her team.

"I'm here" Louise came running in, "Sorry, it just gets so cold in this room, so I went to the locker and got my jumper and then…" She noticed she was rambling. She stopped talking and took out the notebook that was religiously attached to her and put her head down.

Louise was a student with three months to go before her graduation and had been with Shana for field placement for over eight months. Shana has molded her into what was missing from the team. She knew that Louise would not be going anywhere.

Shana started her briefing, "We have thirty cases to go through, and not all are The Widow Hunter." Shana didn't even have time to address them with a good morning.

"First thing we need to do is filter out what cases we believe is the work of The Widow Hunter"

She leaned over and started to open one box "I want the room to be divided into thirty sections, each section having one of these cases here." She pointed to the cases in the box. "According to the date, we will start backdating with the first case being located there." She pointed her finger to the far-left end of the room, "We will work our way clockwise."

"Also, I want a magnified map of California up on the wall, with an 'X' where each of these murders was taken and the number of people killed. The exact date located on file and…." She paused "let's just start there." She knew that with that current information, she could later indicate what more information was needed. She didn't want to complicate things. Simple was always the best.

Within forty minutes of team collaboration, eighteen cases out of the thirty were identified, compared, and put forward to Shana as being the work of The Widow Hunter. Two cases were seen as a criminal impersonating The Widow Hunter and the rest, unfortunately, were unsolved homicides that took place around the same time or were somewhat similar, they were placed aside for now.

Shana was a visual critic type of person who liked to see things up in front of her. The large map of California had arrived, and they placed it on the back wall. Even with all the technology, she had in her lab, sometimes the good old butcher's paper and a marker were much quicker to get hold of.

The locations of the murders were marked with an 'X.' Also, concerning the victim's 'F' was to represent a female victim, and 'M' was for that of a male victim.

"Ok, the cases that have no link I need them packed and out of the room. Let's focus on what we have."

The eighteen files lay across the room. Starting with the dates, followed by the victim's details, then the autopsy report, and finally the crime scene photos for each case all lined up accordingly. Shana was walking clockwise from one side of the room looking at all the photos to the other. The team had done a great job; they focused on detail and even the slightest of similarities. They understood the work of The Widow Hunter. *Good progress*

Shana turned around and stared at the large map of California covering the back wall. She stared closely at the marks made on the map by the team. Trying to see if a pattern exists, if somehow, she can see the next steps of The Widow Hunter. She looked at the dates, reading out loud "Ok let me see! You started here?" The team also looked and saw what she was seeing, she was a force to be reckoned with.

She was distracted by her phone ringing, it was Detective Grant, "You were right, first store, Beverly Hills. His name is Albert Lophus. His wife tried to file a missing person report yesterday, but she was sent away. They said that she had reported him missing after not being home by ten pm when he was due at six pm. He was never late, but you know the rules." Shana knew the rules all too well. A person must be missing for more than twenty-four hours before a report can even be considered, let alone filed. "On her way out, they told her if he is not in by tomorrow, she can then come back and file the report."

While relieved that the lady was alive to date, Shana was also empathetic to the poor lady. The detective went on, "His wife's name is Jane. John just notified me that she's back at the police station."

"Has anyone told her what has happened?" Shana asked while looking at the map,

"No, not yet I'm heading there now. Did you want to tell her? Being a female and all?"

Shana responded, trying to be polite, "Not my job detective." Sexist remarks seem to roll off her back these days.

As much as Shana was brilliant at her work, she could come across as a bit of a bitch when she was extremely focused. She was strong and only showed her soft heart and emotions to those close to her. She loved her team, but when she needed to use tough love, she had no problem. Being in a man's world didn't affect her, she knew with confidence that she was good at her job regardless of her sex.

"You need to get her in protective custody, twenty-four-hour surveillance won't do it, detective. You need a plainclothes officer at her side twenty-four-hours a day. Do not let this woman enter a bathroom on her own…. Let me work on catching this psycho."

"Got it. Keep me updated, and don't forget to eat Shana!" Detective Grant cared a whole lot for Shana. He was the same age as her father and at times it felt like he was her second father within the police force.

"For sure," Shana replied smiling.

Shana put the phone down, this time placing it on silent, and headed to the map. She didn't want to be distracted *'Speak to me'* she murmured to herself, *"Where to next you freak?! Where to next?"*

She ran her finger across the map. The location of the first 'X' being Redding, there was one female located there. She then ran her finger down the map slightly until she reached Chico *also one female body*. A little further down she reached Yabba city, again one female body, then down a little further to Sacramento – *also one female body*. Shana then drew her focus even further down heading north to south on the West Coast and looked at Concord. Here The Widow Hunter had one male and one female victim, the same for Modesto. The Hunter makes his way to San José killing one female followed by Fresno, Tulare, Ridge, and Crest. He then stopped over at Bakersfield leaving two bodies. There were two stops before heading to Los Angeles and Thousand Oaks' both destinations having one female body victim, followed by the most recent victims in Los Angeles, one female, and one male.

Shana critically analyzed The Widow Hunter's tracks and noticed the clear line down the West Coast seaboard of California heading to Mexico. Shana could see where he was heading, but that was not enough information for she needed to know a pattern of where he was heading.

A little frustrated, she turned away from the map and then looks back. *"Ok now let's focus on the dates. Come on... something just jump out at me!"* She took a moment to breathe. She stared and stared until the numbers become blurry. She blinked to regain a clearer look, and then a eureka moment occurred. *There it was!* She looked over the dates one more time to confirm her findings. The dates of the killing were part of where the answers lay! She was quick to pick up a green marker to note the new evidence. First, she joined all the 'X' markings, from the first murder to the most recent.

Then she stopped and stared a little closer, ran her finger over the lines, and stopped at the location where two killings had taken place. "He killed one male at Concord, then continued down and killed another male in Modesto. The woman of these men was alive at that time, there was a week between the killings." Everyone was listening in, no one daring to talk not wanting to break her concentration.

"Concord male, he had been married for three years, no children – killed in a car accident."

She looked at her team to confirm if the information was correct. Wong quickly jumped in, "Yes, that's right. The brake pads were removed from the car, and a long-running metal wire from the gas tank to the socket of a headlight was also found. The fuel tanks had a hole drilled in it."

Louise looked puzzled, "Why drill a hole in the fuel tank?"

Tim was quick to answer her, "Fuel can only ignite by spark if there's enough oxygen to support the explosion. This criminal had a clear understanding of how to get a car to explode."

She pulled out a butcher's paper and threw it on one of the tables. She was seeing something but just needed to be sure.

Shana started making notes.

1. *Redding female 3^{1st} March 1990*

2. *Chico female 11th May 1993*

3. *Yabba city Female 12th April 1995*

4. *Sacramento Female 6th January 1996*

5. *Concord MALE 14th February 1997*

6. *Modesto MALE 21st April 1997*

7. *San Jose Female 30th April 2000*

8. *Fresno 20th May 2004*

9. *Concord Female 10th June 2001*

10. *Modesto Female30th April 2000*

11. *Tulare Female 24th January 2005*

12. *Ridge Crest Female 22nd March 2006*

13. *Bakersfield Male 5th February 2008*

14. *Lancaster Female 2nd May 2007*

15. *Thousand Oakes Female 23rd February*

16. *Venice Beach Male 15th January 2011*

17. *Venice Beach Female 15th January 2011*

Alive to Date–

Bakersfield female

Venice beach Female

When she was done, she stood back looking at the list. "Monica grab some more paper, bring it here, and re-write the dates, but this time write them in the day, month, and then the year numbers only!" Monica was quick to act. She referred to Shana's earlier work for reference. When Monica got to the fifth victim, Shana was already seeing the pattern. It was good news.

1. *3/31/1990*

2. *5/11/1993*

3. *4/12/1995*

4. *1/6/1996*

5. *2/14/1997*

6. *3/4/1997*

7. *4/30/2000*

8. *5/20/2004*

9. *6/10/2002*

10. *4/21/2002*

11. *1/24/2005*

12. *3/22/2006*

13. *2/5/2008*

14. *5/2/2007*

15. *2/23/2010*

16. *1/15/2011*

17. *1/15/2011*

Shana ignored the years that the crimes had taken place and focused more so on the months and dates. Once the years disappeared, Shana noticed something unusual. The dates and months on each line add up to seven and the months only seemed to range from January until June.

She stopped, looked up at the team "Get Detectives Roger and Grant in here." She called for the forensic student, "Get the senior sergeant from Bakersfield on the phone right now. I need you to also get my dad…" she shook her head; it was hard to remember not to refer to him as 'Dad' at work all these years later. "I mean get Chief George in here also." Louise was out the door before the sentence was finished.

She handed Jake three photos of three different crime scenes, all that were photos of blown-up cars. "Give that to imaging on your way. Get them to see if these three holes are identical and please hurry back." Jake took the photos and hurried out, he only needed to go next door.

In between a quick snack and a coffee, twenty minutes later the detectives were all now in the training room. It hadn't taken them long to gather. Jake also finally walked in and nodded. He had the laboratory results; she knew that a match had been found. Shana directed him to the front, wanting him to present the information.

"The DNA located on the hanging wooden shelf is that of a Damien Waltz. He was brought up in Redding, but his house was seized by the estate when his mother was murdered in 1990." Jake explained.

Louise picked up the office phone in the board room and called "Can you please put me through to your senior sergeant? My name is Louise Walker from, Forensic Unit for the LAPD. I have our Superintendent Operations Forensic Field Commander Shana Watson here and we have some new information concerning The Widow Hunter," she paused, then she placed the phone down, putting it on speaker. She turned to Shana "His name is Chief Cormack," Shana nodded her thanks.

Finally, he answered. Shana left it on speaker, leaning in toward the phone. The room now in complete silence.

"Hello, Chief Cormack here!"

"Chief Cormack, my name is Shana Watson. I am the Forensic Chief Superintendent of the Los Angeles District..."

He cuts in "Shana Watson? Is that any relation to Chief of Police, George Watson?"

She didn't care for that question right now; all she needed was to get this case dealt with now.

"Yes sir, the reason for my call..." the whole team all listened in. Detective Grant was sitting casually while Detective Roger leaned on the table with one hand. The others were scattered around the phone.

"You had a murder take place in Bakersfield on the 5th of February 2008, we believe it to be that of The Widow Hunter,"

He once again cut in "I remember that case clearly. I'm sorry Shana but I think you're mistaken. His hands were not tied, nor was he killed in any manner of which 'The Widow Hunter' presented."

Shana was quite irritated at this point. "Sir, if you please let me finish."

At this time, her father walked into the room, closing the door behind him. Shana was irritated that he was late. "Sorry Shana, please continue." He nodded at her.

"Is that Chief George Watson?"

"Yes, it is, and from that deep voice it's no other than Chief Cormack." The two were at the police academy many years ago, each taking similar paths in different parts of the force. Cormack let out a little laugh "How have you been doing?"

Shana was on her last straw of irritation; she turned around and looked at her father '*Now is not the time!*' she mouthed.

He shrugged his shoulders, but could not help but respond "I have been doing great, and yourself?"

Shana would be the only one that would get away with looking or speaking in any manner to the Chief. *Enough small talk.* "Sir, if I can get you back on track. The Widow Hunter is heading back your way, I need you to get the wife of the victim Robert Hobson whom I can guarantee is living alone. She will be the next victim"

"How certain are you Shana?" Cormack replied, confusion lacing his tone. Monica was deep into her computer digging up everything she could find about Damien Waltz.

"Sir, in 1997, two murders took place within two months – one being in Concord and the other in Modesto, these were male victims. The killing was made to look as if they were car accidental deaths. However, this is not the case. All three cases, including the one that took place in Bakersfield, had a hole in the fuel tank. Visually the holes are identical. I have a team confirming that through imaging as we speak." Now she had everyone's attention. "The person who I believe to be the serial killer is Damian Waltz. This is who we are after." Monica handed Damian's file to Shana as she was conversing. Shana went through it in shock. "I can assure you that when his father died, he was seven." Monica nodded, "The dates and months when added together for each murder add up to seven; this number is significant to him. Also, all the murders took place in between January and June. I believe he is heading to Bakersfield to finish what he started. I also believe that the murder will take place on January 24th. With January representing one, then by adding the numbers in twenty-four, you get two plus four plus one, giving us seven. This number surfaced on each date of each crime he has committed,"

Shana continued to flick through his extensive file. "The Redding victim was his mother; she was the first person he killed. He stayed in Redding for three years while officers were looking for the apparent criminal; the crazy thing is the police department did not even place him as a suspect."

The team could hear Chief Cormack whisper to the officer "I need the case on Robert Hobson, the Reddington case and information on where his wife is right now, contact details, movements, everything!"

Shana waited until he was finished before continuing, "I'm sending you Damien's information over now. With your permission sir, I would like my team to be present on-site, and I understand that your unit has its crime scene team and …." He interrupted yet again.

"Shana, you are the only forensic field investigator we know. When can you get here?"

"Tomorrow afternoon?" she looked at the team to see if it was ok with them. All she got was nods from all. They wanted to catch this son of a bitch as soon as possible.

"Tomorrow it is," Chief Cormack paused, "I hope you're right Shana."

"So do I sir." She turned the speaker button off and turned to her team, the detectives, and her father.

"I want to know why he is heading down this way and where he was going. Monica, where is his family history file?" Monica quickly handed it over. She had worked with Shana long enough to know that when she asks for something, she needed to have it ready at that moment.

She flicked through the file, talking to herself but loud enough the team could hear. "He has no home and no current address…"

"Why is it that this killing was different from the others, why shoot the male victim point-blank and why have the hooker?" Shana asked out loud.

Wong was looking over Monica's shoulder while she was viewing the files when he noticed something "What if the hooker was for Damien, not Albert? What if he had Albert meet at the motel so that he was able to get rid of the brake pads, and drill a hole in the petrol pump?"

"But he could have done that anywhere." Tim jumped in.

"No, no not true. He works in an exceedingly high-tech security block where there would be no chance to get into the parking lot. And as for doing it while he was at home, Albert has a security gate. Once you pass it, he drives another mile before reaching the house, and then it's parked in a garage with a high-tech alarm system."

Shana frowned, thinking "Ok so let's say somehow he got him there, then the prostitute came in… it just doesn't make sense!"

Detective Grant then jumped in "It makes perfect sense. This guy cuts women's nipples off." Shana rolled her eyes. That was not a statement that had any good reasoning as to why this case was more dramatic.

"I want his mom's file – a detailed report, not just the crime scene report." Monica was ready for her again as she handed over the file. Shana leaned up on the wall as she read out loud from The Widow Hunters' mother's history. "She was an alcoholic who lost custody of her son at age sixteen. She was on anti-depression medication and tried to poison her son. She held him accountable for his father's death." Shana shook her head "How did the father die?" she flicked through a few more pages, "Oh here it is. Father died while on his way to pick Damian up from soccer practice, a car accident."

"At elementary school, Damian had asked his schoolteacher for help. Informed the teacher his mother was tying him up and forcing him to have sex with her. She would belt him if his penis did not harden. Jesus. These disturbing allegations lead his mother to be transferred to a mental institute for six months between January to June." She paused. "That's why he only kills in those months! It was when he was safe, strong, and felt like justice had been served." She looked down at the file and read out loud "Before she left the metal institute, Damian was going from one foster family to another, causing havoc along the way." She paused, trying to take it all in. *The poor child.*

"In 1988, when his mother was released and Damien was sent back to her, she had found God and begged Damien's forgiveness. They would both attend Church weekly, and the community noticed the transition his mother went through. She was noted as being 'saved.' They were a happy and loving family, and the community thought Damien was wonderful." She snorted. "Not that happy. He must have been picturing murdering her from the start. On the anniversary of his father's death, 3rd of March 1990, he killed her, and we can only assume that is when The Widow Hunter was born."

Shana turned to the map. "He is not flying up. He is driving. This is time for him to reflect and plan. He's had time to know the roads too well."

"I want his picture sent out to all police stations in California." She turned to her dad "Chief, with your permission, I do not want anyone to stop him. I just need them there as backup. He is armed and dangerous. He is perspicacious and won't let anyone cease his plan. Any officer in his way is a dead one."

Her father nodded "Ok, let me speak to the commissioner and get this done. Anything else?" he questioned.

"Thanks, that's all for now." Shana had already turned back to the file, looking for more information.

She missed the proud smile on his face. They would have this case wrapped up in no time.

***

The team was packed and ready to go. Ryan was there to say goodbye just before Shana boarded the plane, "Be careful. Remember, your job is not to physically catch the criminal."

"I know, I know. I'm not leaving the police station, just making sure all goes according to plan. Don't worry, I have Detective Grant with me." She smiled, putting her arm on the detective's shoulder. The detective looked at Ryan and smirked with a slight wink.

Ryan looked at Detective Grant, "Don't let her out of your sight,"

"It will be ok." He assured him. "We all have her back."

A quick kiss was exchanged between Ryan and Shana, as they were within the team's presence. She smiled at him softly, before heading towards the plane, not looking back.

Ryan stayed until Shana disappeared in the distance, and there he was reminded of her attributes that made him weak. She is such a strong girl, very driven, extremely intelligent but her sincere empathy can get her in trouble. *He had every reason to be worried.*

***

CHAPTER 6

*'Let us come together today and continue to work
together tomorrow…. Let us grow.'*

Chief Cormack was the first to welcome Shana and her team.

"Hope it was a good trip?"

"It was ok sir." Shana replying politely, shaking his outstretched hand.

They exchanged hello's with the team and Cormack directed them into the police station, having a room set aside for Shana and her team. The team rested the boxes down on the table and spread out in the room, quickly working to distribute their information, set up their computers, and get ready to begin. Tim helped Louise to place Shana's map up on the wall for her to see.

"No officer in California has seen Damien yet. His photo was sent to every police station." Chief Cormack pointed out.

"I figured as much, with not knowing what vehicle he is in, or even probably having some physical changes done to himself. He is good at being discrete, we can see that in his pattern of work. He knows clearly what streets to take and when. He probably knows when police officers exchange shifts and would probably be listening to police radio as well. From previous cases, we can see that most crimes were committed when most officers were not close to where he was, so he knows your whereabouts and where to be clear from." Chief Cormack frowned, all confidence seemingly to leave him. Shana was quick to comfort him "This isn't a problem. He will be here, you'll see!"

"Is there anything else I need to know Shana?" he changed the subject.

"Do you have the information for me on Robert's wife? What are the updates there?"

"We have not notified the victim's wife." He handed over a file.

"Her name is Carla Hobson, and she is currently at work. She works at a travel agency at the local mall only ten minutes away from her home, and five minutes away from here. We have two undercover cars following her around and four undercover police officers currently in the mall within view distance of her."

"Thank you." She didn't want Carla to know. That would be putting her at risk as well as jeopardizing any chance of catching The Widow Hunter.

From the assessment that Shana made, she noted that it would take eight days exactly for when he would kill next. She now had his game plan to her advantage. With Alberts wife, Jane in a safe house she could focus clearly on his next target. Shana's bait to The Widow Hunter, Carla. *Finally, a head start.*

A team was created; some consisted of a few officers from Chief Cormack's team and the rest were Shana's team. They met each morning, going over their briefings, and any extra information was shared among the board. It was slow but very productive.

Closer to the date, Shana sat them all down and gave them an insight into the history of Damien. She also showed all photos from his previous crime scenes so that people can see who he was, what he was capable of, and the urgency of catching him. Questions were always put forward and Shana was happy to provide answers to all of them.

Shana joined in at times with the surveillance team. She would often wonder what it was The Widow Hunter was attracted to. All the victims, besides being happily married, were completely different. Different ages, races, mixed religions… it was very hard to find what they all had in common.

Shana learned a lot while she was on surveillance. She would watch Carla's every move as she went through the motions of her every day. *She was so much easier to read than a dead person.* Carla was very humble. Walking into work, she would give her spare change to people holding charity tin cans outside the mall, and coming home, she would give some food to the homeless man who lived outside her stairway. Shana liked her. In another lifetime, maybe they would have been friends.

Shana's mind drifted as she saw a passing lady come out of the mall with a sympathy arrangement. It made her heartache.

"I wonder if he ever attended the funerals of the deceased?" She asked the undercover officer with her. "I wonder if he watched their loved ones crying in pain. Do you think it excited him, knowing that he would be back to kill her soon?" The undercover officer shrugged. He didn't have the answer, and neither did she. There were still lots of loose ends to this case. She needed some time alone and a review. This all was happening too quickly, and when things were rushed, errors would be the result. She had no room for error. Not now. Shana needed to know more starting with why he picked the women he did.

***

CHAPTER 7

"Are you wise enough to unravel the art of my face; do you see the story my eyes tell? Do my wrinkles tell you I have lived?"

Carla must have some sort of attribution or physical characteristic or *something* that connected all these victims. They had no answers and Shana needed answers.

Shana watched as she parked the car at the mall. Carla applied some lip gloss before getting out of the car and heading toward work, pinning her name badge on her shirt as she went.

On the other side of the mall in view was Detective Grant with some undercover police officer from Bakersfield on the lookout.

Shana was in deep thought *A normal woman going to work*, Shana was intrigued to understand the killer's mind.

Shana told the officer that she was just going into the mall, next to where the travel agency was located to do some looking around. The officer told her that she was not allowed to do that.

"From memory Shana, it was you who told us we should not jeopardize this case." Shana knew he was right, but she just wanted a closer look. Shana lied and said that she had spoken to Chief Cormack, and he said it's fine. The officer needed to protect himself, he may have heard of Shana, but she now was in Bakersfield, and it was their rules she needed to play by. *There was no daddy here, to get her out of this one.*

***

As the officer was on the phone to confirm what Shana had said, she took that opportunity to slowly disappear. Not being able to help herself, Shana casually walked into the travel agency. She had not thought this through, she realized this when someone commenced a welcome greeting. But now it would create suspicion if she just left.

"No, she can't go in and she knows better." The Chief yelled down the phone, frustrated at the officer's stupid question. The officer put the phone down and turned around to notice Shana was gone and could see through the glass windows that she was in the travel agency. It was too late.

At the same time, the detective and the undercover police officer located on the other side were watching Shana walking up. Detective Grant was shaking his head "She can't control herself," he mumbled, knowing that when Shana wanted to do something, *she would do it.*

The officer looked over "Is she serious? What happened to her saying this could jeopardize our whole investigation?"

The detective looked at him, shaking his head "Let's just hope she knows what she's doing. She's solved every case she's ever worked on." He added, in the hope of keeping her credibility high.

***

"Anything I can help you with miss?" A red-headed young lady with slight freckles and a big smile got Shana's attention,

"Just looking for now, thank you," Shana replied to the lady that was working alongside Carla.

At the back of the wall was a bunch of catalogs and travel books of beautiful places from all around the world. Shana looked up and saw the beautiful bungalow that lay in the middle of the water, isolated with nobody around. With the thought of just sitting there, Shana began to daydream about how she could see the beautiful clear crystal blue ocean straight from the balcony. It was heaven, it was the Maldives.

She picked up the travel book and opened it looking for more pictures.

"It's Heaven," Carla said noticing the catalog that Shana had picked up.

"It truly is" she turned around not knowing whether to have a discussion or not with her. She was more comfortable observing, but with such a small travel agency she had no choice but to interact.

"Honeymoon?" Carla asked knowingly.

"Oh." Her subconscious mind drifted for a second, she saw herself being swept away by Ryan on the beautiful sands of the Maldives. Something straight out of a romance novel. She liked the thought, both of them both alone, no uniform, no weapons, but total peace. "Yes, my fiancée and I are looking for honeymoon destinations" she enjoyed that idea very much.

"Well, the Maldives is the best honeymoon destination. When are you considering going?"

"We are getting married in three months, so we are looking at the end of April." Shana needed to make her fabricated story somewhat realistic, and three months seemed realistic.

"Have a seat here and let me see what I can do." She guided Shana to a seat as she went around to the other side of the table and started to type away on her computer.

"You must be so excited; the Maldives is one of the most beautiful destinations in the world."

"Have you been there before?" she was curious as to better understand Carla

"Yes, I have," her grin slowly disappeared, but a fake smile overtook it, Shana could see clearly, she had been there with her husband.

"I can see you're married." She said, pointing to Carla's wedding ring and hoping to get more information, "Where did you go for your honeymoon?"

Carla unconsciously covered her left hand and went silent for a second. "Yes, that's right." The fake smile shined again "I went to the Maldives with my husband. We were there for two weeks, it was breathtaking. The best two weeks of my life."

Shana smiled at her, knowing what she had probably gone through "You've sold me,"

They both smiled. "When is the big day?" Carla changed the subject

Thinking quickly on her feet, Shana responded with "April seventeenth" Portia's birthday was the first date that came to her mind. Then for a split second, Shana thought how great it would be that on her wedding day she will have a surprise cake for Portia. She shook her head remembering that this was all not true.

"I'm assuming everything is organized and you're all ready?"

"Yes, I have an amazing wedding planner. The only thing left is picking out the wedding cake, and I am picky with cakes so this one has been a little difficult."

Carla smiled and leaned over to her bag placing it up on the table.

"A good friend of mine has an amazing cake store. I'm sure your wedding planner would have heard of her; she is a true artist."

Shana found her answer while Carla was searching through her bag. She noticed a many small plastic bottles of Jack Daniels whiskey. *It all clicked.*

Carla handed over the business card of her friend's cake shop.

"Is there a chance that I can head off and get your details or I can come back later? It's just that I have to go soon, I didn't notice the time." Shana said, trying to find a way out of there without upsetting Carla or making her suspicious in any way.

"I completely understand. If I can get your number or email, I can send this information to you, and we can take it from there."

"Perfect," Shana wrote her some fake email address on a piece of paper and handed it to Carla. "Thanks, Carla" Shana got up and was ready to exit.

"How did you know my name?" Carla didn't remember introducing herself.

Shana felt a brief flare of panic before she pointed, "Your name tag."

As she exited the store, she sighed in relief. That was close. Shana made her way straight to the parking lot, wanting to get back to the station; she may have the answers to why and how the Window Hunter picked his victims.

Shana was now in the parking lot, ready for an earbashing. She watched as the Bakersfield officer was marching her way "What were you thinking?" Shana didn't care what he had to say, she probably won't ever see this Bakersfield officer again, and she had more important things to deal with.

"Can you get me to the police station?" she opened the door and jumped into the passenger seat.

"With pleasure!" getting her to the police station was the best idea; she could not cause any problems there.

Shana had not been prepared to be told off by the Chief when she reached the station. It was quite different from their first meeting where he was outside to greet her, this time he was yelling at her.

"What were you thinking? I don't know how you do things back in Los Angeles, or what you get away with, but your daddy is not here to get you out of this."

Shana hated how people sometimes used the dad's card against her She knew he supported her, but she worked her way up and she felt people should give her credit for that. *She was her own person.*

"Chief Cormack, I get that you're upset, but if I had not informed you of this case you would have a dead victim on your hands tomorrow. As for jeopardizing the case, don't worry sir, I just may have a better understanding of this case than you give me credit for." She walked toward the room that was assigned to them before turning back around.

68

"By the way Chief, next time you want to talk to me, could you be as kind to take me aside and not put your vocals on display for everyone to hear? I'm sure my daddy would also appreciate that."

The Chief frustratedly pointed his finger to speak, more so to scream, but held himself back and just marched off into his office.

Shana also did the same.

"I need the toxicology report of all female victims." She said to Monica. It was common knowledge that alcohol tended to stay longer in a deceased body than that of a living person. She didn't need to know the amount; she just wanted to see if it was present. She knew it would be difficult to completely get the amount due to contamination that would have taken place. It also probably didn't help that alcohol was a byproduct of decomposition in most kinds of present tissue. It was a long shot, but it was the only one that could confirm her thoughts.

"Alcohol should be in all the female victims. Just as seen in Damien's mother's toxicology report." Shana was sure of it.

Even though these victims were not alcoholics, the fact that they drink alcohol on a regular or routine basis would be enough to trigger the mind of The Widow Hunter. In all victims, he saw his mother. Shana knew too well that his line of attack would always be after they had a few drinks.

The reports from each murder case were brought in. Shana was right. There were signs of alcohol, for some of the victims it was a small percentage, but it was enough to be located in the bloodstream. They were now on the lookout for any drinking places or bars Carla had attended in the past.

Twenty-second of January – 3:00 AM

The shrill of the phone pierced through Shana's sleep. "Hello?" Shana groggily answered.

"He's here Shana, he's in Bakersfield. He is currently staying at the motel three blocks away from Carla's house. You were also right about the visual changes. He has grown a beard and his hair slightly longer, but it's him." The detective was wide awake.

"Does he know he is being followed?"

"No, no, he has no idea." It was clear that he was excited that the case will soon be closed,

"OK, I should get down to the police station." Shana stumbled as she slowly got out of bed.

"No Shana, it's all good. There is nothing you can do here. Let us do our job, I was just letting you know he's here."

She paused for a bit and then sat back on the bed. The detective was right, what was she going to do, even if she had gone into the police station? She would be sitting there worried. The best thing she could do is get some rest and get ready for tomorrow.

"Ok, keep a close eye but also keep distant, tomorrow he should be preparing. Maybe buying some rope and he will be at the mall, following her every move."

"Shana, get some sleep; I'll see you tomorrow." "Fair enough" She hung up the phone, walking around anxiously. She needed that glass of wine now more than ever. She wanted to continue with how to deal with this case but stopped herself. There is nothing more she can do right now but try and enjoy that glass of wine.

The next day, he did go and buy some rope, and was at the mall, sitting across from the travel agency at a coffee shop, watching Carla's every move. On her break, Carla went and had lunch outside the mall at a small little deli in front of the parking lot. On her way, she stopped at the liquor store and picked up a little bottle of alcohol that can easily be hidden in her bag. *Perfect timing Carla, let him see you bought that!*

Shana, again part of the surveillance team today.

They watched as she spent her day at work as usual, and on her way home stopped by the Chinese restaurant close to her house to pick up some takeaway.

They watched as Carla parked the car in her carport and headed in, opened the door, and closed it behind her. The Widow Hunter was already in his car, up the road, the information of what was happening was being feedbacked to Shana.

Shana was confident that he had no idea that two undercover cars were set at two houses across the street, officers were hiding out in a house up for sale, and one unmarked car parked one house down already to put an end to The Widow Hunter.

Shana was extremely nervous back in the police station, *Now the waiting game,* briefly knowing of what was taking place, and many different thoughts entering her mind. She wanted to be there; Shana couldn't take the thought of anyone else getting hurt.

She couldn't take these reoccurring thoughts anymore and picked up the keys to one of the cars and headed outside. She started pushing the alarm button to see which car the keys belonged to. This could be theft, but seriously, who would report her? Then a car finally beeped, *Crap* she thought to herself, as she saw the car's plate number, clear as day *'CORMACK.'* She didn't have

71

time to go back in. She got in and drove the Chief's car, trying to block out the repercussion that will follow.

Shana drove to where Carla lived, slowing down as she entered a road four blocks away, observant and extremely cautious.

In front of her, she saw sirens and police cars. She could hear screaming and two gunshots. She jumped in shock and pushed the accelerator with aim of getting to Carla's house. Was she too late? Who was shot?

Carla was outside being held by two police officers as she tried to reach the body that was on her porch. It was Damien – The Widow Hunter. He was shot in the leg and had a direct shot to the heart.

Carla looked up as Shana was running to make sure no one was hurt, confusion coloring her features. The detective and Chief escorted Shana to the side. She shook her head at the scene around her. The medical examiners from the local forensics team move to take the deceased body away. Some police officers were collecting evidence from his car and backpack. These included a rope, surgical knife, camera, electrical tape, gloves, alcohol wipes, and bleach.

"What are you doing here?" Chief Cormack asked, tone hard but quiet as to not alert Carla.

"I …. I just wanted to make sure that if it had not gone according to plan. I don't know what I could have done, I just needed to be here. I was going crazy at the station." She tried to apologize but he waved her off. A tired sigh escaped him.

"Just… stop. Thank you for your help but the case is closed. You can go home now." He clenched his teeth as he noticed the car, she had pulled up in "And get my car back to the station!

She nodded in agreement, "Can I just talk to her?"

The firmest 'NO' she had ever heard was said to her. She made her way down the small steps of the patio and headed to the car, just like a little girl who had been sent to her room.

As she got halfway into the front garden, a detective called her back.

"Shana, Carla wants to talk to you."

She subconsciously thanked Carla, she turned around and headed back into the home. While entering the front door, she passed the Chief, "how do you always get your way?"

Shana smiled and shrugged as she made her way to Carla. "No Maldives and no wedding I assume." She was shaken up.

"No, no Maldives, no wedding. I'm sorry Carla we couldn't tell you, it would have…."

She cut her off and placed her left hand on Shana's hand, "You're lucky you didn't tell me. You did the right thing; I would have killed him." Carla stuttered as fresh tears fell. "I would have killed him." Shana held her, apologizing continuously.

They spoke for a bit; Carla was settling down and relaxed in the presence of a woman. Shana had a trustful face, a personality that created comfort and also one that created compassion when need be.

As Shana was heading out to let Carla get some rest, they said their goodbyes. Shana had one more unanswered question that was dwelling in her mind. She turned around as she reached the door.

"Carla, can I ask you something?"

"Go ahead" Carla nodded.

"Your husband died three years ago, yet you still wear the wedding ring…. Why?"

Carla looked at her hand and touched the ring. She spun it a couple of times and then took it off.

"I was waiting for the day when my husband can rest with his killer dead. Now, I can rest."

Shana had saved two lives that night, not just Carla's, but that of the widow from Venice beach. It was later discovered that she was to be the second victim after The Widow Hunter had killed Carla.

With that, she gave a small sarcastic salute to the Chief and a goodbye. It was time for Shana and her team to head home.

***

CHAPTER 8

*'Learn yesterday's problem, take its lesson and use it today,
move forward knowing a clearer tomorrow'*

PRESENT

Shana is alone in her store, pacing back and forth waiting for the
photos to develop. She looks a few times through the window,
seeing if there was anything unusual, anyone, watching her.
Shana no longer feels safe. Her phone is ringing. Shana looks
down on the caller id and saw the name *'Dad.'* She isn't in the
mood right now to talk to anyone. *She is afraid.*

There were so many unanswered questions. This case was amiss
from the get-go. There was so much going on. Shana had an
exceedingly tough time letting this case go. But when she saw
what was happening to her, waking up at four in the morning to
go over the case, having dinner with Ryan with the case open on
the dinner table. It had consumed her. When she finally let go of
the case, she could not bring herself to look at another case. It
affected her in ways she never thought was possible.

The Wise Monkey's case had entered her dreams and consumed
her daily thoughts.

Shana remembers what happened in that case and a small tear rolls down her cheek. Shana wipes her tear away, but as she closes her eyes she remembers. She remembers why she is so afraid.

It was the case that took place a few months after The Widow Hunter. Her mind took her to the beginning where it all started.

***

CHAPTER 9

"Close your eyes and take a step back in time,
relax, and let the mind unwind."

Flashback.... The past.

The shrill ring of her phone tore her from the depths of her dreams. Stifling a groan as she saw the time, she answered.

"Get down to the police station now."

"What happened?" Shana figured it was a case and a big one at that. Her father would usually give her some sort of description of what crime scene she is attending, or at least say good morning. He sounded almost disturbed. "Just get down here" he hung up.

Shana shrugged to herself but was up and ready to go as quickly as possible. She knew it had to be a big case and was she eager to get started.

As she entered the police station, the first thing she noticed was unfamiliar faces. She saw Ryan at the end of the corridor with a lot of people in between, she raised her hand to get his attention. He made his way past the officers, Ryan then pointed his hand to an interview room, indicating to Shana to meet him there. Shana nodded and headed straight to the room. She shouldn't have been as surprised as she was to see her team in there waiting for her.

"Your dad didn't tell you?" Ryan was surprised when she asked what was going on.

"No Ryan, if he had would I be asking you?" She snapped, frustrated.

"Just tell her what is happening," John interrupted.

"Remember the family that was killed six years ago in New York, the dismantled bodies?"

It took longer than she liked to admit to remember it, even with her memory. *I need coffee.*

"Yes, yes, the little boy, mother, and father all dead in Long Island, right?"

"And what has that got to do with us? Is he here in LA?" She wasn't sure how she felt about having to deal with another potential serial killer. They were coming down from the high of closing The Widow Hunter case a few months ago.

"Yes… well maybe. To be honest, we aren't certain yet."

"What do you mean?"

As Ryan was about to explain a little more about the case, Shana's father walked straight in.

"There you are, come with me." He pointed at Shana. Ryan continued to walk with her, as the Chief took off before they could reply. Shana and Ryan were swaying between people to keep up to Chief. Shana had never seen the police station this full before.

As the Chief nearly approached his office, he leaned over one of the officer's desks, who was already holding out a file for him. The Chief thanked the officer with a head nod and kept going. Shana looked at the officer and turned to Ryan "Is he new? Who are these people?" Just as Ryan was going to answer Shana, her father turned around.

"Ryan, you don't need to be here. I need to talk to Shana." Shana shook her head; she hated the way he treated Ryan and it was all because he was her boyfriend. The Chief walked behind his desk and opened the file.

Shana looked at Ryan, placing her hand on his, giving him a cheeky wink. Ryan smiled and headed out.

"Do you always have to treat him like shit?" She sighed. Ryan was already working late shifts and placed on the worst possible jobs all because of who he was dating. Ryan is a much bigger person, never complained. Ryan took it all, in hope that he can prove to the Chief he was worthy.

"Sit down, Shana." His voice tinged with a little dash of worry while, pointing to the chair.

"What's going on Dad?" she asked as she sat quickly, distracted by the seriousness of his tone.

"You remember the New York murder of the family that took place?"

"Yes, Ryan mentioned it. What about it? Is he here?"

"No, I'm sure he has fled, probably on his way out of LA as we speak. The crime scene, however, is waiting for you."

"What crime scene?" She gasped. "Oh no, oh God he killed a family here?"

"Yes, his work is getting more artistic and more gruesome. Shana, this is the worst crime scene I have ever seen." He paused,

"Roger died today." He blurted out, seemingly not knowing how else to tell her.

Detective Roger was someone Shana loved and trusted. She had known him since she was a kid, and he was her dad's righthand man at work and away from work. Shana felt sick to her stomach with the news. The murderer was here, and now he had taken the life of someone she knew. *It just got personal.* She remembered the Chief Forensic Scientist in New York who was on this case a few years ago; it was someone she highly admired. Dr. Lynn. If Lynn could not have solved the case, what hope did she have? It has been an open case for many years. Lynn was one of her teaching professors at the university. Shana was overwhelmed with endless questions going through her mind, how had Roger died? Why had he struck in LA, and how will she find him?

She looked over the New York case on her father's desk. During the time of investigating, seven police officers, two federal agents, one detective as well as three forensic team members had died on the case. She was afraid. Shana put the folder down and turned to her father.

"Dad, what happened to Roger?" She did not want it to be true.

"He was found two blocks from his home." Shana's mind was drifting; Roger's brother lived two blocks away with his family. *Oh no.*

"Not his brother?" Shana pleaded.

"Yes Shana," he put the file down on the table and got up, pacing the room.

"Roger was heading home after his shift. You know Roger, he headed to the pub for a few drinks. We received surveillance from the pub saying he left around two am. He must have passed his brother's house and noticed some lights on or something that made him stop the car and go into his house."

"Did he call you? Did he call anyone?"

"Yes, I received a missed call, but it went to voice mail, he didn't leave a message." He continued "He must have walked in while the killer was at work, shots were fired. He…he died instantly." Shaking his head side to side

"The killer then fled, but only after he completed his work. There was no other car at the scene, so we assume he fled in Roger's car. Probably had the siren going until he got to his escape car. We can't find Roger's car."

Shana got up and put her hand on her father's shoulders to comfort him. "Dad, I'm so sorry. I'll find him, but primarily, I need to get to that crime scene."

"Shana, you don't know this man, he won't stop, and if he knows you are trying to track him down you will die. It's a fucking game to him."

Shana took a deep breath in. She knew every word her dad was saying was right, but she had a job to do.

"I have to go," Shana was heading out to the crime scene, once she had gathered her team, to find out what's going on. She didn't have time to think about the repercussions.

"Shana…" her father yelled as she was halfway out the door "I want Ryan stuck to you on this case. He will be there when you stay up late, at the crime scene, when you're in the office when you're walking to your car." Then he paused a little "Even when your home."

Shana was a little shocked, but a part of her felt relieved and happy. Her father would have never liked the idea of her moving in with Ryan, and now he is asking that Ryan be tied down to her in every step she takes. She raised an eyebrow and shrugged her shoulders "You're the boss" she nodded.

She headed to the forensic unit, bypassing all the people running around, some on phones, some talking to other members of the department. It seemed everyone was on some sort of energy drive; phones were ringing, and everyone was moving quite fast. She headed to the elevator, got in, and pushed to go down to the lower floor, her sanctuary. She was alone in the elevator there, she valued those three seconds she would get alone before dealing with one of the worst murder cases. She gave herself time to reflect on Detective Roger, time for her to mourn his death. Then just as the elevator beeped, she took a deep breath in, fixed her clothes, and held her head up. She needed to show confidence to her team, and she needed them at their best, now more than ever.

The doors opened and the team was standing there, all looking at Shana.

"Sorry to have gotten you all out of bed. What do we have?" she walked into the team, expecting the New York file to have already been viewed and understood by everyone before her arrival.

Jake was the first to speak. "We went further than the New York case. Six years ago, a family in Long Island was killed, it was a massacre, they were a family of three. The dismantled bodies were that of the father, mother, and also that of their six-year-old son." He paused.

Shana tried to remember the details of the case, it was slowly coming into play, she needed to be refreshed.

"Ok, Jake we will continue the details of these cases when we get back. Right now, we need to see his current work."

Shana pointed to her field officers and headed in the direction of the garage, it was time to find evidence, to finally catch the murderer.

There was no room for error in this case. She needed everything to be perfect. On her way to the crime scene, she wondered back to what her father had said. Roger had called him, but he missed the call. Roger was his best friend; he would never have missed Roger's call.

While Ryan was driving her to the crime scene with three forensic unit cars following, she took out her mobile phone to make a call. Before she made the call, she altered the caller id off her phone to private.

Ryan looked at her, trying to figure out what she was up to while trying to focus on the road, "What are you doing?"

"Trying to figure something out." She continued her process, not wanting Ryan to know what she was doing and unsure why.

Her father's phone rang, and rang and rang, then paused for a second, and then a different type of ringing tone took place, then a female voice, "LAPD Chief Watson's phone, how may I help you?"

She stared at the phone, wishing her father had not lied and it went to voicemail. Chief George's phone was linked back to the police station. Roger would have defiantly spoken to someone. Why did her father lie? What was he hiding? Her gut was telling her something is not right.

She needed answers. But to get them, she needed patience. She needed to deal with this after she had seen the crime scene.

Ryan didn't ask any questions. He continued driving to a strongly lit-up street of police cars, where they could now see the yellow tape blocking off the crime scene.

***

CHAPTER 10

悪因悪果
"Evil cause, evil effect."
Japanese Proverb

She made her way past the police tape and to the front door, in the opposite direction an officer was running out, slightly bumping into Shana's shoulder, making it to the front of the yard to regurgitate.

"Great work officer, just contaminate my crime scene." She shook her head, making sure that all the other officers had heard, she hoped it would stop them from repeating the same mistake.

Shana felt that an officer's job is to enter the house, make sure that no one is there and that the people who are alive are assisted, and those that are dead are to be left in the positions they are found. Nothing more, nothing less. Now, she would have to gather the officer's vomit and label it in case there was other evidence found around it. *Did no one respect the crime scene these days?*

The house was now empty. The streetlights were out, so instead the police department had gathered some highway lights which were placed in the direction of the house and on the footpath. With neighbors hovering and by-passers stopping to see the action as the bright light directed at the house made it feel as if it were midday, and the sun was shining brightly.

The usual routine took place. All who knew Shana or had worked with her in the past waited outside until they were called in. *'Here comes the magic,'* some would whisper. Shana stepped into the house, noticing a few things laying on the floor, but it was otherwise a perfect home. She closed her eyes and let her senses guide her. This time going to her safe place before a crime scene was different. She was not in the yard, she was in the kitchen, her mother stirring a pot on the stove, Shana's senses smelled a beef and vegetable stew, she took another breath in. Lionel Hampton's album Flying Home was playing. Her mother dressed in the long white summer dress that Shana was so familiar with. Little Shana was sitting on the kitchen table, crayons of all colors were scattered on the table, and Shana was drawing and looking over to her mother who was looking at her and smiling, it was as if the two were having a conversation with their smiles, her long brown wavy hair flickering from side to side, her smile and white beautiful teeth shining.

But this time for the first time, Shana's mother's smile was slowly disappearing while Shana's eyes were closed as she began to imagine and wonder where her mother's beautiful smile was. She was slightly frowning as her eyebrows slightly lifted, she was looking at the drawing that Little Shana had completed. Shana looked over her drawing to see what she had drawn. It was a paper full of black circles, dark circles round and round, and located all over the paper. It was a page of black scribble. Shana then looked at the crayon in her hand, it was red, she looked across the table, and as she did the rainbow-colored crayons were all turning black one by one. Shana was scared, she looked back at her hand and the red crayon too had gone black. Shana jumped off her chair and stood in front of her mom, hoping for some sort of explanation meaning and more so comfort from her mom. *The kitchen was now empty.*

Shana opened her eyes and gasped for air. She no longer heard jazz music; this had never happened to her before. Ryan heard her gasp, and soundlessly steps closer to her.

"Are you ok?"

"I'm fine Ryan." She didn't know what had just happened, but she needed to get it together.

This was not a simple room where she could twirl her way around one room as she normally would.

She wanted to start upstairs and work her way down room by room. After each room, she would call the team in to enter the room, collect evidence, then their normal procedure of evidence collection and digital photography. As she was heading up, she could see the living room to her right, and Roger's body. He was laying on his side and his gun right near his hand, just millimeters away.

She turned her head, wanting to stay focused. Roger wasn't going anywhere – she would be back for him. She continued up the stairs until she reached the second level.

She walked past the upstairs bathrooms and entered the main bedroom. The door slightly opened; the smell of a butcher was in the air.

She looked across the room, not a lot seemed to be moved out of place. It was a large bedroom with a king-size bed in the middle, the sheets indicating that someone was in the bed, the pillows out of place. However, everything else seemed normal. All except a foot visible to Shana at the end of the bed. The size indicated a man was behind the bed on the floor. Shana slowly made her way over.

As she looked over the body, she quickly turned her face away and covered her mouth, then let go to gasp for air, she stood straight up with her back to the body. She took her recorder out of her pocket with her gloved hands slightly shaking; She calmed herself down with a few deep breathes. She turned around and pushed the record button.

"White male victim looks to be mid-forties" she paused to turn away again. The man was staring directly at her.

His eyelids were glued back with having no hope of closing his eyes, forced to have to witness every single thing that had taken place to him.

His hands had been tied but the ropes were removed after he was killed, the marks noticeably clear around the wrist.

"A type of glue was used to keep the eyes opened, being placed on the eyelid," Shana moved to the top of his fingers, she noticed "dislocations in his crucial region, slight blue defense marks located on his hand, trying to stop a sharp object, clean-cut, located on the palm, and also the inner arm."

His thighs opened widely. Each time she looked down; she had the urge to want to vomit. The smell was so strong.

"A few of the bottoms located on the floor around him indicating that the shirt was ripped off his body."

"A large amount of blood loss on the carpet in between the victim's legs and around his outer and inner thighs."

Shana was able to see the internal organs of where the penis and testicles were supposed to be located.

"The testicles, penis, and scrotum have been removed. It looks as if it was an elliptical incision, the testicles also were extracted with a precision cut." She looked around the room to see if she could locate the missing organs, but they were nowhere to be found.

She wanted to move along; she wanted this body at the morgue as soon as possible to have an in-depth medical understanding of what took place.

However, just as she was getting up, she noticed the shirt that was ripped open and was then folded back on the body, with a bloodstain on the inside staining the front of the shirt.

She questioned the situation out loud "Why would he rip the shirt, and then close it?" Logically the reason would be that he was hiding something or wanted to surprise the person who found the body.

Shana used her pen, and slowly moved one side of the shirt over followed by the other. She found something very was unusual. He had used the victim's blood to what resembled that of Asian writing, she was not sure which, however. She stared at it as if waiting for a translation to occur.

She took her phone out and took a quick photo of the writing; she wanted to know what the killer was saying.

She looked over and over, "Was that a letter 'h' (悪ん) at the end of the writing or was that part of it" She continued to talk to herself.

She had what she needed, she looked around the room, wanting to move on quickly. She called down to two members and asked them to come up and investigate the room. Normal routine, crime scene photos, collect evidence and be thorough.

She then led them into the room, with a brief indication, trying to prepare them for what they are about to see

She then called in Wong knowing he spoke over five languages. Shana was hoping he would translate what she saw, or at least find out what language it was in. But as she was just about to head down the stairs, she looked toward the end of the hallway. She was not sure this case was going to be easy. She started to question herself.

She could see the little fingers of a child part in the hallway with the rest of the body in the room.

"Shana?" she slightly trembled as Wong broke her concentration,

She wanted to ask him, but she put it on hold. "Come with me" Wong followed her as she walked to the end of the hallway, "wait out here."

Shana walked into the room; the bed was unmade to illustrate the child was probably asleep before the murderer entered. Shana assumed that the child was probably woken by a screaming parent or was he the first victim? Then maybe his father was coming out of his bed to help him, only to be surprised by the criminal. Could two people have been involved in this? Questions and assumptions consumed Shana's mind as she continued investigating.

That poor little boy, so innocent, his golden-brown hair so fluffy. He looked to be around seven years old. His eyes were also glued back, just like his father's. Shana hoped that the child didn't have to witness his tragic death. The blanket that was placed slightly over his shorts, made her angry.

She started with the child's hands; "visible bruising, abrasions, fractures are visible on the arms and hands of the victim, a few cuts also seem visible and one cut leading to the back of the arm." A brief description was all she could stomach. Even though she was great with detail, the real detail was in the autopsy report. She continued with the description of the room and the location of the boy.

Shana stopped recording as she looked at the defense marks.

Seeing defense wounds shows the fight they had in them. The victim wanted to live, wanted to survive, wanted to just get away, to defend themselves with every ounce of energy they have, they did not want to die. The fight that humans have in their last hope of defending themselves was the reason why Shana did what she did. She would now fight for their soulless bodies.

Shana clicked the recording button again, *"Child's room is located toward the end of the hallway on the left-hand side. The room looks to be untouched, bed unmade, some trophies have fallen to the floor that seems to have been located on the nightstand."*

She didn't want to touch the body this was more of observation before her team joined her.

"The same type of glue probably was also used to keep the eyes opened," Shana moved down trying not to look the little boy directly in his eyes, trying to keep her breathing at a normal rhythm.

Looking at the left side of his head and then rotating to that of his right, "Victim's ears have been removed, ears are not located near the body and are currently missing." She closed her eyes for a second emphasizing what she was witnessing. Shana took a deep breath in before she continued.

"Visible injuries appear on the neck. There are scratches, abrasions, and scrapes, with some blood located on the victim's nails, these marks are also probably defense marks. The combination of lesions indicate erythema, abnormal inflammation, and redness of the skin," she used her pen to slightly lifting his chin, revealing the neck, "Very faint bruising clustering in the sides on the neck close to the jawlines, even extending to the chin. Some chin abrasions are visible. The ligature marks around the neck hinting towards manual strangulation." She could see the bruises left behind. It was evident it was by hand.

Shana was hoping that the little boy had died before having his ears cut off, or even his eyes glued. This however was unlikely; the sole purpose of the criminals was to have the child's eyes open during the whole procedure.

She didn't want to remove the small blanket that he had covering his upper thigh and genital area. She didn't want to find what she had found in his father's room. She took a minute or two to collect herself. She was a professional. *She could do this.*

With her pen, she lifted the blanket slightly to find that the genitalia area was all intact, a small sigh of relief came over her.

Shana then saw bloodstains on the child's shirt, the bloody hands of the criminal. She gently pulled the child's shirt back "What have you left this time?"

There again she saw Asian script, in the little boy's blood. 聞かざる

This one, however, was a little longer than the other one. She took out her phone and took a clear picture.

She looked around the room and continued to record her findings. Shana then started her outward spiral analysis of the crime scene, starting at the location of the body being located at the entry of the room and working her way around the room. Making sure every part was covered.

When she finished, she took one last look at the little boy, and leaned over, "I'm going to find this son of a bitch, I promise."

Shana needed to remember this is a job, but who was she kidding? This job had a way of sucking you in so much more when children were involved. *It consumed you.*

As she headed out of the room, she saw Wong waiting for her. "Wong look at me." Wong seemed to be all over the place.

He looked up "Are you ready for this? Do not think for one second that saying no will undermine your professionalism. I just need you to be honest – are you ready for this?"

She knew he was ready, but also, she knew that with forensics it's best to slowly get someone into fieldwork, better than throwing them into the deep end straight away. Wong was great technically and with the camera, but she knew that he could do so much more.

He nodded, "I can do this." He was amazing in armed robbery crime scenes and worked well with collecting evidence. He was also quite talented at analyzing gun residue and weaponry analysis.

Shana put her hand on his shoulder "Ok," He took a few deep breathes before going in.

Shana moved towards the bathroom to have a quick look. But paused, remembering the strange symbols.

"Wong, do you know what this says?" she took out her phone and showed him the writing on the father's and little boy's body.

"This is Japanese. This one says 'Shizaru,' this is an incredibly old scripture, my grandfather had this tattooed on his palm. It symbolizes the principle of doing no evil," Then he pointed to the second photo "This says 'Kikazaru,' it is a name, I think. I'm not sure."

"Ok, that's fine for now. I'll need you later though." Wong nodded.

Wong made his way into the little boy's bedroom, while Shana walked into the bathroom.

Just as she was heading down the stairs, she noticed a photo on the wall she had missed on her way up. In a beautiful family portrait, the father was sitting on a chair, with his son on his lap, his wife on a chair beside him, and finally, a beautiful girl standing with her hand on her mother's shoulder and her mother had her hand on top of her daughters. She was a beautiful girl; she looked a lot like her mother. Shana thought it was a delightful photo that conveyed their closeness as they smiled happily for the camera.

Then she looked back upstairs, there were only two bedrooms, *where was the girl's bedroom?* She looked again to make sure that she had not missed anything. Shana was right there were only two bedrooms, one was the boys, it only had one small bed and could not have fit two people in that bed, or that bedroom.

She continued down the stairs when Shana was distracted by the noise coming from outside. With police lights lighting up the street, it seems all the officers have decided to have a meeting right outside her crime scene. The noise was getting louder and louder as she had made her way down.

Someone had tipped off the news. Journalists, news broadcasters, and radio stations were all located at the front, being pushed back by police officers and told to stay behind the crime scene tape and off the lawn.

Shana was disappointed. It seemed journalists these days pay off some police officers to get in on the big news. Sometimes they do more harm than they do good. Getting the public worried and alerting them early can lead to massive destruction in the case. An autopsy needed to take place, research needs to be done thoroughly, and psychoanalysis of the criminal needs to be made to understand what they are dealing with. With this information, they can build their case, know what they need to keep to themselves and what information they need to release to the press. Any incorrect information given to the press can be damaging to the case, Shana had experienced this in the past.

She poked her head out, calling out to Detective Grant, "Keep them as far away from the house as possible, the less they know the better."

"Someone's already tipped them off. FBI is flying in."

She shook her head in disappointment, "just keep them as far as possible." He nodded.

Shana continued to look for an extra room or a place where the girl would have been located. There was no such room. She was puzzled.

Shana walked down the hallway and entered the kitchen, the kitchen was not quite as clean as the rest of the house, understandable as the woman lying on the floor appeared to have fought for her life. She was just meters away was the phone, which she tried to get in hope of calling the police.

Shana leaned over the body; the lady was turned on her stomach. The basic discoloration that appeared on her back was blood heading to the floor which told Shana that she had been turned over after she had been killed.

Once her heart had stopped beating, this victim, this wife, this mother, was definitely on her back. Her back had pressed up against an object because her back was touching the floor, there are white spots, kind of bleach looking, they are located on the parts of the body that had direct contact with the floor.

But this was moved within an eight to twelve-hour gap, her body was cold and stiff.

The victim was put in a position where her legs are straight, her head on the floor, with her nose touching the ground and her hands above her head. On her elbows, it was clear, with gray areas visibly showing patterns of postmortem lividity.

On her naked back, there also was Japanese writing. The criminal must have brought a paintbrush with him.

This time 見ざる was found on the back of the female victim.

Shana again took a quick photo of the writing,

She recorded her findings, "the woman's hands were not tied, and some defense marks are visible on the back of her arm," She had to follow a protocol before moving the body. She made note of the woman only having her underwear on, which from looking at the back seemed to not have been moved or replaced That was a good indication that no sexual encounter took place.

"A pool of blood was around the head and face, indication an open wound." Shana resumed.

She then looked over at the writing. *Same technique as the other two.* The letters start so dark and so clear, but then slowly get lighter and lighter as if he only dipped in the victim's blood once.

Before calling in more members of her team, she left the body for a second. A gut feeling was leading her to further analyze the kitchen. The kitchen was open to the dining room, and the dining room was open to the lounge room.

Returning to the body, she found the reason behind the pool of blood around the lady's head.

It appeared that the eyeball had been removed with surgical care. Moving to the other eye, she opened the lid and saw the same thing. This killer had removed both eyes without making much of a mark on the lids and had taken them with him. *With care, not anger. But why?*

Shana leaned over and saw the knife near the kitchen bench. There was blood splatter on the kitchen bench and the knife. *'Could this be what the criminal had left behind or was it the blood of the victim?'* the only way Shana would know is after they take it back to the lab.

A Ginsu fourteen-piece stainless steel black cutlery set had once sat so neatly on the kitchen bench. Now they were all over the place. Shana could see that the victim tried to grab a knife to defend herself. The killer was much stronger, but that didn't mean she was going to give up.

There were visible blood stains and splatters that were located slightly away from the body, she must have been punctured roughly three feet away from the body. There were blood smudges on the kitchen floor indicating the body was dragged, the clean kitchen was covered in blood. There were hand marks positioned on the benches and the sink and the bottom of the fridge as if she were using the fridge to try and get herself up. *It was horrific.*

There were several impressions on the kitchen floor, different from the foot impressions of the barefoot of the victims. She had seen these prints before. She looked closer and then it came to her. *The criminal was wearing protective disposable shoe covers.* The criminal was extremely cautious.

Again, applying the outward spiral search, Shana started at the center of another crime scene and works outward, making recorded notes along the way and using her observation skills to foresee the crime scene.

Shana then called in Julia and Jake. One to start with photography of the scene and one to start forensic photography of the body. She stood by while the photography of the body took place. She continued to watch as her team, performed and notices their facial expressions. She saw anger, disgust, and them questioning why. Shana was grateful for those reactions; she never wanted her team to lose empathy.

After Julia had finished with her photography, it was time for Shana to turn the body over.

Julia placed the camera and stood behind her as she went to assist, kneeling on the ground close to the victim's shoulders and Shana near the hip and lower thigh.

"At the count of three," Shana instructed

"One… two… three" the body was turned over.

"Good God!" Julia squealed, covering her mouth, forgetting to be professional.

Shana grabbed her with force, one hand on her chin, making sure that she didn't look at the body anymore and the other on her shoulder. "Look at me Julia."

"Breathe in through the nose out through the mouth," Shana breathed with her. She didn't need Julia to faint right now. The other member taking photos around the crime scene had stopped subconsciously to also follow Shana's breathing instructions to Julia.

Jake was a strong man and worked in the field much longer than Julia. He didn't want to show that he too was affected. With his back turned and his hand on the kitchen bench, he secretly did as Shana was telling Julia to do. It was working. Shana then reached into her pocket and placed some eucalyptus oil on the tip of her finger and placed it under Julia's nose, besides hiding the smell, it acted as a kind of a wake-up call as well.

She knew that Jake was also affected, and clearly understood that he was trying to be strong.

"Jake," He turned around, his face flustered.

She leaned over and placed some oil also under his nose.

"I know you don't need it, but just in case."

Shana told them to take a few minutes off. She wanted to make a few more notes with the front of the body now the true artwork of the criminal was now visible.

It was clear where the blood was coming from, the majority of it anyway. The defense marks are all so much clearer now all located on her hands, palms, inner arms, and fingers.

Shana could see abrasions, which involved scraping off the skin on a rough surface. She looked around and found where these could have come from. The side of the wall leading into the dining room was a feature wall that was composed of sand and cement. The victim was using the wall as a means of getting up but was dragged most probably by her feet. The victim was grabbing on the wall for her life.

"Abrasions on the palm and the tip of her fingers, incision cuts were also located on the palms of her hands and her left index finger. This was a sharp cut done with a knife with exceptionally clean edges. A puncture is located just below the thumb, on her right hand, her left wrist appeared to have a small chunk of skin removed and unseen."

"The victim has her eyelids also glued back, however; it was not as clean as the other two victims. The other two had had their hands tied but there are no marks around the victim's wrist to indicate that she was tied. With the amount of visible defense marks, it was obvious that she was continuously trying to stop him." Pausing for a second, again taking a breath in aim maintaining her professionalism

"The eyeball has been removed with surgical care and then gorged out in anger over something." Shana looked around. 'He must have taken them with him with the others' Shana held herself as much as she could but looked closer, a surgical scoop and a knife scapula were used, and these are also consistent with the marks on the victim's hands. "The criminal was trying to make a clean-cut, but the victim trying to defend herself. There are a lot of laceration and error cuts where all are located around the eye. He then must have removed the dismantled eye from the eye socket with severe tugging and straining. The face was slashed. The victim's lips looked incredibly dry and ripped. It indicates her lips were glued together, most probably to keep her from screaming. However, it seemed this didn't stop the victim. The pain of her eyes being taken out was enough; she wanted to scream for help." Shana had never seen a human being so brutally damaged with defense marks. "It was probably her cries or the noise she was making with things falling in the kitchen that triggered Roger. This woman was not just fighting for herself … *this woman was fighting for her family.*"

She pushed the stop button on her portable recorder and called Jake and Julia back in. They seemed to have got themselves together and were ready to collect evidence.

Where is the daughter's room?' she thought the only thing down here was a lounge room, a kitchen, and the dining room, with a brief hallway.

While wondering, she walked towards Roger. From the positioning of Roger's body, Shana pictured how he would have come in. Roger must have walked into the house; Shana wondered, *'did he have a key?'* He probably tiptoed into the lounge room, hearing the noise most probably coming from the kitchen.

The criminal must have been packing, ready to leave by the looks of things, as the woman was taking her last breaths. Roger entered the living room; the killer must have heard him. Shana tiptoed around where she thought Roger would have come in, and as she did a squeaky noise from the wood floors echoed in the quiet. This would have alerted the killer, *'Damn'* The killer was also tiptoeing in the hallway to surprise him.

Roger would have had his gun in his hand ready, the safety was off, and his gut feeling told him that something was wrong. Roger was known for his intuitions, his gut feeling was never wrong.

Shana started to visualize what had happened. Just as the criminal was making his way into the dining room, moving slightly faster than Roger, he must have stepped on the floorboard right on the angle of one that made another small squeaking sound. This must have made Roger jump and shoot; however, he shot the wall. Shana walked over to the wall where the bullet hole was, it was in line with that of the hallway. The killer shot back with such precision. Shana could see that the entrance wound was on the forehead, a clear shot.

The entrance wound was usually much smaller and somewhat symmetrical to that of the exit wound. The entrance wound seemed ringed and had a visible residue of gunpowder present. Using her feet to measure Shana felt that the shot was taken from roughly five feet away.

The exit wound located on the back of Roger's head was quite large. This takes place as the movement of the bullet through the body tends to slightly slow down and cause a somewhat combustion with the tissues closest to the existing and surrounding muscles. The exit wound had bled profusely, with blood splatter around the back of the room where Roger's head was facing was visible, as Roger fell to the floor blood was pouring out profusely. This was illustrated by the pool of blood found.

From what Shana could see, there were only two bullets – one from Roger which landed in the wall, and one from the criminal which landed in Roger.

She called in the crime scene unit from outside to start with the lounge.

They came in to cover the crime scene, looking not only for the weapon involved but also for bullet shell casings and if there were any loose rounds.

Shana let the team do their job as she went through into the hallway in line with Roger's body, then kneeled close to his head, pointing to the direction of where he was shot "This is where he was shot from" she spoke to herself. Shana placed her hand on her temporal bone slowly massaging her head, right above her ear. A small migraine was making its way and she just didn't have time for it right now.

Shana walked through the hallway past the kitchen where the crime scene unit was working its magic. She made her way to the door leading into the garden, Shana opened the door, a small outside laundry with an outside toilet attached to it. The garden was roughly fifteen by thirty feet quite a small garden, the grass however was freshly cut, and no shrubs seemed visible.

A small table for four with a nice umbrella hanging was located not far from the BBQ area. No other object was in the garden. It was probably the simplest garden Shana had ever come across.

Shana put her head in the laundry room and the outside toilet. Nothing out of the ordinary.

She picked herself up and headed back inside the house.

"Ok, I need you all to listen up." She also tried to get the people's attention from upstairs analyzing the crime scene.

"I need a thorough investigation here. I want every digital photography to be perfect and all evidence collected. The New York team is flying in. We all are aware that the same thing happened in New York, but this is LA and one of our own was also taken."

She took a breath, looking at Wong "Once you're done with the room, I need you at the station,"

Wong nodded.

"A person is missing from this crime scene," Shana continued. She then called over her best computer whiz Tim, "we have lots of work to do, I want ALL the detailed New York files on my desk." Tim was ready to deliver.

Her gut instinct said that there were more cases like this, she just needed to find the link. She made a mental note to find out more about the other cases with the same pattern. The more the cases, the easier it would be to better understand the criminal's pattern and hopefully catch him.

With Asian calligraphy, Shana knew she needed to be looking internationally if there is a link to other cases. But her main concern now was that Shana first needed to find out where the girl was and focus on the crimes that have taken place in her jurisdiction.

It was going to be a strenuous kind of day.

***

CHAPTER 11

弱肉強食
"The weak are meat; the strong do eat."
Han Yu

Shana later discovered that Roger had tried to save his brother's family. Steven was Roger's younger brother and Kate his wife, they had two children a boy named Douglas and a girl named Katherine, who had started college last year. The family shared a close bond. They had moved from Florida where they lived for over 20 years, but when their daughter was accepted at the University of Southern California for a Bachelor of Law degree and fortunate to be placed on scholarship, the family decided it was best to move close to their daughter.

The sun was making its way over LA as Shana sat in the office. The New York file was right on her desk. *Case NY3450.*

She knew the detective that was on the search for the girl, He was vigilant and impulsive, but he was also the best with missing people cases. If anyone needed help to find a person, they would go to Graham.

"Graham, have you found the girl? Have you found Katherine?" She yelled out to him.

"Shana, I'm working on it, I just got the information now!" he snapped.

Shana took a breath, and then in a gentler voice asked,

"Ok Graham, let me know the second you have something."

"I sure will," he commenced typing away, investigating any significant links from her financials, her mobile phone, and any other useful information that can assist the team in finding her.

Shana's fear beleaguered her with the uncertainty that if it were the criminal that had taken the daughter, why was he out of character, given that he had not kidnapped anyone in his previous cases. This poor girl is scared and alone somewhere, dead, or alive. Whatever the situation was, this unfortunate girl was deserted. In any case, Shana needed to fill in the pieces.

Wasting no time, Shana familiarized herself with the New York case and figure out what they may have missed.

The New York case comprised many similarities, it was a family of three, not four, and the father had his lips removed. The child in one case was a young five-year-old girl, who was also strangled and had her ears removed.

The mother had died the same way. Her eyes also gouged out, however, with much fewer defense wounds than that of the most recent victims. The bodies were positioned the same way; however, none illustrated any form of Japanese calligraphy. *It painted a confusing scene.*

Shana looked at the photos, trying to get an understanding of the criminal's intent, the insane character behind this. He was either of Asian descent or was acquainted with one. The question was what the symbolization of Japanese writing was.

She needed Wong to hurry and get back from the crime scene to help her understand the meaning of the writing.

Equally, the houses seemed clean. Most of the mess was caused by interference or things the family used to try to get away, like a dropped lamp. Other than that, all were in order.

Overall, the biggest difference between the two cases was the fact that an officer was at the scene. Roger had seen who this person was. But it wasn't like Roger could tell them who it was. Roger's few seconds face to face with the criminal made Shana wonder – *were words exchanged or was it a quick shoot-out?*

***

CHAPTER 12

*"I have lost a loved one in my life,
compensate this pain with love"*

A week before Roger's death

George picked up the work phone and was about to dial, then hung up. He reached for his suitcase and pulled out his cell. *Just to be safe*. He called Detective Grant.

"Meet me at Rutter's in five."

"Make it ten, I need to drop the kids at school. I'll drop them off and be there shortly after,"

"She's your ex, Grant, you don't have to run errands at the drop of a hat for that bitch." This was an old argument that they both constantly had.

"I'll see you in ten."

Grant was George's best mate; they had met just before they joined the force at eighteen. They were each other's children's godfathers and brothers in all but blood. Three years ago, when George was shot on duty and nearly lost his life, his only option for survival was a blood transfusion that came from Grant. They knew each other's weaknesses, strengths, and secrets. They supported each other and covered for each other. Their arguments don't last long, and when they did argue, after a lot of cursing, they end it all with a beer and some football talk.

Rutter's was a local bar where the two hang out and on occasion, the local bar would become the work-related escape for countless police officers. Given that the Chief and Grant were regulars, they had possession of their corner, slightly isolated from the bar, yet in full view of the widescreen TV where the news or football was visible. More importantly, it was private, meaning they were reassured they can converse without others prying or listening in. It was a family-owned business with bar food but was well-known for its burgers. They had farm-grown organic eggs in them, and the fries were deliciously spiced, crispy, and salty.

George was at *Rutter's Bar*, sitting in the usual place waiting anxiously for Grant, looking at his phone. The bartender, a sweet 45-year-old woman who was familiar with him coming into the bar, knowing that he was probably was on shift and brought over some house coffee. George smiled and thanked her. Everyone in the bar knew who he was, *after all, he was a regular.* Grant walked into the bar, greeting the bartender, high-fiving the waitress, and hugging the lovely 56-year-old wife of the owner.

George watched and waited for Chief to join him. He wanted to get this conversation out of the way quickly and come up with a game plan.

"I'm here, and if you're going to bad mouth Patricia, then I'm out of here," Grant said, defending his ex-wife and not in the mood to fight with him.

"I don't give a crap about Patricia. There's bigger shit to deal with."

They both looked at each other.

Grant sat down. "Roger's acting up again?" George nodded. "I told you he's weak, but you had to take him in and baby him. He's not your son… fuck fuck!" he snapped, angry at the thought that Roger could blow the whistle at any time.

"Grant, he did not receive the letters. I've gotten them instead, maybe he was too paranoid with the feeling of being followed." George was both trying to defend Roger and find a solution.

"You know what I don't fucking understand is for the past two weeks, I've been receiving shit, and I fucking haven't told you or the little bitch." The last comment was referring to Roger.

George was astonished "Why the fuck wouldn't you tell me?"

"Because you would make me move in with you." George sighed as he leans back, but he knew better. Patricia hated George and moving in with him would mean no chance in hell for any sort of reconciliation. He understood yet was undeniably frustrated.

"As long as Patricia's happy." Grant's look said that he was done with this topic.

George then changed the subject, "I spoke to Tateyuki. He had three families butchered in Japan before he hit New York. If hits in LA we're screwed."

Grant was visibly angry, "Tateyuki, the fucker said they killed the serial killer, that's what we paid him to do."

"They thought they did." He paused, unsure how to tell Grant the rest. "He faked his death; his lover had dug him out after they buried him."

"This is fucked up." Grant got up, putting his arms on his lower waist while he leaned forward, trying to breathe properly, "This monster is after us. I have to get Patricia and the kids out of here."

George nodded, knowing nothing he could say would stop him. "Fine but do it discreetly. He's watching our every move."

"You have to get Shana far away from here George!" he was pacing now, the thought of something happening to Shana scaring them both. But George had no choice, he was in charge, he worked hard for this, and with Shana always in his presence and her boyfriend close by, it *should* be ok. He didn't like it, but it was what it was.

"I can't..." George wanted to explain but Grant was quick to jump in, raising his voice.

"Are you fucking crazy? Are police stripes worth more than your daughter?" George tried to explain himself but Grant cut in. "You know if he hits LA, Shana WILL BE working on this case?" George didn't have to answer vocally, his eyes were doing the talking. "You're fucking with me, right? Are you fucking serious?"

"Shana will be in charge of the crime scene of an international mass murderer with whom we have had fucking contact. She could be a victim. Is it getting through to you?" Each word is hissed through tightly clenched teeth.

George was done with being silent. "Sit down. He wouldn't hit in LA he is just trying to scare us!, we don't even know if he is here on American soil! don't you think we would have had our mate at homeland security let us know!"

Grant chuckled in disgust *"Your manipulations know no boundaries. What the fuck is going on?!"* he yelled as he slammed the table out of anger.

It was George's turn to stand, "It's going to be fine." He whispered as he placed some money on the table and rushed out. He came intending to talk about Roger, it ended up being about Shana. They needed to discuss a plan, and George thought it was critical time that was wasted.

"You're making a big mistake." Grant rose his voice so that George could hear on his way out.

Both were fired up with anger. Both acted on it, their quick impulses always got the best of them. Grant sat in silence as he grabbed George's drink and threw it back.

The fear was that they both knew Shana was a brilliant investigator and there is no denying that she is overly dedicated and intelligent. She won't stop until the puzzle is solved. It wasn't Roger that they should be worried about, it was Shana. They're going to lose her. Grant pushed the drink away at that thought and walked out not saying bye to the people he just greeted so lovingly. *His gut confirmed something was going to happen, and soon!*

Had they known Roger's death was coming, they both knew this conversation would have been different.

***

CHAPTER 13

"My pride is my wrongdoing."

Grant and his wife took Shana in for a while after her father was shot on duty when she was twelve. Like family, they took amazing care of her. He always knew how to make her feel better. Grant treated Shana as if she were one of his own. He would always look out for Shana and George.

At times, when Shana's father and Grant were arguing, Shana would get a bucket of water and throw it on the two of them, telling them to cool down. This would result in the pair chasing her and tickling her. She may have lost her mother, but she felt like she was blessed with two amazing fathers.

Shana always tried to get away with her teenage mischiefs. She once asked her father to go to a rave party that everyone was going to. Her father knew that pills, drugs, or alcohol most certainly would be sold or distributed. Thus, her father would answer with a firm and affirmative *"No!"* After begging for weeks, she gave up. This did not mean Shana would not try to do things her way. Saturday night came.

"Ok, Dad I'm off to bed," stretching her arms into the air followed by a phony yawn.

"It's Saturday night. Don't you want to stay up and watch a movie with your favorite person?" her father questioned. It wasn't like her to go to bed so early.

"I would love to, but it's that time of the month and I have a few cramps."

"Ok baby girl get some rest then. Want some tea?" He was suspicious now. When had that ever stopped her?

"No, but thanks, I'll just sleep it off." Shana then kissed her father on the cheek and headed upstairs to *'sleep.'*

Shana, at times, would forget that her father had an elephant's memory. He was a single father and was always on the lookout, for he knew all too well her moods and most of the reasons behind them. George began to analyze the situation, ironically like it was another case. *I sure don't remember those mood swings that tag along with her junk food snacking,* so Shana did not have her period. Her father's eyebrows rose as he remembered that tonight was the rave party. *She better not have!"*

Just as he was going to head upstairs, his phone rang. Grant outside. George explains what had just happened with Shana and the funny feeling he had that she may not be telling the truth.

"Hey, don't bother going upstairs, I'm just outside," Grant was laughing "I'll see you in a sec…. with Shana,"

George hung up and headed toward the door until he received another call, which distracted him.

During their conversation, Shana had tried to sneak out, given that she had planned her escape for weeks and she was so excited.

She opened the window; it was a simple short jump. She had her clothes on and ready to hit the rave. She danced and pranced silently on her tiptoes in excitement as she placed some pillows over her bed followed by her blanket. *Perfect*! Those pillows were a great disguise. Shana locked her bedroom door and jumped out of the bedroom window, landing safely on her legs. As she was bouncing back into a straight position she was startled by Grant, who was watching her every move and waiting for her calmly, chuckling to himself.

She turned around, startled, and jumped as she saw Grant standing there waiting for her. He knew her all too well.

"Oh, come on, are you serious?" Shana sighed, knowing that it was all over.

"Sleepwalking, I suppose?" Grant replied sarcastically.

"Can't you just be one of those cool godfathers and ignore this? Come on please, you never saw me." She begged that just this once she could do something exciting.

Grant shakes his head "No sorry my dear. Come on, let's go inside."

Two minutes later, the doorbell rang and with a sense of urgency in his tone, George ended the phone call and opened the door.

George was angry but happy that Grant had got her before she had headed out. Turning up to a rave party looking for her would have been a disaster.

"Get your butt upstairs. You're grounded." He growled, pointing to her room.

"How can I be grounded if I didn't even make it to the front yard?" she tried to reason and plead with them.

"Stop being a smartarse. You were thinking of going and you acted on it. If it weren't for Grant, God knows where you would be!"

"Ohhh you're so melodramatic! Both of you need to seriously relax. I'm not a hostage!" she had her hands on her hips and a very typical teenage scowl on her face.

"Get upstairs. We'll talk later" her father replied as she was making her way past the lounge room.

"Fine! But I can only open the door from the inside, I was planning to climb back in!"

Her attitude was grating on his nerves. "I don't care! Just get upstairs." He snaps.

"FINE!" Shana stomped up the stairs to her bedroom.

A massive bang takes place and then another one follows.

Grant and George look at each other before nearly running into each other to get up the stairs, only to see Shana standing near a door hanging on one loose door hinge.

"I can get in my room now." She smiled; arms crossed. George was speechless. "Oh, and I guess we need a new door." She parted with, as she walked in into her bedroom.

George was furious and opened his mouth to yell, but Grant grabbed his shoulder.

"Let's have some beers, and let it cool off. She's a teenager. It is what they do."

George nodded; Grant was right.

They both sit on the couch, drinking beer, trying to calm down. Grant looked over at s friend, "She did tell you that she couldn't get into the room since it was locked from the inside."

George looked at him and they laughed.

"She reminds me of me more and more every day. It's scary."

They both sit back and put their feet up to enjoy their beers as they watched TV, and randomly laugh as they remember what just had happened.

***

CHAPTER 14

"We have just scratched the surface.
The crack is made, now it is time to dig."
R. Chaalan

The journey of finding the Wise Monkey Serial killer was in play.

"We got a hit on the girl," Tim called out.

Shana quickly made her way into the room after hearing the announcement from the hallway.

"Her last call was made two days before the crime. It was at her home. Calls before that were regular calls to her mother and father's cell phone. A few other numbers were also called. The phone has been unused for the last three days. The phone is still on, and we are trying to track it down to find its location, we're waiting for it to come in." Tim explained as they waited anxiously for the green light to come on suggesting a possible location or whereabouts. Finally, it was zooming into the location before a street name appeared on the screen.

"Look here." He pointed to the address.

"The dot is not moving. Either it's just her phone or we get the phone and the body. This corner is a cut-off dead-end quiet street."

"Good work Tim," Shana said gratefully, taking a long breath in, this was good news. She made her way to Detective Grant and explained the situation while they both walked out toward his car.

As she was heading to the car, Shana stopped and turned to Tim. "She has been missing for three days in this report, from her last phone call, but then the lecturer said she has been absent for four. Where did the extra day come from?"

"We're getting some surveillance tapes from the university," Tim responded in hope of letting her know that he was already on top of it.

"Find out who her social network is. Who she spent time with, find out whether or not she's seeing anyone, in a relationship, when was the last time someone saw her? Thanks, Tim." No one knew social media like Tim.

She got in the car and then they were off. "God, I hope she's not there."

"Me too," Grant said cynically. There were enough dead bodies for one day.

The whole drive with Detective Grant was pure silence. Grant had nothing to say, it was undeniable that he had a great deal on his mind.

As they pulled up to the location, they parked the car on the corner a few feet away. It was a corner filled with oversized bins. Not a human insight, as silence overpowered the clamorous streets of the city. Shana visually analyzed the dusted area and came up with the assumption that this place would be capable of secreting a dead body without any risks or chances of getting caught.

Grant leaned over to inspect the oversized debilitated bin.

"Move back Shana," Grant said, and Shana did as he instructed.

Covering his mouth from the odors the bins were releasing, Grant flipped the bin over. It was full of trash, moldy with compost and God knows what else. An unbearable foul smell filled the air. They both jumped back to the cloud of flies and cockroaches crawling out. Shana knew this was not a good sign, flies liked bodies.

Shana took out her phone from her side pocket, she had the victim's number saved in her phone. Trying to slightly turn her head from the smell that the wind was blowing her way, Shana dialed the number and as she expected, it was ringing from the bin they had opened.

Grant looked at Shana and Shana glanced back at him.

"Seriously, you're not going to make me do it, are you?" Shana was not dressed accordingly.

He nodded and smiled "You picked your job Shana and I picked mine. I'll stand here and call the crime scene unit or back up. Did you want a bottle of water?" his humor did not help the situation.

After Shana went through her forensic analysis of bin diving, with her now stale gloves. Shana had come across a large shoulder bag. It was Katherine's college bag; it had her college books, her phone, wallet with money, and her credit card all in it. It appeared untouched. Fortunately, there was no discovery of her body. Shana was relieved.

Shana placed Katherine's bag in the evidence carry case to take it for further DNA examination or testing at the lab, maybe a fingerprint, anything that could link them to the sociopath criminal.

Detective Grant drove Shana back. "Shana, maybe stop off at home for a quick shower?" Shana nodded, she knew it was on the way to the station and she would be quick. She was glad it was Detective Grant in the car and not anyone else.

***

According to the surveillance tapes, the victim was evidently at the college campus at the date of the crime, but not in class. She was seen walking into the college. Another tape shows her going to her locker, followed by her leaving the campus. But during the time of the crime, she was missing on campus, that was the last of her.

Friends described the victim as disjoined and quiet. It was said she *'was one that usually stayed to herself, no boyfriend although there was a guy who had a crush on her,'* but nothing more than that.

All this was not enough to help solve the pieces of the case, but more importantly, help Shana find her. Shana was relying on the victim's bag for any critical clues to her whereabouts. A unit was sent out to further investigate the area where the bag was found. Street surveillance tapes up and around the area were viewed over and over, lamentably there was nothing.

Finally, one of the neighbors called the police station to return a call made from one of the detectives.

"I'm not a hundred percent sure, but I could have sworn that her car was parked out the front a day before the family died. Have you found the car?" The concerned neighbor was curious.

The detective thanked her for the information but truly felt that she may have had muddled it up since surveillance shows the victim at college. He brushed it off, as it was an old, confused neighbor, trying to help, it was useless.

A day later, the car was found parked at the Marina in San Francisco, seven hours away from her home and college. The car was called in and was being towed to LA for further investigation. It was isolated and empty for gas.

Shana went back to the drawing board; this came with weeks of sleepless nights and living on coffee. Scrupulous investigations and continuous analysis of the crime scene were repeating itself. Shana was becoming impatient. The comparisons of the New York case were not enough evidence, and nothing was talking to her. She had a deep gut instinct that there was something she was missing. She needed to further investigate the writing that was left behind by the killer. She called Wong in to assist, in hope of a better understanding of what was taking place.

Wong was way ahead of her, he had already made a few calls and done some research concerning the writing.

Shana was eager to resolve the case "Wong, please enlighten me! What do we have?"

"Ok, can we do this in your office?" Shana made her way down and approached Wong on the open floor where the forensic team was located and there were quite a few people around all who were working on the current case. Chief George had made his way down to Shana's unit to check up on things, he was in the distance speaking to Julia and Jake regarding updates.

Even though Wong had briefly whispered, it caught the eye of some of the work colleagues, but more importantly that of Detective Grant who just came in to give Shana some updates. Shana noticed Wong stop talking. Wong had something to say, and it needed to be said alone but right now there were too many eyes on them. *Her curiosity was peaked.*

***

CHAPTER 15

*"Your actions are nothing more than a reflection of
who you really are."*

Detective Grant did not like what he saw. He walked straight up
to the Chief bypassing Julia and Jake.

"Why can't he discuss it here? Why does Wong want to take her
into the room? He's fucking Japanese, you better pray…"

The Chief was quick to cut in, "He's just trying to impress her
with his perspicacity and information. Why do you think that no
translator was going to be called in to find out what was written?"

"He played it safe in New York, now he is making his point
clearer and you know his sole aim is in taking us down George!"
he continued, "just go in there, you're the Chief. Go find out
what the fuck is going on!"

The Chief shook his head, feeling that Grant was overreacting,
but took his advice in any case.

The Chief walked up to Shana's office and barged through the
door without knocking. Wong was plugging in his laptop, the
Chief wondered what he was about to show her. It wasn't even

on the police network because he could have just used Shana's computer.

"How's it going?" he asked.

"Yeh good, good. Wong is about to share some essential information with me," Shana's answer was full of hope for a lead.

"Is that right Wong? Hope it helps get this prick. What did you find?" he made his way to the screen.

While noticing the Chief making his way, she saw clearly how Wong was quick to open as many files as possible and close files that were related to the file. By the time the Chief had made his way to view those files, Wong had different files open to show Shana. Shana was very conscious as to what Wong was doing, she felt a little uncomfortable but didn't want to question him in front of her father. *Shana frowned as she watched him.*

Wong started babbling out information he had on file "In Japan, the Monkey's role in guarding against demons originates from the Japanese word for monkey Saru. According to the legends of Japan's Mount. Hiei shrine-temple multiplex, this makes the Monkey an 'expeller of demons.'"

"In Japanese, zaru an archaic verb conjugation in the negative, like the word 'DON'T' is vocalized in the same way as the suffix for monkey," so when the phrase was translated, someone used the clever play on words and related it to monkeys. Another well-known phrase and variation of the same theme are more commonly quoted as *Monkey see, Monkey hear,* and *Monkey do.*

The Three Wise Monkeys and Japanese History and culture was the start to better understanding the case, the criminal, and the danger that's coming. *And sure enough, the danger was coming.*

Wong started with the basics. "The criminal had used a bamboo brush, with the head of the brush being that of fine chicken feathers. It consisted of a long tip compared to that of the handle. The Japanese use a special technique called the Jofuku, meaning to dip once. This style of writing is when the artist only dips their paintbrush once and this is how the narrow lines are produced. The aim is to finish writing what you need before the ink runs out while doing this with perfect strokes and no hesitation."

Shana was intrigued, her father looked bored.

"That's why the writing seemed to fade out toward the end. Ok, what else?" Shana took notes as Wong continued.

"This criminal must have studied in-depth the Wise Monkey Philosophy, it stands for the mantra 'see no evil, hear no evil, speak no evil and also at times do no evil'." *Pausing before going onto the next slide.*

"The Japanese folk religion had taken this into a deep part of their culture; together with the Chinese Taoism and the Ancient Shinto influences they had come together to form in-depth symbols of what is known as the Kōshin faith."

"What is that?" Shana asked, intrigued with new knowledge and learning.

"Ok, let me first explain what Kōshin means. Kōshin is comprised of two characters – Kō" he wrote both symbols 庚申]. "In Japanese, 庚, the Chinese zodiac stem that is said to be associated with metal and the planet Venus, and Shin 申, is the ninth branch symbol of the Chinese zodiac and the character for a monkey."

"I remember seeing that SHIN symbol," Shana remembering where she had seen it.

"It's a common tattoo these days, and even though it's an old ritual, they say that the Kōshin festival continues secretly today." Wong continued, ignoring the Chief's harsh stare.

"You see Koushin 更神, means 'exchange of the Gods.' The Koushin Day is when the spirit residing in the human body is said to rise to heaven, it is a time of meeting and exchange."

"Seriously, what is this crap?" The Chief was not at all amused.

Shana gave her dad a firm look, then looked back to Wong *"Please continue."* Wong nodded and went on.

"The first Kōshin ritual in Japan supposedly occurred during the reign of Monmu around 679AD, or around the time of the forty-seconds Emperor. I was able to get some information from Dr. Marcos who has great contacts in Japan and has informed me that there are recorded documents held by the Shitennōji Temple in Osaka. Another reference to the Koushin practice occurred in the Shoku Nihon Kōki of 834 AD."

"So, there are indications that it does exist! But Wong, what does it mean for the case?" Her curiosity peeked as to something so far back in history was being carried on until today.

"Yes, well the Kōshin festival was held on the sixtieth day of the calendar. It has been suggested that during the Kōshin festival, according to old beliefs, one's bad deeds might be reported to heaven unless avoidance actions were taken. It has been theorized that the Three Mystic Apes, instead of Seeing, Hearing, or Speaking, may have been the things that one has done wrong in the last fifty-nine days."

"The three Mystical Apes have become what we know today as the Three Wise Monkeys?" Shana making sure she was on the right track.

"Yes," Wong continued "The Sanshi keeps track of the good deeds and particularly the bad deeds of the person they inhabit. Every sixty days, on the night called Kōshin-Machi, if the person sleeps The Sanshi will leave the body and go to Ten-Tei (天帝), the Heavenly God, to report about the deeds of that person. Ten-Tei will then decide to punish bad people, making them ill, shortening their time alive, and in extreme cases putting an end to their lives. Those believers of Kōshin who have reason to fear will try to stay awake during Kōshin nights. This is the only way to prevent The Sanshi from leaving their body and reporting to Ten-Tei."

"Is the criminal playing the role of Ten-Tei?"

"To be honest, Shana it's too early to tell." Wong shrugged.

"You're telling me this is practiced today?" Shana finding it hard that people even today believe in these things.

"Yes, and it is quite common more so with people of hierarchy positions. You could view it as the Mason's being mostly American, and the Kōshin being that of the Japanese. However, there is also a huge Chinese and Indian influence. Even today, certain Japanese shrines and temples continue to perform the Kōshin rituals. For those who still believe, most are elderly Japanese." He paused before he got back on track. "So once the sins are reported, depending on this report, the Court of Destiny might decide to shorten the individual's life. To prevent this, people stayed awake on Kōshin nights being the eve of the Kōshin day, gathered around scrolls of Shōmen Kongō. This practice eventually became known, in Japan, as the Kōshin Machi 庚申會 the Kōshin Vigil, Kōshin Gathering where names it was given."

"The reason he wrote in red is linked in with Japanese culture. For the Japanese, red is a national symbol of blood and passion on one hand, and a religious symbol on the other, as the color is reserved for the robes of the second-highest abbot in Zen Buddhist practices. For those who practice Feng Shui, red is used to attract positive energy."

"How come I have never heard of this?" Shana questioned, curious as to why she had never read anything about it.

"Because that's how they prefer it. The Japanese people are very conservative, and what happens behind closed doors stays there. Hence the Monkey wisdom."

"The association of The Wise Monkeys with Japan's Kōshin cult reflects the crucial importance of the number three."

"He kills in three's!" Shana exclaimed.

"The Japanese word for monkey is Saru this word is phonetically linked with the negative ZARU, which means 'not,' thus, the names of the Three Monkeys are Mizaru 見ざる (no see), Kikazaru 聞かざる (no hear), and Iwazaru 言わざる (no speak). Those were the words that were located on the bodies. All expect Iwazaru, which means 'No Speak,' instead of the word (No Do) is exceedingly rare that the 'do no evil' comes into play. The only time that "do no evil" is present and is judged is when a person had been cheated, a spy, a traitor, primarily it's the removal of the gentile area."

"This victim, must have done something personally to him, for him to punish him?"

"My thoughts exactly!" Wong agreed with Shana.

"What are you going on about? This can't be the case. We all know Roger, and this was his brother's house. He has no idea who this person is, Rogers brother-in-law was an accountant! So, what he cheated him with fraud taxes…. please!"

"Dad, please. We have to take everything into account. If this is too much for you, I'm sure there are other things you can do?" She didn't want Wong to be distracted. But there was also a hidden agenda, Shana had a sixth sense, and this one gave her suspicion that her dad was hiding something. The Chief simply shook his head and stayed put.

"To be spared all evil in life, one must not hear, see, talk or do evil. This is unfortunately present and even seen in today's teaching of Buddhism. The Three Wise Monkeys, sometimes four, were introduced to Japan by a Buddhist monk of the Tendai sent from China, around the eighth century AD This was probably passing on knowledge gained from Indian Buddhists. In Japan, the monkeys were at first always associated with the blue-faced deity Vajra, a fearsome God with three eyes and numerous hands. Their characteristic gestures of covering their ears, eyes, and mouths with their paws were a dramatic pictorial way of conveying the command of the God."

"Well, looks like this guy has read a few books." The Chief made a point about the killer.

"Yes, but…" Wong tried to continue and but was cut off by the Chief,

"I mean how many biblical references do we get concerning serial killers? Let's be realistic here, reading a book and referring to a crime may get us just that little closer, but we need to focus on the hard evidence."

"Reading a religious book is not going to help you catch a terrorist now… is it?" Wong said.

Shana looked at Wong, subconsciously telling him to back off. She could see that Wong understood.

"Yeah, you're probably right."

While Shana was amused by the whole conversation, she thought differently. It's those studies that lead to a better understanding of the criminal's frame of mind, and even being able to foresee their next actions.

Understanding whether it be the Bible or the Quran, or book reference that the criminal refers to was of high importance. The killer was attached to this history, it could have been this point of reference that has triggered their actions.

Thinking about it made sense. *How many cases*, Shana thought to herself, *has she come across, that the belief was a teaching from a religious group, ordering them on what to do next.*

"You finished interrogating my team Chief?" She was protective of her team. She loved her father. But withholding information was a habit of his. Shana knew all too well he was hiding the real reason for her mother's death. Shana would play the fool for now; it would only be a matter of time before the truth would resurface.

"You don't agree?" the Chief looked at Shana knowing his daughter was not stupid but hoping that once just once she can bypass something.

But it was too late.

"No, and you know I don't agree and Wong, you don't either. On that note Chief, since this is boring you, could you please leave me and my team to do our job?"

The Chief looked at Shana and shook his head. The history of The Wise Monkeys was bound to come up, it was obvious, it was written on the bodies.

But that's where it needed to stop.

The Chief then moved to walk out, but before he exited the door, he stopped and turned around,

"Yes?" Shana questioned his motive, looking at him with a straight face.

"Never mind." He left closing the door behind him.

"Sorry Wong, please go on" She apologized for her dad's behavior.

"Shana, there is some information here that I think is best discussed somewhere else."

"I figured as much when you hide those files, tell me what you can, and we will plan for the rest later. Are we looking at a Benedict Arnold role?"

Wong nodded. "I believe so."

"Ok."

There was an understanding, the name Benedict Arnold was a well-known name. The one-time war hero chose a path of betrayal after becoming disillusioned with the cause. Thus, what it represented was a huge problem, with a slight insight into the solution, knowing there is a Benedict Arnold around, is better than not knowing.

"Let me get into the Monkey business." Wong tried to make light of the situation. Shana responded with a smile.

"The Three Wise Monkeys usually can be seen on paper scrolls that were used in the Kōshin ceremony, whereby the role of the Monkeys is to be understood as messengers."

"So, they were the ones who would work with Ten-Tin?" Shana questioned Wong.

"Yes, but some temples also show Three Monkey's statues, and in rural areas in Japan, many "Kōshin" stones (Kōshin-do) still can be found. The first record referring to the Kōshin belief is by a celebrated Japanese priest called Ennin, also named Jikasu-Daishi. He visited China in the Tang Dynasty and witnessed Kōshin practice there on November 26, 838. He wrote that he observed a practice similar to that of Japan."

"What I am understanding is that this ritual is practiced in both countries?"

"Yes." Wong agreed with Shana.

"Fundamentally it's a life practice about not to see, not to hear, and not to speak. In brief, in my opinion, if we can ignore something that may cause trouble, it's possible to avoid troubles. However, it's not easy to practice it in our real lives, how do they go about this?" Shana started to pace.

"That's about getting in the nitty and gritty of it all, but you must know Shana, only those who are invited into this cult have a deep understanding of it. However, if you are born into it, you have no option to leave it. Some have tried, and this has resulted in death."

Shana shook her head in disbelief.

"There are many leaders who followed this philosophy. Mahatma Gandhi was said to have a small statue of the Three Monkeys, and he was known to be a firm believer and the practices of this wisdom. Even today, a larger representation of the Three Monkeys is prominently displayed at the Sabarmati Ashram in

Ahmedabad, Gujarat, where Gandhi lived from 1915–1930 and from where he departed on his famous salt march."

"Wow, I am familiar with those statues. You see them everywhere, but I had no idea they had such an in-depth meaning. Or to even think that a string of murders has to do with these teachings, it baffles me."

"The rest, we will discuss later," Wong said. He could see Shana had a lot on her plate. As he packed up his belongings, he handed over a piece of paper to Shana. "This is the person you need to get in contact with. He will be difficult to get hold of, so you'll be needing Portia for this one."

Shana simply nodded, looking at the piece of paper. It was the contact details of Dr. Marcos. Shana knew of him, but she was never privileged to be in the same room with him. Dr. Marcos was a hard person to get hold of, and if you're not in his circle of trust, then prepare to be treated terribly.

Shana knew this all too well. She was prepared.

***

CHAPTER 16

"In times of need, slowly plant the seed and hope that through the lines, they will read."

"I don't see you enough," Portia complained. Shana's shift work was driving them apart. They barely had time to even chat on the phone. The worst is when Shana is on a high-profile case which is most of the time, and when that happens, it's months without meeting. When they were to finally meet up, Portia could see her mind is elsewhere. There was no winning.

Shana handed Portia a small gift bag showing off her Mona Lisa mysterious smile.

"Bribery doesn't work." She reluctantly smiled. It was hard to get angry at Shana.

Portia was excited. She loved receiving gifts. She opened the gift bag to see an object wrapped up in tissue paper. She placed the gift bag on the ground on the side of her chair at an outside Italian restaurant, after unwrapping the gift she looked in amazement. "What is it?" She asked in confusion,

"It's a small wooden sculpture with the Three Wise Monkeys sitting side-by-side," She started pointing to each monkey.

"This one has his eyes covered meaning see no evil, this one has his ears covered meaning hear no evil, and the third one has his mouth covered meaning speak no evil." Shana had bought it from a flea market the weekend after Wong's meeting. Besides the fact she was working on the case, she thought it would be funny and safe way to start a discussion on the case with Portia without her being annoyed. Also, she needed some insight.

"The Three Wise Monkeys," Portia rose an eyebrow for her to explain.

"Hear no evil, see no evil say no evil? Have you not heard of them?"

"Ahhh the three of the wisest of Wise Monkeys. I remember seeing them at the market stand in Thailand, and in Cancun. They even had little Buddha's to replace the monkeys." Then she paused for a second. "Thanks, I guess."

"Aren't you wondering why I gave it to you?" Shana asked.

"No, and I don't want to know, because I am hoping it has nothing to do with a case that you're currently working on." Portia tried to escape from the whole conversation.

"What makes you think that?" Shana smirked.

"Shana, seriously it's not every day we meet. Let's talk about us, boys, you, me, perfume, stress-free stuff. Please I beg you."

"Ok, can we at least have a schedule? Thirty minutes work and then the rest just us?" Shana used her puppy eyes to her advantage.

"It's not like it will change anything, go." Portia sighed and put her hand under her chin and leaned forward on the table.

"Ok, first I love you," she was grateful to Portia that she had the chance to explain.

Shana sat and explained all the stuff that Wong had told her. She spoke of the history and the origin, and the crime scene. She spoke of the family that was found and of the missing girl. Shana was going over everything in detail. Portia sat listening attentively to everything Shana was saying, trying to take it all in.

"You're telling me there's no news about the girl, even now?" Portia is astonished that this killer may have kidnapped her.

"No, and that amazes me. But I'm not giving up on her."

"I know you won't, but from listening to what this person is like, it would be out of character for him to kill her. She doesn't fit the profile, but then again…" Portia trailed off, taking a moment to think "He may have been spying on the family, thinking it's a family of three and was surprised when he was at the house, so he didn't know what to do."

"No, I don't think she was there at all. I don't see how? Roger was there and she would have had time to exit."

They both sat in silence, confused, and going over their thoughts. *Portia's mind went somewhere else.*

As they continued chatting, the topic changed, and they went on to talk about their lives and memories of their childhood. The conversation was then filled with laughs, something they both had missed very much.

Portia has been physically exhausted; the case that she has been on in the last three days has been overwhelming. A young girl was directed by the specialist to the mental ward where she was being diagnosed. Portia had a lot of concerns with what the specialist had diagnosed her with. As a result, Portia decided to dig a little further.

Not only was she attacked by the girl when she was in the room alone with her but was threatened and told that if she were let loose from the hospital, she would kill herself. Why would someone want to be locked up? It's usually them acting as if nothing is wrong aiming at convincing the doctors they were normal to get released.

Portia would have loved Shana's insight on this. But she held back, *and it was a good thing she did.*

Shana then seemed to remember something just as they were getting up to go their separate ways.

"Portia, how well do you know Dr. Marcos?"

"Why?" Portia asked, perplexed at the mention of his name.

"Just wondering if you're able to pull a few strings." Portia was agitated, feeling as if this whole meeting had a hidden agenda.

"It was nice seeing you too Shana, and next time you want to ask me to get you in contact with someone, just pick up the phone. You don't have to go through all this trouble."

"Seriously, come on, it's not like that! Wong mentioned that you know him, that's all, I just remembered. Honest to God." Portia sighed as she saw Shana was trying to be honest.

"Yes, I do know him, very well," Portia said trying to brush it off. Even though she didn't believe Shana, she didn't want to argue "I apologize I can't help you there. He doesn't like your type of people. The police, forensics, or any form of government."

"Could you at least try?" Shana begged.

"Trust me, I'm telling you exactly what he would say, *no chance in hell.*"

"Fine, I'll try and figure something else out." Portia could tell her friend was irritated and it annoyed her. She had asked for help under the cover of the first catch-up in a long time from a man who was notoriously determined to never speak to authorities.

A friendly yet cold kiss on the cheek goodbye and both girls headed in opposite directions. Walking away, thoughts of work overwhelmed both of them. Shana said something about her case that triggered a thought, with this in mind Portia was eager to get back to work instantly.

***

CHAPTER 17

"Hide me from the truths of my reality, for it is easier to not know, than to know and bear witness to the truths."

A room cut off from the world. Scheduled and empty, white cushiony walls, the floor was soft, a small slight bounce with every step, mimicking walking on the moon. A mattress covered in white rubber, but nothing else. No bathroom with a mirror to see themselves. No reminder of the past. No understanding of the future. No technology. Nothing.

Some patients would go crazy walking themselves from wall to wall. To most. This made the sane insane. If you believe something you become it.

The nurses would first come in with empathy, work to the best of their ability, eager to make a difference. But in time like the ones that have been there before them, they have lost any sense of emotion, lost all empathy. From the daily routine of medicating the patient, washing, keeping an eye on them, to being hit by patients, verbally, physically, mentally, and emotionally abused by the patients who know no better. The amount of work they do daily was in no correspondence to the defective salary they were receiving. This in turn created a robotic-like structure for the nurses, a dreaded routine. Forgetting at times that each patient is an individual and each individual is different from the next. Everyone has their own story to tell. But they stopped listening long ago with sentiments slowly faded. Short-term stays in this ward, in this institution, were rare. If you have been sent here, then prepare for an exceedingly long stay – might as well call it your new home. This place is for good.

Portia knew all of this too well. At times she would truly try, but at times she in a way gave up. One patient many years ago when she first began, she had invested all her time and energy organizing their one-day outing in which Portia thought was suitable and would help, it took a lot of convincing. Her senior knew too well the repercussion but had allowed it. Knowing that the only way she would learn from her own mistakes. The patient went out and stabbed his mother and then killed himself. Luckily, the mother survived. But that patient was gone for good.

Since then, Portia knew she needed to toughen up. People would act in a certain way to get what they want. He wanted to kill his mother; psychologically he was acting sane to get to do this. Crazy, but true.

Sometimes the dreams would haunt her, she would see patients wandering through narrow corridors, and she would hear patients yelling from rooms, some felt they were on fire, others psychologically believed they were being attacked. Some would scream about their lost ones and many reenacted crimes they had done in the past.

Portia's main focus in the study was schizophrenia. When diagnosed, the patient loses contact with their past in order of helping the patient move forward. In saying so, the patient must be medicated for the rest of their lives, you are no longer a normal person, no longer an individual. You come in one way, if they were allowed to glance at themselves in a mirror, the patients would no longer probably recognize themselves.

***

CHAPTER 18

"To camouflage, is to go unnoticed. Picking the time of when to hide and when to reveal is critical."

An overly confident police officer made his way into the police station.

This particular officer came in casually, walked across the hallway, and made his way to the elevators to head down a level. The elevator doors opened, and he was on the forensic unit level. Her team was all working, some looked up at him smiling as he made his way to Shana's office. No one asked any questions.

Walking in casually, he landed at Shana's desk. He picked up the photo placed on her desk and figured it was Shana as a child with her mother and father in a family portrait. He took the photo out of the frame and placed it into his pocket. He was ionized with adrenaline; this was all a game for him. *And he was winning.*

He knew exactly where each camera was located. At the location of each camera from the hallway to the elevator and Shana's office, he had his back turned, the back of his head and body was all one could see. He wore black gloves and carried a police motorbike helmet on the other hand; it was a little larger than usual, but no one noticed.

He pulled out a package from under the helmet and placed it on the floor right in between Shana's desk. He didn't want the package to be picked up by anyone else.

He had one last look at Shana's office and then headed out. The elevator opened, and he made his way up and walked down the hallway to the exit doors in front of him. He was stopped before he reached his destination.

"Hey dude, can I get some help with this?" a fellow officer said, patting the officer on the back in a friendly manner wanting his help to move his desk with aim of making room for the newcomers coming in from New York.

He looked at him directly in the face with no expression or emotion and sadistically turned his back. He was not going to help him. He couldn't help him. He was in line with the camera, one slightly turned, and he would be exposed. He turned and walked away.

"Thanks, dude, thanks heaps," John said sarcastically.

The officer placed the helmet on his head, as he was making his way down a few steps walking toward the motorbike parked across the road. The officer then disappeared. His work was done for the day.

Shana walked in with her weak skim nonfat latte in one hand and a pen in the other, ready to sign off on some evidence files she needed to look over. She looked up Wong was working away at his desk when Shana called him in "Wong, sit down" Her tone was serious.

"I want you to have a look at this file here," She handover the file, it was his room evidence collection in the current case.

Wong was confused, why was Shana showing him this? His mind was working a hundred miles per hour; he knew he had not missed anything, and the processes of the collection were perfect. He looked at the photos. Shana should be asking him more about the writing that was located on the bodies. He had additional information, which was a fundamental necessity, but he needed to be sure he could trust her. Wong had a feeling that this was going to happen, the deeper he dug the more dangerous it got.

He looked over the photos, and there it was. Shaking his head, thinking this was how they would get rid of him. He was set up. Wong had a certain way of taking photos. These photos were not Wong's photos. He felt that Shana should have also picked this up.

He sat down, wondering how this was possible, and reflected when it suddenly came to make sense. He knew exactly what had happened. The Chief's best friend, Detective Grant had come up to him. He needed him to head to the Japanese consulate, to meet with Lyn Wangton,

"Hey Wong, heard about the Japanese writing, I need you to head to the Japanese consulate and see Lyn Wangton, he will be someone we will work with" Wong was a little fidgety trying to get his stuff together, he was eager to go. The thought of him being set up crossed his mind. Picking up his essentials to head out, he remembered something, and he looked at the detective.

"Let me just inform Shana where I'm heading," Wong suggested as he walked toward Shana's office.

The detective grabbed onto Wong's shoulder "She has more important things to deal with, anyhow she knows." He slightly positioned him and moved him in the exit direction.

He handed over the address. Wong was picking up his forensic camera to place in the locker.

"You're going to be late; you know what the Japanese are like give me that and I will put it in, just go." Rushing him off, Wong wasn't thinking correctly. Even though a part of him didn't like the idea of anyone touching something that he was responsible for, but the thought of helping solve this case, being a key player, and moving up also took control. Having an authoritarian figure telling him he will take care of it, seemed like nothing wrong. Wong did as he was told. After all, it was no regular detective, it was a sincere person who was the best friend of the Chief, and everyone knew he was like a father to Shana. He would be an idiot not to correspond.

He headed off to the consulate.

He had waited at the consulate for Mr. Wangton for one hour and fifteen minutes, being told constantly by the receptionist that he was held up in a conference.

Wong was getting up to leave a couple of times but was stopped by the receptionist, who would inform him that Mr. Wangton is just finishing up.

But then something unusual happened. The receptionist received a call.

"Yes. Yes, he's here" paused listening to what the other person on the phone was saying, the receptionist then nodded in agreement "Ok, Bye."

She was suddenly very apologetic, "Mr. Wangton has been called into another conference and will not be able to see you; however, we have your information and will call you to make another appointment,"

"I can wait." After all, he had already waited. He also didn't want to go back to the office empty empty-handed, he needed the progression into the case.

"No, sorry he is flying out this evening and has back-to-back meetings until then." Wong had tried, but there was nothing more he could do.

His one hour and fifteen waits, was perfect timing to get his camera taken back to the scene, take some photos without contamination of the evidence resulting in it, not being admissible in court. His collection of clothing had also been contaminated and the worst part was in the logbook he had twenty-four items of evidence collected. However, in storage there were only twenty-one items of evidence, hence, three items of evidence were missing.

Wong sat in Shana's office his worst nightmare had just come true. He was set up!

"Wong." Shana tried to get his attention from his inner musings.

"Can you see what's wrong with these photos?" she pointed out certain things that were different in each exact photo. In some evidence that had been collected and the photos not taken.

"Are the photos the only issue?" he waited for Shana to tell him also that there was an error in the collection of evidence.

Shana tilted her head, curious, "Yes, the evidence collection was…"

He cut in, he was furious but trying to hold himself, he knew he was being let go. He respected Shana and knew this was not her doing. *She's not like them.*

"Please, just stop." He held his hand up not wanting to hear anything more.

"I... I...I ...didn't take these photos." Wong pleaded, desperately wanting to confess and tell her everything. He was going to lose his job anyway.

"Look, I know this case was a little hard, and you are nervous, but I had to go in and clean your mess. I can't have this on my team, this is not like you. I don't know if it was the case or things happening in your life. I will write a referral for any future employment." Shana put her head down, not knowing what else she could say.

Wong shook his head in disbelief; he did not want to say anything more. There wasn't any point. She didn't want to listen.

"Is that all?" he wanted to pack and get out of there. His face was reddening, and he felt like he couldn't breathe – he was hurting.

"I'm so sorry Wong." Shana placed her hand on her head, taking a deep breath in. She liked and trusted Wong.

"Don't be, it's not your fault or mine." He stood up, moving to head out.

"Shana" referring to her first name as if she was a friend now, not a boss, or a work colleague, "Please be careful, and have a look at these photos compared to past photos I have taken."

Just as he was at the door, Shana called his name one last time. "Wong, Benedict Arnold sends his regards."

Wong looked at her and tried to smile. He knew he had to leave. And that she had a plan. Shana was in control. Wong needed fresh air; this was all too much for him.

She sat alone on her office chair with the door closed, holding back tears. She didn't like what was happening. She loved her team and hated how her father had control. Just minutes ago, he was talking about the reputation of the team, and if Shana didn't fire him then he would.

She wasn't going to get her father near Wong, so she did it. Expert witnesses needed to have 'no flaws,' thus, an error in collection evidence as big as this would ruin the integrity of the police station and her forensic unit, most importantly her career.

As Shana looked up, she noticed her empty frame. It once held a photo of her mom and dad, and her being held by them. The only family photo she had. She looked around. There was no photo. With all this moving around and looking at her feet, she hit the package under her table.

Shana was puzzled. She picked it up and placed it on the table. The words *'Be Wise'* were noted on the front of the package. The thought of The Wise Monkeys came to mind.

How does someone walk in and place a package on her desk without being seen? Shana was furious *what the fuck is going on?* was all she wanted to scream right now Her mind was running through options, reading over and over the words *'Be Wise.'* Finally, she sat down and thought about what could happen. She put on a pair of gloves and carefully opened the package, she pulled out ten drivers' licenses belonging to various men. There was also a note.

Do not try to escape The Sanshi from leaving your body and reporting to Ten-Tei. Why do they stay awake on the fifty-ninth night? Are they afraid?

Why is it you choose what not to see, what not to hear, and what not to speak? If you can ignore something that may cause troubles, does not mean you will avoid troubles. I am the Heavenly God!

I cursed them. They have lost their senses. I have done as Amascut did to Apmeken's. Look deep in the eyes of a person

153

and you would know that their eyes could speak. But to be that of a good person you don't allow your eyes to seek.

Hear deep what the mouth says, and you know that the mouth will speak, but to repeat what you have heard, would be then just to cheat.

Listen to what I tell you, and hear me loud and clear, for if the ear does not pick up all I have to say, you can no longer speak or see.

To see, to speak, and to hear, give the capability to do. But to do with not thinking is Evil in itself.

Why is it I do what I do? What is it you do not see what I do? Who is it that hides your eyes, and blocks your ears?

My work is the work of God, my work is the art of God. Do not come looking, do not try and see, but see what I have done, and praise my artwork.

Look into history and you will know that I was called. I am Ten-Tei.

Be wise.

The work of the monkeys never stops. It's here to stay.

Look into countries beyond what you see, do not trust others. Just trust me.

Hear no evil, speak no evil, Do no evil .... Say no evil Shana .... And you shall live.

She then put the letter down and flicked through the driver's licenses., All middle-aged men, from all around America: Arizona, Florida, Texas, Georgia, California, New Mexico,

Nevada, Washington DC, Oregon, Uttar. *Who are these people?* Shana thought to herself *Why all these licenses, why this letter? What on earth does it mean?*

She started to pace the room, looking back at the letter, then back at the driver's license. She was thinking, analyzing, and contemplating.

She then looked back in the package and found another paper folded. She opened the letter, after reading it she placed it in her pocket. *No one needs to see this one.*

She placed the driver's licenses in the photocopy machine, *her team needs to see this.*

She called in Jake and Monica into her office. Considering it all, Shana was not ready to tell her dad, she was being *'wise.'*

She handed over the evidence and placed it in a bag for fingerprints; she wanted this done as soon as possible. Shana needed to stay hopeful, follow procedure, and most importantly, follow her instincts She handed photocopies of all the driver's licenses to Jake and Monica. She asked the two to get information on all the people found on the license.

"If they are deceased, I want to know how they died, where they died, and who else died. Any family members and where they live. I want to know everything." Shana explained as she leaned in as if to share a secret with them. "This part of your job involves you not talking to any other member of the team; you know I had to let Wong go?"

They both nodded. The work environment was becoming too frantic and highly pressured, it was becoming a burden. Firing people seemed to be an easy task now.

"I need you to be discrete. I also need this information like yesterday."

"Yes ma'am" Jake responded on the behalf of both.

Walking out of the office she notices the team now looking at Shana. She had no idea how firm she came across, but it was enough to have all eyes on her. She knew that they all felt a loss, with Wong leaving they were hurting, they lost a friend, and feared their jobs. They, including Shana, needed to get emotion out of the equation and focus on the job.

"Use Brendon's office," Shana suggested, pointing to Brendon's room. His office was perfect, clean, and organized. More importantly, it was empty as he was off enjoying his paternity leave.

They grabbed their paperwork, Jake grabbed his laptop, and both headed into Brendon's room closing the door. When Shana spoke, they listened.

Jake and Monica adjusted rather quickly in Brendon's office. It was less chaotic and far greater privacy to discuss the case or research-related findings.

"What's going on Jake? I'm a little scared." Monica said, confiding in her work colleague with who she had attended university. They always had a strong friendship.

"Nothing Monica. If you worry, then you're more likely to make a mistake. Stay alert, relax, and let's just do our jobs."

She nodded, "Jake?" as she was placing the papers across the table ready to get to work.

"Yes, Monica?" Jake replied a little frustrated because he too was scared, and annoyed that he didn't have any answers for Monica.

"I know that Wong didn't take those photos. He handed in twenty-three items in front of me, and I saw them…"

"How do you know what it was about?" Jake questioned, not even knowing why Wong was let go.

"I was listening in; I was near the copier when they were talking." Jake looks at her disappointed "I didn't mean to," Monica continues "Listen to me, I always look at the way Wong works because I wanted to adapt to his ways of working, no one is as thorough as him. Jake, he was my mentor."

"Monica, stop! Do you want to join him?" she shook her head. "We are small fish. We are two steps into the ladder trying to make it in this world. If we try to play superhero and take out some of the people higher up the ladder than us, they can easily stumble down and bring us down with them." Jake pinned her with a glare.

"But Jake…" Monica was infuriated, trying to get a word in, wanting to do the right thing.

"No buts Monica, this is bigger than you and me. Just let it go." Jake said, knowing Monica was right, but he also knew how the world worked.

"What if that was us, what if that was me?" She looked at him for some sort of empathy. He looked her straight in the eyes.

"It's not."

Jake then uploaded the names into the computer and pressed enter.

They both looked at the screen in silence, waiting for some information to come up, both lost in their thoughts. The room was silent. The information all started to roll up on the computer.

It was evident that all the ten males were deceased, and all had families of three who were also deceased.

Each case was different. There were no eyes taken out, there were no ears removed, there were no genitals or tongues removed.

They both looked at the screen, trying to make light of it.

"We need each autopsy report," Monica said, knowing that there was a link and it needed to be found fast.

"I'm already on it," Jake replied as he instantaneously had another screen open on the computer filing a request for information. Under normal circumstances, this course of action would have taken around a week, but this was no normal circumstance. They sat, looking over the information presented as they waited for the crime scene photos and autopsy reports to be accessible.

All it took was one phone call from Shana. Jake and Monica sat there not exchanging words but trying to scrutinize the case as they waited anxiously for the information to come through both trying to figure out what the link was, using it as their escape from discussing what is currently taking place at work.

Finally, the boisterous '*ting*' sound from the computer indicated a message is present. They both looked at each other, amazed at the information that was now in front of them. This was way bigger than anyone realized.

***

CHAPTER 19

"I have hidden them deep for a reason, do not rely on the naked eye for truths."

They had thought that the case was a serial killer having just been involved in two to three families. But it turned out to be a serial killer with many years and years of unnoticed work.

How could people have missed the link? The element was one tiny thing that had them all linked up. It was conspicuous that each specific investigator that was assigned to this case had died, more so killed.

The federal police network popped up on the screen stating that some information was withheld. They had never seen anything like this. They pushed the locked folder to the side and focused on what they had available. Monica, however, was curious to know why the FBI would be holding information concerning this case, and why had they not informed them there was a link.

They got the information they needed to support their argument and were now ready to bring Shana in. Jake picked up Brendan's phone and called into Shana's office.

Shana answered immediately. "Did they send over the information?"

"Yes, please come." Shana was waiting for that call; she had the phone down and was there in seconds.

She closed the door and hovered over them as they sat on the computer screen.

"What do we have?" she looked at a wealth of information and autopsy photos on the computer.

Jake replied, "All the deceased bodies are male and from America. Each male had families of three including a wife and one child."

"Each family was killed around the evening; however, each killing was different." Monica added, "Some victims were shot, others strangled, poisoned, stabbed, or even one family placed in a tub together and electrocuted."

Shana shook her head, just the thought was devastating.

"Ok, what else do we have?"

"Every detective working on each case was killed." Jake showed her the information, "Look Shana, if the family was shot, then the detective was shot. If the family was slaughtered, then the detective was also slaughtered, and so on. *This man is crazy!*"

"Was one detective electrocuted to death?"

Jake turned and looked at Shana and replied "Yes."

"Good God!"

"I need to notify Detective Grant before it's too late." She ran a hand through her hair. "First, is there any link besides the family of three that can connect the killer to the two other murders?"

Monica started to pull up photos to show Shana "We ordered the autopsy reports, each body had been cut in certain areas. They were classified as defense marks, but because of the present case I was focusing on the eyes, ears, mouth, and genital area and we found the link."

"All bodies had a needle-like insertion in the eyes, mouth, ear or genital area; it was as if he injected a chemical or something into those sections of the body, but the autopsy report just said it was a purple bruising, which the forensic pathologist thought something was injected. After testing the blood, they found nothing, it was then left unanswered." Monica said, trying to be clearer in explaining herself "Remember the Fitroid case?" Shana nodded.

"Well, with Fitroid case, he would kill his victims with the so-called needle of death. We couldn't even pick up the chemicals from the blood, but after further analysis, we were able to spot a purple circle the same as these ones." Monica pointed to the autopsy photos on the screen.

"But why shoot them, stab them or whatever he did, and then inject them, or vice versa?" Shana paused for a second thinking, then continued "and what could he inject that would not show up in blood work?"

Monica smiled "That's what I initially thought, but then I looked even closer and see this area the slight lump here?"

Shana looked close but could not see what Monica was talking about,

"It was hard to see at first, and not all the photos of the victims show it, except it is visible in these," Monica replied as she dug into Brendan's draws and pulled out a magnifying glass.

"I can show you this better on my screen. I have the program built-in, and we can view it on the larger screen, but for now," Monica placed the magnifying glass on the screen, *"right here."*

Shana could not see anything, "Monica if the pathologist couldn't pick it up, you want me to?" Monica used her computer program to zoom in and make the image clearer. There it was a slight lump on the ear around where the light purple ring was, where the needle injection was.

"That could be from an ear-piercing," Shana said sarcastically, trying to figure out the relevance.

"No, it's a fraction too high," Monica said passionately as she moved to the other photos, showing Shana very imprecise light purple circles in the eye of one of the victims, on the lip of another. However, none were evident in the genital area. Monica had magnified the photos via the computer, but that wasn't enough to see it. On top of that, she placed the magnifying glass to better illustrate her point.

"Well! What did he eject? Anything on the other autopsy reports?"

"We just looked briefly, but just like the other case, they were picked up, blood work taken, and then left unanswered. I think he injected something after the victim died. He wanted us to find this, but we didn't. Now he removed those parts in the body in the hope of making it clear to us." Monica didn't know what else to say to emphasize her point.

Shana was thinking and speaking out loud, "We were not seeing the link; he was talking to us, and we were not listening?" Shana was now pacing, deep in thought, and speaking out loud "He injected something, but not a chemical substance," Monica looked over curious to know the answer "Could he have injected an object?"

"Yes, my thoughts exactly, a liquid would not have left a slight lump." She knew what needed to be done "Shit, we need those bodies dug up. Shit, when was the last body buried?" Shana had an idea.

"These were all in the last five years Shana. We're good with digging up the bodies. Even if decomposed, if we search thoroughly enough, we could find them." Monica was eager to get started.

"Let's work on the most recent, find that information. Get it to me. I want to know the locations and who was working on each case."

"We have so much work on our hands, it's time to get the pieces together." They both nodded, "I'll talk to the Chief and get us everything we need, you just make it happen."

Shana was heading out when Jake stopped her "Shana, some of the information is said to be withheld by the FBI, so we were not able to attain everything,"

"That should not have happened. Autopsy reports should be open to us, are you sure?" Jake then went over to show her, there it was.

"Leave it with me." Shana had nothing else to say.

"Ok" Jake replied, happy that she was on the case, so to speak.

It was now time that Shana needed to update her father. *It was a wise thing to do!*

CHAPTER 20

"Slowly discovering yourself in the middle of the chaos,
involves unbearable pain. The confrontations of it all
will make you insane."

"Dad, we need to talk." Shana barged into her father's office. The Chief was in a meeting. There was an unusual Asian man in his office. The man seemed uncomfortable and his face slightly red, it seemed as though Shana had interrupted an argument of some sort.

"Sorry, I didn't know you had someone with you," Shana said apologetically.

"I was just leaving." He replied while picking up his paperwork and throwing it into a suitcase as if he were waiting for a distraction so that he could get out of there.

He walked past Shana and then turned around looking back at the Chief, "just get it done." And then stomped out.

Shana then closed the door behind him, confused as to what just happened.

"What was that about?" she turned back to her dad.

"Just some political enterprise that's trying to get the force to support something, nothing exciting."

She shrugged and sat down.

"What's up?" Her father asked as he was clearing his overflowing desk from the paperwork that he and the man must have gone through.

Shana glanced over the paperwork while talking to her father "I received a package today, from the killer." At this point, she viewed a document on her father's desk that was titled *Psychiatric Ward Los Angeles* – She couldn't see the ward number. That was where Portia worked. Why this document was on his desk puzzled Shana. She made a mental note to ask Portia about it later.

"What? Did you open it?" her father looked up at her, worry all over his face.

"It's already been opened." She replied, calming him down.

"Sit down Dad." Shana whispered calmly, hoping to slightly change the subject as she became inundated with curiosity "Why do you have a document from Portia's work?" Shana was curious to see what lie would be told this time.

"Um…. Some domestic violence cases are about a man beating his wife for many years. We finally made a convincing case and got him charged, however, he pleaded insanity, so he is being tested to see if this is the case." He said. "Get back to what you were telling me."

Shana hated abusive men; she had seen her fair share in her line of work, "Hope he gets a real jail term." She blurted before she leaned forward eager to update her dad about the case.

As far as she was concerned, she was in spitting distance to closing the case. With the help of the murderer, she would have all the information she needed to trace him down, catch him, and happily lock him up and move on to the next case.

"I didn't know exactly if the killer dropped off the package or someone working with him. I just came back from being with the team looking at the surveillance. He was dressed as an officer. He knew where each camera was and only gave up his back, there was however one instance where he was seen having a conversation with John, that's where his neck slightly turned but nothing close enough for us to work with," Shana took a deep breath.

"Shana, what about the package?" Her father questioned, impatiently.

"It had ten driver's licenses, all-male men who and were married and had one child. Each family was killed in the last five years, and each death was executed differently."

"Besides the link of them all being a family of three, do we have anything else?"

"Each detective working on the case was killed in the same manner he had killed the victims, if one family was shot then the detective was shot, and so on."

"I got that part." He interrupted looking closely at his daughter "and the other link?"

"Each body seemed to have something injected in it either in the location of the eyes, mouth, ears, or genital area. We're talking about something exceedingly small. At first, I thought it was a liquid injection, but in all the autopsy reports a liquid injection was rejected. Monica pointed out the slight lump, so with your approval, I want to dig up the bodies and see if this is the case. Overall, the killings have taken place in the last five years, so concerning decomposition, let me deal with that."

She stopped and looked at her father.

"Dad?" trying to get his attention from his daydreaming "Did you hear anything I said?"

"Yes, do what you need to do. Bring past the papers and I'll sign them,"

That's all she needed to hear. She got up quickly to gather all the required vital documentation ready to place on his desk by the end of today.

"Shana?" her father called as she was heading out "Roger was shot at the crime scene, but yet the victims all had certain body parts removed and strangled."

"We thought of that. He wasn't the detective working on the case. Remember it was assigned to Detective Grant. You need to talk to him and make sure he is extra careful. I'll work my hardest, but please Dad just tell him to be safe."

He nodded his head in agreement.

"Shana," just as she nearly disappeared in the hallway, she turned back to her father's calling.

"Yes sir?"

"Be careful, don't get too cocky, and don't underestimate this killer. Don't think he sent you that information because he is providing you with answers. If he can kill these families in five years and not have anyone pick up on it, and the only way we could find the link is him wanting to get our attention, then we have to remember he is much smarter than we think!"

"It will be ok," Shana replied also nodding in agreement and headed straight towards her office. She needed to uncover a lot of things from this case. The first thing was getting those documents signed.

***

CHAPTER 21

"The cherry blossom waits patiently for spring; the timing could not be more perfect as the blossom is now liberated."

Everyone had to be at the six am meeting. No excuses. All those involved in the case were now present. An agreement has taken place between the Chief and the head of the FBI unit. The combined task force focused on catching the killer was all now in the room. Everyone in the room had the same agenda. To catch this criminal.

Time was of the essence. After going through each case, from the beginning to the most recent, Shana then focused on what Monica had found. She presented these findings through digital visualization techniques so that everyone knew what was going on. She also went through the surveillance camera. John was told that he would need to describe who he had spoken to. Furthermore, from John's current description they could only say that he looked Asian, but whether Chinese, Japanese, or any other part of Asia was yet unknown, given that the case followed the Monkey theory, Shana was only able to consider and put forward that he may be of Japanese descent.

John was shaking his head; he was in close proximately to the person who may have been the killer and he had not known.

Ryan turned to him "Don't beat yourself over it, how were you supposed to know?"

"A small object was placed in the bodies. Our main concern is to find what this is and move forward from there. A lot of traveling will be involved. For the next four weeks, you all will be working eighteen-hour shifts. You'll have your acquired breaks, but we are limited with time. The press already has hold of the two cases, we aim to keep this information internal until we can find something that will link us directly to where the killer is before he strikes again."

Shana continued with other important information concerning the case, covering every detail, before telling them to go and pack and prepare whatever they needed to.

For the first time ever, Shana noticed the fear in Detective Grant's eyes. She called him in for a private discussion after everyone left, telling him to take extra precautions. She was concerned and needed him to understand that this was a serious matter, and he needed to have someone constantly with him.

"Dad has Ryan by my side in everything I do, who figured he would ever do that, but it's because he knows how serious this case is" she took his hand.

"You're like a father to me, and sometimes more. I'm not ready to lose you, please take this seriously." She knew how stubborn Grant was.

He smiled and brought her closer in for a tight hug, "I'm not going anywhere. You see the difference with the other cases is they didn't have you working on them. So, I ... we will be fine."

She looked up at him "Please, just have someone always with you. Will you?" she then moved back and grabbed his hands and looked directly into his eyes. *"Promise me!"* Shana pleaded.

"Promise me." Shana drew his attention by trying to catch his eyes.

The detective gave in. "Ok, I promise, now go! And find this psycho."

"I will." She responded, heading back to the main room in her department.

Shana sat in her office, looking around. In four hours, they would be flying out to one of seven locations to begin digging up the bodies.

She had never been in a position of digging out a body. It was a lot of paperwork and going through specific area departments was a headache. Normally it would take a while and would be much more exhausting, but she had her dad's help which truly simplified things.

Shana sat gazing out of her office watching her team getting the equipment they need in place. Those who were coming with her got themselves ready to head out, the ones staying behind were ready to meet the rest of the team. She then glanced up and was noticing a security camera, located in the communal area.

She started to think to herself, how was it that a person walks into the police station, and nothing is picked up. How does someone get this type of information? She needed another glance at the security tapes.

She picked up the phone not taking the negative finding that *nothing was found* on the security camera. Shana felt optimistic.

"Can you link me into the security footage we were looking at yesterday to my office?"

"Sure, right now?" Tim questioned.

"This second please," Shana replied, anxiously determined to go through them before departing, just one last time.

Tim walked in and gave her the access security code. Each link had a brief explanation to it, stating the location of the camera and the time. Fortunately, these two significant factors can also be viewed on the footage, playing a huge part in the evidence to support the criminal investigation. She started following the man from him walking up the stairs, to the entry and exit of the building.

His head stayed down, positioned to perfectly avoid the cameras. It was evident that the whole way through, there were slight movements. He wore gloves and was covered from head to toe, except his hair which was jet black and totally in place, Shana continued to critically analyze his every movement, specifically to the section where John had called him for assistance.

"Need to slow it down here." Shana speaking aloud. His head slightly jerked to see who was calling to him, but not enough to get a glimpse of any facial recognition. Shana kept winding back the tape repeatedly, hoping each time she was going to find something.

By happenstance, Shana jumped off her seat and hit pause. There it was, she found something. She just needed it magnified. She ran up out of her chair and headed to the common room.

"Jake! Monica! My office." Monica had a stack of papers in her hand and was about to get them filed and ready to join Shana in digging up the bodies. Monica dropped everything and looked at Jake. Shana had already disappeared into her office and was waiting for them.

"First Wong, now us Jake?" Monica whined as they dropped everything and headed to Shana's office.

"Seriously, stop being paranoid," Jake muttered.

They entered Shana's office and closed the door.

"I need this magnified with that new equipment you had shipped in from England."

Monica sighed in relief and looked at Jake who just shook his head.

"Sure." Monica responded, "What is it you're after exactly?"

"Look here," Shana replied, pointing to the computer screen. She enlarged it as much as she could, but it was a little blurry, but enough for them to see it.

The person who had delivered the packages had left a piece of information about him, and they found it,

"It looks like a tattoo," Jake responded looking closely,

"I'm sure it is," Shana said, hoping for the best.

When John had spoken to him, there was an unexpected turn which had his hair slightly move from his neck revealing a small tattoo.

Forensic technology could play with this pigmentation and increase the image and figure out exactly what this tattoo is.

Many cases in the past have had a lot of help with people tattooing themselves, piercings, or any type of body mutilation. This is seen in another form of fingerprint detection. No two tattoos are completely identical. And if they have yours on file and compare it to when they will find you. Monica took some notes down and then ejected the tape and headed to what she called her 'specialty room.' Jake and Shana were only steps behind.

Time was crucial they needed to be at the airport in less than an hour, Monica knew that.

This great machine had come in only a week ago it was Monica's new baby. She was experimenting with it using closed cold cases to get her familiar with the machine.

She placed the tape in and waited, the machine was making some slight noise. Shana looked up at Monica confused as to why it was making that noise.

Monica giggled "It reminds me a lot of the slot machines." Jake shook his head; she was like a little girl at Disneyland when she was near her machines.

Shana smirked, releasing a smile, "It better hit jackpot for what we paid for this baby."

"Oh, it will," Monica said nodding in reassurance while looking at the machine.

Suddenly, there it was on a wide highly defined projectile across the room, the screen zoomed into perfection.

The tattoo was perfect, it was as if the camera had pointed directly at the tattoo and taken the picture.

Shana smiled and Monica smiled back proudly. The beautiful tattoo of the monkey with the cherry blossoms was now coming to life. *Soon this tattoo will tell them a story.*

Unexpectedly, and without warning, the machine began to deliver an abundant amount of information about the tattoo, including details of what the tattoo meant its history and cultural links, and other vital information. In particular, it directed back to the Japanese culture, the cherry blossom, and the monkey.

Shana was thinking to herself this was money well spent. *They were all extremely impressed.*

"The Japanese cherry blossom is interpreted as 'transient of life.' The cherry blossom tree has short blooming periods and is very fragile. There is an old story attached to cherry blossoms that values sacrifice." Monica looked at Shana, for indication on whether to continue. Shana nodded.

"It is said that there is a Jiu-Roku-Zakura (the Cherry tree of the sixteenth day), in the Iyo district of the province. This tree grew on the lands of Samurai for over a hundred years. When the Samurai became old, the tree began to die. The Samurai was incredibly sad looking at his cherished tree die. He was a brave and honorable man. Thus, he thought of a way to save the tree's life. He sat under the tree and committed Seppuku or the ritual suicide, under the tree. This act gave the essence of the Samurai's life to the tree. The tree within one hour of the Samurai's death, on the sixteenth day of the month, began to blossom flowers and continues to live even today."

"Thus, the cherry blossom tree holds many spiritual beliefs and meaning. These beliefs are set deep within the fundamental teachings of Buddha. A fallen cherry blossom flower also holds many emotional connections within the minds of the Japanese. A fallen cherry blossom is a symbolic representation of a fallen Samurai. Each fallen cherry blossom is a representative of a Samurai who lost his life in battle."

"Men wear cherry blossom tattoos symbolizing Samurai. In ancient Japan, people threw parties to showcase their beautiful blooming cherry trees where the members of the high society graced these occasions. For some, the cherry blossom is a symbol of humanity and hope. Then it links in with the monkey part of the tattoo." Monica explained.

Shana waved her hand gesturing to continue.

"In ancient Japan, the monkey was the messenger of the Gods. Monkey was the symbol of a harmonious marriage, fertility, and safe childbirth, as well as the protector against disease and demons. It was believed to be the Japanese monkey who made and followed the practice: Speak no evil, hear no evil, and see no evil."

There it was again. Shana thought quietly to herself as she continued to listen.

Shana wondered if Wong had more to tell her about what he had found out about those writings. She had other plans for Wong.

"Monica, send that information to me, and good work. I'll see both of you at the airport," It was better they all meet at the airport then leave from the police station together.

Shana didn't need to go and say goodbye to anyone at home, Ryan was coming with her. Everyone she needed to say goodbye to was at work, all, except one.

She entered her office after all her goodbyes and picked up the phone, ten minutes before she was heading out. John was going to drop Ryan and Shana off at the airport. The men made their way to the car, knowing that Shana would follow. They knew she had one more thing to do before she left.

"What time are you heading out?" Portia knew exactly why Shana was calling, her sixth sense always worked well especially with Shana.

"And a hello to you too?" smiling at the fact her best friend knew her way too well.

"Hello, so when are you flying out?" Portia repeated.

"Heading to the airport in ten. I can't believe Dad's making Ryan stay with me in everything I do. He's stuck to me like glue."

"Please, it's not like you're complaining. You have been waiting for this day."

"True, true" she leaned back in the chair, knowing that this is probably the only time she would get of peace talking to the person who she genuinely loved most. Her best friend.

"You're overworking yourself. You know, you can have a break sometimes, hear of annual leave?" Portia voiced, sounding like she was going into therapy mode.

"Portia, stop, chill for a second I'm not your patient right now. Speaking of patients," Shana remembered the conversation she had earlier with her dad about the abusive husband being located at Portia's hospital.

"I didn't know you were working with Dad on one of your patients?"

"Um, oh what patient?" she spluttered.

"The abusive patient?" Shana continued.

"Who told you? That is confidential information!" Portia declared defensively. Shana frowned. This was not like her, not even close to her character. Portia would breach her patient's privacy only with Shana and talk about her day in detail.

"Relax, what is wrong with you? It's not like I care. He could stay there for all I care as long as he never touches his wife again."

"Yeah, I'm sorry Shana, just a little uptight," Portia explained, trying to make light of the situation and cover her outburst.

"When was the last time you got laid?" she tried to add humor to lighten things up. "Is everything ok? Is there something I should know?" But Portia's silence spoke volumes to Shana. Shana was a little curious now; *her gut told her something wasn't right.*

"Just too many patients to deal with, a week of firing and hiring has me worked up, I'm so sorry,"

Shana wasn't convinced, but she needed to head out soon "We will talk when I get back."

"For sure, maybe we can talk and see each other. Hey, maybe we should Skype!" Portia tried to laugh it off and change the subject.

"So funny, try not to work too hard, love you." Shana was getting up ready to hang up and head out.

"Love you too, Shana…. Please be careful." Portia always worried about her.

"You too." Shana hung up and headed out. It was time to go.

As she was heading out, Tim was at his office, he was one of a few staying behind for any emergency assistance.

"They never found the daughter. She was apparently at college around that time having left the house a day before the murders took place. No one knows where she is. It's like she has disappeared from the face of this earth." Tim is updating Shana with what he has found. Shana responded immediately. "That's not possible, I want more information on her. I want the surveillance that says she was at college that day and what witnesses had seen her. I need this to be your priority. I want this girl found."

"Ok, leave it with me. I'll start from scratch."

Shana hated the word *'disappeared.'* This meant she would not be able to find it, and that's not what she wanted to hear, she wanted answers. With that, Shana headed for the door.

First stop Atlanta, Georgia.

***

CHAPTER 22

Exhume – 'to dig something buried, especially a dead body out of the earth; disinter' (Collins English Dictionary – Complete & Unabridged 10th Edition, 2009)

Forensic pathologists would agree that autopsies are best if performed within twenty-four hours of death. Nevertheless, they can be exhumed, the condition of the body may limit the information that can be obtained from an exhumation autopsy. Although in this case even though decomposed, the object should be ok, or so Shana hoped.

Shana felt at ease in South Florida. This State was already in the process of unearthing unidentified bodies that had been buried.

As the body was placed and ready to be analyzed, the team kept in mind that this particular family had died from strangulation. The slightly decomposed body was placed on the morgue bed. There it was the object they were all here to examine was exposed, ever so small, responsively sighted by Monica.

"There it is," Monica exclaimed, pointing with her fingers, leaning over to pick up the tweezers ready to gather and collect the evidence to analyze it. Having the whole forensic team

out here digging up the corpses after having to spend so much money to do so, Monica was so excited that she was right and that it was all worthwhile.

The forensic pathologist leaned over as to see what Monica was talking about, Shana also leaning in.

"There, there." She pointed, making sure her nail didn't touch the body. There it was a small bone-like material and much smaller than a grain of rice, nearly invisible to the naked eye. That was the green light to start digging up the remainder of the bodies.

"Is something's on it?" Shana couldn't see anything. But there had to be - a criminal who wouldn't just place something there without anything on it would be a waste of time.

Firstly, photographs were taken by expert digital forensic photographers before viewing or adding chemicals that could ruin or damage the evidence. The object needed to go through a process of exquisite analysis. Then it was ready to hit the lab, both geared up to find out what it was.

The naked eye can view only what the naked eye can see. The wonderful microscope was now in full play working its glass lenses through, minute light rays are separated and spread apart to allow the object to appear much larger. The microscope will be able to tell them exactly what the object is.

Ryan walked in as they just had placed the object under for viewing.

"Heard you found something?" they both looked up; he had a large Ice Slurpee in one hand and a half-empty bag of fairy floss in the other. He looked like a child that just come back from an amusement park.

Shana looked up and smiled, his red lips were stained from the strawberry Slurpee,

"Nothing yet just placed this under," Shana replied as Ryan glanced over, trying to see.

"Looks like a grain of rice." He said looking at where the object was placed.

"Yeah it does, however, it feels a little harder, and weighs a little more, maybe a bone?"

"Wow," Ryan responded as he moved to the back of the room, to let them get on with her work,

"Reminds me of the Ripley's Believe It or Not dude" he suggested while using the back wall to lean on, placing his Slurpee on the side.

Shana looked over, and as did Monica. "Is that where you were today?"

"No. No, this was a while ago. There was a man, he felt like he won gold when he found the best grain of rice to write on. He was inspired by some dude called David Pay to write on grains of rice. David could write the entire alphabet in seventeen seconds and can write up to three hundred and thirty-three characters on a single grain of rice, and guess what?"

Both Shana and Monica, excited to look through the magnifying glass, but not wanting to be rude and continued listening to Ryan blabber.

"He did this all with the naked eye. No magnifying glass, no microscope, nothing, just holds the grain of rice with his fingers and writes. His goal is to write the Lord's Prayer twice on a single grain of rice." Ryan explained as he stopped to take a small sip of his Slurpee, "Isn't that awesome?"

"Yes, Ryan it sure is. Now can we see if the Lord's Prayer is written here?" Ryan smiled and knew it was his cue to be silent and let them get back to work.

The forensic analysis was now in process.

It was absolute silence as Monica was looking into the microscope. People outside listening in, attentively eager to find out what it was. It felt like a surgery taking place and the loved ones were left thinking the unknown in the waiting room, awaiting some sort of positive feedback.

Suddenly, the writing on the object appeared, again the Japanese writing. It was so clear, so perfectly written. Thankfully, a Japanese translator was ready on sight, knowing that this writing may be like that found on the bodies in LA, thus, within minutes it was translated. Shana was glad he was there.

'See no evil... see no me' That was it. This small object of insertion was taken out of the eye.

Shana paced slowly back and forth, trying to figure it out. This allegory for the Three Wise Monkeys kept Shana curious and mentally exhausted.

She kept repeating to herself "See no evil... see no me, see no evil... see no me." Over and over.

She then looked over at Ryan, Jake, and Monica. "When can we get the other two bodies up; his wife and child?"

The Chief of the Atlanta District was all ears listening to every word, he had the answer Shana was after, "We can get the rest of the bodies first thing in the morning. Shana now would not be a good time, lots of burials are scheduled for today and we don't want to be digging up bodies while people are burying them."

"That's fine. In any case, the team and I need to rest. We can start again tomorrow." Shana replied, given that her team went straight to work the moment they got off the plane. Rest time was good.

***

The next day came quickly and as expected a similar object was found in both coffins, with a viewing of the autopsy reports, they were able to see where the insertion was following what Monica had pointed out, from the light purple circles and the slight lump.

The little boy, in this case, had it located in his ear and the mother in her upper lip.

After a similar analysis, the object found in the girl consisted also of Japanese writing, translated to:

"Hear no evil... hear no me."

Whereas the object in the mother translated said:

"Say no evil, speak not to me."

"I wonder if it is the same thing that is written in each body. We need to get these bodies dug up and analyzed now." Shana demanded, as she got on the phone and made a few calls to confirm their comings and that the bodies were ready in the morgue upon their arrival. All bodies need to be exhumed and the sooner, the better.

Shana also knew she needed to take Wong's advice right now. She needed to contact Dr. Marcos. She needed his help.

Shana also got on the phone with Portia; she knew that Portia was her way in.

Dr. Marcos was one of the best offenders profiling, also known as criminal profiling. He used a behavioral and investigative tool that is intended to help investigators accurately predict and profile the characteristics of unknown subjects or offenders. Offender profiling has many names including personality profiling, criminological profiling, behavioral profiling, or investigative analysis.

Shana had dealt with professional theorists in the past who have a way of understanding criminals based on physical, mental, and psychological attributes. But Shana also knew that Dr. Marcos goes a step further and how he does it is unlikely to be shared. His analysis of criminal profiling and continued development of psychological profiling of offenders is far advanced than anything she had come across.

"I need Dr. Marcos here." She said as soon as she heard Portia's voice, time was of the essence.

"Don't you ever just say hi? How are you? Or at least let me finish the word hello?" Portia sounded frustrated.

"Hi and, how are you? Now please Portia, I need Dr. Marcos here!" she was desperate.

He was one of the professors at Portia's university and he and Portia became acquainted, hence a strong friendship formed. Dr. Marcos was not too fond of the American way of dealing with forensics, he felt that a conspiracy plan was in play, and many people who worked years in the police force, the forensics unit, or even the CIA, or FBI, would say he is not far off.

"Shana, he has a conference on this week and also has to head toward Washington as an expert witness for some case," Portia explained.

"Portia, I'm not asking, I need him here. Please just make it happen." She sighed.

"The case I was telling you about, there are ten families we are currently in the process of digging up, all over, and they are sending the evidence we need here, that's twenty-one people in total. Then heading to the New York family, that's another three, and the family that took place in LA that's three with their daughter missing. Portia, he has left evidence in the body, linked with some Japanese cultural thing. Listen I need insight, I need this." She took a breath and continued "This arsehole is not playing games; he wants us to understand him and I fucking don't!"

"Ok leave it with me," Portia said calmly, taking a big breath in reassuring her that she really will try.

"Thank you." That was the only thing Shana could say.

It only took a few hours for Portia to get back to her.

"He'll be there in eight hours, you have him for a week, and I told him that we know each other professionally not personally. He will cost you big bucks. Good luck."

"What no hi, no how are you, not even wait till I say hello?" Shana replied sarcastically.

"Now you know how it feels, I have to head out," Portia replied.

"Thanks!" Shana replied, smiling from ear to ear, and extremely grateful.

"Yeah, bye," Portia said hanging up the phone.

She was a little worried about how blunt Portia had been, but it was something to worry about later. *For now, Shana was fortunate.*

***

CHAPTER 23

"When the fool spoke, the wise man answered him with silence."

Dr. Macros arrived in Atlanta. Shana had a car waiting for him as he got off the private jet. She smiled as he walked down; behind the smile was a sigh of relief.

She ran in to greet him.

"I'm not here for you, I'm here for Portia. You must have left a good impression on her for her to recommend me being here. I overlooked some of the documentation you sent my way on the plane. Also, you can, later on, answer the question as to why Wong is no longer on the case." Dr. Macros said while holding copies of the case in a folder and making his way to the car.

Shana didn't care about the reasoning of how he got here, she was just grateful that he was here and eager to hear his insight.

While in the car, he opened his documents and an old diary.

He smelled of mothballs, with years of experience and wisdom illustrated in every wrinkle embedded on his round elderly face.

He had a distinctive mustache, with the tips rolled to perfection.

His suit was one size too big, and his brown leather briefcase looked to be the same age as him. He had no sense of humor and was a straight shooter, additionally, he was never married.

With his exceedingly high IQ came along with it a slight stutter that only brought itself to the surface when he was just about to reveal intense news. Shana was simply happy to be in his presence, regardless of what he thought of her.

"I appreciate you taking the time, Dr…." it didn't take him long to cut in.

"This person, this killer," he pointed to the files "is someone I have never come across. This person is serious and frustrated that his work had gone unseen. The only way I feel this could have taken place is with some work happening from the inside, a coverup."

Shana sat back, thinking to herself, *here we go again.* This was Shana's biggest fear, the chance that he may be right.

"I beg to differ, Dr. Marcos. The evidence was hidden so well, that it was not picked by the naked eye. The rings only appeared late in the autopsy period, and also did not indicate the cause of death. I am also angry that this went through without being picked up, but I can promise you that it was a simple error."

Dr. Marcos stared at Shana directly in her eyes, his eyebrows slanting up; he was not at all impressed.

"You poor young girl, with your experience in this world and your mother's death, you would think that would have toughened you up a bit. You're saying eight cases – that's twenty-four bodies – all had autopsy's and none of the pathologists picked up on a slight lump or a slight purple ring, but your staff picked it up on a photo?"

He was right, it sounded too suspicious. But Shana felt the urge to defend herself.

"Dr. Marcos, I know that you had read up on me, and please know that I respect you, but I ask that you never mention my mother's death, as this has no bearing on the case. Also, to answer your question, yes unfortunately what you are saying is true. Monica is an expert in digital forensic photography and has an eye for detail, and no I feel there is no conspiracy. You're here for criminal profiling and we are happy to pay you whatever your desired asking price is, which I hope that would allow you to invest in a suit that fits you." Shana stopped to catch herself, he had pushed her to her limits by mentioning her mother and didn't realize that she had gone too far. Her tongue spoke before it checked in with her brain. She started to worry *What if he left, he didn't have to be there.* She then tried to defuse the situation.

"I'm sorry Dr. Marcos... I *"* he cut in, Shana held herself knowing that what he was about to say, he will probably result in her asking the driver to turn around head back to the airport, all because she couldn't control her tongue.

"I had it coming, shouldn't have mentioned your mother. In any case, I have gotten in contact with a friend of mine from the Japanese consulate. He is expecting a call from me in one hour, and I would like this conversation to only include myself. I will then collaborate with you on my profiling. I would like to see some of the bodies, his family history, basically anything that you haven't given me, oh and the surveillance video, I want to see the tattoo and his body."

"I'll get Monica to assist you in everything you need. I understand you like to also work with no interference and have an office, secluded and ready for you, also concerning our travel to the other locations I know that you are also coming with us, I have accommodated your needs as much as I possibly can."

"Shana, why is it that you are attending, each location and observing as the evidence is being collected? Why not get each department to do it, and then send the information over to you?"

He asked an exceptionally good question, she trusted him enough to be honest with him.

The car stopped, and the driver got out opening the door to let Dr. Marcos and Shana out. Shana thanked him but said they would make their way up. She then closed the door, locked it, made sure no one was close by to hear what she had to say. She then explained to Dr. Marcos what she needed to say in complete confidence. Bringing to surface the letter and information she had not shared with the whole team as of yet.

With Shana's upfront honesty and trust in Dr. Marcos, he had a newfound respect for Shana, *He knew she was one of the good guys.*

Dr. Marcos went through the files he had, and the information given to him by Shana, he was taking it all.

With each body came an object, each object had some different writing on it. Covering Atlanta, Portland, Washington, Alabama, Florida, Alabama, Florida, Idaho, Colorado, New York.

Each evidence collection was attended to and viewed by Dr. Marcos and Shana.

The evidence collocation was made, photographed and toward the end of the two weeks, they were all ready to head back to Los

Angeles. The case intrigued him so much that he stayed longer than the time intended.

During this time, Shana learned quite a bit about Dr. Marcos, the real person. His life his dedication, his loneliness, and that his high school sweetheart had been kidnapped, raped, and killed. Shana now understood why his life took the path that it did, why he had chosen this career path.

After the death of his high school sweetheart, Dr. Marcos found a way to work with the FBI and manipulated them to reopen the case, not letting them know that he knew her.

Not only did he help catch the killer on the case he was working on through his amazing profiling and analysis, but he finally found out who killed his beloved girlfriend, many years ago. His analytical, strategy, and determination were not comparable.

Nevertheless, the truth of the matter was that many, many years later, he still had so much anger and hatred toward parts of the world that Dr. Marcos was never able to open his heart to another. How is it, this strong, passionate man manages to live life all alone? With all that intelligence he must know how affected the mental state could get without human interaction. *Shana was puzzled, she also felt sorry for him.*

***

CHAPTER 24

*"You will be judged by the circle you are in. Look to the circle
and see what reasons are behind that judgment."*

Shana couldn't figure out what had changed, even though it was
good to be back in Los Angeles. Dr. Marcos had been a little
distant, they shared so much on this two-week trip, besides the
relative information concerning the criminal, she felt like they
had become friends.

But lately, he had not answered Shana's calls, and not turned
up to the meetings they had scheduled. He was silent on the
plane home; Shana could have sworn he was pretending to sleep
the whole way back to indirectly avoid her. Criminal profiling
lecture was set in place for next week to be given to the team to
better understand who it was they were looking for.

Shana couldn't do it anymore. She knew he had a meeting the
second day, as she had glanced over and seen it in his diary.
Shana did something that she thought she would never do.

She followed him.

Dr. Marcos sat outside in an isolated café, in beautiful Beverly
Hills. The waiter approached him with a smile as he placed

the coffee on the table. She sat at a small park across the road, partially hidden by trees. She could see him, but she doubts he could see her. It appeared that Dr. Marcos looked as if he did not worry about the world. Drinking his coffee and reading a paper, his old brown leather briefcase protected firmly between his feet. Shana tried to call him. She wanted him to pick up and invite her over. She saw him pick up his phone; Dr. Marcos looked at the phone and simply shook his head before he turned the phone upside down, placed it on the table, and continued to read the paper.

Shana was so annoyed and curious. She was paying him to do a job that he was not doing. She had enough and was ready to walk over and to confront him when she stopped immediately.

Three men had approached Dr. Marcos and sat down. Shana quickly made her way back behind the tree, looking closely. All three men were in suits, and their prominent cheekbones and slight obliquely set eyes, lead Shana to believe they were of Asian descent. *'They had to be Japanese,'* Shana thought.

But as she looked closer, there was a familiar face. It was the same man that was in her father's office when she had barged in weeks ago. *What was he doing here?* That was supposed to be some domestic violence case. Shana was confused and felt out of the loop.

Then Dr. Marcos pulled something out of his suitcase, she couldn't quite see it from where she was.

The older man then got up and slammed the table as he looked at what Dr. Marcos was showing him, the other two men calmed him down. *'What was he angry about?'* Shana's mind was running. The same man then grabbed Dr. Marcos by the shirt while pointing to what he had pulled out, something in a yellow folder, *'what is going on'* Shana murmured to herself. She wanted to go in and help Dr. Marcos, but her gut kept saying to wait.

The other two men had calmed him down again and then they all sat down talking. Looking around making sure they didn't draw too much attention. Shana then looked to the far-left corner. There she saw Wong standing. *'What on earth is going on?'* too much was happening.

What was Wong doing here? She had fired him. Then Shana stopped for a second and thought maybe it was a coincidence he was in the area. She kept looking back and forth keeping her eyes on Dr. Marcos and the three men and then she would turn to Wong. Wong then walked across the street walking in the direction of where Dr. Marcos was sitting. He then made his way into a convenience store about three shops down to where the café was. *It better be a coincidence.* Shana thought. But Shana knew better.

As the men then got up the leader continued to exchange words with Dr. Marcos while being close to his face. Dr. Marcos looked helpless.

After they had left, Dr. Marcos was placing some papers and an object in the yellow file.

Shana was going to approach him and ask him point-blank to explain what the fuck is going on!

Shana was ready to cross the road when she saw Wong exit the convenience store and make his way to Dr. Marcos, where he handed over the file. Wong looked over and noticed Shana as he was walking off.

"Wong stop right there…. Wait" she tried to cross the road, waiting on two cars to get out of her way, and trying hard to keep Wong in view distance.

195

Wong walked a little faster in the opposite direction, crossed the corner, jogged to a car that was already running, the car had no number plate. Wong jumped in the passenger side of the car and was gone.

She didn't even bother chasing. She knew where Wong resided and would catch up to him later.

She walked back as Dr. Marcos was walking off in the opposite direction; he had quickly placed a sum of money on the table, eager to get out of there. He did not want to speak to Shana.

The truth of the matter is. He no longer knew who she was. He couldn't trust her.

"Dr. Glen Marcos!" She yelled, not considering that she was in a public place not caring who was around. She was angry that things were being done behind her back.

Dr. Marcos turned around, shaken up from the previous conversation he had with the men earlier.

"You speak of conspiracy; you speak of integrity, what the fuck is going on Marcos? Who were those men? And what the fuck was Wong doing here?" She would normally never speak like that to anyone, let alone someone of his prestige, she even left his title out. She no longer cared.

"Shana, I, I, I ...." Dr. Marcos was nervous, his stuttering started to take place and his hands began to shake uncontrollably. Shana noticed this, and her empathy quickly took over, she grabbed his hand and sat at an empty bus stop, he took her hand and followed her lead. He also sat down.

She had her hand over his. "What's going on Doc?"

"Shana, p..p... please," he stuttered, "I'm so sorry, but this is bigger than you and me."

"Why are you not telling me what's happening? We're on the same side Doc." Shana paused; he didn't respond "Are we not?"

"Are we Shana? Because if that's the case, then there are a few things that you haven't told me, things you left out. I'm sorry that I cannot, I can't tell you anything!"

"What are you talking about Dr.?" Shana was confused "And what things have I not told you? I told you everything I know, in detail. I have shared the documents with you! I've even shared confidential information with you and yet you say I'm holding back information?" Shana explained, looking at him waiting for a reply or some answers, "Why were you with Wong? And why were those three Asian men with you?" Shana asked again, as Dr. Marcos sat there quietly not answering any of Shana's questions or concerns. This time, Shana had lost all her patience "Please don't make me take you in! You know I have grounds to do so, you are withholding information! Please don't make me have to resort to that!" Dr. Marcos shook nervously.

Shana could see what Dr. Marcos was thinking. Shana grabbed his face, she brought it closer to hers. "Look at me Marcos, look clearly, we are on the same side" Dr. Marcos eventually looked into her eyes.

"Were you involved in putting Lorraine away?" He asked her directly

Shana was confused. With all the names of the people that had dealt with she could not remember that coming across the name Lorraine. Shana was frustrated and couldn't take any more of these games there is a killer on the loose and her job is now on the line. She needed results, fast.

"Who the fuck is Lorraine? Stop playing with me, Doctor."

"You have no idea?" he shook his head "ok Shana I will answer all your questions, but not today, they have someone following your every move."

Shana jumped in "No one followed me here, I snuck out."

Dr. Marcos continued "You can't be sure! You want answers! Then we do this my way" Shana nodded. She didn't care, where; she just needed to know what was going on. "We need to go somewhere isolated. You need to make sure no one is following you. Shana, once I have handed this information to you, I don't know how much longer they will keep me alive!"

"What are you going on about?" Shana was confused.

"Look just don't worry about that right now." He placed his hand on hers, Shana looked up. "Promise me that you will come alone." Shana nodded.

"I promise you." Shana was getting nervous. She wanted answers, however, at the same time she was afraid to know, her gut instinct knew from the beginning there was more to this case than she had thought. People were working hard at hiding things from her. Why did her father lie to her? And why did Portia go along with what her father had said? It was exhausting. She didn't know who to trust anymore.

Dr. Marcos could see Shana was thinking a thousand miles an hour, "Listen, Shana, meet me tomorrow at a place named Lion's Lighthouse in Long beach,"

"Shana, you need to look at me." Shana did as he requested. "You cannot tell a soul! You cannot speak to anyone; this is bigger than you and I and you cannot trust anyone!"

Shana had to ask one question that has been on her mind "Is someone internally involved in this Dr. Marcos? If there is corruption within the workforce, need to know Dr. Marcos! This is something that cannot wait until tomorrow." Dr. Marcos just ignored her. He got up and waved at a taxi, it stopped directly in front of him. He walked to the taxi and opened the door. Shana was a step behind him. "You can't go Dr. Marcos you can't do this! I need to know!"

He hopped into the back of the taxi "I promise I will let you in on everything tomorrow I just need you to keep your end of the bargain, do not discuss this with anyone, not even your best friend Portia."

She looked at him, a little embarrassed that she had lied about knowing Portia on a professional work level and not personal, *'how silly of me to think that he wouldn't find out, he does profile for a living, and he understands everything'* She shook her head.

So much was going through Shana's mind and her headache was getting stronger.

She got up and was ready to make her way across the road when she felt someone following her, a slight shadow only a meter away. She stopped walking and was about to look over her shoulder when she noticed an Asian man looking directly at her only one store down. She continued to look at him until he turned his head looking through the window of an antique shop right between the coffee shop and the convenience store. Shana didn't know if she was being paranoid. She then turned around to notice no one behind her and continued to walk toward her car hoping she was not being followed. She turned around again after she had passed the man and saw that he was standing there looking at the antique store. She was a little more relaxed now, thinking to herself, *'false alarm,'* not until the hair on his neck moved with his head as he was trying to look closer at an object in the window, there it was. The tattoo with the cherry blossom monkey. It was the same tattoo of the person who dropped off a package. It was a distinctive tattoo with the same hairstyle. Right in front of her, was the possible criminal.

She slowly reached for her gun, she didn't have a backup, but she had no time. He could be the killer; he had to be the killer. She could kill him now and figure the rest out later.

She had no idea how this was going to play out. Shana held her gun pointing in his direction and paced slowly closer to him. The man looking in the window being able to see her reflection, but not moving, smiled to himself. He waited until she spoke.

"Freeze and turn around slowly," she yelled at the top of her voice. Bystanders moved out of the way as they saw a gun being pointed toward him in broad daylight. He placed his hands in his pocket casually, Shana afraid he was getting something "Put your hands up, I said freeze." He then turned casually in the opposite direction of Shana while having his back to her, "I said freeze! Don't make me shoot you." Shana's hands shook. He continued to walk away from Shana "I WILL SHOOT YOU!" Shana placed her hand on the trigger and was ready to fire, being left with no other choice. She walked slowly toward him as he tried to walk away. He then froze. The sidewalk was now empty, there were no bystanders – it was just him and Shana.

Just as Shana was aiming ready to shoot, she felt something poke her in her lower back "This gun is pointed at your spinal cord. One shot will have you paralyzed for life if you do not do as I say."

Shana had her gun pointed straight at the man. She was so scared and knew that a gunshot at close range would completely break through her bones and all the surrounding nerves.

"Breathe Shana, you can put the gun down now."

Should I shoot the killer, and risk my life? What if he is not the killer and the killer is the one with the gun behind me? Shana had no choice. Shakingly she placed the gun down slowly on the floor.

The man leaned over grabbed the gun, Shana kept her hands in the air, as the man behind her emptied her gun, and he then launched the gun a few meters away.

Shana looked in front of her, as the man turned around, and bowed at Shana, and laughs. Shana was furious. He got on his motorbike and drove toward Shana, the man that was behind Shana jumped on and they sped off. Shana turned around to see who he was. But she could only see his back sitting and holding on for his dear life on the back of the motorbike.

Shana quickly picked up her gun and the bullets, watching as the motorbike swerved in and out of traffic and disappeared before her very eyes. She had no chance of finding them. Shana got in her car and took her anger out on her steering wheel. She didn't know what to do. She picked up her phone her hands shaking. She called her father, but just like before, it rang out, she hung up. She called Ryan, the same thing she couldn't talk to anyone; she didn't know who to trust. Also, they would ask what she was doing here. She had promised Dr. Marcos.

Shana needed to know what it was Dr. Marcos knew because whatever it was, he was getting close. The killer must have been there watching their every move. Shana had no choice but to wait. Tomorrow six she would find out what Dr. Marcos knew and then maybe just maybe she can finally bring that son of a bitch in.

***

CHAPTER 25

"They say the human mind is the point for the discovery of truths. The heart is that of falsehoods."

Shana entered her apartment physically and mentally exhausted. All she wanted to do was keep busy until it came time to meet with Dr. Marcos.

As she sat on the couch, slouching back taking a second to relax, Shana closed her eyes. A strong hand leaned over and grabbed her shoulder.

Shana jumped up frantically straight to the table where she had placed her gun and pointed it straight at the man standing in front of her.

"Shana, what the hell is wrong with you?" It was Ryan.

She quickly put the gun down, and tried to get hold of herself, for a split second she forgot that Ryan was living with her, and a week ago she had given him the key to her apartment.

"I'm so sorry," she tried to laugh it off. "I had a really bad day today."

Ryan jumped over the couch and planted himself next to her and put his arms around her.

"Tried to call you a few times today, as did your dad. He freaked out when I had no idea where you were. You can't just disappear like that." Ryan was worried.

"Now, where were you?"

Shana remembered what Dr. Marcos had told her '*Don't trust anyone*' and how hard it was for her to lie, and easy for anyone to pick up on, she tried in any case.

"Oh, nowhere fancy, just needed some time to myself. Spoke to Portia, and meet for coffee, nothing major."

Ryan moved his arm from around her "Shana, Portia is in NY for a conference, so there is no way you could have to meet up with her." Ryan replied sarcastically "Unless you had taken some sort of jet this morning, and somehow miraculously got back, after a quick cup of coffee. Come on seriously."

She was angry that she was caught out but angrier that she couldn't tell him.

"Listen, Ryan, please I just wanted time alone. Sorry I lied, but I just need to be left alone for a bit."

She hoped he would understand and drop it, but she was wrong.

"Shana you can't just disappear. I am willing to keep my mouth shut and give you your space as long as you're in seeing distance of me. You want to sit in the park and be on your own, then fine! I'll sit a block away and just keep an eye on you, it's fucking that easy."

"I don't need a babysitter. Please, Ryan, I don't need this shit right now, just leave me alone. You can sit in the bedroom with the door open and watch me in silence." Shana replied cynically.

Shana needed to plan a way to get out of Ryan's way early in the morning, so he would not follow her. There was no way she was going to jeopardize her meeting.

Shana sat on the couch going over some of the evidence of the case. She went back to what had happened earlier with the three Asian men, Wong, the gun on her back, and the man with the tattoo. It kept repeating in her head until she lay on the couch and dozed off.

The house phone rang.

"Can you get that?" Ryan yelled from the bedroom.

He came out and noticed Shana asleep on the couch; he picked up the phone, which was in the kitchen.

"Hello,"

"Ryan, I'm assuming your mobile is not working?" Ryan shook his head, wishing he had not picked up the phone.

It was the Chief.

"Where was she?" he was not in the mood for small talk.

"I tried to find out; she said she just wanted some time out. She went to the park, probably just to get away for a bit... Chief I'm so sorry I...."

"Save it Ryan if anything happens to her, so help me God, you're accountable. She wasn't at the park, and you know it."

Ryan's subconscious mind wanted to say, 'then you go, and fucking ask her and leave me the fuck alone you psychotic fuck,' but what came out of his mouth was completely different.

"I tried to see if this was the truth, but she wanted to be left alone."

"Where is she now?" was the quick response.

"She's lying on the sofa; she just dozed off while going over some paperwork." Ryan felt the need to be descriptive and accurate with everything he said to the Chief.

"Where is her phone"? He asked as if some amazing idea came to him.

"On the table?" Ryan answered confused as to why he is asking.

"Get her phone without her knowing,"

"But sir?" Ryan questioned, not liking where this was going.

"Don't 'but' me son, and just do it. She may be in danger." Ryan went and picked up the phone quietly.

"Sir I don't know her code?" Ryan didn't want to do this. The Chief knew all too well it was Shana's mother's birthday. Seconds later Ryan was in, and now going through her phone. The Chief wanted to know who she had called today.

"It was you sir, but she called, and she must have hung up, there is no time duration." Ryan replied as he continued to scroll down the recent call list "Also the same as Portia, and myself. She had called us but must have changed her mind. There are also two new messages." Ryan wished he held back his tongue.

"Um." Fidgeting as he clicked on it and the message came up. He read it to the Chief.

'Alone Shana. I trust you.' The message read. It was simple, short, and precise. Both the Chief and Ryan went quiet trying to critically analyze what the message meant.

"Ryan, you need to make sure you delete the message and place it back exactly where it was."

"Yes sir," Ryan answered as he followed the Chief's instructions and deleted the message.

"Ryan, you are not to mention this to Shana. Please son listen to me, this is way over our head. I feel that Shana is being set up to be taken down."

Ryan was concerned, worried, and angry with himself for leaving her today.

"I will have a few people following her tomorrow; I have a new project for you to do, starting now." The Chief explained while Ryan questioned her father's motives, why he was not staying with Shana if her life was at stake?

"But sir, I want to stay here and protect her; no one is going to protect her like me."

"You will be protecting her, but in doing something else. I need you somewhere else, you will drive with John. He is heading to the airport in forty minutes to pick up the Chief General from Japan. You will drop the Chief off at the hotel and keep surveillance on him until tomorrow evening." Ryan was furious; he didn't want to leave Shana's side.

"He is familiar with the case and has some information for us. He must be looked after. By him coming to America, he has placed his life at stake!" the Chief responded, emphasizing the importance of the job.

The Chief hung up the phone and Ryan stood staring blankly at the phone for a while.

He looked over at Shana sleeping peacefully; he was confused. He didn't want to leave, but Shana's father was his Chief and a possible future father-in-law. He had to do as he was told. Ryan returned Shana's phone quietly back to where she had left it and leaned over gently to move Shana's hair off her face. He then leaned closer and kissed Shana on her forehead and whispered, *"Please be safe, I love you."*

He went to the room grabs his backpack and quietly left the apartment. Not before placing a blanket over Shana.

***

"Who is this guy that we're going to pick up?" Ryan asked as he jumped into the passenger seat of John's car heading to LAX airport.

"Some important Japanese dude I reckon, something to do with the case," John answered casually.

Ryan with a little confused as to why John didn't know more information about who he was going to pick up.

Ryan had the feeling that something was wrong "Don't you feel that things are getting a little too secretive about this case? My gut tells me something's not right John and you know my gut never lies." Ryan replied, wanting to see if John shared a similar reaction.

"Dude, if I were you, I'd do just as I am told. Can I remind you that you are dating the Chief's daughter? You don't want to fuck this up. *She's worth it.*" They both went quiet. John continued "This is a nice and simple job; all we have to do is pick up the

Japanese dude then drop him off at the hotel and just keep an eye on him until tomorrow evening. What's so suspicious about that?"

"That's the point John; it's too much of a simple job! Why are we, qualified police officers, doing such a simple job? I'm telling you something's not right. It's to get us out of the way." Ryan then turned to John, who was shaking his head. "You know the Chief made me go through Shana's phone." John looked at him confused "Because we had no idea where she was today. If she had woken up, while I was going through the phone what would I have done? I'm an idiot; I'd probably have told her, *Your daddy asked me to.*"

John couldn't help himself; he laughed hysterically. "Are seriously laughing?" Ryan said in hope that John would empathize with him.

"At least you got her dad's approval to go through the phone. Did you find anything exciting?" John laughed.

"It's not funny John, there was just some message from Dr. Marcos about some meeting or something like that."

John smirked as they continued on their drive. Ryan's thoughts took over him as he sat quietly worrying about Shana. On the contrary, John was looking for a close Starbucks Café craving a coffee with a blueberry muffin.

Ryan had it hard, he was continuously in tough and challenging circumstances because he was dating the Chief's daughter. John, on the other hand, was always there to make light of every situation, John was an optimistic character, and he was the kind of brother that Ryan was never blessed with.

As they both were lost in their thoughts, it was as if something had just hit John. He turned to Ryan and asked "Dr. Marcos has been distant for a bit lately. Last I heard, Shana was frustrated he wasn't returning her calls or coming to pre-meetings about the criminal profiling that's happening tomorrow. Don't worry Ryan, it's probably about that. If it were a life-threatening situation the Chief wouldn't have you and me here." John explained as he saw a sign leading toward the 24-hour Starbucks Café and turned right before parking the car. They both got out given that they had plenty of time to get to the airport. *A coffee break was a great idea.*

***

CHAPTER 26

"The reaction of fear that I feel is the confrontation of being a step closer to the truth."

Shana woke up suddenly and sat up looking around, noticing the bedroom door closed. She tiptoed around the house quietly with the aim of not waking up Ryan, she quietly turned the handle on the bedroom door and looked in to notice the room was empty. In a way, she was relieved, even though she wanted him there and she loved him dearly, she needed this time to be alone. She couldn't have him follow her to her meeting with Dr. Marcos. Shana continued to look around the house to make sure Ryan was not there. She then went into the bathroom and had a shower, brushed her teeth, and got into some comfortable clothing. Coffee was all her body could take right now. She sat at the kitchen table waiting for time to go by. Finally, it was quarter past five. She tied her hair back grabbed her gun and put some files away in a briefcase. As she was heading out, she remembered she had left her phone and quickly ran back in and picked it off the table.

She was about to message Dr. Marcos she then changed her mind. *'He knows we are meeting today.'* Soon she will know everything she needed to know. Shana got in the car and made her way to the beautiful Long Beach pier.

***

Shana had no idea that she was being followed. He made sure to keep his distance but was able to see where she was heading. He didn't know where she was going, but he was aware of who she was meeting. He watched as Shana swerved in and out of lanes and shook his head at her risky driving skills. He continued to drive, following her to the destination.

Detective Grant, continued to drive behind Shana, keeping his distance and continuously behind her every move. He had forced George to stay back and that he would follow Shana, it would not be right if he came, he needed to be present at work. He needed to stay at the station. As Grant continued to drive, he received a phone call it was the Chief "Do you know where she's heading?"

At that point, Shana pulled a crazy turn just missing oncoming traffic.

"No, I'm still following her she's heading towards Long Beach, I think I'm not quite sure. Seriously, how did she even get her driver's license?"

"Just make sure she doesn't see you and stay safe. Do you want me down there? I can come down?"

"No! Me and you together here, we might as well hand in our badges! I'll be fine, all I'm doing is being a spy, just relax George!"

"Listen, Grant, please just be safe, look out for my girl. Don't go playing MacGyver on me right now and do some Rambo shit! Just call me if something's up!" the Chief replied anxiously.

"Yeah" he replied. The Chief may have been his best friend but right now he was a pain in the arse. "I just don't want Shana to get any idea that anybody was following her, the more information we have the better we know what the hell's going on."

Grant was getting pissed off, "You're the one who fucking put Shana in charge! I told you it was not a good idea, and why did you let her bring in the old dude? Dr. fucking Marcos, how about you let me fix the shit you got us into Chief?"

The Chief was not in the mood to fight right now, "Look Mr. Fixer, fine. Just don't kill anyone, find out what's happening, get back here and we will figure out what to do next! GOT IT?"

He recognized he had struck a chord, he could hear that the Chief was worried about his daughter, and worried about him. His main concern was what information Dr. Marcos would unravel to Shana, they could both lose her forever.

The detective continued to drive behind Shana and then noticed she was in the clear direction of the Pier. She started to slow down, making it clear that she was looking for a parking spot. The detective parked a couple of blocks away on the side of the road and waited until she had made her way to the lighthouse. Grant was happy that she was meeting in an open area. He slowed then drove a little closer and continued to stay in his car. He found a spot where he was able to see everything while also be slightly hidden.

He noticed Dr. Marcos sitting at a bench with his brown leather suitcase in his hand and waiting for Shana to approach him. He stood up as he saw Shana coming his way. They exchanged handshakes and both sat down. Grant watched patiently to see what was happening.

The detective could see Dr. Marcos opening his briefcase and some papers were handed to Shana. A conversation was taking place; Grant wished that he had some sort of device that would let him hear what was going on.

He couldn't take it anymore and called the Chief.

"He's handing over some papers I don't know what he's handing over and me sitting here watching is meaningless. I'm just going to go up to them and find out what's going on! I'll grab the paperwork."

"Listen Grant don't fuck this up! If you do that, then you open a can of worms! We can't have that right now just sit back and keep an eye on her, we can find out that information later. We will follow him home and grab that crap, you hear me?" George demanded, however, Grant was exasperated and ended the call, although knowing the Chief was right. Grant was just looking for an easy solution the waiting game was not his type of game, and he was sick of it.

Just as the detective threw his phone on the passenger seat in frustration, he heard the two back doors of his car open and then the passenger door open. He leaned over to get his gun, but he was not quick enough the Asian man was quick to block him.

The man behind that passenger seat simply said one word.

"Drive!" he sat back relaxed, with the man sitting next to him behind the driver's side holding a gun to Grant's neck. With two guns pointed at him, the detective had no other option and began to drive. He didn't know where he was heading but he knew the result would most likely be his death.

Grant had to be quick on his feet, He thought to himself if he was going down, then they are all going down with him. He aimed to crash and hope that he came out alive.

Grant started to speed faster and faster, swerving in and out of traffic uncontrollably, not listening to the direction of the person in charge.

The men were not expecting this, they all started to argue with each other, each one having a different idea of what to do next. One wanted to just shoot him. The man in charge was screaming and telling him not to. The louder their voices got; the faster Grant was driving.

The man in the passenger seat couldn't take it anymore. He punched Grant in the stomach, in the hope that he'd understand how serious they were. This did not affect Grant. He didn't care; anger had taken control of him, he was in total rage, no longer in his right state of mind. If he was going to die, then he was going to take them all down with him he drove fast aiming for the bridge. *Fuck it!* he thought. He was going to take the car off the bridge, this would be his only way of protecting Shana and George.

However, that wasn't his fate. As he was approaching the bridge a motorbike passed by and shot the passenger through the window the blood splatter followed immediately after. The men in the back started screaming and yelling at each other in Japanese, not having had expected that to happen. Grant had no idea who the person on the motorbike was but was grateful that there was one down in the car. He continued to drive, he aimed for the midpoint of the bridge, the highest point. The men knew exactly who he was, and the way they were acting showed signs they were scared, with the other man still pointing his gun at Grant, telling him to take an exit. Grant was not listening. He mumbled to himself "*Fucking Amateurs*" They could not risk shooting him now, if the car crashed or stopped, the man on the motorbike would finish them off. They all knew that.

The motorbike was swerving in and out of traffic and went into the far distance ahead of Grant's car. For a second, they all thought he had disappeared.

The motorbike then turned and stopped, facing oncoming traffic with Grant's cars approaching at full speed. The man pointed his hand to the left instructing Grant to take that side while he stayed put. With that, Grant knew what to do. He pushed a button allowing the back window to open. He slammed his brakes now bringing the car to the left-hand side of the man on the motorbike, who had his gun in the perfect position to shoot at the back seat. Grant continued to accelerate. *He got him, but he did not kill him. Damn!*

The boss leaned over his injured friend, who had a bullet wound in his shoulder, and opened the door, pushing him out of the moving vehicle. He rolled a few times and stayed put. With one hand on the steering wheel, he turned his other arm to grab the man who had no weapon and then spotted that the boss was trying to grab the gun off the floor behind Grant's seat. Grant took hold of the Asian man's hand, but he had quickly leaned over and grabbed the gun with his right hand. Spontaneously, Grant slammed his brakes; the boss dropped the gun and it bounced all over the car floor. Grant, holding the man's hand, tried to lean back to get a better hold of him, but the boss used his free hand and bent Grant's hand backward until it cracked. Grant screamed in pain. The boss quickly got out of the car and held a gun at the first car he saw. The boss pulled the man out of the driver's seat and jumped in. He was now driving in the opposite direction, but he stopped and picked up the man he had thrown out of the car earlier and drove off. Grant turned, wanting to follow them. The man on the bike had another idea though.

Grant, struggling with his broken hand, tried to start the car again. The motorbike rider began to make his way over to him.

Come on! The car started just in time and Grant sped off. The motorbike rider quickly followed him.

The motorbike made its way past the back of the car until it was side-by-side. He looked over; the passenger side window open; he lifted the shield of his helmet *"Pullover detective!"* Grant had seen those eyes before. Grant smirked at him, finally able to get hold of his gun and pull it out, with the adrenaline running, he blocked out the pain of a broken hand, and he shot at the motorbike, just missing him. The motorbike pressed on his brakes to get out of the shooting range of Grant. *It was too close.* The man pulled his gun out from behind him and pointed it, closing one eye, and using the other to be exactly precise, he pulled the trigger, not once but twice. He had shot the back-left wheel first, and then the back-right wheel.

Detective Grant's car was now sliding out of control. He placed his whole body weight on his foot as he intensely slammed the brakes as the car went out of control spinning, smoke filling the air as the tires continued to burn until his car crashed side on with the cement medium on the bridge. Grant's head smashed on the side of the window, making everything blurry for a split second. The adrenaline was still there, and he knew that if he wanted to survive, he could not stop. To get out he needed to get to the passenger side.

The motorbike rider removed his helmet and parked his motorbike safe from incoming cars and walked up to Grant casually. Grant tried to grab his gun, but his arms wouldn't let him. When the rider saw this, he laughed and shot Detective Grant in the shoulder to weaken him even more and placed his gun back in the back of his jeans before making his way to the passenger side.

He leaned in and grabbed the detective's broken arm, squeezing it.

The rider continued to pull on his arm until his whole body was now outside the car on the road. Grant screamed in pain.

The rider then knocked him unconscious. He dragged his body across the road, not caring about the scrapping that was taking place between Grant and the road.

Casually, he picked his body up and placed it on the motorbike. He placed each leg in a clip that he had earlier created so that Grant's legs would not dangle in his way. He pushed Grant's head forward so that he was able to see in front of him. He finally placed his helmet on, got onto his motorbike, and disappeared. Bystanders were very confused, yet no one dared to intervene.

Finally, a bystander decided to dial 911.

The police finally arrived fifteen minutes too late. The mobile phone was by car. The unmarked police vehicle was now demolished and a dead person on the passenger side. The Chief was called and informed one of their unmarked police cars had a dead body in it and a random phone.

The Chief dropped everything and was out the door. He sped toward the crime scene. He called Shana, hoping that she was ok, worried that something had happened to her, *what if she was the dead passenger?* George was calling over and over but there was no answer. George knew if the killer had Grant, then he would never see his best friend again. He also knew all too well what follows. He no longer cared about his badge, he needed to rescue his friend and find his daughter.

The Chief arrived at the scene already blocked off to the public. He ran up to the car, looked in, and a sigh of relief. It was not Shana. But he knew who was in the car. A member of the NPA Japanese international team. *Why were they with Grant?* The Chief looked over and noticed a police officer over the car, while keeping an eye on the police officer close by, he stuck his hand in and down the side of the driver's door. He grabbed the black envelope and stealthily put it in his jacket. Now all he needed was that mobile. It had to be Grant's and if not... well it would give him somewhere to start. He knew that this was probably placed in an evidence bag. Shana would be called in no time to attend this crime scene and further investigate what took place.

He needed to get hold of that phone before she did. He noticed a young police officer holding the evidence bag. The Chief walked up to him casually.

"Is that the phone you found by the car officer?" The Chief asked.

"Yes sir" the officer replied, standing straight, he was after all in front of the Chief. *His boss.*

"Good work son. I'll take this from you."

"Um, sir should I put it in evidence, first or..."

"Son! I said I'll take it from here, what was your name again?"

"Paul, sir. Paul Proctor."

"Well Paul Proctor, you did a really good job, and I'll keep that in mind, with your future advancements in the police force." The Chief then took the bag off him, folded it in two, and placed it in his jacket.

"We understand each other." He pierced him with a stern firm face, hoping that he would understand that the Chief didn't need a wise-ass rookie talking back to him.

"We understand each other sir." Proctor knew what the Chief meant. *There was no phone.*

"Good work Proctor." Nodding his head as he walked off *"Good work."*

The rookie looked at his partner confused, but both didn't say a word, just shook their heads, and made their way back to their police cars.

The Chief had one more look at what was left of Grant's car, and then headed to his car, and drove off. He needed to get in contact with his Asian buddies to find out what the fuck was going on. But more importantly, he had to find a way to get to Grant.

Time was of the essence.

***

CHAPTER 27

*"Sometimes the puzzle you are spending so much time
trying to figure out… Has missing pieces."*

"Dr. Marcos, thank you for meeting with me."

Shana sat down on the bench. Dr. Marcos was looking around; Shana could see he was paranoid, observing that Shana came alone. "I can assure you I came alone. Nobody knows I am here. Now please!"

"I don't know where to start Shana," he opened his briefcase.

"How about at the beginning?"

He smirked. "That's the problem, the beginning! This case is a huge test on your part Shana; it's a test of your integrity. Have you ever thought about why it is that you're a forensic pathologist? Why it is that you are the youngest Chief forensic team leader? You're the 'A' to 'Z' of any investigation."

Shana was offended at the question "Because I worked damn hard to gct here."

He nodded, "I didn't mean to offend you, and you're somewhat right, but the progression stage, promotion after the promotion was so quick." Shana was hurt and offended at what Dr. Marcos was saying. Even though there was some truth to it, she didn't want to think she had gotten to where she is because of her father. That would have killed her. "It's not because of your father; it's because of your mother!"

Shana was very confused "My mother?" Shana questioned "Dr. Marcos, my mother died when I was just three years old."

"Shana let's come back to that later. Let me tell you everything!"

"This case goes back many years." He handed over some papers for Shana to look at as he continued to explain them.

"Let's go back a little into history first, to Japan. In 1938, a Japanese communist party was secretly formed. This party was originated from the likeliness of Russia and China. This group is so secretive it has no comparisons to the American CIA or not as kind as the KGB." Dr. Marcos explained.

Dr. Marcos continued "An international gathering of world leaders and hierarchy political groups needed to be created to stop what was happening. This Japanese party was not only martial arts experts and knew their way with the Samurai sword, but they were also mobsters and criminals, who would kill at any possible chance they had. There was no discretion. Man, woman, and children were all treated equally. Honor killings were an everyday ritual. Even if they had only just heard that something was wrong or someone was doing something wrong, this was enough for them to kill."

"Are they still around?" Shana asked,

"Yes, and they are getting stronger because they know that there are people out to get them. Shana, if you are in the honorable stage of this party, where only twenty people lay, then whatever wrongdoing you do, you will be supported wholeheartedly by the rest of the party."

"You're saying the killer is in this party, he is in the so-called top twenty?" Shana questioned.

"Yes, but there is more to it. His family, going back to his great grandfather, had blood ties to this group, the creators, the profits if you like, so even if those nineteen people do not agree with his wrongdoing, by law, by fear, they must follow,"

"Basically, they cover for him or help him out?"

"I don't know. Sometimes one or the other, sometimes both. Shana, this is where The Wise Monkeys came into play through the belief of hear no evil, see no evil, say no evil and do no evil."

"So, by turning a blind eye, turning a deaf ear, not repeating what is said, and all in all not doing anything about it, makes them think it's ok?"

"Yes, but it's more than that, the killer whose name is Sogoto thinks he is Ten-Tin, the honorable God, and the person who all people report to on the sixtieth day. His killings were done publicly before the very eyes of the party. That is why when he kills here, he makes sure the person can see what he is doing. The last thing they see is evil and are not being able to speak of it once their souls have gone."

"Good God!" Shana uttered. "Then why has he come here, why America?"

"A better question would be why countries like Russia, China, or Germany before you say why America."

"I'm confused," Shana responded blankly.

"You seriously have no idea?" Dr. Marcos explained pointing to the papers he handed her.

"Oh God!"

"You may want to leave God out of this one. Seven families in Russia, six in China, five in Germany and we are now adding up the ones here in the United States."

"Why?" Shana couldn't get her head around it. *An international serial killer.*

"Simple. All the people he killed were all together at one point in time in their lives."

"How?"

"I have to give gratitude to Wong for this." Dr. Marcos suggested while handing over another document to Shana, with black and white photos.

Shana looked closely, trying to figure out what she was supposed to be looking for.

"Wong did the right thing by coming to me; he also knew that you would contact me."

Shana shook her head wondering how he felt. 'How did he get this? What am I looking at?'

"This is a document your father should have burned many years ago. You know Shana, the Japanese ambassador that Detective Grant had sent Wong to meet didn't exist. Wong made a few calls and came across a man whose wife was killed eight years ago in Japan by Sogoto's team; he raped her in front of her husband and then let him go. The man escaped to America. He was never able to forget. When he heard that Wong was looking into this case, he handed over some information that he trusted Wong with. After he gave this to Wong, he killed himself. He could no longer take the guilt and he couldn't keep running."

"Wong let him kill himself?" Shana was surprised.

"Shana, he couldn't stop him. Had he not killed himself, Sogoto's or his men would have found him and made him suffer for days on end. After he handed the information over, he directly killed himself, no one, not even Wong could have stopped him!"

"How did all these men know each other?" she looked at the photo, so many men in a room, but none seemed aware they were being photographed. "A photo of all these people together that was not meant to be made public. The person who took this was bribing your dad. Those three men I was with were trying to get your dad and Detective Grant to give them the information they needed,"

"Grant? My dad?"

As she said this, something got her attention. A car screeched as it took off at high speed. Shana looked over to notice a car speeding off. *idiots,* she thought to herself.

"Did someone follow you?" Shana did not want to distract Dr. Marcos from telling her more. She had so many questions.

For a split second, she didn't know whether she should get up and follow the car, the back of it resembled Detective Grants, *'probably paranoid.'* Then Dr. Marcos grabbed her hand. "Sit back down Shana, there is more you need to know!"

The car was gone. Shana did as Dr. Marcos requested.

"Tell me more about the Asian man. What are their names, what do they do, and more importantly, why are they in America?" Shana questioned, trying to get back on track with Dr. Marcos. "Tell me how this all links into my dad and Grant."

"As I said, Shana, the three men are a part of the largest police force in the Japanese community, however, their boss, is a corrupt police officer. These three men have gone against their boss and were signed up with the FBI and CIA in capturing Sogoto and taking down the corrupt boss. Long Din is their leader, his daughter, his son-in-law and his grandson were killed by Sogoto. To avenge one's death is common, you could say it's a tradition that's passed down. His son-in-law had secretly taken these photos you see in front of you. He brought him into the force and now felt responsible for their deaths."

"How did we not know this? The other killings in other countries?"

"Shana, if seven of those families were killed here in the United States and they were not able to link them, then what makes you think they would have in the other countries? He has his connections, but more so a lot of people fear him. More importantly, he is precise, a perfectionist, always a step ahead. He has watched his grandfather, and father before him. He has learned, and he has come to be the most dangerous man alive!" Dr. Marcos started rolling the ends of his mustache, enough to calm himself down a little.

"Defamation is the worst type of sin within Japanese culture. People hold their reputation up to the highest level. The way Sogoto got through the justice system is through bribery using the information to test the person's integrity or worst-case scenario making up information that seems so realistic that even that person starts to doubt himself. He could make people kneel to him, after all, he truly believes he is of a higher power."

"A God?" Shana interrupts anxiously, her mind traveling a thousand miles an hour.

"Look at their photo, what do you see?"

"It's a bunch of men in suits, what am I looking for?" Shana asked as she looked closely at the photo.

"This photo was taken twenty-eight years ago, look there." Dr. Marcos pointed at two men standing at a table talking to each other. One had a coffee in his hand.

Shana gasped. "Oh, that is my dad and Grant!"

"Yes, it is" Shana brought the photo closer to her to confirm she had seen it right.

"My dad has never been to Japan," Shana murmured. She was confused and at this stage, exasperated. Her entire world seemed to be flipping upside down.

Shana looked at each face in the photo more closely and then it came to her. *"How, why?"* each person in that photo was the same man that were on the licenses that were delivered to her by the man on the motorbike. He was the killer. *Sogoto!*

"This is why my dad didn't want me on the case! That means Grant is next!"

"I saw the man yesterday after you had left. The one that dropped the parcel and the letter I showed you at work. He must have followed you."

"Are you sure?" his frown lines showing ever detailed wrinkle.

"Of course, I'm sure. Someone he is working with had a gun to me that's how bloody sure I am. I knew it was him when I saw the monkey tattoo!"

Dr. Marcos went back through his suitcase and showed Shana a photo, "This one?"

"Yes! Yes, that's it."

"Shana, that is Sogoto!"

"Why did he not kill me? He had the perfect chance." Shana is slightly irritated with all the game playing.

"He never just kills someone. He makes them suffer, emotionally, physically, and mentally, before he takes their life away. He has a plan, and he would never deviate from it, no matter the circumstances."

"He looked me straight in the eyes!"

"He knows who you are. Oh, hell he knows who I am, don't underestimate him."

"All the people around the world who were killed by Sogoto are from the elite group that was organized, that bloody NPA."

"The man who I meet yesterday caught two of the ring leaders. Three months ago, a banquet was held by a Japanese man he used to work with. Sogoto cut off his penis and testicles and went on the internet and organized the banquet dinner charging 70,000 US a head where he cooked and marinated his body parts."

"What are you talking about Dr. Marcos? I'm sure that's illegal! And what has that got to do with anything?"

"The funny thing Shana is I heard, but not a hundred percent certain, that cannibalism or whatever you want to call it is not illegal in Japan. That it was a delicacy." He shrugged his shoulders.

"This man felt the need to punish himself for 'doing evil' and to do this publicly was getting his honor back. The police went undercover to the banquet and captured two of the leaders. Since they could not charge them with anything illegal, they had no choice but to kill them and make it look like an accident."

"Did that work?" she turned her body completely toward Dr. Marcos.

"it was as if he knew what was happening before it even happened. The undercover police ended up dead, and he sold off their organs also. So, no it didn't work, he is always a step ahead.!" Looking in the sky as if to find answers, Dr. Marcos continued.

"He started his killing in Japan, working his way around the world until he got here."

"When is my time Dr. Marcos?" Shana's voice tone lowered in fear.

"Shana, this is the part that puzzles me. He has a special interest in you. I do not know! But I assume soon."

For the first time, she wished Dr. Marcos would have lied.

Shana's phone was vibrating throughout her whole-time conversing with Dr. Marcos; however, she was too intrigued to even look at her phone. She was finally irritated with the phone that she pulled it out of her pocket and placed it on vibrate.

She placed the phone on the bench and continued to listen as Dr. Marcos filled in the gaps, then finally asked the question that was puzzling her.

"When I first got here, you mentioned my mom?"

"Yes," he hesitated.

Just as he was about to explain, Shana's phone was vibrating again. It was Monica. It rang out again, and then again. *And then again*

"I think you better answer that." Dr. Marcos suggested he saw the worry in Shana's face. She nodded and answered her phone.

"Monica, what's wrong?" feeling a little guilty for ignoring the calls for so long. Knowing that with the number of calls she made, *something was wrong.*

"You haven't heard." Monica panicked.

"Heard what Monica?" Shana now had gotten up off the bench and walked slightly away from Dr. Marcos.

"There was a massive car accident, a car chase, a kidnapping; I don't know where to start!" Shana could hear the panic in her voice.

"Well can you send someone to the crime scene and find out? I'm a little caught up right now,"

"Yes, of course, it's just that, Detective Grant is missing. Bystanders said that he was knocked unconscious and placed on a motorbike and taken away. There is also one dead man in the Detective Grant's undercover cars!"

Shana was thinking back to the car she saw speed off earlier "Where was this?" Shana asked anxiously.

"At Queens Way, Long Beach" Monica replied. Shana moved the phone away from her ear, she couldn't believe it. She was only minutes away.

She was so angry with herself. She should have followed the car. She straightened herself up.

"Get down there, and do what you guys have to do, I'll be there soon" Shana instructed.

"I just got here,"

"Monica, I need every clue possible to find out who took Detective Grant." She said, not realizing that she was pacing, she was really worried.

She hung up and made her way back to Dr. Marcos.

"Sogoto has Grant!"

He shook his head, but he didn't seem surprised "There is a dead man in his car also. I need to get to the crime scene; it's not far from here,"

"Ok," Dr. Marcos replied as he quickly packed all his paperwork in his briefcase.

"Do you have any idea where he may have taken him?" Shana asked, hoping that he might have some sort of clue.

"No. I'm sorry Shana, but don't count on him being alive when you get to him."

Shana's eyes were watering up and her face reddening. She didn't like the negativity that was coming out of Dr. Marcos.

Just then Shana received a message from Monica's phone. It read 'Dead Asian passenger.' Shana scrolled down to see the photo; she then showed it to Dr. Marcos.

"This was one of the men you were with yesterday. Why was he in Grant's car, and why is he dead?"

Dr. Marcos was quiet. "The same way you got in contact with them to meet you yesterday, you will also get in contact with them today." Shana was firm!

"I will find Detective Grant, and I will find him alive!" Shana insisted.

"Shana I am happy to help, but I have to be somewhere right now, I'll meet up with you later" Dr. Marcos was scared, and he was trying to flee the situation. Shana was on top of it.

"I don't think so, Marcos." Shana couldn't believe her ears; she knew very well he had nowhere to go.

He got up, ignoring Shana, and began walking away.

"Shana, you're on your own here."

"Dr. Marcos, STOP!" He continued to walk away,

Shana had no option but to pull out her gun, *"I said stop."* Ignoring her demands, Dr. Marcos continued to walk away. Shana shot her gun into the sky, scaring him, the sound making the birds flee the trees making the Doc stand suddenly and turn around to face her.

"Grant is dirty!" he yelled in a panicked explanation to get her to see past the lies.

She went straight up to him, grabbing his hand and placing it behind his back in a lock. She whispered in his ear "Dr. Marcos you know I don't like doing this, but you have left me with no other option." She forced him to come with her. "Now let's find out if you're right! But right now, the detective who was a second father to me is kidnapped. *So, I am not asking I am telling you!* You are coming with me." She walked him down toward where her car was parked. Dr. Marcos had no choice. "You'll contact those men, and we will get to the bottom of this."

"I also need to know Wong's dealings with this case," She opened the passenger seat, and placed Dr. Marcos in the car, and activated the kids lock, he had no way of getting out "Sorry, but I need to do this."

Dr. Marcos had no choice when there's a gun involved, "Seems you have made your mind up. I just wish it weren't clouded. You don't know who to trust? Your dad lied to you, Grant lied to you, and Roger lied to you." Rolling his eyes

"Roger? Detective Roger Rodriguez?" Shana asked as she sat in the driver's seat ready to go.

"Yes Roger, don't look so shocked. Your mother lied to you. Even your best friend Portia."

She didn't let him finish "Stop with my mother, just stop. Don't tell me they lied, *tell me what they lied about!*" Shana slammed both hands on the steering wheel, having had enough of what he said. She stopped and took a breath in, not wanting to let Dr. Marcos think she had no control.

"The guilt trip is not working right now. I have a job to do so right now my mind is intact with me getting my job done Dr. Marcos, and I apologize but you have to help me do this one." She grabbed the seat belt and locked him in. She was ready to go.

Dr. Marcos stayed silent as Shana sped to Queens Bay, she was there in minutes.

Shana pulled up to the tape blocking off the streets, annoyed that the street was already bombarded with journalists and social media heroes. She took her handcuffs out and attached one side of Dr. Marcos's hand and the other to the steering wheel. She leaned into his pocket and took his mobile phone from him. "You won't be needing this right now." He looked at her with disappointment.

"You're making a big mistake." Shana ignored him as she walked up to what was left of Detective Grant's car.

She took her phone out. And called her dad, but it rang out.

Her dad was not picking up. Panicked, she saw Tim, Jake, and Monica at the scene. Shana made her way to them, a little relief at the sight of familiar faces.

"What do we have?" She looked at Monica.

"There is some blood in the back of the car, we have a unit looking into it. It looks to be that there was more than one person in the car."

Shana shook her head realizing that Grant was also unarmed.

Monica pointed to the back seat of the car, showing Shana the blood trail also on the side of the door. "I think there was someone also behind the passenger."

Shana looked closely in the back seat, she had a gut feeling "There were three men in the car with Detective Grant, I'm sure of it."

"My thoughts exactly." Monica agreed.

Shana walked around and looked at the car. She looked at the dead man. He appeared to be in his early forties, nicely dressed. *A bullet wound through the neck.* Shana quickly placed on some gloves and examined the crime scene more closely.

She leaned over and slid her hand in the dead man's jacket. He had an expensive wallet on the inside, and Shana opened it up and took out his identification.

"Haruki Ogawa" was a part of the NPA, which was a branch of the National Public Safety Commission.

"What is NPA?" Monica asked as she noticed the badge in the man's wallet. "The Police Law, it's a conforming with principles such as rule of law and local autonomy, it aimed at providing an efficient police structure on a democratic base. The structure consists of the national and the prefectural police. Formerly, most police agencies functioned as guards for the Imperial Family." Shana answered.

"The Imperial Family?" Monica asked, having not heard this term before.

"That part is not important. They know there is a mix of centralization and decentralization, in saying so the police administration is the responsibility of prefectural governments. The Criminal Investigation Bureau is probably the closest thing the Japanese have to our FBI." Shana explained the general information she learned from Dr. Marcos earlier.

"I am assuming they're here to help us?" Monica was confused.

"Yes and no. They're here with apparent support from our CIA, and FBI partners, but as you can see, they didn't do a good job at protecting them. They're here against their Chief commander's will. Monica, we had three vigilantes on the run in America after the most dangerous man in the world and have no support from the NPSC." Shana responded.

"Make that two." Monica interrupted quickly to correct Shana.

Shana nodded her agreement.

She quickly made her way to Dr. Marcos for a quick question. With the window open and the Doc handcuffed to the steering wheel, she leaned against the door.

"Do we notify the national police in Japan then?"

"They do not have 'national police.' Their National Police Agency is but a body with the task of coordinating activities between the various prefectural police forces. The most powerful of which is the Cabinet Intelligence and Research Office, from what I gather, they were getting orders from there." She remembered the papers, she glanced over earlier with Dr. Marcos as they were walking over to the car.

"Do you know who these people are? I need to find Grant."

Dr. Marcos stuttered over his answer, "Generally, Japan has never had much of a need to deal with matters that FBI handles regularly, the crime rate is quite low. People are too scared to commit a crime, or more so Japan keeps it hidden from the media, so no one knows for sure. Besides, prefectural police can cross prefectural boundaries with NPA authorization, given that Japan's a unitary state and its internal subdivisions are not given rights that are codified in the Constitution, with much power in the hands of the central government in Tokyo."

"You need to call the men and find out where they are!" Shana handed over her phone to Dr. Marcos. She sensed he was nervous, but she was limited on time and needed his help.

"Shana I am sorry; I don't call them. They call me!"

"What do you mean? Make them call you!"

"Shana, I don't think you understand. I don't have their numbers; I don't know how to get in touch with them. They found me! That's how they work!"

Shana was frustrated. It seemed like she was pushed up against the wall today. But she refused to be held back. Walking away from Dr. Marcos and back to the crime scene, she let her thoughts wander, *there has to be something that can tell me where you are Grant.*

Shana was now aware of the NPA. But how can a committee that was brought together to keep the world safe, have such a corrupt leader?

Shana made her way back to the passenger side and leaned the body forward. She placed her hand in his pockets, to find anything that could link her to where the other two men are.

Monica came up to Shana, as Shana was taking out some scrambled-up receipts and a small packet of matches. *Perfect* She loved it when a deceased body had hotel matches on them. It made life so much easier.

Shana knew exactly where this hotel was. It was the *Holiday Inn* located on Willow St. Long Beach, not at all far from where she was.

Jake was running towards Shana; he had a concerned look on his face.

"Shana, we have a problem," Jake said concerned.

Shana got up, placed the matches in her pocket, and for the first time not following protocol playing by the books was not working.

"What?" Shana asked, hoping for good news. Jake's frown said it was bad news.

"The witness, a man who was driving by, said it was two men. One who had been shot and was being assisted by the other held a gun to that man and took his car." Jake said as he pointed to some middle-aged man across the road.

Shana was not shocked; she had figured as much.

"Has he said anything else?" Shana asked.

"Nothing more than what he has already told us, he is creating a fuss about his car and needed to get to work."

"He won't be heading to work. Monica, get him to the station and get a full description of the two men, and the man on the motorbike, plate numbers, and the type of bike – anything."

"But Shana…" Monica interrupted.

"No buts Monica, just do it." She then turned to Jake. "Jake, you take care of this crime scene; I have to go do something."

Shana saw blood in the driver's seat and a bullet hole. From the location, she could see that Grant was wounded. He had been shot in the left arm close to the shoulder where the bullet must have gone into Grant and then out and straight into the car seat. It took a lot of force for that to happen. Someone standing in front of them maybe.

"Jake!" Shana called out, seeing that he was collecting bullet shells.

"There is a bullet shell right here." She pointed "I want it photographed and pulled out of the seat then analyzed right now. As in this second!."

"No problems," Jake said as a friendly smile appeared on his face. He saw the urgency. Shana moved out of the way while he started to take photos.

Shana then remembered Dr. Marcos's documents from Wong. On one of those documentations, Jake's name was on it. He had signed out some paperwork and must have handed them over to Wong. While Jake was photographing, Shana asked him, "I know that you are in contact with Wong, and I want to know everything that he has asked of you and the information you have presented to him."

Jake put the camera down. She watched the color drain from his face. He knew he fucked up.

"Shana, I'm so sorry, it's just that…"

Shana was furious. She leaned forward, her face in front of his,

"You know what you did was wrong! I don't know how this all started Jake, but we were always a team. All of us! Not working with me and going against me puts you in a corrupt category. How did we end up divided? You have until this afternoon to present everything you know!"

Jake looked at her, "Shana I wanted to tell you, but Wong and Dr. Marcos said not to…."

"Dr. Marcos also knew?" Shana raged.

"I'm glad you know, I want to tell you everything Shana, more than you know. I promise you we are on the same team, I promise…" His words stopped. A force pushed his body and fell straight onto Shana's body. Shana tried hard to catch him, but his weight didn't allow for it. She fell to the floor with Jake's body on top of her, the hard surface of the road on her back.

For a split second everything went quiet. Monica ran out of the car. Her face looked as though she was screaming, but Shana could not hear a thing. Shana pushed with all her might and pulled Jake's body up slightly looking at his face, wondering if he had fainted. Shana didn't want to confront her darkest fear right that moment. She lifted his shoulders, with his head dangling over hers, and there she saw his blood dripping. Shana's reflex was to lift Jake's head and her bloody hands let her know what had happened. Jake was shot by a sniper in the back of the head. *Did someone just kill Jake?* She felt numb and slightly sick.

Shana looked around as everyone surrounded her, guns facing up, and people taking cover. *On a fucking bridge! How is this possible.* The sounds of the police sirens came rushing back as they went looking for the man that has shot Jake. From a far distance, Shana could hear the siren of the ambulance and above her, the cries of Monica. Shana moved Jake's body to the side; while Monica took Jake's hand and begged him to come back. Shana shook with all the chaos that was happening around her.

Shana slowly rose to her knees, reaching to place a hand over Monica's as Jake's lifeless body lay there. Her knees cemented on the road, her body covered by Jake's blood, and her glaring eyes gave away how furious she was. She had one thought and one thought only *I'm going to find you and fucking kill you.*

***

CHAPTER 28

"To rise once again, a part of me had to die. But the rebirth has made me stronger and wiser. Now I understand."

Shana slammed the door of her car, shakily trying to wipe the blood off her neck and chest. She completely forgot that Dr. Marcos was right next to her, cuffed to the steering wheel.

Shana was disgruntled, she had just lost one of her finest team members to a single sniper shot, and worse, no one could find the killer. People were running all over the place, but Shana couldn't focus on that. The shock of what just happened was starting to set in. With that, she removed the handcuffs of Dr. Marcos. She needed to make sure he was safe also. "Shana, we dug too deep. We are all probably next."

"Why didn't you tell me Roger was also working with you?" Shana asked, looking for someone to blame.

"You didn't ask?"

She looked at him, filled with anger and hurt. She grabbed his chest and pushed him back into his chair. He groaned "I don't know what you have found or what you know, but you are going to tell me everything. No one else is going to die on my count.

241

If you hadn't gotten Jake involved, he would still be alive. No more lies, no more riddles! Do you hear me?" she yelled.

Shana looked directly into Dr. Marco's eyes not letting go until he had understood her demand.

"Ok." Finally, he answered. Shana then let go and sat back in her chair, her eyes slightly watering up. Monica approached the car, trying so hard not to cry. Monica leaned into the open window on Shana's side.

"Shana, please don't make Jake's death go to waste. Don't let them cover this up!" It was all starting to come to the surface, Shana was starting to see, there was inside involvement.

She looked up at Monica. She needed to get in the mind frame of the killer, she needed to solve the puzzle and start putting all the pieces together. "I promise you! It won't."

She closed her eyes and took a deep breath in and with that her mind went to the crime scene and to the matches she had picked up earlier, Shana exhaled. She opened her eyes and pulled out the matches from her pocket, Dr. Marcos staring at her. Monica stood there blankly, waiting for some sort of response,

"The Holiday Inn, it's a start" Shana had a good feeling.

Monica nodded, trying so hard to believe her. She looked over at Dr. Marcos who was giving her a nod of approval.

As Shana turned to head toward the car, Monica blurted out, "WAIT! I overheard a rookie giving your father Detective Grant's phone. It was left behind."

Shana nodded, that could be the explanation of why her father was not answering the phone, he too was out looking for Grant.

Shana tried calling her father and when he didn't answer, she tried Grant's phone as she drove off.

"He won't answer." Dr. Marcos suggested.

"Of course, he won't." she snapped, looking across at him, "He has gone to find out who took his best friend," Shana said as she breathed heavily "for someone as extremely intelligent as you, I would think you would give things the benefit of doubt before you're quick to judge."

"Oh, but I have," Dr. Marcos replied honestly.

"I hold you accountable for the murder of Jake. Until I find out who pulled that trigger, in my eyes you're the murderer. How is that for the benefit of the doubt?"

Dr. Marcos didn't bother replying. He sat in silence. Both of their minds were working overtime. Shana's thoughts were to her father saving Grant and killing Sogoto. Finally, they arrived.

She parked the car, and then again replaced the handcuffs on Dr. Marcos.

"Shana, let me go with you. If they're here, maybe I can talk to them."

"From how they were talking to you, I don't think so," from the conversation she had witnessed just yesterday, they didn't seem to like Dr. Marcos very much.

She got out of the car, "You have done enough damage."

As she made her way to the entrance of the Inn, she continued to try her father's phone "Come on Dad. Answer," again nothing.

She knew she needed backup. Someone she could trust. She wasn't going to play hero with these men. She called Ryan.

"Hey, have you calmed down now?" Shana had forgotten about their argument; she had a million other things on her mind.

"Ryan, have you heard?"

"Heard what?"

"Jake is dead." Shana blurted out.

"What, why was this was not announced on the police radio? Where are you? Are you ok?" His tone was worried and a little scared. She took a second to breathe deeply.

"He was killed by a sniper at a crime scene just now. Detective Grant has been kidnapped, one guy from the NPA is dead, and the other two are missing and my dad is nowhere to be found! I have called his phone a thousand times. This all has to do with this stupid case!" everything came out in a rush.

"Where are you now?" Ryan remained calm.

"I found hotel matches in one of the Asian man's pockets, I need your help. I just got here. Ryan, I don't know who to trust anymore!"

Shaana heard Ryan call out to John, letting him know he needed to step out. "Grab us some lunch on your way, Sitting around doing nothing got John hungry." Shana shook her head. You could always rely on John's stomach to lighten the mood.

"Ryan?"

"Where are you, Shana? I'm coming to you. Just stay put!."

"I'm at the Holiday Inn in Long Beach, on the corner of Willow and ……."

"Where?"

She repeated, "at the Holiday Inn, Long Beach on the corner of……"

"Shana, I'm already here!"

Shana looked up at the Holiday Inn, completely confused as to why Ryan was already there.

"What?" Before Ryan had a chance to explain, Shana could hear shots being fired.

Shana jumped at the noise of gunshots on the other side of the phone,

"Ryan! RYAN!" For a second, Shana froze.

"I think the men you're looking for are here!" Ryan's voice was a whisper.

More shots were fired. She opened her mouth to speak but he beat her to it. "Shana, get an ambulance, John's down… NOW!" He wasn't asking her; he was telling her.

Shana was quick to hang up before quickly calling in backup and an ambulance all while running toward the building. She hit the stairwell and ran up. She had no idea where she was heading, then halfway up the stairs, there it was a gunshot. Shana flinched, placing her back to the wall, looking over and seeing a clear way. Her heart was racing, and she hoped to God that Ryan was ok. She continued running up the narrow staircase, following the sound of gunshots and making her way through the hallway after reaching the end she made her way through the exit door, running up the stairs. Ryan leaned over into the hallway, his gun ready to fire, but they were much quicker. He wasn't sure, but he thought there were only three of them. He threw himself inside a room as bullets began to fly again.

Ryan could slightly see, from where he was that they had made their way into the room that he and John were meant to be protecting. He couldn't get a shot from where he was.

They all left the room, minutes later, heading to the stairway. Ryan had one chance, he leaned out of the room and fired his gun, from the retaliation he knew he had most probably missed. He jumped back.

The door of the stairway was in open view. They were making their way out. Ryan now could see there was much more than just three.

As Ryan carefully followed, he noticed Shana going up the stairs. Just as she turned the corner for the last flight of stairs to where the sound was coming from, she now faced to face with about seven men, four which had a gun pulled at her. Even though she too had her gun drawn, she had no chance. Her hand shaking like a leaf.

Ryan now in hiding with his gun drawn, knew the precaution of shooting, there was no chance of any of them coming out alive. He paused, continuing to point his gun.

The leader came up close to her. Ryan had never been so afraid, the thought of losing Shana killed every bit of life in him.

The man calmly reached over and takes the gun off her.

They could see Shana was nervous.

He said something in Japanese to the other men. Then he looked at Shana and in broken English, "Not just yet! Soon! But not just yet" the men giggled, one then hit Shana's temple with the back of his gun.

Shana fell to the ground, unconscious. Ryan closed his eyes, taking a deep breath in *She's still alive* he thought, trying to make better of the situation.

The men impetuously left the premises.

***

CHAPTER 29

*"The wound left scars that created tissue much
stronger than skin."*

Laying on the stairway completely knocked out, Shana mentally
went back in time.

She was in the playground at her local park. Little Shana was
skipping her way to the swings.

Little Portia is also there.

"Let's see who can go higher!" Portia said excitedly as she sat
on the swing and started to go back and forth to gather speed.

Back and forth they teased each other, but all too innocently as
they laughed.

"Shana, slow down, girls please be careful, you're going too
high," her mother called in the distance.

"Yes ma'am," Portia replied giggling as she slightly slowed
down, but was eager to win.

"Shana!" her mother said again, Shana was pretending not to
hear, she wanted to win.

The Park was only down the road across the street from their house. It was an open area. It was perfect. They jumped off the swing and climbed the house made of wood to get to the top of the slippery slide so she can go down; she looked in the distance and could see her daddy's car pull in. He parked in the driveway, and then pulled a small suitcase out of the boot of the car. Shana jumped up with joy *"daddy's home! Daddy's home"*

Little Shana pushed her way past the kids and slid down as quickly as she could and ran through the park to her father.

"Shana! don't cross the road" her mother yelled.

Shana wasn't listening; she was so excited that her daddy was home.

"SHANA!"

Her mother yelled, running behind her.

Shana's father heard his wife's voice and turned around. He looked up across the road and saw his little angel running toward him. He quickly dropped his suitcase and quickly ran across the road, stopping a car on the way, and meet her on the other side, just in time before she had crossed the road without looking,

He grabbed her and twirled her around.

"I missed you,"

Shana hugged him so tight; she also knew that with his travels usually came gifts.

"Daddy, what did you get me?" she said with her little hands on her hips, to see if he had remembered what she had asked for.

He laughed as he crossed the road with her, and put her down, as Portia and Cherie arrived at the house. He hugged and kissed his wife.

Shana's mother looked at him, hugging him tightly and staring into his eyes,

"This is the end of it, right? No going back?"

Little Shana was observant, she looked at the carry-on. Her mother said her father went to Australia for work, but the papers hanging out of her father's suitcase had *'Japan'* all over them.

He was supposed to get her a stuffed koala and kangaroo.

Shana waited anxiously. Her father then handed over a jigsaw puzzle, Shana frowned, "That was not what I wanted."

"Shana baby, I was working, and I had so much work to do…"

"You forgot me?" Shana was upset, hurt and on the verge of crying, when her mother walked in.

"Honey, you had left this bag in the car," her mommy said.

He looked up at her after looking in the bag, giving her a silent thank you. *She had him covered.*

"One koala is for you and the other is for Portia and one boxing kangaroo for you and one for Portia."

"You tricked me" she grabbed her dad and hugged him, and then started to pretend the boxing kangaroo was attacking him and had the help of Portia and her boxing kangaroo, he pretended to be hurt, as they all laughed and fell to the floor.

"Thank you, sir," Portia said smiling.

"My pleasure Portia, hope you didn't think I would have forgotten you too?"

While Portia was in the toilet, Shana looked at the jigsaw puzzle. It had pictures of animals all over it, like a family zoo. After dinner, she turned it over to notice a sticker on the back.

The price was in Yen and a sticker on it simply said Duty-Free Japan Airport.

She was Little Shana, as long as she had her kangaroo and koala, she was happy. She ignored what didn't make sense. Until now. A repeated voice started talking as she slowly was becoming conscious.

"Shana! Please Shana. Wake up." She gasped awake; it wasn't her mother calling her, it was Ryan.

He held her in his arms with her legs collapsed on the stairway, calling her name repeatedly until she finally came back to consciousness.

"Stay with me Shana. Stay with me."

She had the worst possible headache and when she reached up to touch her head, a lump throbbed under her touch. The light felt blinding as she squinted against it. It did nothing for the pounding in her head.

Police officers and the crime scene unit were now walking past them. Shana was groaning as Ryan pulled her in for a hug, glad to have her back.

"Ryan? What happened?"

"Don't talk." Ryan's eyes were red, he choked back tears as he notified her "John's dead, Shana. The Chief is nowhere to be found."

Shana instantly got up, a wave of dizziness causing the throbbing to pound louder. Ryan tried to tell her to take it easy, but she ignored him. She had things she needed to do.

Physically leaning on Ryan for help, she made her way down the stairs to the front desk. Shana showed the license of the victim she had taken from the pocket to the concierge, "Where is this person located? He is staying at your hotel." Ryan was right behind her. Shana kept placing her hand on the side of her head where the bruise was, hoping it would not get any bigger. It really hurt.

"I'm sorry ma'am, I cannot answer that." The lady was a little taken back.

Police were now circling the lobby and going upstairs to attend to the people who had been shot. They were also still on the lookout for the people who attacked them.

Ryan slammed his hand on the table, anger taking over. "Listen here, lady. As you can see this is a matter of life and death. Two people have been killed in your hotel and four wounded." He pulled out his badge and threw it on the table in front of her. "If you do not want to be taken down to the police station for obstruction of justice, answer the question and direct us in the right direction. Do you understand?"

Shana looked over. With all the commotion she had forgotten that Ryan had just lost his friend.

Shana could see how much damage was being made to people's lives with this case. The lady was overwhelmed by the amount of police in the hotel, people being evacuated, and two dead people upstairs.

She quickly got on the computer and looked up the information.

"They were on level six. Room number 601, they checked out early this morning." She answered.

"You said they? How many were there?"

"I'm not sure, sometimes two…four…. Five …. Maybe six…." She shrugged, not sure of the exact number.

"Has anyone been in that room since?" Shana asked softly.

"No ma'am." Shaking her head, happy at being able to finally give an accurate answer.

Ryan then took his badge off the table, and Shana took back the victim's license before they headed straight to the room, bypassing all police officers and detectives along the way.

One officer stopped them on the way,

"Shana, have you seen your father? We're waiting on some guidance."

Shana didn't know what to reply, she too was trying to get hold of him.

"He's on top of it. He has placed Edward Leach in charge." She thought quickly on her feet.

"Oh ok, I had no idea." The officer didn't question it. Leach was most likely next in line to take George's job, and the way things were going, probably sooner than expected. He was a hardworking man and great at making things happen.

She nodded and gave him her fake smile and continued her way to the room. As she was outside the door; she quickly made a call to Senior Sergeant Leach.

"Shana, glad you called. Have you seen the Chief?"

"That's the reason for my call, just got off the phone with him, and he is currently on top of something big and unable to contact anyone. He has asked me to notify you and for you to take charge until he gets back."

"Oh ok, thanks for letting me know. Tell him that I won't let him…."

She hung up before he could finish the sentence. She didn't like how excited he sounded at the idea.

Both Ryan and Shana pulled their guns out just in case someone was in the room. Making eye contact, they nodded. Ryan knocked. No answer.

Ryan was about to barge the door, Shana's hand stopped him, silently pointing to the housekeeping trolley. Ryan grabbed a few swipe cards and inserted them in; the light on the door handle went green.

They raised their weapons and made their way in; the hotel room was empty.

Shana went straight to the trash can, any information would help. It looked as if that the room had just been cleaned out, however.

She went straight back to the trolley and went through the garbage bag located on the bottom. After tossing through the rubbish, Shana found a crunched-up paper that had some writing on it, *'Berth fifty-five.'*

Shana looked at it and then handed it to Ryan, not knowing what it meant.

"I know exactly where this is," Ryan had been there before. They had a lead.

Shana followed him, just before she made it to the stairway, she came to a frantic stop. "Oh no."

"What's wrong?" Ryan asked, worried.

"I forgot Dr. Marcos! I handcuffed him to my car,"

"What?" Ryan was confused "Why would you do that?"

He pointed to the lift right near the stairway after she wobbled slightly.

While in the lift, he asked "Shana, what's going on? I should have been with you today, but your dad got me on this assignment. Now Detective Grant is missing, and your father. And why would you handcuff Dr. Marcos to your car?"

"Oh, Ryan it's me who needs answers. Trust me, so much is going on, and for the first time I feel like I have no idea what's going on." She sighed heavily.

"I need you to start at the beginning." Ryan leaned in so Shana could rest her head on his shoulder.

The lift beeped as it finally reached the ground floor. They both got out and she all but ran to her car.

"What has he done?" Shana was shocked, the steering wheel was gone, and so was Dr. Marcos.

Shana turned to Ryan, noticing him frowning and his jawline flexed as he clenched his teeth.

Ryan looked at her, "In case you didn't hear me. John, my best friend is dead, Jake your employee is dead, your father is missing, so is Grant and now Dr. Marcos has taken off. What the fuck is going on?"

"You want answers, Ryan?" Shana replied exasperated "Then help me find Dr. Marcos."

"Ok! How far can a man with a steering wheel attached to him go? We'll take Johns' car," They both headed across the road,

"First we need to get to Berth fifty-five."

"Where is Beth fifty-five? What does it mean?" Shana had never heard of it.

"It used to be a seafood restaurant, but it has been closed down for some time now. It's just an empty storehouse, It's on the port." Ryan answered.

She looked at him, not at all surprised that he knew that information. If it had something to do with his favorite type of food, then he knew about it.

"Shana, what's going on?" The tone in his voice indicated he wasn't going to stop until he got answers.

"Look, I don't have all the answers. But what I do know is that all the people that were killed were at one point in time in Japan. The people that had Grant in the car are from a group called the NPA. It's like this vigilante group. They are linked with the FBI, KGB Russia, and the Middle East. Don't ask me what they do, I have no idea. They get rid of things. Anything that affects Japan is straight away destroyed. It's like if you had something bad to say, or do, then to get rid of you would be the best solution, and this is where The Wise Monkeys comes into play." Shana explained.

"What has this got to do with the killer and the men at the hotel? Why would they kill Jake?" Ryan asked.

"I don't know Ryan. Those men at the hotel let me go. They said something to each other in Japanese than he said soon or something like that to me, and they all laughed. I don't know what happened after that, they could have killed me, but they didn't!"

"Ryan, this isn't the first time, I had my gun pulled out on the guy who dropped off the parcel, he was meters away. I had him, his name is Sogoto, and he is the killer."

"What, when was this? Why didn't you tell me? I should have never listened to your father." Biting his lip, not wanting to say anything more.

"A guy came from behind me; I dropped my weapon and in no time, they both disappeared. Why can't he kill me and just get it over and done with?"

"What would that bring?" Ryan frowned, hurt at the thought of losing her.

It was a slow reaction from Shana's end, "What do you mean you should have not listened to my dad?"

Ryan bit his lip; he shouldn't have said.

"Ryan! What did my father say?" Her tone was sharp.

"Shana, PLEASE now is not the time" Ryan tried to divert her, but she wasn't having it. Who knows when a perfect time would present with the way things would be were?!

"Now is a perfect time!"

As they were pulling into the industrial area, he knew he had no choice.

"I was supposed to be with you today, but your dad made me go and babysit with John. He knew you were going to meet with Dr. Marcos."

"How did he know I was meeting with Dr. Marcos?" Placing her hand again on her head, feeling a migraine that she was trying to ignore coming on.

She was confused; she knew she had not told a soul and was positive that Dr. Marcos would not have said anything. He didn't trust any of the cops after all.

"Honest to God, it's not something I would do. He was worried and, in a way, so was I, and then it was..." Ryan was now rambling.

"Ryan, what did you do?" she was furious, he only ever rambled when he was lying.

"I went through your phone while on the house phone with your dead. His idea I swear!"

"And anything else you want to tell me?"

"I read the message from Dr. Marcos about your meeting and deleted it?" Ryan coming clean.

She opened her mouth to yell at the lack of respect when something caught her eye. She frowned.

"That's dad's car."

Shana thought to herself *'what was he doing and more importantly was he still alive?'*

Ryan accelerated toward the car. Shana tried to jump out of the car the second it came to a stop, but Ryan held her back. "We do this the right way." He said before grabbing the radio and calling in for backup. Shana tapped her foot, itching to just get in there. Ryan nodded and let go of her when the confirmation that backup was on the way came through. *"Now we can go."*

Both seized their guns tightly, they were ready. Together, they headed toward the building.

***

CHAPTER 30

"A thousand players and only one me. Checkmate!
Who called it? It's a mystery, you'll have to wait and see."

The Chief knew what he had to do. He got in his car and drove off, furious that Grant was gone. He knew what the killer was capable of. Just the thought of what he would do to Grant was enough to make him sick. He swerved in and out of traffic at high speed not knowing exactly where he was going, the noise of his phone ringing irritating him more. He knew he needed to stop. He *had* to find Grant. He knew he was short on time, and he would be damned if he wasn't going to save his friend. With that, he swerved his car to the side of the road a few kilometers away from the crime scene, a street with less traffic flow, and came to a stop.

He grabbed the folder that he had taken earlier and went through it. It had images of Jake and Wong meeting with Dr. Marcos; it had photos of the seven men coming out of their hotel. He continued to flick through them; he knew exactly who they were, but there was nothing in this folder that could direct the Chief to Grant now. The same with his phone. The Chief was going in blind, and he hated it.

He got out of the car unable to breath properly. He slammed his hands on the bonnet of the car his eyes watering up, he had never felt so helpless. His phone had not stopped ringing, he didn't want to answer it. What was he going to tell his team? His phone constantly ringing. But he couldn't function anymore.

The phone rang again, this time it was Grant's phone. He saw the number was private and quickly he answered. He didn't say a word, just listened.

"You don't answer your phone anymore." His tone was condescending.

"Lucky you had your friend's phone." There was a pause "He sends his regards by the way."

The Chief squeezed the phone, and his face reddening with anger. "You fucking sick fuck, I'll find you!"

"Yes, I can see that. I mean it's only been fifteen years you've been looking for me, right?"

Sogoto spoke so calmly as if he didn't have a worry in the world. It only made George angrier.

"You son of a bitch."

"Yeah, listen I'll be quick with your friend. I'll try and make it as least painful as I can."

Quick to change his tone, the Chief understood he was not going to take the conversation anywhere. The Chief decided to try and negotiate. Pride has no play anymore and there is life on the line, a person who he valued more than a brother.

"Listen to me, we both know it's me, not Grant you want. I'm the one working the case, I am the one you want, I am the one who was there, it's me who gave you that scar."

"You know what? You're right, I want you both." He paused, then chuckled. It sent shivers down George's spine.

"Chief, I'll see you at Berth fifty-five."

The Chief quickly started his engine, "Where is that?" he demanded. But Sogoto had hung up.

Sogoto turned to the table where the detective lay. His clothes to some extent ripped and hung off his body. He looked over at Grant, it was time.

Sogoto was extremely excited. He would do a little now, and then come back for the rest. He wanted to take his time with this detective. They did have a history after all, and this was fifteen years in the making. The look of sheer fury was all over Grant's face.

"Detective Grant, we meet again, Let's go back a few years ago. You looked over my file and threw it to the side." He slightly paused and continued.

"Do you remember?" Sogoto hissed, seeing his sheer fury now replaced with anger and fear.

The detective Was trying to think of a way out, he felt helpless.

"Allow me to refresh your memory. The team you organized for the NPA," he laughed and walked around to the other side "You thought I was not good enough." Sogoto placed his hand on his chin as if he was thinking Unstable, inexperienced, his father is a psycho, were just some of the words you used about me."

Sogoto saw the second recognition dawned on Grant. It was very satisfying.

When he was in Japan and the team was being organized, for the NPA, some would call it a team of government vigilantes, he remembered holding the killer's file. Sogoto had applied to be a part of the NPA. He was in a room filled with men around the world, that were actually after him, just casually among them. But he remembered that there were never images of Sogoto, not until the tattoo was revealed, and this was way before Shana had picked it up. It was the Chief fifteen years ago who was the first man to have contacted Sogoto and live.

The secret society would never speak of Sogoto, or dare take a photo, for they would see no evil.

Sogoto left him with his thoughts. And Grant did just that, he remembered just like it was yesterday He was in an office in the middle of Tokyo. A large sign on the wall 'Interpol National Central Bureau' was part of Japan's Organized Crime Department He was sitting on the table with his leg on the seat, as he leaned forward going through a list of files. The Chief was by his side as they both were looking at the files. The Chief, the detective, and the Chief of NPA were all looking for one thing, a single man with no history or close family ties, and someone they could trust.

There it was, as clear as light, he picked up the killer's file, and looked over. Grant closed his eyes as he remembered.

"This guy just looks fucked" the Chief chuckled.

"This guy is unstable and inexperienced."

"This guy doesn't need the NPA he needs a psychologist, look at this" Detective Grant said as he leaned over to show the Chief what he had found. "His father faked his own death intending to find his wife, who ran away from him. She came back to the surface when she thought her ex-husband had died, and so he found her and killed the poor woman. Shit he also killed his other son and then killed himself, the only reason this guy is alive right now, is because the school bus had a flat tire, His father is a psycho."

The Chief looked up at him and replied, "we're not here to counsel," as he put his hand out to take the file of him and placed it in the rejection stake.

Only meters away was the killer, listening in, taking it in, and knowing that they had rejected him. He was a leader; he was a God! And to hear those words from these two people, well, Sogoto took note of everyone there. He now had a plan.

The detective turned around, "Hey son, can you get me some coffee?" he asked, looking at Sogoto not acknowledging that it was his file that he was looking at,

In the process of getting the coffee, Sogoto made copies of all those that were accepted, all thirty of them.

Grant tried to apologize while straining against his bonds.

"Say no evil, detective, say no evil." He leaned forward tightened the steel caps on his head that he had in place to keep his head from moving. No one would be able to hear his screams. He was isolated. He ran his fingers over the surgical mouth gag. Sogoto removed the tape off Grant's mouth and opened his mouth enough to fit the gag in. This mouth gag came with built-in steel tongue depressors to hold Grant's tongue in place.

Grant screamed, trying to fight the device away, but he was weak. And he knew that pleading didn't work. The tongue is said to be one of the strongest muscles and with simple ease, Sogoto finally captured his tongue in the device and spread his mouth open with the gag.

He then leaned over and grabbed a scalpel, and with such ease and with two simple strokes, he sliced Grant's tongue off. Grant was slowly choking on the blood, it was going everywhere, leaking down his neck, he was trying to swallow and spit, but both were hard without the tongue. Suddenly, the table bed Grant was on turned upside down allowing the blood to pour onto the cemented ground. Sogoto was not going to let him die just yet. He had too many ways to play.

Grant could see from the corner of his eyes Sogoto leaving. Then he heard the sound of a motorbike until it was too far in distance to be heard.

Grant took a breath in He felt his end was near.

George arrived at Berth fifty-five, it looked empty and the only thing there was an old car parked on the side.

He took precautions and took out his gun from the glove box. There on the righthand corner hidden away was another gun, loaded and ready to go. He placed one pushed slightly into the side of his pants with the handle hanging out. And the other in his hand. He got out of the car, placing Grant's phone in his pocket, just in case Sogoto was going to call. He walked slowly to the warehouse.

The area seemed empty and quiet. It was an isolated industrial area, away from the roads, and traffic. It was located right against the water where it appeared a few boats lined up. The water was slightly dark green, with a huge algae intake, and the smell of fish filled the air.

Sogoto, a very smart man, had organized the NPAC team to also be there.

George got closer. He could hear people talking on the inside. The five men sat around talking, anxious waiting for Sogoto to arrive. Some were under the impression that Sogoto had come to the end of the road. He slowly kept his back to the building as he made his way around the side. As he turned the corner, he pulled up his gun, and so did the man. Both froze, having nearly just killed each other. They took a deep breath, with the gun still pointed at each other.

"What the fuck are you doing here?" they both asked in a firm but soft voice, so as not to let anyone inside hear them. It was the Japanese NPA officer Kenzo.

"Sogoto said he was going to be here. He wanted to end this." All dressed in their suits, as they stood by the large, now open warehouse roller door. They were not afraid. George looked at each one, he had hired each one of these men fifteen years ago.

"End what? You were going to meet with him?" George sensed a setup.

"Yes, I called Grant. He was supposed to be meeting me here. We went to pick him up, but…" Cutting in, George didn't want to hear the bullshit information they were feeding him.

"Detective Grant was taken." George explained, *"Sogoto took him."*

The Japanese NPA officer Kenzo was shocked, but then they all pulled their guns up again at each other.

"He killed one of my men." Kenzo was furious. They were all fueled with anger and both sides wanted to avenge their friend's deaths. Revenge was pumping in their blood. Then just like that, they all put their guns down simultaneously. They all knew this was a time they needed to work together not against each other.

"They killed him today." George confirmed what Kenzo and his men were saying.

"You mean he was here on American soil?" He knew they were speaking about Haruto Junkyu; he was supposed to have been protected. But when you're a spy, everyone wants you dead.

"Yes, I brought him in. He was about to do a press release about the involvement of the UN. This would have opened doors to the integrity commission into everything,"

"You son of a bitch, you had to kill Junkyu!" George responded angrily; "He was a good loyal man and just trying to do the right thing."

"NO! It was your people who killed him. How did they know where he was staying or that he was even here?" The NPA officer replied who also wanted to avenge his death. The Japanese thought it was the American's and the American's thought it was the Japanese.

During the whole chaos of it all, Sogoto was preparing himself, wishing he somehow could hear what was being said. Sogoto's sniper was ready and was slightly amended and mounted with parts of a Zastava M93 black arrow, a rifle that had a hundred years of combat history and always proved to be accurate and reliable. It was his grandfather's gun, but for right now, it was Sogoto's best friend.

"You know how his mind works. He has sent us here to die. He is not here, but they are." George said, pointing to where the five men were standing minutes ago. Now the roller door shut.

Kenzo nodded and looked up.

"He's watching us." They both looked up looking at only a few buildings around them.

"I say we get out of here; we can deal with these guys later."

The Chief would be wasting his time here, time was crucial, and they needed to find Sogoto to find Grant. There was no time for a fusillade.

"And what do you recommend?" Kenzo was curious as to what the Chief's plans are.

"He's close, so we go looking for him." Kenzo nodded in agreement, they knew it was a setup that was meant to result in bloodshed. They knew better and if they all looked hard enough, there may be a chance they could find him.

George hears the shot and the glass breaking, George quickly took cover, with the screams of the man inside and the broken window George knew exactly what happened. Sogoto's aim was perfect, through the window he took down one of the five Asian men. This was quickly followed by four men streaming out of the building, yelling and with guns out.

By that time, George and Kenzo ran to the car, they noticed the two men in clear sight who began firing away. George had his gun out and was ready, *"Son of a bitch"* as he fired back. He shot him in the hand then again while falling to the floor and in the chest. *One down* everything went silent, George quickly pulled his right hand out from behind the car, grabbed Kenzo, and pushed him toward him.

He was bleeding immensely. George grabbed Kenzo's hand to place pressure on the wound slightly below the collarbone.

"Stay with me, stay with me." He kept repeating. He needed him alive; he needed his help in finding Sogoto.

The men were endlessly shooting. George fired back and managed to strike one of the men in the foot when he bent down looked under the car. He then got up to look over and shot the same man straight in the chest before taking cover again. *Two down*

"Two down," George yelled. Kenzo held the Chief's leg to get his attention for a second, and with his left hand, he pulled something out of his pocket and handed it to Chief. The Chief took it without hesitation and knew what he had to do.

Kenzo nodded, in the minutes he had left to live. George returned a nod, reassuring him he would take care of it. A feeling of relief took over.

Kenzo's left hand hit the floor, and his right hand released slowly, falling to George's foot. He was gone.

George stood up to take one shot but felt a burning pain rip through his shoulder.

"FUCK!" he screamed in pain, as he fell to the floor to take cover. The adrenaline blocked most of the pain, but he knew this feeling of shock was temporary the pain was coming. George then grabbed the gun from his back, while trying to get to the side of the car. He took a breath and looked out through the back window He saw one man behind an old, rusted garbage can. As the man leaned hesitantly forward, he made his move. George got up for two quick shots and got straight back down.

He then went back to behind the car, taking cover again. Guns were firing at the vehicle and the men yelling at each other back and forth in Japanese. In pain, he adjusted his shoulder slightly and then leaned over, picking up the man and placing his arms under his, and used it as if it was a bulletproof vest.

Both men surged forward, and he shot one to the left and one to the right, both went down. He dropped the body and moved to find more cover. One man was getting up to take out George, but

George quickly shot his hand from trying to get the gun. George walked straight up to him the last man alive. He was wounded, and unarmed, lying on the floor screaming in pain.

"Where is Sogoto?" he growled, the gun pointing straight at his head, with George's foot on his hand, right where he had shot earlier.

The man pleaded and yelled in Japanese. George realized that this man spoke no English. *He is no help to me* crossed his mind before he shot him point-blank in the head.

He then turned around to head back to the car, placing his hand firmly on his shoulder to stop the bleeding. Now that the adrenaline had worn off slightly, he felt the excruciating pain. He knew he didn't have time for a hospital. Besides, they would ask too many questions.

As he walked slowly back to the car, pain tore through his thigh, sending him sprawling to the ground with a heavy *thump*.

George rolled and looked up to see Sogoto walk toward him. George tried to reach his gun, but Sogoto was quick to kick the gun away.

"You son of a bitch, you're DEAD!" George yelled. Sogoto leaned over and placed his hand on George's wound. His scream was guttural.

"No, I'm still alive, but I don't think you will be for long. If by chance you don't make it, I'll send Shana your regards,"

George tried to grab Sogoto's leg as one last chance of fighting him off, for his daughter's sake, but he was too weak. He was losing too much blood.

Sogoto just shook his foot and George's hand fell to the floor.

271

He threw a piece of paper on him, "Your friend is here, you have ten minutes to get to him alive, after that…." He turned, got on his bike, and left. George couldn't help but think of what Grant's last minutes of living would involve. Sogoto's unrepentant torture no doubt.

***

As Shana and Ryan made their way toward the building, Shana's eyes were glued to her dad's car.

Once Shana and Ryan passed a few cars to see the building, they were in full view of lifeless bodies lying around. Asian men dressed in black suits.

"Those were the men at the hotel!"

"They had masks." Ryan corrected her.

"Not this guy." She pointed to the dead man behind the bin. "He took it off slightly in the hallway, trust me I remember him."

Distracted by noise, they looked up "There is someone alive behind the car." Ryan was shocked. He kept his gun raised and ready.

Shana made her way to the other side of the car, hoping it was her father. Her stomach sank when she saw that it was her dad. They ran over and she skidded to his side.

"Dad? Dad? Please, please stay with me." She was pleading, holding her father's head up. Ryan immediately called checking the eta for the ambulance and backup as he kneeled to the Chief.

Shana held his hand crying, pleading for her father to be ok. Ryan leaned over, to check his pulse.

"He has a pulse Shana. It is light but it's there," Ryan uttered, in a small relief.

The Chief's eyes were faintly open. Shana felt mixed emotions, she smiled then began to weep uncontrollably "Dad, please stay with me, please."

"I'm not going anywhere." His voice was barely a whisper, "Shana,"

"Dad please don't talk; the ambulance is on the way. Just stay with me please."

"Listen." Waving his hand around with the little energy that he had,

"Get me in the car, we need to go here." He shakily held out some paper with an address on it.

"Dad, we can go there later, let's get you to the hospital now."

"Listen, Shana," her father whispered,

"Grant is there, a…and if we don't leave now, he will be cut up into piec…es." His eyes watering up, words a broken harsh whisper.

Shana stared into them for a couple of seconds while they continued to water up.

"OK…. OK," She nodded in understanding that this needed to be done. She had some bandages and a few little bits and pieces that would stop the bleeding and give him a boost of energy. He would be good for at least an hour.

"Shana, he's badly injured… you can't." Ryan tried to plead some sanity across the two, "Taking him and putting him in the back of the car can do more damage than good. Look, he is bleeding a lot; he needs a hospital!"

"You can help or stay here," she said as she heard the police and ambulance making their way to the scene. She knew if they had arrived before she left, then they would not allow her father to go and make her wait for a special unit to try for Detective Grant. By that time, he would be dead.

Ryan ran to get the car and drove it to them as close as possible,

The Chief's adrenaline was coming back into play. Shana opened the boot and took out the first aid kit and threw it in the back seat. Ryan had never seen the Chief like this, it was an angry Chief. He was shot two times yet with the way he was acting, one would think he was hit with a mere bat a couple of times.

"Where are we going?" Ryan asked as they drove off, turning the corner. He looked in his review mirror and saw a large number of police cars and ambulances flooding the area. They got out just in time.

Shana handed over the bloody paper to Ryan. The address was clear, and he knew exactly where it was, it was five minutes away.

Ryan placed the siren on "Hold on" he drove in and out of traffic at high speed, while Shana was in the back with her father cleaning up his wounds as much as she possibly could and closing them up to stop them from bleeding. She handed him over two tablets. He didn't even ask what they were. She needed him strong enough to save Grant, and she was there to do the same thing.

"Should we call for backup?" Ryan suggested,

"NO!" The Chief yelled. "Son just drive. I'm fine." The Chief shakily sat up and took a few deep breaths.

"Dad, Ryan is right. We need backup." Shana tried to talk some sense into her father.

"I said no," he started to load his gun.

"Dad, what's going on? Who were those men, what did they want?" Shana asked, unable to keep the questions in any longer.

"Shana, the main thing is to save Grant. We can talk later."

"Dad, why were you in Japan? Why were you and Grant in Japan?" he looked at her, confused,

"We're here," Chief said changing the subject, as much as Shana wanted answers, she knew it was pointless. They would be having a very long chat later though.

"It's on the right." Ryan pointed to an old youth center that now sat as a vacant building.

"Ryan, do you have your vest on?"

"No sir, it's in the car." He opened the boot.

He took out two vests and handed one to Shana and the other to Ryan.

"Dad, what about you?"

He shook his head, "Put them on,"

She wasn't going to argue with him now. Both Ryan and Shana took the vest and put them on. All three had their guns ready and headed toward the building.

Each one looking out for the other, the padlock on the door was open as if it were an open invitation.

The Chief was limping, but it didn't let that stop him from making his way in. Shana and Ryan were a step behind, all three having their backs to the wall at all time and their guns close to their chest. The hall was old and the building rusty and dark, they continued to move forward. The hallway had many rooms. The doors leading into each room had a small window where they could look in as they passed. They quietly peaked into each window as they passed slowly, cautiously, and quietly moving across to the next one.

Then the Chief heard a sound, the noise of groan in pain. He pulled his hand out stopping Ryan and Shana, then directing them with his hand to the sound.

They stopped at a room with a different door, a new door, and a large clean window, large enough for all three of them to see who was in the room. To their horror, they saw Sogoto and Grant who was attached to a metal bed. Sogoto looked up and smirked at them before turning back to Grant's body with the scalpel in his hand ready.

"You son of a bitch." The Chief tried to smash the door. Ryan tried once and then twice; the door was not moving. Sogoto was not even paying attention to them. She was locked on Grant, who faced them, pleading with his eyes.

The Chief then shot at the door once, twice but nothing happened. Shana leaned in placing her hand on the door.

"This is bulletproof glass placed in a titanium door. There is no way we can get through this. He must have planned this."

Sogoto's started cutting; he sliced Grant's right ear off and threw them toward the door so that the Chief could get a closer look, George was now banging on the door, wailing, and screaming, falling to the floor unable to breathe. He looked over to see Shana screaming and Ryan trying to restrain her. They were all helpless.

The Chief fumed with anger, he looked in the room, looked around, "There has to be a way in."

As the other ear was thrown, their rage magnified. Ryan tried to get in through the other room, shooting the walls down, but there was no chance. He had cement rendered them.

"There was no way in that way," Ryan confirmed.

"Dad, over there, look!" Shana pointed to the hidden vent to the left. You could get into it via the roof. Sogoto had it covered, but he missed a fine hair-like opening that caught her eye. Ryan and George ran off to get into the vent.

Shana was sick, sick to her stomach as she stood watching, helpless. As he cut, Grant's eye out, she stared unable to move her eyes from what was happening. Grant was crying and moaning, his first eye thrown across the room.

His fingers and feet moved vigorously trying to get out of the lock he was in.

When he cut his second eye out, Sogoto looked at Shana and smiled. He moved his hand toward her as if to hand over the eyeball.

Shana looked him straight in the eyes filled with anger *"I will kill you,"* she screamed, banging on the door.

"You hear me, I will kill you!" Sogoto shrugged his shoulders and threw the eye to the side.

He then looked up toward the noise coming from the roof. The Chief and Ryan were making their way in. Ryan shot all over the room, hoping that he would at least wound him enough to stop.

They couldn't see properly from the roof as it was tilted. Ryan broke the glass and just kept shooting.

Sogoto grabbed his scapula and as he looked at Shana, slashed Grant's throat. Shana fell to the floor crying. He casually picked up his jacket, moved some old carpet, and looked to be walking down.

Shana's tried to stem her sobs and focus. He was heading downstairs, there was no sign of a downstairs, he was underground. Shana frantically knew she had to find a way down there. There had to be an exit point. Shana ran out of the building, circulating it.

At the same time, Ryan had gotten into the room and ran over to the bed. It was too late. Grant was dead.

He saw the stairway that led downstairs and with the Chief right behind him, he moved down them. While halfway down the stairs, they heard the sound of a motorbike. They began to sprint, knowing if he left this building, they may never catch him again.

Shana was on the outside of the building. As she turned the corner, a motorbike flew out of a thin fibro wall, and Sogoto drove off.

Shana aimed her gun, firing a whole round of bullets at Sogoto. Sogoto turned around and fired once.

Shana felt a heavy plunge on her chest with enough force to throw her whole body backward. As her back hit the cement she elevated her head up using her arms used to stop her head from hitting the ground, she felt hot pressure on her chest and found it difficult to breathe.

She had been shot!

George and Ryan completely furious, ran out hearing the shots fired, but they were too late. Ryan turned and saw Shana on the floor before running to her aid. George limped straight to his daughter's side.

She looked at her father "He's gone, Grant is gone, Dad." Her eyes watering up.

The Chief then pulled the vest off, he was so grateful he made her wear it.

Shana was sitting up but finding it hard to breathe.

George now fell to the floor, the pain of the night catching up to him. It hurt him more to admit, but there was nothing he could do for Grant. He needed to go to the hospital.

"It's time to call it in Shana. Your dad needs an ambulance, and they need to get Detective Grant out of here." Ryan pleaded, trying to do the right thing.

"Make the call," Shana replied, giving Ryan the green light. He picked up the phone and called for an ambulance and the crime scene unit. She had to get into autopilot, block out emotion and focus on the case, at least let those around her see that. She could not risk being pulled off the case for something as little as a conflict of interest, not now.

Her father was nearing critical condition. He needed hospital hours ago, but he was as stubborn as she was.

Ryan stood over them as Shana sat on the floor leaning over her father; she moved over his jacket and noticed how much he was bleeding.

She looked at him worried; she knew this amount of blood was not good news.

The Chief noticed her face change as her eyes watered and worry overtook her.

He held her hand as firm as he could, getting her attention. He looked her straight in the eyes "We're fighters. It doesn't hurt."

She knew it hurt; she could see how much he was trying to hide his pain.

A sigh of relief as the sound of the ambulance was getting closer and closer. Both Shana and her father got in the same ambulance. Ryan was about to follow them in the car when he was held back by the FBI.

This FBI officer was tall, well-groomed with his perfectly combed gray hair. You could tell he took his time to make sure everything was the way it should be, and he was about to do just that with his job.

"You have a lot of explaining to do son, you're coming with me." Shana looked up as they closed the ambulance door, knowing they were all in trouble.

Ryan risked his job and integrity by following the Chief's orders even though knowing they were wrong. The police should have been notified; better yet the FBI should have been notified, but it was her father that didn't allow it. He was smart enough to know the Chief was hiding something, and he was getting annoyed at all the bullshit excuses. He walked with the FBI to the car.

***

CHAPTER 31

"You don't need to move slow to get in touch with your instincts. They'll let you know when you need to be. Just be prepared to listen."

Shana sat in the hospital waiting room, bruised heavily from the bulletproof vest. There were a few people ahead of her for x-rays though so all she could do was wait.

She tried to call Ryan a couple of times, to see what was happening, but couldn't get a hold of him. She had a sinking feeling in her stomach.

She knew she had a shit load to deal with back at the office, she should have called for backup. But she didn't. She knew that she would be interrogated, the day from the very beginning had gone all wrong. She had nothing else to do but think.

For the first time in her life, she had questioned her ethics.

She continued to try to call Ryan again with no answer. She then figured he would be in an interview room right now, with the FBI, and the police investigations unit.

She paced. She just lost John, Jake, Detective Grant and now her father was in the theater room, hanging on for dear life.

The phone rang. Shana jumped up, startled, hoping it was Ryan.

Shana, seeing the caller ID, answered "Monica?"

"Shana, where are you? The FBI is looking for you. They have a special investigation unit, and they have been all over the place!" her voice slightly shaking.

"I figured as much" She shook her head in disappointment at what was to come.

"Have you got anything for me?" She hoped that any information could get her closer to Sogoto and then all that had happened today could be forgotten.

"I'm sorry about Detective Grant, his body was transported to the morgue twenty minutes ago to undergo an autopsy at a different hospital. We have all been told to step back from the case." Shana paced faster and was incredibly angry she had put her team in this position and placed the integrity of the unit at risk.

"Shana?"

"Yes, Monica?" She wanted to apologize to her,

"I called in a favor, a fellow friend of Jake and I was at the crime scene as their unit was taking over. He found a fake ID with Sogoto's photo on it at the scene. It must have fallen out as he was getting away; it is slightly covered in Detective Grant's blood. Normally he wouldn't tell me this, but he knew that you and Chief had gone MIA." Monica gasped, "I didn't mean it that way!"

"All good. Please continue." She didn't blame her for thinking the way she was.

"The name on the ID was Morgan Kans and after some research, he is to board a plane heading to Japan in forty minutes. The exit is LA airport." Shana had one last chance. If Sogoto got on that plane and left it was over, she had no jurisdiction in Japan. This was her only chance.

"Shana, please don't let Jake's death go unnoticed. Tell me what I can do to help." Monica's voice was small but strong.

Shana was looking outside, she noticed four FBI cars pull up and a bunch of men and women walking up to the hospital. She knew they were there for her and her father. She needed to get out and head to the airport.

"You have done more than enough, Monica. We never had this conversation." Without waiting for confirmation, she hung up the phone and ran through the hallway aiming at exiting from the back. The FBI was not far behind. She quickly made her way into a near room and hid. Within seconds they too were now in that room.

Holding her breath, she waited and hoped he would not find her. Just then his partner called to him, and he left. Shan then quickly made her way straight for the fire escape door; it was locked, and she could see in the distance more FBI agents were coming in. Thinking quickly, she opened the closest door to her left. She found herself in the doctor's locker room. Shana sent up a small thank you to whoever was listening.

She placed a lab coat on with the surgeon's cap and face mask. She tied her hair in a bun and opened the door slowly and headed out. She needed to get to the airport.

The FBI was nowhere to be seen as she walked down the hallway, trying to avoid attention. Then suddenly, she turned the corner and she walked straight into the FBI agent's shoulder. He then quickly grabbed her hand, Shana's heart leaped into her throat. He then looked up straight at her.

"Sorry about that doctor," the agent apologized with a small smile.

"Not a problem. Careful around those corners, we have more important injuries to treat rather than clumsiness." Shana responded with a nervous joking tone.

"Yes ma'am." He nodded, smile widening.

She nodded and continued to walk out the door; it was in plain sight. *Only a couple of steps.*

"Excuse me!"

The FBI agent had come back. She stood frozen, staring at the door. A part of her wanted to run forward and try her luck, but where would she run to, and more so, how would she explain running from the FBI?

She closed her eyes and slowly turned around.

He approached her and placed his arm on her shoulder. Shana opened her eyes, ready to surrender.

"You dropped this." He handed over a name tag that was supposed to be pinned on the lab coat.

"Thank you. Thank you very much, sir." Shana replied anxiously.

He nodded and made his way back to his partner. She turned around, took a big breath in, and continued walking forward through the doors and on to freedom.

That was so close she thought as she walked out toward the main road.

She was safe for now. In her mind, she kept thinking about how she would come back with good news for her dad, for Monica, for everyone. The case would be dropped, the investigation canceled, and all would be well. She needed to get to him before he got on that plane.

But right now, she needed a car. She saw a car about to leave the car park and stood in front of it until it came to a stop and pulled out her badge.

"Sorry ma'am, I'm going to have to use your car,"

"But I have an appointment to go to, um I..."

"This is a serious matter and people's lives are on the line, do you want to be held accountable?" Shana warned her. The 40-year-old lady in a business suit, trying to make a living, nodded.

She exited the car, took her briefcase and Shana quickly made her way in. The lady had her favorite CD playing at full blast. *'Hit the Road Jack,'* by Ray Charles. Shana put the volume down slightly and opened the window of the car "Thank you" and drove off.

She had to get to LAX airport and quickly.

***

CHAPTER 32

"If it is out of my hands, then why does it drain my mind and bury my soul?"

Monica had an agenda. She wanted to kill Sogoto, no questions asked. She could not live with herself, knowing the man that killed Jake was alive. Monica secretly left the office without anyone detecting, as she took one of the available police cars from the front; she needed a fast car with sirens to get to the airport. No one even noticed or asked any questions; everyone was too busy looking for Shana and waiting for her dad to come out of the operating room. Monica had her friend fax over the fake identification. She embedded the image of Sogoto into her head. She parked the police car right on the side of the international departures and left it on. She notified the security guard on her way in. He nodded, no one was going to mess with an officer, even though she technically wasn't one, but who was going to ask? She knew exactly where to head. International Departures at the Japan Airlines International terminal. She quickly looked up the computer screen; there was a departure from Los Angeles LAX – Final Destination Osaka, Japan Kansai International. The stopover would be Tokyo. So, this was the only chance, if there had been a stopover in the States, they would be able to get it wherever the stop or change was. Unfortunately, this was a flight with one stop to Japan.

The plane, being a Japanese plane also meant that the minute it went up in the air, America no longer has jurisdiction over it. They can ask and plead for it to make an emergency landing, but the Japanese won't. This had happened in the past, when that plane is up in the air, refused to turn around, and the armed robber was gone for good. They couldn't have this happing in this case.

***

Shana drove close to the curb of international departures entry and parked the car, with the front tire slightly on the footpath. She ran off, heading to the Japanese airline international baggage drop-off and boarding pass pickup.

"You can't park here." The tall man in a security uniform was quick to attend to her car as he noticed her running into the airport.

"Then tow it." She didn't care right now.

Shana ran through the door and to her surprise, the first person she saw was Monica. Oh shit! She would be placing her job on the line and her life at risk by being here!

"What are you doing here?" she grabbed Monica's arm spinning her around. She shook off Shana's hand, as she came to a stop.

"Shana, I'm here to help. I'm here to find him."

"Monica, this is not part of your job." She was not ready to lose another colleague and didn't know how she would explain Monica's presence here to the FBI. She needed to leave.

Monica leaned into her jacket and got out her badge.

"I no longer work for you, so therefore you cannot tell me where I can be." She handed over her badge to Shana and walked off. Shana held the badge in her hand, thinking to herself how much meaning the badge once had, and how now it felt like just a cold piece of metal.

Time was crucial, and she knew she needed Monica.

"Monica," Shana called out to her, "Ok listen, we work can together." She said, handing back the badge to Monica.

"Cormack sent me the photo." Monica opened her phone to show Shana the photo of Sogoto, not knowing that Shana had stared straight into his eyes earlier. "I know what he looks like." Shana mentally shuddering at the flashing memories of Grant's mutilated body.

"We should split up, keep your phone close. I'm heading into Gate 54; you take all the other gates from forty-eight down."

"The minute you see him, call me... don't do this on your own." Shana pleaded. Monica nodded.

Shana made it to Gate 54 just in time, all passengers were on board. She flashed her badge and made her way onto the plane. She ran past the air hostess and put her gun away, not wanting to scare people and get a reaction of screaming passengers. It could cause Sogoto to react to a hostage situation. She got into the front of the plane and explained to the captain that they may have a serial killer on board. The captain gave her fifteen minutes before the plane was said to take off. Shana couldn't believe his response. Had that been her as the pilot, she would stop the plane for as long as needed be, to be certain a murderer was not boarding her plane. It annoyed her how some people were,

But for now, she just had fifteen minutes to work with. There was no way he would be armed. Going through an American airport, they would have picked up anything that could cause harm.

Shana made her way past first class. She looked to her left and her right, and she saw the wealthy dressed in their designer labels. A young twenty-year-old woman holding the hand of a man old enough to be her grandfather. She continued to move forward. People's eyes followed Shana, wondering what she was doing.

Shana tried to be as calm as she possibly could and made her way through business class. Men and women in suits, all getting ready probably to head straight to appointments, meetings, or conferences as soon as the plane landed. She could not fathom that type of lifestyle.

She continued to walk forward. The curtain in front of her indicated the division of economy from business class was at hand's reach. She pulled it slightly and made her way into economy, a long line of people was there.

She continued to walk looking right and left, continuously making sure he was not on the plane. She couldn't see him, a part of her was shaking *Where was he?*

"Can I help you find your seat?" an air hostess with a little too much makeup and a smile that looked too fake to be genuine approached her.

"Oh, I'm fine just making my way to the seat, it's over there." Pointing to the back of the plane, not having time to explain to her why she was on the plane, and what she was after.

"Well please hurry and be seated we will be departing any minute now." The hostess replied bluntly, moving out of her way so Shana would make her way to the seat.

Shana made her way to the end with nothing.

She then made her way to the other side and walked down glancing over every face, every person. *Where was he?!* As she got halfway down toward the front of the plane in economy her phone rang, it was Monica.

***

Monica ran through the airport as Shana had requested, taking the left side while Shana took the right. As she got to Gate 44, a security guard came from behind, his gun digging in her back.

"Walk with me." Monica did as he wished, she was hoping that it was Sogoto; at least she had found him.

He walked her into the disabled toilet, where he quickly smashed the front of her body on the wall making sure she did not turn around to look at him. He held her there as she writhed in agony.

"Call Shana and tell her you found Sogoto." She fought against his hold.

He grabbed her head and banged it against the tiled walls of the bathroom, Monica was not following orders. Emotionally she was numb, however physically she was in pain, her tears rolling down as she tried to gasp for air.

He took her phone out and called Shana. He placed the phone near her mouth, with the other hand holding the gun to her head.

She was in pain, bleeding from her forehead, but she did as he said.

"I…. I found him he is here!" Monica spoke, hoping Shana would not come.

"Where are you?"

"Gate Forty-Four," Monica replied quickly and Sogoto hung up.

Of course, he would not have been stupid enough to get on a plane directly to Japan. He was going to stop off somewhere then go. It would have been too easy. *Idiot!*

***

Shana was quickly making her way to the exit of the plane. The captain was standing there waiting for her.

"You're good to go." She waved as she continued to run off.

"Are you sure?" he sounded confused and a little relieved. Where was that emotion when she was telling him there was possibly a serial killer on board?

"Yes," she replied as she turned and continued to Gate Forty-Four. She ran as fast as her legs could take her; however, it was an empty floor. Not one person in sight.

As she picked up her phone to call Monica, she saw her run out of the public bathroom.

Shana ran to her, seeing that Monica was distraught and bleeding. She got to her before Monica had fallen to the floor.

***

CHAPTER 33

"Little does she know that his distance is only a physical absence and not that of the mind."

Shana noticed the blood and bruising on Monica's face and felt her blood boil.

"What happened? Where is he?"

"He's gone." Shana was furious, thinking that Monica had tried to take him on her own. She should have waited.

"He wasn't alone. Someone made me call you. It was not Sogoto, I couldn't see his face, but I had a clear view of his neck when he left – there was no tattoo. Nothing! I didn't see his face, he's gone!" Monica's tears left a streak through the blood on the left side of her face.

"We are dealing with just Sogoto…. We need to find out who else he is working with."

Monica was slowly getting up; they both knew that they had a long road ahead of them.

"Excuse me?" a young man tried to get Shana's attention. She was not in any mood to be interrupted.

"What?" She snapped, holding onto Monica's arm to help her stay steady.

"Are you Shana?"

Shana nodded. "The air hostess on the plane you were just on, said you dropped this,"

Shana was confused. Why would an air hostess get someone to give her something and how did he know who to give it to?

Shana grabbed him by the collar, causing the young man to whimper.

"She gave me this, she said it was important!"

He handed over a photo of Shana that was taken of her while in Atlanta uncovering bodies at the graveyard. He had also been there.

Shana grabbed the photo and the letter off him and let him go. Sogoto was playing games.

Monica leaned over, knowing that the photo was taken in Atlanta as she was also there.

They both leaned in as Shana opened the letter.

"So close, but NOW ……. So far… look up … Goodbye!"

They both looked up at the plane that was just about to take off. Shana and Monica looked at one of the windows that had a picture against it; it was a red background with a skinny monkey winking.

Shana started to wonder, she had a better understanding of Sogoto's ways now, but with him in Japan and her here, she had nothing.

A blurred image of him cutting up Grant blinked in front of her. She was too busy trying to catch him, he was not worried, and he had everything planned perfectly. He knew that the ID would be found, and it would lead Shana to the airport, he knew that she would not bring anyone with her, because it was personal now.

Shana smiled, she knew his game plan, but it was too late. "Monica, it's not two people we are after…. It's just Sogoto!"

Both now standing looking outside the glass window "How so?!" responded Monica.

"We know Sogoto is always well planned and organized. Sogoto must have covered his tattoo, it's easy to do." Monica nodded. This could have been possible,

Shana continued "He must have had surveillance on us for a while now. He knew us personally. He knew by killing Jake that you would turn up and that was what he needed as a distraction. He loved impulse, he loved being close and getting away clean." Monica closed her eyes in pain.

"Sogoto would have presented his ID, most probably that of the NPA group. He would have got off the plane, came to you, and then casually got back on the plane in perfect timing."

Silence fell over them as they reflect on what had just happened.

"Can we stop the plane?" Monica broke the silence.

"No Monica," Shana sounded defeated. That was it, he had gotten away.

Shana and Monica headed out to the front of the airport where the car that Shana had come in was being towed, she looked over at Monica.

"Can you drop me off at the hospital?"

"Sure," Monica pointed to the police car two cars down.

Monica got in, as did Shana, both lost in their thoughts.

Shana going over everything in her head, trying to figure out what went wrong. So many loose threads, so many things she didn't know so many unanswered questions.

Both didn't exchange any words. Monica pulled into the emergency stand at the hospital right near the sliding doors.

Shana opened the door, with no energy left in her body, "Thank you." She turned to Monica and got out of the car. Shana couldn't keep running from the FBI, and more importantly, she needed an update on her dad.

"Sha-na?" Monica said, trying to get Shana's attention, her voice trembling as she was holding back tears, anger, a small gulp between the two syllables of Shana's name gave it away.

"Yeah?" Shana looked back.

Monica simply handed over her badge; Shana held her hand out, knowing that Monica would not do this if she were thinking in the right state of mind.

"Monica, are you sure? Take some time off and think about it. I don't want to lose you as well." Monica placed the badge in Shana's hand and closed Shana's fingers over the badge with both her hands.

"I have." She was holding back tears.

"I 'll clear my stuff out tomorrow." She placed both her hands on the steering wheel to illustrate that the conversation was over, and she was done.

"Monica?" Shana whispered, it hurt her to see her colleague ... her friend hurting so much.

"Please Shana, just go." Shana nodded and stepped away from the car, watching as it drove off.

Shana turned and looked up at the hospital. Shana wondered if Portia would be in her office today. Portia also ran the secured psychiatric ward, on level nine.

She approached the front desk and asked about her father. Within minutes, a doctor came out and said that he was in recovery. He had lost a lot of blood and was very weak; he had to undergo surgery, multiple blood transfusions, and also will need lots of physio. He also informed her that he sent the FBI away and told them that there is no way he was physically fit or mentally stable to answer any questions until tomorrow.

She nodded, holding her hand out to exchange handshakes.

He was going to make it, he was alive. She needed to wash her face; Shana was drained.

Shana entered a bathroom and looked at herself in the mirror; she had aged five years in this past week. Her hair was brittle, mascara marking under her eyes, her blouse was considerably dirty and bloodstained. She stared into the mirror looking at herself, staring long and hard, her eyes watering up. The veins on her neck swelling, as she looked at herself with anger and disgust, she looked deeper and deeper into the mirror, and out from behind her was Sogoto.

She jumped and turned around, taking her gun out and pointing it.

There was no one there. Her heart pacing a hundred miles an hour, her hands shaking. She opened the tap and let the cold water pour out. She placed both hands under, and washed her face, she used paper towels to clean herself, she felt so dirty but just needed to get herself together. She was a mess.

She looked in the mirror one last time before she exited the bathroom. Her subconscious mind, repeating *be strong, be strong, be strong.* She tried to get her breathing back to normal. She exited and headed toward her father's room.

Shana took her time walking through the hospital hallway to her father's room, she was tired, exhausted, and confused.

Shana opened the door and there was her father sound asleep, the morphine present in his body allowing him to rest. There were tubes attached to him and a heart monitor beeping loudly, the oxygen mask covering half his face. His skin color was so pale. She placed her hand on his leg as she was making her way to the other side, the room small, with a little sunlight coming through the curtain.

***

Portia stood outside the door of Shana's dad's room, with the door slightly opened, and listened in.

"I'm here now, you're going to be fine," Shana whispered. She sat on the chair right next to his bed and placed her elbows on the bed right next to him.

Shana started to cry.

She calmed herself down, not wanting to upset him, she was conscious of her behavior and placed her hands over her face she took a deep breath.

"I lost him, Dad. I tried, I tried…. He just got away."

Portia wondered who she was talking about. Who got away?

"I don't know what else to do?" then she paused.

"Monica left. I guess it was too much for her, she was always remarkably close to Jake, I... I was thinking I should leave also; I don't know Dad, I failed."

"Why is everyone so secretive? I have no answers." Portia's eyes watered up as Shana stood up, pacing around while continuously questioning everything that had taken place, questioning herself.

"You need to toughen up Dad. You need to get better. You, Grant, Portia, and Ryan were the only family I have left."

"Now Grant's dead, and you're in here, please I beg you, please get better."

Portia silently cried as she listened to the helpless Shana, a girl she had never met before, a girl so hurt, so vulnerable, so confused. This Shana was a stranger. She had never seen her best friend so defeated and confused before. Portia could have assisted her with some answers. But she knew she couldn't, and even if she wanted to, now was not the right time.

Portia covered her mouth, to cover any noise when she heard that Detective Grant was dead. She knew how much Shana loved him; how fond she was of him. Portia also was fond of him; he too was like the uncle she never had.

Portia waited, not knowing if she should go in to assist her friend, her sister. But she knew better. Shana needed to vent. Portia turned around heading back down the hallway, to the elevator. She would give her time, then be there to help her pick up the pieces.

***

Shana continued to vent and talk, and even mentioned Ryan and how he went through her phone.

All her questions were being asked, everything that was going through her mind not only in the last week or last month but years, she went into wanting answers about what happened to her mother. She wasn't getting any answer obviously, but it felt nice to just get them all out there.

Her frustrations of not getting answers made her thoughts go too deep places. Her father was in a deep sleep.

She sat on the chair and held her father's hand, she felt an enormous amount of guilt override her. She should ease up on him a little, he too needed the benefit of the doubt, but it was hard. She was caught between emotions and truths.

She placed her head on the bed, leaning forward while on the chair, placed her arms on the bed, with one hand holding her father's hand.

"I'm sorry Dad," she truly was, she also was exhausted and drained. Shana closed her eyes and immediately fell asleep on the chair. Her body needed the rest.

Hours later, Shana woke up to the nurse coming in to check her father's blood pressure. Realizing she had fallen asleep, she got up and apologized to the nurse.

"You're fine. The doctor said it was ok for you to stay. That chair over there is a recliner and probably would be more comfortable laying there though."

She pointed across the room to a green recliner which she then helped Shana move closer to her father's bed.

"I appreciated it." Shana smiled gratefully that her father was being looked after by a nice nurse.

"His blood pressure seems to be normal; he just needs some rest. But looks like he's doing well,"

"That's wonderful news, thanks again."

The nurse made her way out of the room and closed the door behind her, Shana was in the corner, so the detectives were unable to see her, she listened in "Sorry I was advised by the doctor that you will not be able to see him until tomorrow morning, he's currently asleep and unable to speak with you."

"Is his daughter in there? Shana?" they asked the nurse directly.

"No one else is in there sir, now please you do your job and let us do ours." The nurse lied. Shana was relieved. She needed the time to think, and she didn't quite have the answers they were after. She needed guidance from her father.

She was so grateful to the nurse. Shana laid back in the recliner chair and stared into the ceiling as her thoughts again took over. This time she also rested her eyes.

***

CHAPTER 34

"The foundation of a friendship requires mutual agreement in the solid ground."

Shana had not yet heard anything about or from Ryan. She didn't want to use her phone, knowing that it was most likely bugged and most probably they would get surveillance on her. With the phone off she felt safer.

She picked up the phone near her dad's bed and called upstairs, hoping Portia stayed back at the hospital.

"Portia, my dad..." Shana didn't know how to tell her.

"Stop, I already know. I saw you sleeping, so I let you get some rest. I knew you would call me the minute you got up. He's ok Shana and so are you, I'll see you in a minute."

"Thank you," was all Shana could say, she knew deep down it was Portia who informed the nurses to lie. Portia was very ethical, so for her to do that was huge.

Shana knew she could confide in Portia, and she was ready to share everything. She needed Portia's expertise in helping Shana mourn the death of Jake and Grant. She needed someone to hold her.

"Shall we go somewhere and let your dad rest?" Portia asked Shana as she popped her head into the room.

"Yeah sure," Shana replied as she was following Portia down the hospital hallway.

Portia entered the cafeteria, which was off premises within those hours, however, Portia had access with a swipe of her card. The door opened, and they were there alone. Portia turned on the lights and placed two chairs that were packed away off the table and slid one over to Shana and one for herself.

They both sat down. No one to bother them, no interferences, or disruptions, now they finally had some time alone.

The only thing available was the coffee vending machines and the snacks vending machine next to it.

"Here, it's not the best of coffees, but it will have to do," Portia said, handing over the coffee to Shana as they walked and talked.

"It will be just fine," Shana said as she took the coffee gently from Portia's freshly manicured hands, certain that she wasn't in the mood to drink or eat.

"Here eat this, it's turkey." Portia offered as she took the sandwich out of the brown paper bag that she had bought earlier and handed it to Shana. It was a sandwich sealed in a triangular package with a big print across the package highlighting it was a healthy choice, very typical of Portia.

Shana smiled and took the sandwich. They both dug deep into sandwiches, "Finally, some food." Portia quietly uttered.

A couple of minutes later it was as if the sandwich was fuel to Shana's body that finally got her to talk.

"You can't trust anyone, Portia," Shana stated softly.

Portia looked worried as if the comment were targeted at her as she swallowed her last bite before replying "What makes you say that?"

"Everyone around me, Portia." She looked Portia straight in the eyes, the sandwich falling back to the plate. "Everyone, I don't know who to trust."

"Except you, you're the only person I know I can rely on. You're the only person who would tell me how it is," Shana said as Portia sighed in relief.

"Start from the beginning," Portia suggested with the intention of at least helping her best friend,

"Ok," Shana told Portia for the first time from beginning to the end of everything that had taken place in the case, walking her through it as if Portia was there. She went into detail and explained the involvement of Dr. Marcos, Ryan, Wong, and Jake's devastating death setup. Shana further explained what Sogoto had done to Detective Roger and Detective Grant, to her father, forcing her to go with no back up to where Sogoto was, to the NPA officers, the Chief Officer of United Nation Japan all dying.

Portia sat and listened attentively. She wanted Shana to get it all off her chest, it was clearly eating her.

They both sat in the cafeteria, until the early hours of the morning, Portia listening and Shana talking when finally, Shana came to the end of it. She looked up at Portia, her eyes glazing, and tired.

"What do I do now?" Shana was so tired.

"Take a break, rest, eat, look after your dad. And look after yourself, then you'll know what to do." Shana nodded as Portia continued, "You can't make any decisions right now, worst decisions in our life are made on impulse."

Portia was right.

Shana hugged and kissed Portia on the cheek goodbye as she headed back to her father's room.

As they got closer to the room, Shana and Portia could hear people talking in her father's room. Shana started to speed up to the room to find out who it was but was held back by Portia.

"Let me go and see what's happening, you wait here," Portia demanded as she pushed Shana into a small room that was filled with all hospital goods. Shana wanted to see who it was her father was talking to. Portia knew that it was probably safer than Shana staying put.

Portia continued to walk closer toward her dad's room, the door slightly open, enough to place a pin through it. She listened in.

"You know it's the right thing to do. It's not only your job on the line here Chief."

"What am I supposed to do? Sit at home and watch soap operas? You're kidding me, right?" George replied, trying to emphasize the need for something to be done.

"Listen, George, let me make it clear and concise. If you don't retire, then an investigation will have to take place. There is no way we can even think of getting out of that, and we'll all go down." Portia now was listening in closely, waiting for George's answer. Portia clearly understood his selfish need to protect his arse.

"Or you can retire; we have agreed with the investigating unit that you are under a lot of stress and acted inappropriately and that you feel it is now time to retire."

Portia continued to listen in, wondering what it was that the FBI agents had hidden, the more she heard the more corrupt they all sounded. The more she feared that what she was hiding from Shana was not what she was supposed to be doing.

"Chief, listen, you should have called us all in. The detective, your fucking mate is dead because of you."

"Don't you dare say because of me? I'm living with this as much as you guys are. I was trying to fix things, but it seems all you fuckers care about is your arses. I'm not retiring, and they can investigate. I have a few internal people I can talk to; I can make this go away!" the Chief snapped.

"You can make this go away?" The FBI agent replied sarcastically laughing, "You can't make this go away. It's on every channel on every broadcast, in every paper. It's not just the FBI or internal investigation you have to answer to, it's to EVERYONE!"

"I'll figure it out." The Chief muttered, not taking in what they were saying.

"Let me make it simpler for you." The FBI agent said as he approached the Chief "Because you do not seem to understand the urgency of all this. They have received a 'go card,' saying they will not look into the case and leave it as is, if he, meaning you Chief retires, it all goes to rest. The killer is gone, no more serial killer and the investigation is closed. It's Japan's problem now!" the agent explained.

"If you do not retire in the next two days, your daughter will be the first to be investigated. We will plant evidence, and we will make sure she never works a day in her life again, and that her reputation is ruined. We will make her life and yours as miserable as possible." The agent threatened. Portia was outraged but knew that the FBI agent needed to fight harder, he had to break George first. "You will be investigated, and we will be certain that when we all go down, we will state that Shana was a part of this…A big part of it."

George tried to get out of bed, but with the number of drugs and wires attached to him and his pain, he couldn't move.

"You son of a bitch, you go near my daughter and I'll fucking hunt you down, you piece of shit. You hear me?" the Chief yelled.

They were heading toward the door as Portia quickly moved away and walked in the opposite direction.

"We look forward to receiving your resignation tomorrow before midday, if not George…… well" he shrugs and continues "let the games begin."

"Fuck you," was the last response Portia heard coming from George.

Portia walked back to where she left Shana.

"What was that about?" Portia was again put in an uncomfortable position, not knowing what to do, questioning her option, to be honest with Shana and tell her what happened.

"They were asking a few questions, but your dad was too tired to answer, so they said that they would come back."

"I thought I heard yelling" Shana replied confused.

Portia shook her head thinking fast on her feet, "Probably the room next to him, they all seemed civil. I honestly believe everything will be ok,"

"Ok, I'll go see him." Portia knew Shana's father needed some time to think, and she sure hoped that they would not get Shana involved in all this and just retire.

"Um, I think you should just give him some time to himself. He just got up, go have another coffee and maybe get him one on your way,"

Shana walked into her father's room. He looked up at her and smiled. She put the coffee down and sat next to him.

"Welcome back Dad," she smiled as she put her hand over his.

"Shana, come closer I want to talk to you." Shana did as he asked, happy that finally she will get some answers but worried at what the answers would be.

"I know that you have a lot of questions, but what I'm asking is that you trust me. There are things that I can't tell you, and it's for a good reason."

"When you talk to me, I need you to be clear and concise. Do not talk to me like I am your little kid anymore.... Go it?"

"Shana please just listen to me." her dad urged as he placed his hand on hers "I'm retiring."

"What?" Shana questioned confusedly, "Why?" She knew too well that her dad lived to be the Chief; he couldn't possibly do anything else. *Retirement?*

"I have my reasons, plus, I think I have been shot enough times in my life to call it quits."

"You love your job, you live for this, what will you do instead?"

"Probably take up golf," he replied smirking.

"You hate golf. Seriously, this is not a funny matter. I need you to be straight with me, is this something they are asking you to do?" She was confused. Shana knew her father too well; he would never quit, never willingly at least. Her gut feeling was never wrong.

"No, Shana it's simple, I'm tired and I'm exhausted. The house is paid off, I have some cash saved. I just want to rest, invest in some small business, and more importantly, spend more time with you,"

"But what would I do without you at the office?"

"You will continue to do what you do best" Shana didn't want to; she could not imagine the day she would go to work and her father not being there. It was mind-blowing.

"Dad, can you at least take some leave then come back? Think about it, you're stressed now, you just got out of an operation." Shana suggested, hoping that somehow, he could change his mind, or at least negotiate with her.

"Minds made up little girl, I'll make it official tomorrow morning," While shifting in the bed trying to get comfortable.

"Also, the FBI will approach you. But don't worry I have spoken to them, so don't worry about them investigating further into this case and speak to Ryan and see what he is doing."

"I have been trying to call him, his phone is off."

"It should be on now. Give him a call and see what he has told the investigators. Shana, tell him not to say anything. It will all be ok,"

Shana looked at him suspiciously, how on earth would he know that Ryan's phone would be on? There is no way. They probably kept him in the interview room all night and knowing Ryan he would not have spoken a word.

"You know how crazy this all sounds right? A conspiracy? Dad, what is it your hiding'?" He didn't respond. Shana got up and took the phone and dialed Ryan from the hospital phone near her father's bed.

"Hey, how are you?"

"I've been trying to call you. Where have you been? What happening?" Shana asked.

"Well besides, being locked in an interview room by some FBI power trippers for four hours nothing much."

"Did you tell them anything?"

"What was I to tell them? I don't know what the hell is going on. But I did hear your dad's resigning, everyone at the office is gossiping about it. Is it true?"

"But he didn't make the decision until now?" Shana replied, confused as to how people already know.

"Just rumors Shana, relax? Where are you?"

"Still at the hospital,"

"The FBI needs to talk to you also, but it seems you have disappeared off the face of the earth."

"Yeah I know I'll talk to them today; I just need to get myself together,"

"Anything you want me to do?"

"You have done enough Ryan; I'll be in the office later." there was nothing anyone could do.

"Shana, the FBI has let me go but I'm due in for questioning tomorrow,"

"Just say that you followed the Chief's orders" she looked over at her father, who nodded.

"You sure? That could cost him though."

"Cost what Ryan, his retiring. Let's just make this go away please." She was frustrated and just wanted to end this conversation. She also felt bad that she has placed Ryan in this position.

"Well, I'm heading to John's family today; I need to be there. I'll keep my phone on me. Keep me updated."

"Will do, please give them my condolences."

"Will do" Ryan sounded so distant, so empty and so hurt.

She hung up and turned to her father. "I need some answers, you keep telling me that there are things I don't need to know." he tried to talk but she didn't let him. "But I need to know, start with telling me. Why were you in Japan, and who were those men from NPA, and what were they doing in your office?"

He looked at her, both staring in each other's eyes hopelessly, "Shana, the less you know the better,"

Frustrated and angry to his reply, she hit the side of the bed,

"Grant is dead, and you're here telling me you're not going to explain why. Either I will investigate, and I will not stop until I know what's going on, or you be clear with me... because I will find out. So, stop wasting my time Dad and please tell me what the hell is going on."

"Yes, I was in Japan." Shana took a breath in and sat down, knowing that she finally was getting answers. It was a relief.

"But I was there to initiate dealings with the United Nations in creating an interaction correspondence group similar to that of CIS, focused on international crimes, or more so international serial killers."

"But with different laws in different countries how is that possible?" Shana interrupted, knowing that it was difficult to do.

"Let me finish. It was a meeting with leaders of the high economy countries coming together and creating this team so it would include people from all around the world coming together to work together under specialized law and specialized forces."

"The only reason I was in Japan was some NPA people showed interest, we had no idea at the time that they were corrupt and were trying to take down the American integrity by showing the system does not work. After the serial killing took place in America two years ago, NPA and other Japanese teams pulled out, and were no longer on board, embarrassed that one of their most terrifying killers was on our grounds." George explained.

Shana was astonished by the information, yet part of her didn't buy it.

"There is a specialized group that dwells on teachings set by a historical leader focused on The Wise Monkeys, where if one does nothing, even if evil is right in front of them, then they shall live."

"Yes, that's right" George confirmed.

"Dad, Sogoto was not new to you. You had a history; you didn't think to tell me? You knew all the murders were linked?" Shana felt betrayed.

"Yes, Shana unfortunately you are right, BUT there was a good reason. The specialized team, even though at that time included no Japanese participants, were working on catching him."

"Let me see if I have this right, the CIS, NPA, KGB, and whatever other specialized groups that is out are all working together to catch this person?" Shana questioned.

"Yes."

"Ok, but where were they all when he was here in America?"

"It doesn't sound right Dad, you're talking specialized forces, the biggest brains in the world could not catch this scum. I don't know what you take me for?"

"Shana listen, I couldn't tell you anything, and we were all informed to stand back. A large group in Japan bigger than the NPA wanted involvement. One of the men who was head Chief had his whole family wiped out by Sogoto. It was our way in, we agreed that on their term we will follow through with the case."

"You agreed for him to kill as many American families as possible here, let me play cat and mouse, and then what exactly?" Shana asked sarcastically.

"Catch him hands down; he had nearly been caught twice, before. We were building a tight case" her father replied.

"Building a case? How about watching him kill your best friend?" she snapped.

"Shana stop right there. If I could, I would have shot him right between the eyes then and there, whether the specialty group allowed me to or not."

"Fine, but what happens now?" Shana asked, drifting from the question knowing if her father had a gun to his head, he wouldn't have fired.

"He goes back to Japan. We leave it with them, and we also send some officers over who will work closely with the Japanese group to make sure they get the help they need." Chief answered.

"And who are these people exactly?"

"That, you don't need to know."

"Send me with them." She wanted to track him down, she knew him well now.

"Sit down Shana; this is not our fight,"

"Not our fight? I have Grant dead, Jake dead, John dead, Grant dead, Roger dead, eight families dead, THIS IS MY FIGHT!"

"Shana, Japan is a foreign country with different rules and legislation. They play dirty, it's not the place for you. They don't care about your insight, they will eat you for breakfast, literally."

"Dad, please make it happen. Get me to Japan."

"Now is not the time, and I can't do anything anymore, I'm resigning, Shana. Let's just respect the death of Grant, see his family, make sure he gets taken care of. That's our prime concern now."

"But…"

"No buts… Please." He reached over and grabbed an envelope that was on the bedside table.

"Hand this letter over to Sergeant Wilson, he is expecting this." he handed a sealed envelope, "Make sure he gets this,"

"Your resignation?" Shana asked as she looked at him disappointed and her stomach turned.

"Yes," he replied.

She shrugged and replied, "Seems like someone dropped it off and asked you to fill it out, or wait let me guess, you asked the nurse to go pick up one for you?"

"Shana, please just do what you're told for once."

"This conversation isn't finished," She knew she needed to confront her work colleagues and speak with the FBI, and internal investigation the earlier the better, she wanted this out of the way.

She needed to go back to being a leader, a leader for her team, and find a way to catch the son of a bitch that got away.

"Ok I'm going into work, and I'll hand over your stupid letter, but I'll be back with some proper food and more of an understanding of what's going on."

"Ok, fine just go now," he answered, slightly smiling, and watching his big girl walking out and closing the door behind her.

***

Shana headed home. It was early in the morning, and she needed a good shower to clean herself and her problems away. She also needed to head to work. She got the coffee machine ready, went in had a shower, and put on her suit.

She had another cup of coffee, and looked over some photos around her house, some with her mother and some with her father as she got older and when her mother was no longer around. She glanced at photos with Detective Grant and apologized to him. She took the blame for what had happened to him.

She looked into Grant's eyes and then remembered what Sogoto had done. She could no longer look at the photo. She put her coffee cup down, took a deep breath in, and headed to her office.

Shana drove into work, not knowing what to expect. She parked the car as if it were a normal day, she held the letter her father gave her in her hand, looking at it, wondering what would happen if she was not to hand it in. What if he changed his mind later?

She placed the letter in her bag for safekeeping. Sergeant Wilson was the first person present in the unit.

"Good morning sergeant,"

"Good morning Shana, I'm sorry for your loss,"

"I am sorry for your loss too. Wasn't Grant also a friend of yours?" Shana was a little pissed, he knew very well what Grant was to her. She wasn't liking the attitude she could hear clearly in his tone.

"Yes, of course, I know you've had a hard few days."

"You have no idea," Shana replied as she continued to walk across the hallway to the escalator to go down to her level.

"Shana, I think you forgot something?"

"And what could that possibly be?"

"A letter from your father? He called and said you're dropping it in."

"Oh that, it seems I forgot it at home. I'll get that for you tomorrow, but I'm sure there is no rush?" For some silly reason, she didn't want to hand over the letter to this man.

The sergeant walked up to Shana while waiting for the elevator, the doors opened and she entered, Wilson entered with her, it was just the two of them heading down.

"Shana, I know your games too well. If you know what's best for your dad, you get that letter out of your bag now and hand it to me. It's what your father wants." Being a little condescending.

"Is it? Or is it something that you have talked him into?"

"Shana, listen to me and listen carefully," he said as he leaned in, with one hand pressed up against the wall, closing in on Shana, and the other on the stop button of the elevator "If you don't hand in that letter now, you're jeopardizing what you call a great man's career, so if this is the outcome you want, then you keep it. But since I am in charge now, I ask you to pack your bags and get the fuck out of here,"

"You're firing me or are you threatening me, sergeant?" Shana replied in shock.

He grabbed her bag off her, took out the letter, and then handed her bag back to her. He was much stronger than she was, she tried to hold on to it, but he yanked it out of her hands.

He let go of the stop button and then the lift opened, "Now get out, pack your stuff, and go on annual stress leave like a good girl. No one has any questions for you, I have covered this and cleaned you and your dad's mess." He paused.

"Three months of leave, then be back here doing what you do best!" He knew he couldn't fire her; she was irreplaceable.

Shana got out of the elevator furious. The doors closed and the sergeant was gone - to think she once respected him. She didn't know what made him turn into the biggest arsehole she had ever met. Shana was maddened by the whole incident.

Shana wanted to tell him she quit, but she knew it would be an impulse decision and that she would have no way of digging more into this case which she had to do.

Shana walked into her office and past what was left of her team furious, she noticed Monica in the distance, clearing out her desk. Shana didn't bother saying hi or even taking notice of the people in the room. She went straight to her office and closed the door.

Shana slammed her bag on the table and sat on her chair. She felt out of place, this used to be her second home, more so her first home, because at times she spent more time here than in her place. Now it felt... empty.

She sat looking around her office. Looking out to the floor where all her team was, the momentum was down; the esteem of the team was down, the team appearing damaged. This was a team that had been in place for six years. This team was a family.

Shana looked at her desk and saw a letter. From Jake. She opened the letter intrigued to see what it was. A transfer letter. Jake had been applying to other forensic teams around California, and this was his request for transfer with an accepted job. He was planning to leave.

Shana was confused. As she held the letter trying to figure out why Jake would have wanted to transfer, Monica knocks on the door, asking to come in. Shana of course let her in. Monica looked as though she had had no sleep. She walked in and closed the door behind her.

"That was his letter of the transfer request," Monica said after noticing the letter Shana was reading.

"I can see that, why?" Shana asked, looking at Monica for an answer.

"We were seeing each other for over a year, and we knew it was wrong, it was hard hiding it, but two months ago…" she paused her eyes watering up as she couldn't hold her tears back this time "He proposed. We were planning to get married at the end of the year, but if this was to take place, then we knew that we could not work together. We knew that you wouldn't allow it, so as much as he didn't want to leave, he applied to transfer, letting me stay."

Shana put the letter down, feeling so guilty and at the same time so ignorant and obtuse for not even noticing. She had been so caught up in work that she didn't even stop to look at her team, their needs, what they were going through. She had failed as a leader.

"I'm so sorry, Monica. Had I known, I would have done something, or at least recommended some options."

"We didn't want to bother you with it; you had a lot on your plate."

"I'm so sorry; you should have bothered me with it."

"It's too late now, I just wanted to thank you, for everything, on behalf of me and Jake. We both loved working for you," Shana held back tears, but now she wanted to hug Monica, however, she couldn't, she felt as though she didn't even deserve a thank you, she was so angry and disappointed in herself.

"I'm so sorry, is there anything I can do?" as Monica was walking out, she turned and looked Shana straight in the eyes and paused.

"You catch that son of a bitch. You do what your good at, you track him down and you make him pay for what he did. You make that bastard pay for killing Jake."

"I will Monica, I will I promise."

Monica then got a hold of herself, "When you're ready to make that promise and mean it call me because that's the only case I would ever work on again."

Shana didn't know how to take it, she had initiated that Shana's promise was deceitful, that she was a liar. Shana didn't want to defend herself; Monica was angry and deep down Shana was playing the blaming game, and she was blaming herself for everything that was going wrong, this was just another one she would blame herself for. She had pushed Monica away and she let her team down.

Shana sat at her desk. She pulled out a paper from her pocket, a paper that was sent to her the day she received the package. It was a paper that she had not told a soul about, except for Dr. Marcos.

You once had a mother but like mine, she was taken.

You once had a father but like mine, he was a liar.

You once had a friend but like mine he was evil.

You once had a job but like mine, you will soon hate.

You once saw evil and then caught them, but now you let them flee.

You once heard evil, but now you turn a blind ear.

You once said evil when you spoke of me, I will show you how evil I can really be.

You will not catch me so do not try, have you ever wondered why?

Your father will not tell you, but his time will come.

You once did evil, but by killing your father it will not be evil you see it will be justice. For both you and me

We shall meet again. I promise you!

***

CHAPTER 35

*"I cannot keep turning the pages back and forth, for now,
I have no choice but to close the book."*

She read over and over it trying to get something to jump out at her, something that could help her, but all she could pick up was that her father was seen as justice to Sogoto, she wanted to know why. Sogoto may be crazy but was impressively smart at it.

Ryan then broke her concentration by barging into her office.

"They tell me I don't have a meeting today. Seems that it all has been sorted, so either your dad has some connections in really high places, or some internal corruption is seriously taking place." he vented.

"Just be grateful, with the interview out of the way, nothing on your records and you can go back to work, nice and easy." her tone was dead, showing no emotion.

"Shana, where is your heart? A detective died, one of your work employees who you have known for six years DIED, my best friend DIED, and you telling me no paperwork that's it, the case is closed…. Who are you?"

"No, that's not what I'm saying. Let me meet with Dr. Marcos and figure out a strategy, I won't let this go, but for now, we have no choice,"

"We have no choice? Bullshit Shana! We always have a choice. Something is not right here, and you have known it for a while, but you can't bear to face it, so you crawl into your little shell and believe whatever it is that pleases you."

"Ryan that's not true. What do you want me to do? I fucked up! I know," her defeated tone made Ryan grab her and hug her. It was hard to stay mad at Shana.

"You're right. Let's take a break from this case for a while, spend some time together. We can't bring them back but let's not let their deaths get in the way of us. I'm sorry baby."

"Don't be sorry Ryan. You did nothing wrong; I know I am all over the place." She hugged him back. "They…" she pointed to people upstairs "have said that if I don't take leave, I'm out of here. I'm on leave for three months. I don't know what to do, my team's broken, Jake is gone, Ryan, I'm …"

"Stop Shana. Go home fill the tub up, light some candles, get a glass of wine, soak yourself. Then get some sleep. Your leave starts now."

"You don't know but once you're in there it will relax you. Shana, I have always listened to you. I have done what you want and been your dad's slave since I fell in love with you. Please for once, listen to me."

She loved him, she leaned in and hugged him so tight. She was grateful for him, and she would do as he said, she owed him that.

"I'll see you after this shift." He hugged her one last time before he headed up the stairs back to work.

"Hey, since we both have some leave now, how about that honeymoon trip to the Maldives?" He turned on the stairs to tease her. *"Very funny!"* They both laugh trying to turn a bad situation into a good one.

Shana went into her office, grabbed a few things, and closed her door. She looked around her office as if to bid it farewell. It was a strange room, somehow it did not look like the room she was once familiar with. It had lost its warmth.

I'll see you soon; I'll be back better and stronger.

Shana was heading home. It was all surreal, she had a dream as a little girl of opening a little store by the beach. Developing photos for the locals and travelers. Looking at each happy image that was captured. Maybe that was her calling. Then she would not just leave…. She would quit!

She had no set plan for the first time.

But she truly did have one thing on her mind. One thing that she needed to do… She couldn't wait to get home to do it, and that was to sleep.

***

CHAPTER 36

"Take a stumbling rock and turn it into a steppingstone."

Present

The whole case had played back in her head like it was just yesterday. Six months has passed since she has last seen Sogoto or went back to her previous job.

Shana sits in the photoshop with the doors locked, overlooking the photos she has just come to grips with. She needs to be in control. In the past, she had let the emotions run; this time she can't let that happen.

She places the photos across the bench, placing them in order of when they were taken. She looks at each photo.

'Ok, Sogoto you want to play? Let's play.' Stretching her arms over her head, interlocking her fingers, she tips her head and stretches her neck. Shana is preparing herself for the biggest race of her life.

She walks over to where her filing cabinet was and pulls out a USB and places it on her computer. There before her eyes were all of Sogoto's cases. She couldn't go back. Her three-month leave was enough time for her to decide that. Shana left. But not without secretly placing all the information on a USB.

Sogoto was back, he had some unfinished business. Shana knows that he had her father to kill. Possibly even herself.

As Shana flicks through the photos, she focuses on a necklace that was around the victim's neck. Shana would have had that noted. She is certain that there was no necklace when the forensic team was at the crime scene. She looks closely at the photo. She has seen this pendant before she looked more closely at it as if to examine it. A beautiful perfect little horseshoe, sparking, probably white gold. Shana knows the horseshoe symbol was for good luck in many cultures. *Where have I seen you,* she thinks.

"Oh, dear God," she says out loud as she leans over and grabs the photos she had on the wall of her family. And there in front of her, was a photo of Shana at three years old sitting on her mother's lap, and before her; she could see her mother was wearing the same necklace. *Identical.* Shana places the photo with the others.

After the case, Dr. Marcos had disappeared to Paris, working on conferences, and teaching there, but Shana knows exactly where he was.

Shana can't ask Ryan for her mother's autopsy report, because he will not even be able to obtain it. She had tried while working but not even the Chief could get his hands on the file. She had thought that due to conflict of interest they would not show them. But now she knows there is more to this story than meets the eye.

Shana isn't going to call Dr. Marcos, knowing he wouldn't give her the time of the day. She is going to make him come to her.

Shana quickly looks over the photos of the crime scene, seeing if there is anything else that was distinctive.

Then she remembers Wong saying that he didn't take these photos. *He was right!* Right in the reflection of one of the photos, Shana can see that it was not Wong who is taking the photos. But she can't see who it was. He is in a suit. Wong never wore suits.

Then she looks back at Sogoto's photos. She looks closely at the photo, seeing that someone is behind the wardrobe. The light shadow on the floor gave it away. She gasps as she had figured it out. It is their daughter, their girl. She was living on campus, and she was visiting. It was clear as day!

Shana has a plan!

She jumps in her car and heads to the person that will get Dr. Marcos back into the States tomorrow. She hates what she has to do. But she knows that there is no other way.

Dr. Marco is the only one who is able to get his hands on her mother's file, and he is the only one that knows what next steps were needed to be taken.

First, get Dr. Marco, second find the girl, and the third figure out what happened to her mother.

Shana drives for what seemed hours until she was in Chino Hills. This suburb was built over hills and valleys on the borders of Orange and Los Angeles Counties. Shana remembers reading about this area many years ago. Being called 'California's best-kept secret.' She now sees why. Shana turns right into a cul-de-sac; Shana pulls in front of the house and parks her car. She takes a deep breath in. What she was about to do is so out of character. But it feels right.

She opens her glove box, and she pulls out her gun. Shana places the gun in her pant behind her back. *'Please forgive me for what I am about to do'* she speaks to her mother, Dr. Marcos, and God.

Shana makes her way into the gorgeous Tuscany home.

She knocks on the door and waits. The door is a large mahogany solid wood with a custom iron grill. Shana touches the door, having not seen anything like it.

"Hello, how can I help you?"

An elderly woman answers the door. "Hi, sorry to bother you, I was wondering if Mr. Health Bolt was here."

"That's my husband. He's out the back, come in," *country people are so hospitable.* Shana walks into the house. It is a large home. She follows the woman into the large living room where she sees a wonderful rock-carved fireplace with a large mantle. Shana looks up and sees the high ceiling fans. She continues to walk on the beautiful shining hardwood floors and sits on the sofa, while Mrs. Bolt goes out to the covered lattice patio to call her husband.

Shana is nervous. She knows all too well that this was stupid. But under the circumstance, she has no other option.

"Hello, I am Heath. How can I help you, my dear?" He answers calmly while he adjusts his glasses. He seems a few years younger than Dr. Marcos but has the same fashion sense.

"Sir, I want you to know that what I am about to ask you, is quite a lot, but I please ask that you understand where I am coming from."

Health sits down and his wife sitting close by.

"I know that you are in contract with Dr. Marcos." at this point Shana notices as the woman grabs her husband's hand, worried at what was to follow.

"Ahhh, Dr. Marcos, I'm afraid you're mistaken. I haven't heard of that name before." he gets up, clearly thinking that that was the end of the conversation. "I'm sorry we were not able to help you."

"Sit down Mr. Bolt." Shana knows he was lying.

"Sorry, young lady but you're in my house and if you don't leave, then I will have to call the police. You're mistaken, I have never heard of that name before."

Shana then pulls her gun, giving him no option. "Sit down Mr. Bolt!"

Mr. Bolt did as she orders, reaching out for his wife's hand again.

"What do you want?" Mr. Bolt asks quietly.

"I know that you are the only people that Dr. Marcos cares about, I know he has no family, and I also know that the only person he trusts a hundred percent is you, his only real friend."

"I don't know who you're talking about?" it was a plea, not a statement.

"Mr. Bolt, is your sisters' name Cecile?"

"I don't know a Cecile?" he is defensive now. *Why couldn't people just be honest?*

"Oh, but you do, we both know that Cecile was Dr. Marco's girlfriend back in college, I also know that it was Dr. Marcos who found her killer......Your sister's killer and I know that he

331

spends one month here, every year." Shana knows this is true because it is the anniversary of her death.

"We haven't seen him in three years" Heath adds, answering on behalf of his wife also.

"Oh, I know that he has been in France." She pauses a little for a dramatic effect, "But you also know that, because you call each other at least once every two days."

"I haven't spoken to him in three years. You have to believe me." Health is being protective now. *Interesting.*

"Are you sure?" Shana now stands up, directly pointing the gun at him.

"Yes, I am sure, He gave us closure, my family…. All of us when he found the killer."

"I know and I am also aware that the murderer committed suicide as well!"

"That was a good thing; he was going to hell anyway! Who cares? We don't know where he is, we are normal people living with what we have left of this world!"

"You see Mr. Bolt, I looked into the suicide; it is my job as a forensic pathologist after all. And after looking into that case, I came across some amazing information, which indicates it was not a suicide." the color drains out of his face. *Bingo.*

"That can't be true?" Mrs. Bolt speaks, knowing her husband was not capable of killing anyone.

"Oh, but ma'am, it is! You see if I was to present this newfound evidence, then the case will be reopened. They will figure out that Dr. Marcos was working on the case, and then his relationship with the victim would come into play. Do you know what that means?"

"Marcos is not that person; he would never do that!" Her voice is shrilly now.

"Oh, you are so blind, Mrs. Bolt." Shana sort of feels a little sorry for this naive woman.

"He would be the number one suspect; can you guess who would be the second in line?"

"These are just silly threats, she is making. Nancy don't listen to her!" Health is trying to convince his wife that Shana is just fabricating information.

"Oh wow! She has no idea, does she?" Shana genuinely thinks that she would have known.

"What is she talking about Heath?" Mrs. Bolt didn't know what to believe anymore.

"Are seriously listening to this crazy girl with a gun?" Mr. Bolt snaps.

"Mrs. Bolt, are you familiar with Chapman's Protocol?" Mr. Bolt stands trying to get Shana to shut up. Shana directs her gun at him.

"SIT DOWN" His wife grabs him and pulls him down.

"Well Dr. Marcos did catch the killer, and he did a great job in doing so. But that wasn't enough. After he was in jail, some people were paid off to bash him enough to get him sent to the hospital from San Quentin Prison."

"Shut up!" Health yelling, not wanting his wife to hear the rest. But Shana is determined to finish the story.

"Sit Back Down, Mr. Bolt, the next time you stand up, I will make sure that you won't be able to stand! Do you understand?" Shana's voice is louder now.

"Please, I don't know what it is you want, but we didn't do anything." His wife is borderline hysterical now.

"You didn't have anything to do with it, I know Mrs. Bolt, but your husband and Marcos had other plans."

"Health is this true? Oh God! Health, tell me she has no idea what she is talking about?"

Health doesn't say a word, his head is down, knowing that there was no way he can stop Shana from talking.

"Heath! Did you kill him?" She is in hysterics, shaking her husband by his arms, trying to get a response.

"Sit down Mrs. Bolt." Shana is letting her determination of getting Marcos here take over. She feels her empathy come back to the surface, as she gently guided Mrs. Bolt to calm down and sit.

"Heath, you flew out to San Rafael Airport, which is minutes away from Marin General Hospital that same night?"

"Oh God!" his wife is crying. Health turns to take hold of her hand to calm her down "Don't touch me! DON'T TOUCH ME!" she screams, disgusted that she is now looking at a murderer.

"Listen to me, Nancy. I could not rest until he died. You saw the crime scene photos of my sister. You saw what he did to her, a lifetime in jail was not enough. I couldn't sleep, knowing he was somewhere, he was alive! I just couldn't!"

Nancy is now sobbing. not knowing what to say. The man she has been living with all these years is a murderer.

"Who killed him? Was it you or Marcos?" Nancy needs to know.

"Nancy, it doesn't matter!" Heath couldn't answer.

"It matters to me! Who killed him?"

"It was a quick death, Mrs. Bolt. An intravenous saline drip was exchanged with the one the nurses had placed. It was then induced with a lethal injection consisting of an ultra-short-acting barbiturate in combination with a chemical paralytic. Enough to have him dead within seconds." Shana feels the need to explain.

"What do you want from us?" Heath is screaming, wanting Shana to stop talking. She knows that she has spoken too much.

"I need you to pick up that phone and explain what I just said to you to Dr. Marcos."

"What will that do?"

"You tell him, he has 24 hours to be here, or I go public with your case," she smirks and leans back in the chair.

Health gets up and goes to the phone, he must know the number off by heart. No one knows the location of Dr. Marcos. The only thing Shana was able to figure out was he was in France.

"The time differences?"

"You're seriously worried about waking him up?" Heath's wife is furious.

Health nods picks up the phone and calls Dr. Marcos. Shana watches with her gun by her side, as a reminder that she is serious.

Health explains what Shana has told him. And within minutes, he hangs up.

"He will be here on the first plane out."

"Great, now that wasn't so hard! Looks like we will sit here and wait."

"I want to be left alone!" Nancy has reached her breaking point.

"I'll be out of here the minute he arrives, and everyone can get back to their normal lives, while I continue trying to figure out mine." The last part is muttered under her breath.

"I have a roast in the oven. Can I at least check up on it and turn the oven off?"

"Great idea! Let's all make our way to the kitchen then." Shana isn't letting them out of her sight. Not until Dr. Marcos was in *her* sight at least.

Shana follows them into the kitchen. She watches as Nancy opens the oven and checks the roast; she is shaking. Shana sits on the stool while Heath sits on a chair at the dining table all in open view. His head is down as he is in deep thought.

"Are you hungry?" Nancy asks Shana, breaking the silence.

"Oh no I'm fine, but you can go ahead and eat, just pretend I'm not here."

"I don't have the appetite." she doesn't even bother asking her husband.

Nancy sits on a stool across from Shana and the silence reclaims them.

Shana knows that she had to call Ryan; he was going to pick her up at seven. She has to call Portia; she was expecting her to sleepover.

Shana picks up her phone and stands in the hallway, where both Nancy and Heath are in her line of sight.

"Hey, I was just thinking about you," Ryan answers happily.

"Me too, um Ryan I won't be able to make it tonight, something's come up."

"What's up?"

"A friend is flying in, and I have to pick them up, just got last-minute notice."

"I guess we can have dinner some other time," he sounds disappointed but before she can ask why he changes the subject. "I pulled my gun out today, nearly fired it."

"That makes the two of us." Shana's tongue beating her thought process.

"What?" Ryan asks, confused.

"Just kidding, I wanted to pull a gun at some customers." She tries to laugh it off.

"Ok, I better call and cancel our dinner reservations then," Ryan replies, not knowing what to say next. Shana feels guilty, not only is she lying, but she is also hiding information from him, but she can only hope that he will later understand.

"Love you," Shana replies softly.

"Love you too Shana,"

Shana hangs up before scrolling down to get Portia's number. She sees Nancy get up and start yelling at Heath. They are arguing back and forth. Nancy is crying and yelling, and Heath is pleading and begging for her to be understanding and forgiving.

Shana lets them continue as she calls Portia.

"What on earth is that noise?" Portia answers

"Don't ask!" Shana replies looking over as their voices got louder. "I will be coming late," Shana looks at her watch and makes a quick assumption, "probably around 5 am, and I don't want to head home. Also, in the case Dad calls, say that I am with you and sound asleep."

"Ok, what's going on?"

"Let's just say I'm bringing a guest. Do me a favor and get the guest room ready, the room that has no windows."

"Are you bringing a hostage?" Portia asks sarcastically.

"Something like that!" Shana smirks.

"I don't know what's going on, but I'm sure I will know all about it at 5 am."

"Thank you; I seriously can't answer any questions now!"

"Just be safe, Shana do you need me to come get you?"

"No, I'll be fine" as the words come out of her mouth, Nancy picks up a vase and smashes it on the floor in anger.

"I better go." Shana proposes, grimacing at the noise.

"Shana, what was that? Are you ok?"

"Yeah, it's just a lover's quarrel."

"I don't know what the hell is going on, but just be safe!"

"Always" Shana replies as she hangs up and attends to the fighting couple.

"Finished?"

They both turned their attention to her and realize they should not be fighting in front of her.

"Yum, that smells good, shall we eat? Can I help set the table?" Shana hints.

Nancy is giving Shana a deleterious stare filled with anger, but she complies as she hands Shana and Heath three plates to set up.

They sit together at the table and eat quietly. Heath finally breaks the silence.

"Can I ask why you're doing this?"

Shana looks at him, irritated and annoyed at how she has to do this to get Dr. Marcos on board.

"No, no you can't," Shana replies. "Mrs. Bolt, can you please pass the cornbread?" She tries to change the subject.

Again, silence rang as they eat. Shana gets up from the table and makes a few calls. She knows that Marcos has caught a private jet out, she knows a nonstop flight would be around eleven hours. She has a long time ahead of her.

It was getting quite dark, darker than normal, and with no streetlights, it felt as though a black cloud was on top of the Bolt's house. She steps out to the patio, looking up in the star-filled sky.

Heath comes outside to join Shana, while Nancy sits on the couch. All within Shana's eye view.

Shana knows they will not call the police, they wouldn't dare to take the risk, considering the circumstances and evidence Shana has against them.

"I moved here for this reason." He nods, noticing Shana looking up in the sky.

"It's beautiful."

"Are you going to hurt Dr. Marcos?" Heath asks, concerned.

"God NO! Listen, Heath, right now he is the only one that can help me figure out a lot of missing threads. He has the answers, the connections, and since I left…" she trails off, realizing that she has said too much.

"We all seem to find the truth, but not like this." Heath eyes the gun.

Shana then places the gun behind her back, back in her pants. "For now!" she compromises with him.

"Dr. Marcos will be here in five more hours, it's already morning. Why don't you go and get a blanket for your wife, and get some sleep here on the couch?"

Heath nods, knowing that Shana wants to be left alone.

He brings Shana out a blanket and then walks over to his wife and places the blanket on her. She holds his hand, the first step of forgiveness. Shana watches as he sat down, and she lay on his thighs. It is heartfelt.

Shana stays out on the patio, sitting on a chair looking up at the sky. She has had so much time to think to herself about Sogoto's return. She knows exactly what her next steps are.

Finding the missing girl, who Shana knows was alive and her mother's history were all too soon to be exposed. Portia's place would be perfect for all these discussions.

Shana closes her eyes, for a second, extremely tired, but not wanting to fall asleep. She drifts off dreaming, to Little Shana hugging her mom afraid to let go, not wanting to let go in case she disappeared on her again. She pulled Shana away from her and looked her straight in the eyes. *"I'm not going anywhere. I'm here; I always have been now you are ready to see."* Little Shana looked at her confused. *"To see what?"* Shana asked. Shana's mother placed her finger on her mouth,

Shana jumps up from her seat, woken up by the patio door being opened. It is Heath and right behind him is Dr. Marcos.

"Thank you." She looks at Heath, grateful that he complied, and that Dr. Marcos was here.

"I hope you didn't bring handcuffs this time?" Dr. Marcos says, reminding her of what she had done in the past.

"No, not this time Doc. This time you will not want to leave," Shana confirms.

Heath closes the door giving them both some privacy.

"You didn't have to do this; Nancy should have never known!" She knows he is disappointed in her.

"Had I not, you would not be here! no more running. Dr. Marcos, it's time to face this, to tell me everything, I'm ready."

"Are you sure?"

"You have no idea. Sogoto sent over some crime scene photos."

"I figured as much; he has unfinished business to do." He nods.

"I have all the documents in the car; we are heading to Portia's place, best if we stay there. Also, first thing 9 am, I need you to call in a favor."

"A favor?"

"I need all the information including the autopsy report on my mother."

"I can't get that for you, it's classified information." He instantly shakes his head.

"Dr. Marcos, please do not play me for a fool, The Shana that you once knew that would take your word for it, died, so you get that information, or you and Heath will spend the rest of your lives behind bars."

The older man holds up his hands.

"See, that wasn't so hard," Shana smirks.

"Shall we?" Shana uses her hand to guide him back inside to exit from the front and head to Portia's house.

"After you."

Dr. Marcos and Heath exchange some words, Nancy is sound asleep on the sofa. Shana apologizes and heads to the car.

***

Shana pulls into a petrol station and fills the car with petrol and comes back with three coffees. She gets in the car and hands the tray of coffees to Dr. Marcos.

She drives off; minutes later she parks in front of a small cozy house. Dr. Marcos is confused; he has never seen that house before. Shana gets out of the car.

"Are you coming?" Shana hints. Dr. Marcos has not moved from his seat not knowing if he was going to wait for her or come down. He holds his suitcase in between his arm and slides out while holding the coffees. Shana is not going to help him. He follows Shana into the front gates of the house. Shana raises her fist and bangs on the door.

***

CHAPTER 37

"The coming together of minds, a shared history of experience, and a hunger of fulfillment always leads to triumph."

"Ok! Ok! I'm coming!" a voice yells, approaching the door. They open the door, and there in her pajamas, her hair everywhere a messy bun and much skinnier than she was six months ago, pale and stressed, stood Monica.

"Shana, what are you doing here?" tying her hair back as she speaks and trying to fix herself up as much as she could. Shana notices the dark bags under her eyes, the sleepless nights have taken a toll on her, and it is obvious.

"Well, are you going to invite us in?" Dr. Marcos sighs.

"Oh, Dr. Marcos? I thought you were in France?"

"Well, I'm not!" the frustration in his voice is clear to Shana who tries to hold back a grin.

"Well, can we come in?" Shana insists.

"Um, well the house is a mess. How about I have a shower and meet you guys somewhere?" Monica offers, fiddling with her ratty shirt.

Shana moves her to the side and makes her way in, Dr. Marcos following closely. Monica closes the door behind them. Shana looks around and comprehends why Monica doesn't want them there.

The house is a mess, an absolute mess. To her left, she sees Jake's jacket still hanging behind the door and his work boots underneath, as if he is alive and ready for when he needed them. There are pizza boxes, ice-cream tubs, lots of empty tissue boxes, and clothes all on top of each other. The smell of something dead fills the air. Monica had given up on life when Jake had died; she no longer has anything to live for.

"Good God! What's that smell?" Dr. Marcos covers his nose with a grimace.

"Oh, I… umm… am renovating and using this room for storage. Let's…let's go into the kitchen." Monica insists, nearly dragging them through.

Dr. Marcos, covering his nose, followed them into the kitchen, only to see the same mess. Dishes that were not done and piled on top of each other, and dried food lay across the benchtops, but the smell is not as strong compared to that in the living room. Small mercies.

Shana hands the coffee over to Monica, "Get dressed. I have a proposition for you." Monica takes the coffee, had a couple of sips, before putting it down. She swallows and nods.

"Please shower first" Shana needs her to be clean and refreshed.

"Ahhh ok, yes, um I'll be quick, just stay here in the kitchen.. please." Monica nervously nods again and heads out of the kitchen.

"What on earth has happened to her?" Dr. Marcos asks curiously, turning to Shana.

"She was engaged to Jake. When he died, a part of her died too apparently."

"Well, something died in this house, that smell is not normal." Shana takes her coffee and walks around looking at all the mess. She notices the photo frames of Monica and Jake, how happy they looked. Photos of them back to their college years. Shana makes her way around the lounge room and sees a door slightly open, leading into another room; She push's the door open. Shana gasps.

"Dr. Marcos, come here!" He walks in and both look around. A rush of emotions tears through Shana. Shock, worry, and empathetic with what Monica is going through. The surprise is the overriding emotion though.

The room is covered with information from the beginning of the case to what's current. She has photos of Sogoto and cuttings of newspaper articles of information in Japan and around the world. Each case that happened and the crime scene photos all up on the wall, all in perfect order. She has photos of Shana's father, and images of the missing girl. Monica has surveillance tapes, placed at the airport. Monica has everything. Shana is shocked.

"Look here," Dr. Marcos says, pointing to a photo.

"That's Portia." Shana says looking closely. The photos are those that are taken from surveillance cameras. One is with Portia talking to a girl with only her back showing and the other is Portia with her dad.

"Why does she have photos of Portia and my dad? And why is Portia talking to my dad?" Shana is confused. "When did she do all this? She has been working twenty-four hours for the last six months?"

She is not ready to let go. Dr. Marcos was analyzing her, *Not until she has closure.*

She has collages of Jake's autopsy and crime scene photos, the report, with a note she wrote on the wall beside his photos, *'I promise to let you rest soon.'*

Shana looks around. There is John's case report, and there on the back wall is Grant's, the detailed autopsy report. Shana has chills as she reads it and then looks at the crime scene photos of Grant. Anger overwhelms her.

Shana then notices another photo that stuns her, 'My mom! How…why does she have this photo!' she murmurs. Dr. Marcos is lost in thought, gazing at the images and documents that filled the room from the floor to the ceiling and covered all four walls. Computers are set in the middle and five cameras of surveillance that she has physically placed around it.

Shana pulls down the photo of her mother, not wanting it to be in this room, and looks over at Sogoto's photo, *'Very soon, you son of a bitch,'*

"I know he is here, Sogoto is here!" Monica claims, announcing herself in the room and pulling Shana out of her musings.

"Yes, how do you know? What is all this?" Shana replies, waving a hand toward the walls.

"Sorry, I didn't want to get you into all of this, But there is so much. I'm so close Shana! We were blocked off from so much and led astray. But not being tied down, I found out things. I researched, I went undercover, I did it all and Jake will finally rest soon." Her eyes flush with indignance and anger as she fiercely holds back tears.

Shana frowns, worried about Monica's health and wellbeing. She is starting to sound a little crazy to her, but on the contrary, Dr. Marcos knew she was far from it. Monica has done her homework.

"Why is my mother's photo here?" Shana can't help but ask again.

"Oh, Sogoto made mention of her, when I was in the bathroom at the airport. I have tried so hard to get her report, but it is hidden so deep. I have tried so many contacts and even Tim…" She places her hand over her mouth, but it is too late.

"Tim is helping you with this?"

"No, no, it's just I asked him for a favor." Shana knows she was covering up, but it doesn't matter. Shana has already planned to talk to Tim. This now makes it easier.

"Ok, and the photo of Portia?" Shana points to the photo of her best friend.

Monica looks away, twisting her fingers. "Ah yes um… you see… the missing girl?"

Dr. Marcos is quick to jump in, "Let's have this conversation at Portia's house."

Shana is ahead of them, for the first time she was following her gut. Within just a couple of minutes, she has figured out where the missing girl was.

"Let's do that Dr. Marcos, you ready Monica?" Shana requests.

"Yes."

"Then let's go, well take my car. If your car looks anything like your house, then it will be much safer." Shana jokes. "Monica, is there a lock to this room?"

"Yes, there is."

"Good, then lock it for me."

"Ok," Monica replies, as she puts in a special alarm system code, and then three locks also automatically lock not letting anyone in or out of that room.

"Your house will be our meeting point since you have everything in place." Shana nods, she is impressed.

"Meeting point?" Monica questions, a tilt to her head.

"Oh, I'll explain everything very soon" Shana replies.

"Time to make that call Dr." She refers to getting her mother's documents. Dr. Marcos knows exactly what she was talking about. He grabs his phone and calls in the favor. The file will be ready for pick up late afternoon and they will not send it electronically. All is going according to plan.

"Monica, call Tim for me."

"Oh, why?" Monica hesitates

"Please just call Tim for me."

Monica takes her phone out and dials Tim's number.

"Hey Monica, how are you feeling today?" Tim askes as he answers. It was clear by the noise in the background that he was at work.

"Oh good, good, um Shana wants to talk to you."

"WHAT!" Tim panics.

Monica hands Shana the phone, hoping she is not going to yell at Tim for helping her.

"How quickly can you get fired?" Shana asks without a hello.

"Sorry?"

"Do you like where you're working now?"

"Oh, it's ok, nothing like it was, in saying that they've put me behind a desk all the time," Tim replies.

"My question is how long it will take you to get fired and get your butt to the address I'm about to send you. Sogoto is here, are you in?" Shana asks.

"Give me ten minutes," Tim replies anxiously. He sounds almost desperate to be a part of the team again.

"Good, I'll send the address. See you soon." Shana says as Tim hangs up the phone. She hands the phone to Monica, who for the first time in a very long time is smiling.

***

Tim quickly goes over to Louise who, after Shana had left, started a secret relationship with. He whispers in her ear "Shana is back in business and wants us for the Sogoto's case."

"Are you sure?" Louise questions, just as softly.

"Positive," Tim confirms.

"In that case." Louise looks around waiting for the senior sergeant to make his way to the office of the new head of the forensic unit. He was characterized as an arrogant mercenary man. Louise finds the perfect time and jumps on top of Tim. Tim falls back on his desk with everything flying off the table getting the attention of everyone in the office, including the head of the forensics unit - the new arsehole. They are passionately kissing and hugging. Those that know them well are laughing and somehow embarrassed. Tim grabs her arse, as he pulls Louise closer to his chest. Louise leans in as she guides her hand down his shirt ripping it open for all to see.

"What the hell do you think you are doing?" The boss yells furiously.

The head of the forensic unit saw how angry the boss was and knows the repercussions all too well. This will fall back on him; he quickly runs out and yells across the floor.

"You're both fired! Get out of here, now that's it!"

Louise releases her grip on Tim's crotch and Tim lets go of her backside and stands up.

"Just confirming…we are fired?" Tim asks

"YES! YES!" the boss insists.

Tim takes Louise's hand and like little kids getting caught with their hands in the cookie jar, they run out laughing. Tim stops, having forgotten something.

He lets go of Louise's hand and runs back to his desk, "You're an arsehole, and working for you has been the worst experience ever, so fuck you very much." with that he nudges his computer over the desk and runs back to Louise holding her hand and heads to their car, not believing what they had just done.

"Oh God, baby, that was so sexy," Louise says, leaning over in the car to finish what they had started.

"We have to be at this address in five minutes," Tim replies regrettably refusing the offer. Louise backs off, but is excited and put her belt on, the adrenaline was running.

"Don't you think grabbing my crotch was too much?"

"Well after you grabbed my arse, I couldn't think properly."

They both laugh hysterically.

"I love you," Tim says whimsically

"I love you too, did you see his face?" Louise replies before they cracked into hysterical laughter. They laugh the whole way to Portia's house.

***

Shana has one more person she needs to complete her team. Someone she trusted, and someone that can stay working in the police force and keep them up to date and informed.

As she pulls up to Portia's home, she notices Portia's car was in the driveway. Portia must have taken the day off. It was way past five. She gets out of the car and watches as Portia runs to the front. She sees Dr. Marcos get out of the car, followed by Monica. She is shocked, confused, and worried. She quickly goes to greet Dr. Marcos, and then Monica.

She then guides them into the house, while Shana is waiting near the car. Portia walks over to Shana.

"What's going on? I thought Dr. Marcos was in France." Portia asks.

"Oh, he was but he came back as fast as he could when he realized I needed his help, amazing man." Shana snarks.

"And Monica?"

"Oh yes and Monica, well that's a funny story." Just as Shana was going to continue, a car pulls up across the road. Out of the car come, Tim and Louise. Shana smiles as she sees the two of them. Happy they are both there and at the same time, shocked as to how quickly they got there.

"Told you it would be ten minutes." Tim laughs as he walks over to hug Shana. Shana hugs him back. Tim then shakes Portia's hand, having only met her a few times. Louise didn't have the same relationship that Tim had with Shana, so she didn't know whether to hug her or shake her hand. It was a little awkward, but resulted in a friendly hug.

"Wow, that was quick. What did you do to get fired so quickly?" Shana is curious to know.

Tim and Louise look at each other and smirk "Oh well, that's a long story,"

"Well, we seem to have a lot of those lately." Portia snarks.

"I have a phone call to make, and I'll meet you all inside soon."

The first thing Shana did is call up a cleanup unit to clean Monica's house, she wants it cleaned urgently. She knows where Monica leaves the spare key, and because it is a friend's company, they are happy to do it as soon as they had the chance. There is a locked room that she makes sure they would not go near.

Then she calls Ryan.

"Good morning Sunshine" he answers

"Good morning my dear," Shana replies, "It's that time, are you good to go?"

"Now! Are you sure?" Ryan questions. *"Do you have the team?"*

"All are here and a surprise addition," Shana replies

"Surprise addition?" Ryan parrots.

"Louise!" Shana exclaims.

"Can you trust her?" Ryan is apprehensively

"I can, I kind of knew she would come along on the ride as of last year."

"But Shana, Dr. Marcos is in France, did you want me to find a way to get him back here?" Ryan asks softly.

"All done and dusted. He's here right now, and this time I promise you he isn't going anywhere!"

"Ok, let me do what I need to do, and I'll be there in a couple of hours,"

"Ok," Shana replies, aware that there are a few phone calls he needs to make and arrange a few things.

"Ryan, meet us at Monica's house, you won't believe what she has been up to!"

"Ok, um, yes I remember where she lives. Ok done. Baby be safe! Oh, and be easy on Portia, you know it's not her fault!"

"I know, I know!" Shana replies as she hung up, she has been waiting to finally confront her. She is eager to hear her side of the story.

Shana messages a number that was not in her phone book, a number she memorized, embedded deep in her mind. *'It's on,'*

She quickly got her reply *'OK.'* It was clear, concise, and simple. Shana heads inside to where everyone was settling in.

***

CHAPTER 38

*"United, we can make it happen. Divided,
we can make it fall apart"*

Dr. Marcos is in a corner talking to Portia, while Monica, Tim, and Louise sit together. It is just as she had expected. As soon as Shana walks into the room, they all stop. It is now filled with silence, all eyes glazed toward Shana for some guidance, a plan, and a better understanding as to why they are all here in one room and together.

"Sit down please." She points to the lounge chairs in the lounge room.

They all made their way to the lounge room, as Portia passes Shana, she whispers "I need to talk to you!"

Shana whispers back "I already know! Please sit down!"

Portia's face turns slightly pale, but she listens and sits down.

"We have been assigned a special case, off the record. As of now, we are not working for the police department, the FBI, or the CIS. We are directly working with the government." Shana begins.

"You have all been placed under surveillance, and will be followed in all that you do, not only for your protection but also to make sure you're all on the right track." Louise looks up confused.

"Yes, even you Louise," Shana confirms as Louise nods, a little excited that she got to be a part of a specialized force.

"Shana, I'm a clinical therapist, I probably should not be here," Portia mentions, not wanting to be a part of what was taking place.

"Oh, but you are Portia. Monica, would you like to explain to Portia why she is essential to this case?"

"Oh um, I am not sure," Monica replies uncomfortably, not wanting to get in between their friendship.

"Oh, Monica yes you are sure! Please go ahead; since we will all be working together, there will be no secrets." Shana insists, the gleam in her eye sending shivers down their spines.

"Portia is the link to the missing girl. Only Portia and your father know where she is." Monica explains, rushing.

"Shana, I'm sorry. Your father said we need to have kept it a secret for hers and your safety I wanted to tell you." Portia replies anxiously.

"Sit down, Portia," Shana instructs. Portia sits down, knowing that everything is about to be out in the open.

"Portia was under direct orders of my Father and Detective Grant. Sogoto's so-called team found out that there was an additional member of the last family killed, and were afraid that she had seen something, so she was hunted down. The girl was afraid and having studied psychology at university she had figured out an escape, which would be to admit herself. However, doing that would cause some sort of alarm bells, so the girl tried to kill herself, just enough to just get her to the hospital. Then knowing the symptoms of diagnosis for a schizophrenic patient, she put her acting skills to use. Fortunate for her, being isolated in a hospital and locked up was her only protection, she would be fed, sheltered, and no one to find her. Further, this gave her a vital time to try and forget what she had witnessed."

Tim and Louise are visibly shocked; however, Portia, Dr. Marcos, and Monica are not.

Shana looks around and continues "But here is something you didn't know. Sure, you all assumed the girl fled because of what she had heard happen to her family. This is where you're wrong." Shana takes out some photos. Knowing Monica is the expert, she hands them to her, and asks, "Can you see what I see?"

Monica jumps up as everyone leans over to look at the photo, no one can see anything other than the crime scene and Sogoto's hand.

"What is it?" Tim asks agitated.

"Look there the cupboard; there is someone behind there. Shana, if I could get a hold of my machine, I could find out who it is!" Monica pleads, she knows she had something.

"No need to, I'm certain it's the girl," Shana replies as Portia looks up shocked as to what she is hearing,

"There is a plan in a way, but this is the time where I need to know if you're in or out!" Shana states sharply.

Portia and Dr. Marcos place their hands up as to want to discuss their way out of the situation.

"Oh, sorry I'm talking to Monica, Tim, and Louise. You two have no other choice."

They both put their hands down, looking at each other. This new strong character of Shana is too strong for them.

The team nods.

"Get what you need and meet me at Monica's house in two hours. I'll explain everything there. Also, you will all be given your protection wear and guns. Welcome back." Shana instructs with a nod.

Monica runs up to Shana, and embraces her with a hug, "Thank you, thank you,"

"Thank you, Monica," Shana replies as tears glaze her eyes.

"Well, I better get home and clean the place up," Monica replies, ready to take off, waving at Tim to drop her off.

"I took care of that," Shana yells out, letting her rest at ease. Monica runs back and hugs Shana tightly.

Shana returns the kind gesture and pats her gently and then the three of them were off, except Dr. Marcos and Portia. There are vital issues that need to be discussed and Shana has never seen them so nervous. It is quite invigorating.

"Shana, I wanted on so many occasions to tell you, but I don't know how I couldn't!" Portia stammers.

"I know Portia, sit down." Portia sits down, attentively listening to what Shana was going to say next "Now this is the part that I don't understand. What was it that my dad and Grant had on you that you felt the need, or even feared to share this information with me?"

Portia looks at Dr. Marcos for some guidance; he nods his head, reassuring Portia she was right, and it is time to inform Shana of the truth. Dr. Marcos got up and makes his way to the back of the house.

"I'm going to go to the yard for a little bit, you both have some catching up to do." Dr. Marcos insists as he pats Portia's shoulder assuring her it was ok to talk.

Shana lets him walk out "What's he talking about Portia?" Shana questions.

"Oh God, where do I start?" Portia replies, unstrung with the situation she was in. "Eight years ago, I traveled to Italy, you remember?"

"Yes," Shana knowing that they were going back in time,

"Remember how I told you I met a man, an amazing man, and we had a two-week romance like no other?"

"Yes, I remember, his name was Paul, right?"

"Yes - Paul," Portia says as her eyes watered up as if she was extremely disappointed in herself.

"And so, what?" Shana replies impatiently

"Well little to my knowledge, it was Paul Strand."

"Paul Stand! Oh, Dear God Portia! Wasn't he married then?" Shana says, loudly.

"I honest to God didn't know. He was a senator then, and I had no idea. No idea!"

"Senator? You're talking about our President here! A married man with four children! Portia, what were you thinking?" Shana yells back.

"I didn't know, honest to God. I was happy traveling, being free, and when I had met him, he was older with a lot of wisdom and maturity. He never once mentioned he was married, and I did not ask, it's not something you ask. There was no ring, there was no sign!" Portia cries sincerely hurt, and in defensive mode.

She sees the disappointment on Shana's face.

"I was embarrassed and when greedy strangers began approaching me, first with bribery, secondly with money, I was running out of options. I didn't know what to do! So, I met with your father, and Detective Grant was there, and I told them my situation, I told them I needed help and to keep it from you!" Portia recounts.

"What happened?" Shana is eager to know

She laughs and cries at the same time "Well they stopped people bribing me, and all the evidence, the negatives of the photos were collected and destroyed, and for a while, I had no headaches. Shana, I was starting to feel safe."

"And then?" Shana askes.

"And then the issue with Detective Grant, and your dad and……. I am so sorry Shana." Portia stops unsure to continue; she doesn't want to talk badly about her best friend's father.

"Go ahead," Shana responds.

"Well, your dad held those photos and negatives hostage, and when they needed me to cover for them, they betrayed me. I had to clarify time and time again that all these perpetrators were not insane just to get them in jail and not the mental institute. Shana that wasn't it, I had to speak to the lawyers, get them their warrants, I had to comply, or those photos would hit all newspaper and air broadcasts." Portia pauses wiping the tear that rolls down her cheek "I had no choice, Shana."

Shana leans in as Portia who is now crying hysterically, "I'm so sorry, I'm so sorry."

"I promise to get those photos and negatives and burn them."

"Thank you!"

"Do you know anything about my mother's death?"

"Your mom?" Portia asks, her lack of knowledge clear on her face. Shana sighs.

"You don't, a part of me wished you did, but I'm kind of glad because I would have been furious if you were hiding that from me!"

"What about your mom, Shana?" Portia pulls away to wipe her eyes and cheeks.

"Somehow, there is a link. Portia, everything my father has been telling me is a lie, my whole life. She never died from cancer!"

"WHAT?" Portia exclaims.

"I'm sure of it, I don't remember a hospital, and I don't even remember a proper funeral, do you?"

"There was a gathering at the house, she wanted to be cremated. I remember a golden vase with her ashes."

"Yes, I remember that, but we never saw a body!"

"You're right Shana, we never even went to the hospital!" realization dawns on her face.

"It's killing me; do you think she just might still be alive?" Shana hoping she is right

"Wishful thinking my darling, I doubt it very much. There is a death certificate in her name."

"Have you seen it?"

"Well, no! But I know how I can check."

"Don't worry, I got Dr. Marcos on top of it." Shana waves her hand.

"By the way how did you get him here, how did you find him?"

"Let's just say that unfortunately at this point I seem to have my dad's genetics of bribery."

Portia frowns.

"We have a lot to do Portia."

Portia agrees, "What did you want to do with the girl?"

"I was thinking of using her as bait, we have no other alternative. If we go looking for Sogoto then we are doing what he wants us to do, so we make him alter his plans. This will place him in an uncomfortable position. In saying that Portia, we need to make it appear as though some media reporter got hold of vital information about the girl. He will have to stop and get rid of the girl. He needs a dramatic ending to his story and killing the girl, in the end, is not as dramatic."

"You're right, but Shana this girl has been through enough."

"Portia, she can lock herself therefor the rest of her life or do something that could potentially let her live again. I agree it will be hard, but you need to trust me on this. I have given it a lot of thought." Shana places both her hands on Portia's. This is the only way.

"I don't know Shana; she's fragile and hasn't spoken a word in six months. When someone is in the room, it's pure silence, but when she's alone she mumbles to herself, and the nights are worse. You can hear her cries across the hallway!"

"She will be ready! Nevertheless, Portia, a life lived in fear is a life half lived. She deserves a chance to get out of there. If we don't use her Portia……. It will never end!"

They both get up and head toward the back door where Mr. Marcos is located, he turns as he heard the door open. *"Is it safe to come in?"*

"It sure is Dr," Shana advises as Dr. Marcos walks his way back from the yard.

"Good, now all we need is a lot of luck," he replies.

Just as he finishes his sentence, a bird poops on his head.

Shana and Portia laugh as Dr. Marcos gently touches the cold paste on his head. "Is that good enough luck for you?" Shana says as she continues laughing hysterically, trying to get the words out.

"Yes, very funny." Dr. Marcos replies getting a handkerchief out from his pocket and lightly smirking at the two of them as he makes his way past them both to get inside as they continue to laugh.

***

CHAPTER 39

"Take the time to go against the plan, for the strategy that's being plotted is out of your hand"

They arrived at Monica's house, the smell of vanilla filled the air, and everything was cleaned perfectly. It is all back in place. Perfect. The only thing that didn't change was Jake's jacket still hanging on the back of the door and his boots lay straight against the wall near the entrance door. Her house now looks much bigger, brighter, and inviting. It was a work progress.

"Thank you." was the first thing Monica says to Shana as she invited them in.

Right behind her were Dr. Marcos and Portia. Minutes later, Tim and Louise arrive.

Monica pulls some hot muffins out of the oven and places them on the table she unlocks the white door and nods at Shana lets her know that they are all welcome to enter her secret chamber when ready.

A loud knock at the door startles Monica, given that she assumed all involved were present. Shana gets up to open the door, everyone observed as these two men dressed in black suits, earpieces in the ear, and a gun by their belts walked in carrying two large boxes in their hands. One was of African American descent and much older than the white man. They place the boxes on the floor and then take off their glasses as they greet Shana and came further into the house.

Everyone stood up, unknowing who these two men were. Just as Shana is about to close the door, another man appears. It was Ryan.

Shana was happy everyone was here. It was now time to start.

"Please introduce yourselves," Shana instructs as she turns to the two men that had just entered.

"My name is Walt, and this is my partner Steve. We are working directly with the international and local federal governments. Our job is to catch this son of a bitch and kill him. The catching part has not worked for eleven years, so we have corresponded a team, this team we have called 'Wise Monkey' ironic I know, but we want to outsmart him. For that purpose, this team now includes everyone in this room, with direct orders from our President and Vice President." Portia looks over at Shana when this is mentioned, Shana knows what she is thinking but looks back listening to the two men.

Shana has full trust in these two men. They both have given their lives to the job, refused to get married, have a relationship, or any form of human contact, knowing that in this job it would be used as a weakness. They were somewhat like robots, well trained, and determined to focus on the target at hand with no distractions. The perfect person for this kind of job. Shana knows that even though they have been trained to control emotion, that these two did care, they know Shana and have worked with her in the past. They care enough to take a bullet for her especially after she helped get them to where they are. She is now calling in her favors.

"In the past, we have been building a stronger case with the help of Shana, and the only reason we have agreed to this is because of Shana. To be honest you're all most likely to die." Walt is a brutally honest kind of guy, and it showed in his tone.

"Walt?" Shana snaps not wanting him to scare her team when what he was saying was probably true.

"Anyway," Walt continues, ignoring her. "We have provided you with badges under that of the FBI in case you need to get into places or in need of help. You find guns in the boxes, bulletproof vests, and all the other toys that come with protecting yourself."

"We will be watching from a distance, and when the time comes, we will intervene, we will be there, but we will not jeopardize our case, so if one of you wants to play hero, you're on your own. It's an embarrassment that he has been around this long."

"We have been sitting and waiting until his return, this time is now, we don't get another chance, once he has finished what he needs to do, there is no need for him to come back."

"May God be with you all." Steve' deep firm voice adds,

"How do we call you?" Louise questions as she jumps up.

Walt replies, "You don't contact us, we contact you and we will find you. The government agency has a microchip embedded in all the products we will leave behind, so we would know exactly where each person is at any specific time. We definitely will be looking out for you"

"You have all signed yourselves over to us, you no longer work for anyone else. Once this is over, you will all be given your lives back and cleared of any doings, the Vice President has given you the green light. We don't think this will happen and advise you to take up life insurance, but Shana believes otherwise."

"Thank you Steve," Shana cuts in not wanting any negative energy in the place. "We will be fine; I've got this from here."

"May God be with you all," Walt and Steve add as they turn around, heading out toward the entrance door, as they got to the door Walt mutters *"They're crazy?"*

Shana quickly closed the door behind them, and walks back in, "Are we good to go Ryan?"

"Are you?" Ryan replies.

"More than you'll ever know!"

"Then everything is in place!" Ryan assures Shana.

"Ryan will be working with us; he will however not be with us. He will keep an eye on what's happening internally and provide us with what information we need. The government will help with protecting us but will not provide us with everything, but that's fine we have what we need, and we know how to get what we want."

"This is the last time I will ask; I need to make sure you're all in. Walt is right, there is a high risk that our lives are on the line, but if we work together and build a strong team, then there's no reason we can't catch this son of a bitch This is your life, your choice."

Monica is the first to stand up, "I'm in" straight after her was Ryan, followed by Tim and Louise. All eyes were now on Portia.

"I wouldn't want to be anywhere else, I'm in." Portia knows she has to do this, anything for Shana.

All turned their attention over at Dr. Marcos and a second later, he confirms his decision "Oh what the hell, I probably only have a few years to go anyway."

"So, you're in?" Shana smiles.

"Yes, yes, whatever I'm in!"

***

They eat warm muffins and sit around Monica's secret chamber bombarded with Sogoto's work. Each goes through the case from beginning to end. Shana needs to refresh their minds and let them know what Sogoto was up to. Along the way, Shana answers any questions they had. By the time three am rolled in, they have spent the whole day exercising and understanding Sogoto's mind.

Shana then sends them all home and they had plans to meet the next day.

Dr. Marcos is also going to meet a friend of his tomorrow morning to pick up the files he has requested and meet them later. Everyone has left except for Shana and Monica.

Shana has told Portia that she will spend the night at Monica's place since Dr. Marcos had taken her car and she has a few things to go over. Portia needs to show up to work tomorrow and place in her annual leave; her excuse was that she was taking her long-awaited vacation. Monica is packing some of the pizza boxes that they had ordered for the team and cleaning up.

"I know why you wanted to stay behind Shana."

"I just wanted to keep you company!" Shana says guiltily. *Was she that obvious?*

"You want to talk about Jake? Or is it your mother?" Monica asks.

"Do you want to talk about those things?" Shana returns the question, not wanting to force information out of her.

"Not tonight, not now. Please." Her voice is quiet and almost childlike in her negative response.

"Ok, then that's what it will be." Shana knows the time will come when she opens freely it was without a doubt a sensitive topic. It is only a matter of time.

"I have placed a couple of sheets and pillows on the sofa for you,"

"That will be perfect," Shana replies, thankfully for Monica's kind generosity.

"Is there anything else you need?"

"No, I'll be fine. You get some sleep we have a long day tomorrow."

"Ok, good night, oh and thank you!"

"Good night Monica." Monica has nothing to be thankful for; Shana makes her way into the room and looks at all the photos. She glances over and over and then pulls out the photo of her mother from her pocket.

"What is it, Mom? What is it that has you coming up in this case?" she spoke quietly to herself.

Shana is exhausted. She messages Ryan, wishing him the sweetest of dreams and thanking him for being there for her before she fell into a deep sleep.

They all need their rest. Tomorrow is going to be momentous.

***

CHAPTER 40

"Fear is to be hiding as living is to be exposing"

She quickly runs up to Ryan "This is it?" pointing to the file in his hand. Ryan hesitantly nods.

She takes the file and was heading back into the house when Dr. Marcos calls her.

She turns around and he throws her the car keys. She catches them and nods, knowing that it was best she was alone. She fast paces anxiously toward her car and opens the door, her hands shaking. She places the folder on her lap.

Shana takes a big breath in and slowly opens the file; she sees her mother's body and quickly closes the file. She lets out a sob, slamming her hand on the steering wheel. She then gets a hold of herself, knowing that she needed to be strong. Again, she takes a deeper inhale and softly exhaled.

She wipes her tears and opens the file. It is a two-page typed-up document with not much information and three photos.

Shana looks over the medical examiner's report.

Her once beautiful mother, in the white dress. On the contrary, these photos depicted anything but white and purity, rather the photos showed the dress as muddy and dirty. Shana places her fingers, gently over her mother's face. She looks closely at how pale she looked. How beautiful she was.

Cherie Watson and next to it the information about her, from weight 121.25 Ibs to height 5'2" to time of death.

The woman's body was found by hikers about twelve hours from the home at Oak wide Picnic Area, CA. Clothes still intact.

Time of death: estimated three days twelve hours from the time of body found.

The body is that of a healthy white adult female. The scalp hair is curled and long. The conjunctiva are white and shows no petechiae. There is light blood in the nose and the left ear canal. The inside of the mouth is in good condition. The neck is unmarked, showing no signs of strangulation. The chest is of normal contour with breasts unmarked, still wearing undershirt and underwear.

The abdomen is flat and unmarked. The genitalia area represents those of a healthy average adult female and shows the pubic hair to be shaved. The extremities are symmetric and otherwise unmarked. The back is otherwise, unmarked.

Medical examination report

1. *BLUNT FORCE trauma to the back of the head, close to temporal results from head hitting object or object hitting head. The blow produced a crushing effect on the human skull.*

2. *multiple bruises and abrasions extending over her arms, bruising on her arms indicate she was grabbed*

with great force enough to leave a bruise while alive hence the struggle.

Cause of death and Conclusion - determined that the cause of death was blunt force trauma to the head.

Body Identified by husband George Watson.

Shana closes the file. Her mother was murdered. Shana knows too well that this was *not* the work of Sogoto and the fact that her father has hidden this from her scared her. Shana is starting to wonder if he knows anything more. Why was her mother alone in a park and why was she missing for three days? It just didn't sound right. Who closed the case and why?

Shana has so many unanswered questions and it seemed to be more the case since Sogoto had come into her life. Shana knows she has to catch Sogoto, he has information about her mother, and she would be exposing it all to the surface quite soon. If there is somehow a link between Sogoto and her mother's death, she is going to make sure she finds out about it.

Shana grabs her mother's photo and smiles. *I promise you, Mom, I'll find out who did this, I promise you, I will make them pay.*

She places the photo back in the file and got out of the car. She needs to get in contact with the girl. It's time to send out Sogoto's bait and be ready to reel him in.

***

"Portia, you and I are heading to see the girl. Tim, I need you to copy the photos of someone in the cupboard without Sogoto's hands. I want them crystal clear; I also want photos of the girl with her family at different stages of their lives." Shana instructs.

"Consider it done," Portia replies.

"Louise, I need you to find a safe house not far from here, and then call this number," Shana hands her a card "I want you to go with them and set surveillance around the inside and outside of the safehouse, I want it in every room."

"Ok, it's on," Louise responds, taking the card.

"Monica, I need you to relocate Detective Grant's family to another place, as far as possible. Better yet, try to relocate them to another country. They need a new safe house. Sogoto knows where they're located; he wouldn't be here unless he had the answers."

"Ok." Monica answers getting her hands straight on the computer to get things done.

"Dr. Marcos, I need you to find me a journalist who is easily manipulated and wants to make it big and fast. Someone who is not cautious and probably easily convinced, I need him to meet us this afternoon at some isolated café place. Not here!"

"I have the easiest job," Dr. Marcos smiles, clearly having someone in mind already.

"Oh Doc. since that won't take so long, can you have another look at this file? See if anything else pops up?" Shana hands him her mother's file, trusting him with it.

Everybody moves to what they are assigned to do, and Shana and Portia head out.

"We'll take my car," Portia says, not giving Shana a choice. It was a good idea because Shana isn't in the mood to drive.

"Is everything ok? Dr. Marcos told me about the file." She asks once they are in the car.

"Yeah, it's all good. She was murdered, Portia." Shana can't help being a little cold to Portia.

"I'm so sorry Shana; I don't know what else to say."

"Makes the both of us, I will find out everything and soon. I just know it."

"Did they catch who did it?"

"No, and that's just it, they stopped looking, the case was closed, it's like nobody cared"

"Doesn't sound like your father to close that case?"

"My thoughts exactly, but for now let's focus on getting Sogoto."

"Speaking of which, Shana, I think going to see this girl is a waste, she has not spoken in six months, not a single word, and she has placed herself in a different world,"

"She will speak, I just know it." Shana is determined. She doesn't know how, but all she knows is that there was no other option.

"Shana, I have been doing this for years, it's not that easy."

"Please, all I ask from you is to get me in the same room she's in and leave us alone. That's all." Her tone is slightly irritated and hurt. Shana is unable to fathom that Portia has held information from her.

"Ok, I'll get you in, but I'm going to be watching from the other side. Shana, I don't want this girl more traumatized than she already is."

"Do what you have to do, but no one else Portia I mean it."

"Ok!" Portia pulls into the hospital and parks her car at the front. They both got out and head to the fifth floor.

She walks into Portia's work and heads toward the psychiatric ward. It is isolated and dark, locked off at every corner. There is no way a person could get in or out without someone knowing. It felt creepy and uncomfortable.

"Wait here." Shana waits in the hallway, Portia swipes her card, and seconds later walked out with a young lady, very slim, wearing white pants and a white loose blouse, her hair looks as though it hadn't been brushed in years. She looks fragile. The girl takes hold of Portia's hand, afraid of coming into the hallway. It looks as though she has never been out of her room.

"It's ok, come with me." Portia then swipes the door of the safe meeting room across the hall and made her walk in, the girl realizing that Portia was about to leave her got angry. Then all of a sudden she turns and just as she was about to attack Portia, she is quick to push her in and lock the door.

"You seriously want to go in there?" Portia asks, seeing Shana has noticed the girl nearly attack her.

"More than you know" Shana rolls her neck as if she was getting ready for a physical fight.

"Shana, she is filled with rage, she took a bite of a nurse's arm last week."

Shana laughs at the thought of it.

"You're just as crazy as she is, it will probably be good watching the two of you fight, I should have ordered in some popcorn." she shakes her head, slightly smirking

"Very funny."

"Seriously listen to me, I am watching everything. Take this," she leaned over and gave her a small needle, "If she gets out of hand inject her with this, this will calm her down and put her to sleep" Portia instructs cautiously

"I don't need it." Shana gently moves Portia's hand gently out of the way.

"Please, just take it!" Shana takes it and places it in her pocket, knowing that she won't need it.

Shana leans into her back pocket and pulls out her handcuffs, "I have these, if need be, I'll use them, I don't want her falling asleep on me,"

"Fine, whatever just be careful."

Shana looks in through the little window, the girl is pacing up and down the room, clearly uncomfortable. The only thing in the room is a table and two chairs all bounded to the floor, the tables had no hard-edge surface. Shana thinks how good it would be to have a room like this in the police station.

Shana pulls out a file from underneath her blouse, she had not wanted Portia to see what she has brought with her. Portia would have given her a headache on ethics, and now is not the time.

Shana walks into the room. The girl is afraid and walks back quickly to the corner of the room, shrinking in the corner. Shana's heart sinks. The girl is terrified.

"Hey Karen." the girl is covering her face as if to make herself disappear.

"Karen, we both know you're not crazy, traumatized maybe but not crazy."

With no word from Karen, Shana places the file on the table and keeps herself on the other side of the room.

"His name is Sogoto." Shana continues as Karen began to rock slightly, her head shaking, and her knees bent, covering her chest.

"The man that killed your family, his name is Sogoto. Karen, I am so sorry you witnessed what you did, but you have the opportunity to help us catch him now."

There was no verbal response or reaction, but Shana knew with the stillness of her rocking that she was listening.

"I also saw him cut a good friend of mine to pieces. I saw what he did to him, and I couldn't do anything, I couldn't save him. But I have been given a chance now to do something, to put their deaths to ease, to stop him from doing it again and to make him pay for what he did" Shana pauses, the images of Grant surfacing, then continued,

"I don't know how much you saw, but I am sure it's all fresh in your head. It wasn't just your family," Shana opens the file and distributes it in front of Karen right at her feet. It is photo after photo of crime scenes of Karen's family and other victims, the children the mothers, and the fathers. She is pulling all possible strings. Desperate times called for desperate measures.

Karen kicks the photos away, pushing herself deeper in the corner, crying and hitting her head, she was yelling louder and louder as she would glance at the photos. Until suddenly she gets up and launches herself onto Shana, trying to bite her and hit her. Shana finds herself suddenly on the floor with Karen on top of her.

Shana quickly grabbed both her hands and turned her over putting Shana on top. Shana is now sitting on top of her and holding both her hands down. Portia then opens the door, running to Shana's aid.

"Oh, we're fine thanks, just getting to know one another." Portia took that as her sign to leave Shana alone and headed back to the room, worried. Shana knows there would be a conversation between them later about this.

Karen was trying to kick her way out; Shana lets her continue before she is too tired and gives in.

"Listen, you can spend the rest of your life hiding here, but what do you get? What life is that? I lost my mother when I was three years old, and the biggest disappointment to her would have been me giving up on my life. So, wake the fuck up! You have a chance to get the son of a bitch who killed your family, to go back to college, to fall in love and make your parents happy!" Shana hisses "Do you think this is what they wanted?"

"You're a chicken and a coward," Shana whispers as the girl's tears rolled heavily down her cheeks.

"I promise to look after you, I promise to protect you!" She doesn't know whether to play good cop or bad cop roles, she just needs Karen on her side.

"Your brother and parents couldn't save themselves and you can't blame yourself that's pathetic. There is nothing anyone could have done to stop him that night! Not even Roger!"

Karen is crying excessively, that Shana lets go of her hands and got up off her, she picks up the photos of the floor as Karen continues to cry.

"I don't need you. You're too weak anyway, you're too much of a coward to get justice done for your family."

Shana knows that would trigger a response, and she is right.

"He was only six years old, only six!" Shana smiles quietly to herself and turns back to face Karen, as she is lying on the floor, in the opposite direction of Shana.

Shana knows very well that she has no other alternative, she has to leave there with Karen on board, and she is determined to try everything.

"Six years, old. Who kills a six-year-old?" Shana comes closer to her.

"It was late, my brother called me on the phone and told me to come home, he heard Mom and Dad screaming, I was only minutes away. I caught a cab and climbed the tree to surprise him in his room." Karen stumbles over her words – it was clear she hasn't spoken in six months.

"He wasn't there, I heard more screams, I walked in on my dad, he was still alive, on the floor bleeding and tied to the leg of the bed. The man was chasing my mother, and I could hear her fighting for her life downstairs, my knees wouldn't move. I heard him coming up the stairs. My dad kicked my legs back into action. His eyes were telling me to go into the cupboard. I went in quickly, just quickly enough for him not to notice me there. I...I watched it all." she pauses, voice growing thick, before clearing it and carrying on, "I watched it all, I didn't blink, I didn't turn away. I punished myself for not helping, I couldn't move."

She rolls over and looks at Shana, "I saw everything he did, and I saw his face and his smile as he did it, but I thought that that was it. While he was killing my dad, do you want to know what I was thinking?"

Shana nods "I was thinking about how I would look after my brother, how I would tell him that none of this happened. How I would take him away, and make sure that he lives, how I would make my parents proud!"

Shana's eyes water up; it was overwhelming for her to remember back.

"Who kills a child, who kills a woman, why did he kill my dad?"

Shana leans in as Karen lunges and hugs Shana, crying hysterically, both now sitting on the floor and in each other's arms.

"He was six years old, I told him to wait in the room!"

"Let it out Karen, let it all out." Shana hugs her tighter, letting her get it all off her chest.

"He went into my brother's room. Why oh God why couldn't I move, I couldn't move, I heard Uncle Roger get shot. I heard his voice. I... I heard everything, and I couldn't move. After everything was silent and I heard the back door close, my knees fell to the floor, I got up and ran to my father. He was dead, my brother was gone, and then my mother, and Uncle Roger... I grabbed my bag from my brothers' room, and I kissed him goodbye, and I ran to my car and drove and drove."

Shana has to ask, "Why did you come in a taxi but leave in your car?"

"My dad was changing the brake pads for me; he was going to drop it off the next day." She heaves a heavy sigh. "They were good people; I know they would never have done anything to deserve this."

"You're right, Karen, they didn't deserve it."

"My parents need to know what I have done with my life, the pathway I have chosen, I want to make them proud, tell me what to do!"

Karen stands up, wiping her face, and takes a deep breath. "Enough of this shit, I should not be the one behind bars!"

"Ok, Karen, I'm going, to be honest with you. Usually, under different circumstances, I would use you as bait without you knowing, but under these circumstances, I'm telling you!" She tells her, wanting to be upfront and honest.

"Him knowing you're alive, means he will be after you."

"He will kill me!" She moves to go back into the fetal position

"No that's where your wrong, look at me. Please look at me. I need you to trust me, I need you to know that I am making a promise to you that I will not let him hurt you!"

"How can you be certain?" Karen hesitates.

"Because I know how his brain works," Shana answers confidently.

"If I do die, I die trying and I get to go to my family, I have nothing else to lose and more so nothing to live for." She slowly relaxes out of the fetal position.

"You're not going to die. You're going to make it, and you're going to live."

"OK." Karen replies, holding firmly onto Shana, feeling protected and finally alive "On one condition, I want all of Sogoto's files; I want to read everything he had done!"

"I don't think it's a good idea," Shana replies, not wanting to scare Karen off.

"It's not negotiable," Karen demands,

Shana needs Karen; there was no alternative "Ok."

"I need you to promise!" Karen instructs.

"I promise."

"Ok."

"Now, go get washed. I'll send over some proper clothes, and we will pick you up tomorrow afternoon. I want to take you to a safe house, but currently, they're setting up surveillance and making sure it's all protected."

"Ok."

They both get up and head to the door. Portia opens the door, her eyes bloodshot red from all the crying she just did. Just as Karen is going back to her room, she runs up to Shana and hugs her one last time. Portia has to turn around; she is too emotional. Shana also tries to be strong.

Shana and Portia head to the car; It was nearly time to meet the journalist and Dr. Marcos.

"You shouldn't have promised her she was going to be ok," Portia mumbles, trying to be a realist.

"Oh, but I am. I also think a thank you is in order!"

"Sorry, for what exactly?" Portia blinks.

"For making her talk!" Shana exclaims.

"Please, you shouldn't have had those photos, and also I'm serious that you should not have promised her she will be ok."

"She will! Let it go."

"SHANA!"

"Portia not now, please!" Shana can't let emotion get the best of her, the way she had in the past. She is trying so hard to be cold. She places her hands on the steering wheels and grips tightly.

"Fine, I'm just saying!"

"Well, don't!"

Shana's phone rings all in perfect timing; any more talk between the two could have ended up in a significant argument.

"Hey, Ryan,"

"Hey Shana, I spoke to Dr. Marcos about your mothers' report. I brought up some information that may be of interest, but I want to see you ALONE."

"Ok I am meeting with Dr. Marcos and the journalist in thirty minutes, how about an hour from now? I haven't had any lunch."

"Lunch is good; I'll pick you up from Monica's place?"

"No, I'll meet you there, how about that Italian place we used to go to?"

"Ok perfect."

"I'll see then,"

"I love you."

"Me too" Shana replies, not having the energy to repeat the words. She is all cried out and emotionally drained.

***

They arrive at Monica's house a little while later.

"I'm going to head home for a bit, get changed, and then meet Dr. Marcos."

"Do you want me to come?" Portia asks.

"No, this will be fine, but I need you to get Karen discharged from the hospital. Can you do that for me?"

"I'll have it done today. Am I coming along tomorrow?"

"No Portia, it's safer if you just stay put for now. You have done more than enough,"

"Ok, well, I'll head home to get those papers done."

"Thank you," Shana replies. As Shana and Portia finish their conversation, Dr. Marcos makes an appearance.

"Right on time." Shana opens the door for Dr. Marcos, he jumps in the passenger seat.

"Did you get those images from Tim?" he asks.

"Yes, and the information regarding the case, Sogoto's picture and…" Shana replies before Dr. Marcos interrupts.

"You called me a thousand times when you were home, and I told you I would get them it's all here!"

"OK, no need to be so jumpy Doc."

"Oh, Shana, you make a normal person insane."

"Now, please tell me about the journalist?"

"He has a few contacts in the New York Times, also well-known in Los Angeles but more so for his commercials, not his journalism."

"What commercials has he done?" Shana asks curiously.

"That doesn't matter" he waves his hand "The point is he figured out that, acting wasn't for him, and he kind of is trying to get his integrity back. He is excited to meet you."

"He knows that my name has to remain confidential and anonymous, right?"

"Well not as the person who contacted him, but he will mention that you oversaw the case. Not having your name in the article would only trigger Sogoto to think negatively that you were involved in getting this information out deliberately."

"Good point" Shana nods in agreement. She had not thought of that.

"Even if he bad mouths you, you just have to take it." Dr. Marcos says, giving her a warning.

"Bad mouths me?" Shana repeats, hoping Dr. Marcos would elaborate on what he means.

"Saying you ran away, quitting because you couldn't find him, I don't know."

"Oh, you're loving this aren't you Doc?"

"You have no idea," he smirks.

They pull up to the café, and park in the parking lot across the road, Shana can see a man with a camera on his side. He is wearing a gray jacket, opened to reveal an off-green fitted shirt that sat right below the belt of his whitewashed off jeans, with some weird European shoes. He fits the model/actor bill perfectly.

He is unshaven with a short stubble beard that matched his slight caramel blonde wavy hair. He looks to be around the same age as Shana.

"This should be fun," Shana says to Dr. Marcos as they cross the road.

"Don't mention the commercial." Dr. Marcos insists, feeling sorry for the kid.

"Don't provoke me, and I won't." Shana laughs.

"Shana!"

"Fine, fine, I'll play nice."

He stands up to greet them.

"Hi, I'm Andrew." he introduces himself, shaking Shana's hand.

"Nice to meet you." Shana returns the greeting

"Thanks for seeing us." Dr. Marcos steps in.

"You must be Dr. Marcos."

"Yes son, take a seat."

They all sit down and order coffee.

"What is it you want from me exactly?" Andrew asks.

"Well, here's the thing Andrew, we have been bombarded with journalists wanting this story, we have moved CNN, Fox, and all large newspapers out of the way because basically, we want to be able to monitor what is written,"

Andrew is all ears, excitement clear on his face.

"Dr. Marcos here vouched for you. Feels your work has heart and compassion." Tilting her head to the side, hoping he was right.

"Well, I have received employee of the month three months ago," Andrew replies egotistically, not realizing that Shana is making all this up.

Dr. Marcos crosses his arms, not liking the lying that is going on.

"Well, the truth is I didn't want you because after we investigated your history, I came across a commercial you did?" Dr. Marcos groans next to her.

"Oh, that's in the past; I promise it does not affect who reads my articles now." He blushes.

"Ok I believe you; Dr. Marcos are you sure he is the one?" Shana asks, turning to him with an eyebrow raised.

Dr. Marcos has his hands crossed, upset with Shana bringing up something she promised she wouldn't.

"Yes, I can vouch for him," he replies straightforwardly.

"Then you're the man," Shana replies as she hands him an envelope and informed him what she needs to be printed. He is surprised that he would have to slightly bad mouth her, but if it means that he is releasing an article that cause chaos then he is ready for the media attention.

"Andrew, I warn you, you will get a headache from the New Chief of Police, and they will retaliate and probably arrest you concerning further investigating where you got your information from. After you copy and print the article, you are to burn these documents. If you don't, then I'm afraid you will be locked up. Because as much as I hate to admit it, this meeting never took place." Shana is in his face, with her hands firm on the table. Everything is going perfectly according to plan - well for now anyway.

***

After the meeting, Shana drops off Dr. Marcos and goes to meet with Ryan.

She sees him sitting in the restaurant; she smiles and makes her way in.

"When this is all over, let just disappear for a while," Shana whispers in Ryan's ear as she leans in behind him.

"I promise," he replies holding her hand.

She moves and makes her way to the empty chair that is waiting for her.

"Shana I'll get straight to it; I want this shit out of the way. I'm here to help, and I'll do whatever it takes to get Sogoto and make sure nothing happens to you, but after this no more!" Ryan is all but begging.

"Ok, no more!" Shana knows she is putting a lot of pressure on everyone around her, she is overwhelmed, but she needs to stay focused. She is so close to the end.

"I just need you around and worrying about you all the time is exhausting. I always thought with forensics, you would be locked up in some lab, doing some tests, away from the psychos of the world."

"You thought wrong, my darling." She places her hand on top of his.

"You're telling me," He replies sarcastically. "Tell me about your mother?"

Shana hands over the file; Ryan reads it and shakes his head.

"Have a look at this," Ryan suggests as he hands Shana a file. It is the 911 emergency phone call made by the hitchhikers to report her mother missing. Shana reads the transcript, and notices what Ryan is trying to point out, at the time of death; it was around the same time her father had reported her missing.

"That would be crazy." Shana's eyes are wide open. Her breathing elevates.

Ryan can't reply and remains speechless until he suggests,

"You're the forensic scientist. It could be coincidental. Was she supposed to be somewhere at that time, was she meeting someone?"

"I don't know Ryan. I haven't spoken to my dad in days, and he thinks I'm at Portia's house camping out as he told me to."

"That's bullshit, Shana and you know it."

"What?" Shana softly replies, upset with Ryan's sudden outburst.

"What do you take your father for? When Tim and Louise got themselves fired; your dad thought it was a little suspicious. Around the time Sogoto was back, he came into the office to speak to the new Chief. They were in the office together for hours."

"Shit! SHIT!" Shana leans back and gnaw at her thumbnail. Panic is starting to creep in.

"Ryan, he can't have killed my mother. He loved her so much." Shana explains faithfully.

"I didn't say that Shana!"

"I know, but just in case you were thinking it. DON'T!"

"Let's just eat. No more case talking. Let's just be Ryan and Shana. Two simple people."

"Who just meet?" Shana smirks.

"Sorry?" Ryan asks, confused at her request.

"Hi, my name is Shana." She goes into the character of meeting Ryan for the first time.

Ryan smiles, knowing what game they are playing, and plays along.

"Hi, I am Ryan, are you by chance my blind date?"

"Yes, I am," Shana replies, acting a little shy and embarrassed.

"You're so beautiful, I just want to take you home." the love shines clear in his eyes.

"Really? Baby, that was lame! You're a bad first date person."
Shana replies, they both laughed.

"Let's just eat; I'm good at that!" Ryan laughs it off and waves at
the waiter letting him know they are ready to order.

It is time well spent.

Shana heads home knowing that by tomorrow, everything will
be ready. The press release is close by, and by then according to
the plan, Karen will be in the safe house. A few trails lead him to
her, and then they will be ready.

***

CHAPTER 41

"In the chaos of a storm, your only friend is a shelter"

"Shana! You need to get to the hospital now! You need to get Karen out of there now!"

Shana has been woken up by her phone and then alerted by the screaming voice on the other side of the phone!

"What are you talking about?" Shana was now out of bed and getting dressed.

"The press release happened this morning, at five am to be exact! It's all over the news, in the papers!" Portia yells.

"What are you talking about? This was scheduled for tomorrow!" Portia wouldn't stop screaming.

"You promised to take care of her Shana!"

"He was supposed to release it tomorrow, I'm coming now!"

Shana quickly gets dressed, grabs her phone, and calls Dr. Marcos as she puts her shoes on.

She turns the television on, and it is all about Sogoto's case, and a picture of the girl that got away! Shana is fuming.

"What guy did you find?" Shana was yelling furiously as Dr. Marcos answers, "We asked to release it tomorrow, and how did he get it to TV, to everyone, it's everywhere?"

"Well, I guess an eager beaver?" He didn't seem too worried.

"This is not good!" Shana responds annoyed, not knowing what else to say.

"Get to Monica, get the team together, we need to push everything a day forward and now, can you do that without fucking it up?"

"After my coffee, yes"

"Dr. Marcos, PLEASE!"

"Ok, ok,"

It was now six am, so she can only hope that Sogoto is sleeping in, although very unlikely.

Shana tunes in to the morning news on her car radio, and there again they speak of the serial killer; she rushes through the morning traffic to get to Karen.

Her phone is ringing.

"The place is ready, there will be a car waiting at the address I just messaged you, get there in twenty minutes,"

"Thank you," It was Walter, he knows that everything is now pushed a day forward. Shana is grateful that everything was in place, but she has to drive much faster to get there on time. She parks right in front of the hospital and notices Portia's car was there. She quickly calls Portia to let her up, but Portia is already at the door waiting. She hangs up and runs toward her.

**

Sogoto has heard the news. The television is running twenty-four hours in his apartment, and he pauses it when he comes across Karen's photo. He looks at her closely, a recent photo had been taken, and this was with something that looks familiar. It is the same hospital Shana's father was once at. Sogoto knows exactly where it was. *Perfect.*

Sogoto is dressed in a large coat, making his way into the hospital. He is his calm self, and he is ready. He always had a plan. He calls down the person currently at the psychiatric ward and sends the nurse at the front desk for coffee with an easy smile. *Women were easy creatures.* When the doctor arrives, Sogoto pulls a gun out and takes him into the laundry room, hand firmly over his mouth just in case the doctor is feeling brave. He doesn't hesitate before hitting him over the head. Sogoto can't help but smile at how easy this was going as he watches the doctor crumple to the ground.

Dressed as if he was a part of the hospital now, he makes his way to level 5. Once on the floor, he takes a minute to look up and down the hallway. Sogoto stops for a second, this was a little too easy. Karen is walking causally in the hallway; she is waiting for Shana and Portia. Karen is no longer a psychiatric patient that needed to be locked up - she was free.

Sogoto sticks to his plan. He walks past her and bumps into Karen. Ever so gently, but just enough to place a transmitter tracking device on her without anyone noticing.

397

"So sorry dear." He nods before moving down the hallway further. *So easy.*

Now he has other things to attend to. Karen did not even notice. Her eyes are glued to the elevator as the elevator doors open.

He makes his way down, back to where he started. Just as if he had been there before. *So simple.*

***

"Some people are just so rude," Shana says, noticing the doctor that bumped into Karen.

"Karen is ready." Portia hands over Karen. She looks much better in her casual clothes, her collar white shirt, and jeans, even if she was still a little scared.

"Take my car." Portia hands over her keys to Shana, knowing her car was faster, and right now, Shana needs speed. "Thank you."

Shana grabs a hat from her bag and told Karen to put her hair in a bun and then Shana places the hat on her.

Then they are off. Shana places the address in the navigator. Fifteen minutes. *Shit.* She needs to be there in ten minutes. She knows if she was any later, her life will be gone, and then she is on her own.

Shana drives in and out of traffic, taking suburban streets and driving at high speed.

She is one minute away, and in front of her, she could see that the car was about to take off. She sped up, swerving the car right in front of the moving jeep, and coming to a stop.

"I'm here, we're here. Please - please!"

"We have to go now!" they both quickly hop into the car as Shana quickly moves and locks Portia's car to the side. They are off again.

The driver looks over to the passenger, both dressed in similar suits to those of Walter and Steve, Shana knows they were all from the same crew. The best special agents possible. She feels safe for the first time in a while.

"Make sure we're not followed."

He looks over and used the review mirror as they are merging in and out of traffic

"We're clear," the passenger finally replies.

Shana and Karen sigh a breath of relief. They have made it.

Shana's phone rings, it is Monica.

"Yes Monica?" the passenger leans over and grabs Shana's phone and launches it out the window.

"What was that for?!"

"Here is your new phone." he hands over a new phone, "You need a secure line, and this is it."

Shana types in Monica's number, thanking her photographic memory.

"Sorry Monica."

"Shana, we have a problem!"

"Oh God, what now?" Shana asks, terrified as flashes of everything that can be wrong dance in her mind.

"We went to pick up Detective Grant's wife and son but they're not home. We tried to contact them, but we are getting nothing!"

"Did someone break into the house?"

"Yes, and it was left as is. She must have packed a few suitcases after the news broadcast and decided to take off, or……. someone's taken them!"

"Find them!" Shana demands

"I don't know where to start!" Monica yells back.

"Monica, this is what you do! Call Ryan and find them, run the plates!"

"Shana, she didn't take her car," Monica says patiently.

"We will call the cab companies. Shit! Shit! Figure it out!" Shana instructs, fear creeping into her voice.

"Ok," Monica replies, unsure of what more she could do. The rest of the ride is in silence. Something Shana is grateful for. It gives her a chance to think.

They finally made it to the safe house and found Louise and Tim waiting inside.

"I promise Karen, I'll be back." Shana hands over the files she promised Karen as she moves to leave the car, and covertly slips her a pocketknife. Karen takes the knife and places it quickly in her jacket.

"Please don't leave me here, please!" Karen begs, placing both her hands together as if she is about to pray.

"You are with one government agent, two of the best forensic units and all are armed, I just need to make sure everything else is going according to plan, please trust me," Shana reassures her.

Karen nods, slowly letting go of Shana's hand. Shana jumps in the passenger seat while the driver heads back to where she parked Portia's car. There was so much going on, and all because of that idiot journalist. Shana doesn't like to be rushed. Rushing led to mistakes, and they can't afford any mistakes when it came to Sogoto.

***

She gets to Portia's car and drives straight to Monica's house. Ryan is there, and they're looking over the computer. Shana quickly jumps in to see what they were looking at.

"It appears that Grant's wife hired a car that morning. She made a few calls from her cell phone before it was turned off the last call was this number…" Shana looks closely at the screen.

"I've seen that number before, where have I seen it?"

She paces, wracking her memory, trying to remember, "Oh I know. That is her sister's home, they used to go there every thanksgiving, Grant would call us from there. That's one hour from here, she is going there." She gets her phone out and calls.

"Hi, my name is Shana and I know Tina and her son Jay well. I am Chief George Watson's daughter."

"You work in forensics?"

"That's right, I know that Tina is heading your way, and I need to know when you're expecting her, she could be in trouble"

"She called me, telling me that she is going away for a while, and not to worry, that she can't talk to me. I didn't understand it until I saw the news this morning. Is it true Shana? That Asian criminal is back for them?"

"That's a part of his plan., Did she say anything, anything at all?" Shana asks, pacing.

"NO, no she was only saying goodbye. Oh God, why didn't she come here?"

"Did you ask her where she was going?"

"Yes, she said, where she feels most safe!"

"Do you know where that is? Please it's important, her life is at stake. I need you to think hard." Shana all but begs.

"No nothing, Ohhh wait!"

"What is it?"

"She always felt safest in our holiday home in Calabasas, oh maybe she is there!"

Shana quickly writes down the address and asks her not to talk to anyone or use her phone.

"Monica, you stay here." She notices that Monica was making her way to the door

"Why?"

"Because we always need someone on-site, and also if anything happens, I need you to look after Karen, I promised her we would."

"Ok, be safe!" she agrees but Shana can see a little disappointment on her face.

Shana and Ryan jump in the car and rush off to the Calabasas' location.

"Why is she going there? Sogoto would know that address." Ryan points out.

"I don't know Ryan; let's just hope he is too busy with Karen's news that he doesn't have time for them."

"I hope you're right!"

"Me too."

The traffic is heavy, Shana feels a little more relaxed when she sees the sign '*Calabasas*'

They exit the freeway, making their way to the place.

Shana parks right in front of the house; there is already a car in the driveway. Shana places her hand on the hood.

"It's warm," Shana observes, knowing she must have just arrived.

Shana is walking to the house when Ryan hisses her name.

"What's wrong?"

"Look!" Ryan was pointing to the parked vehicle one house down. It is a motorbike, it is Sogoto's motorbike.

They covertly pull out their guns and make their way to the side of the house, with their backs against the wall.

"Oh God, Ryan!" her heart feels like it was about to jump through her throat.

"Shana let's not make the same mistake; I'm calling it in!"

Shana nods, knowing it was the right thing to do

As Ryan calls it in, they hear a woman scream.

"Ryan, we have to go in."

"Ok, but behind me," Ryan instructs, looking conflicted and worried.

As Ryan was walking to the front of the house, he notices a familiar car a couple of houses down. It catches his eye, but Shana had not seen it. It was George Watson's car.

Ryan is confused as to why he would be here. There is no time to tell Shana however, as they are already at the door.

Ryan kicks the door in, and they cautiously walk in. The loud screams are coming from upstairs. As they get halfway up the stairs, the screaming stops.

Shana and Ryan walk into the room to be confronted with two dead bodies, the mother, and her child, and Sogoto standing with his gun pulled at the Chief who was tied down to a chair.

"Do you always have to bring your boyfriend everywhere you go?" Sogoto asks, smirking maliciously.

Shana's hands are shaking, Ryan also had his gun drawn. Her father's mouth is taped, but through his yelling, she understood he was saying *"Just shoot him"*

"Now, George why do you want her to kill me? We have so much to tell her, then she can decide whether it is ME she wants to shoot, or YOU!" he digs the barrel of the gun in his head.

"Put your gun down Sogoto, it's over." Shana is surprised her voice sounds so firm. She feels sick.

"Shana, I'm just going to take the shot," Ryan whispers to Shana who nods.

Sogoto then points his gun in Ryan's direction and shoots him in his leg before they could react. Ryan falls to the floor with a scream, sending the gun flying out of his hand. Quickly, Sogoto kicks Ryan's gun behind him and went back to where he was. Shana runs to Ryan's aid, "You son of a bitch," Shana screams at Sogoto.

Shana couldn't take all of this "Ryan, stay with me, RYAN!" Shana shakes him in panic.

"I'm ok, I'm ok." Ryan groans in pain.

"What more do you want? Just fucking kill us all and fuck off!" Shana shouts anxiously. She had thought she is ready to face him, but it is too much,

"You finished?" Sogoto sighs.

"No Sogoto, it will be finished when you are dead!" Shana is shaking with anger.

Sogoto just laughs, walking around the furniture and stroking things as he speaks ever so casually.

"How did your mother die?" He asks suddenly.

"You killed her!" she snarls.

"No, No, I was going to, but someone beat me to it!"

George is trying to scream through the tape over his mouth. Shifting in his seat, he tries to loosen the tape around his hands,

"Your mommy wanted to leave your daddy, but your daddy was obsessed with trying to catch me. He would drink at the bar every night, and continued looking, the best part was that I was watching his every move."

The screaming and kicking from George are getting louder.

"Now, now George did you want to say something?" Sogoto smirks, barely giving the tied up ex-chief a glance before looking back to Shana.

"Well George seems a little tied up at the moment, so I guess I'll tell you the story."

She is trying to keep it together. Shana doesn't know if she was ready to hear this, even though all she ever wanted was the truth. She takes a breath in.

"Your mother couldn't take your father's absence, late nights, drunken behavior, and obsession with me. She had enough. Do you blame her?"

Shana is applying pressure to Ryan's wound, listening carefully.

"The night your mother died, I was at the bedroom patio, right outside ready to make my way in. I wanted to kill your father first, your mother, and then you."

Shana gawks as he continues "Don't look so surprised, you are sure to know about the NPA by now. After your father fucked up my plan, I thought I'd leave him until the end. Your mother was packing ready to leave, and your parents were fighting."

Shana's eyes slightly watered as she remembered being three years old, and hearing screams as she lay in bed. She had tried to place the covers over her head, to block out the noise. Shana gasps for air.

"George, being the drunk husband, grabbed her trying to stop her. Your mother was trying to get her arms free, but he grabbed her and threw her across the room."

Shana remembers the powerfully loud bang she heard, it had made her jump out of bed, and run to her mother's room. She had pushed the door open, and her father quick to respond, telling her everything was okay. Shana had nodded at the time, but now she saw something her mind did not let her see at three years old, from the reflection of the mirror, she could see her mother's foot on the floor. Lifeless.

"Oh God! No. No." Shana wept, the tears rolling down the sides of her cheeks as she looks at her father, who now appears lifeless himself as he sat there, mourning, and ashamed.

"Shall I finish?" Sogoto asks rhetorically, clearly excited to continue. "Or wait, maybe your father has something to say after all."

He rips the strong reinforced tape off George's mouth. Ryan, even though wounded, tries to hold Shana's hand to comfort her, but she doesn't want to be touched or held. Her skin feels like it is crawling with the new information.

George starts screaming as the tape is removed "You fucking son of a bitch, I will shred you to pieces. I will kill you with my bare hands."

"Is it true?" Shana asks, looking at her father. George looks at her, not knowing where to start.

"Is it true George?!" Shana roars, not being able to say Dad anymore.

"Shana, no it's not true; you're going to believe this psycho? Shana, it's not true."

Sogoto hits George with the back of the gun on his head, Shana screams. In her anger, she had forgotten that Sogoto still has a gun.

"Tell her the truth." He demands as he went to hit him again, however just as he was about to make contact, George speaks.

"Okay...okay, I'll tell her," George replies softly

"Shana, I didn't want her to leave, I didn't know what I was doing. I would never hurt your mother. I loved Cherie, but she wanted to leave me and take you with her. I went crazy, I grabbed her, but she was trying to pull me off. I...I thought I pushed her away from the suitcase, from packing. Instead, she hit the side of the table and fell to the floor. I tried to wake her, but her head was bleeding. Oh God, I didn't mean to kill her, I didn't mean it, I didn't know what to do, Shana I was scared!"

"You were scared?" Shana yells furiously, wanting George to pay for what he did. "You were scared! You killed my mother, and you were worried about being scared? You disgusting son of a bitch, you threw her body on the side of the road, like she was nothing!"

"No that's not true Shana that wasn't me; I didn't know he was going to dump her body there!"

"You didn't know? Who the fuck dumped her body?" Shana laughs resentfully as the answer comes to her. "Grant, Detective James fucking Grant!"

George couldn't lie anymore, he nods, "and you wrapped Mom up and got rid of her? You closed the case and moved along; you have been lying to me for over twenty years! You're a murderer!"

Shana pulls her gun and points it at her father, "You're some piece of work. You corrupt piece of shit of a father. You took my mother away from me and fed me some fabricated bullshit story!"

"Shana put the gun down. If you pull that trigger, then you are no better than him. Baby please, please put the gun down." Ryan grunts, reaching over to lay a hand on the gun.

Shana stands up not listening to Ryan; she wants this monster that was just as bad as Sogoto in her eyes, dead.

"All these years, you're going to pay for all those years." Shana threatens him.

"Shana is this what your mother would want?" he replies, trying to negotiate and convince her to stop.

"Why didn't you kill him then? Why wait? Why not kill us all?" Shana's breathing is out of control, she is shaking and feels like her heart is about to jump out of her chest.

"Oh, I was going to," Sogoto replies, watching closely. "I went to your room and watched you hide under the covers when you were frightened, trying to block out everything. I guess I felt a little sorry for you!"

"No, you didn't feel sorry for me, you felt sorry for you! Your father killed your mother in front of you. This reminded you of you. You looked at me watched as I sat alone in the room, and remembered what you had gone through, and that's when you realized you couldn't do it!"

Sogoto doesn't respond.

"Let me see, after I kill my dad, I mean George..." she is shaking "You will kill us, that was your motive all along. Right?"

"If it makes you feel better than just kill me, Shana. God knows I'm dead inside, kill me and put me at ease." George finally speaks, he looks up straight into his daughter's eyes.

"You didn't just lose your wife. You no longer have a daughter; I'll leave you to suffer."

Shana drops her hand; the gun is getting heavy. She knows couldn't shoot her dad, and Ryan sighs, knowing that Shana did the right thing.

"NO! This was not how this was supposed to go!" Sogoto screams.

Sogoto opens the bedroom window, his eyes glued to them, a noise outside caught his attention for a split second. But that split second was all that Shana needs. Shana finds her moment and takes a shot at Sogoto and got his shoulder. Sogoto is quick to turn around and fire back, but by that time Shana has thrown herself behind a table, tipping it over and taking cover behind it.

Sogoto fires a few more shots before he jumps out the window. Shana hears his bike start and he was off.

"Get me out of this, I can help you," George demands. Shana looks at him and turns to Ryan.

"I'll call for help from the car, I have to go, Ryan, I'm sorry."

"Shana… please we'll catch him later!"

Shana is already down the stairs, she jumps in her car, and in the distance, she can see his motorbike. Shana slams her foot on the accelerator and rushes off.

He is swerving in and out of traffic, Shana knows she doesn't need to call for help. She knows Ryan will call it in for her.

***

"Ryan, he's going to kill her. He's going to find Karen, the last puzzle, and kill her and then kill Shana. He could have killed me now; he is saving me until the end." George begs.

Ryan can't even look at George; he was lying on the floor in pain. He has just called it in, and he has no more energy. Who knew leg wounds hurt so damn much?

"Please get me out of this, I know I have lost her, but I would prefer to lose her alive, not dead."

"Let's just wait for backup." Ryan doesn't even want to talk to him.

"Ryan if she dies, I'll fucking kill you! If you really love her, then please, I beg you get me out of these!" George rattles the chair.

Ryan agrees, George has a point. Who knows Sogoto more than George, and George could go save Shana while Ryan physically couldn't?

Ryan crawls across the floor, dragging his leg toward George. He pulls a pocketknife from his pocket and releases him from the tight grip of the tape.

The sirens are closing in; the police and ambulance are on their way. George needs to be out of there before they came, it was too close. The cars are now parked outside. George is free. As the police make their way into the house, George runs into another room, taking with him Ryan's gun. He walks over one of the dead bodies and jumps out the window, landing on his side. Even though he gets hurt, he gets up quickly, before running through the backyard and jumping the neighbor's fence, and casually makes his way to his car.

He needs to find out where they had located Karen.

George knows something was going on, the minute he sensed that Shana was not at Portia's house he had followed her, finding out they are meeting at Monica's house and noticing Dr. Marcos was there with the rest of the team.

That was where he can at least start.

***

CHAPTER 42

"The lie kept trying to run, but the truth outsmarted it and caught up in the end"

Portia jumps as her phone rings. It is Shana.

"Portia, listen to me very clearly, the coast is clear. Get to my dad's. In his office under the carpet, there will be a door that will lead you to another room. In there, there is a safe, the code is seven, Two, Six, Five, and Three. In there, you will find the negatives and the photos you want. Get them and burn them, this is the only chance you get. He is on to us, I know it."

"I'm heading, there, where are you?" Portia asks, worrying about Shana's tone.

"Just tell me when you have it."

"Ok, ok." Portia quickly grabs her keys and runs out the door, freedom was now close for her.

Portia parks down the road, jumps out of her car, and runs up the house, she knows where the spare key was and makes her way in. Portia runs into George's office and lifts two carpets lying in the room until she finds the secret floor. She is panicking and the carpet keeps slipping out of her sweaty hands. She opens the door and climbs down. In there is a wall of guns, a table, lots of files and boxes, and they're right on the back as Shana said is the lock. It is something right out of a spy movie, the sight of all this doesn't help her nerves.

Portia's hands are shaking as she is turning the lock, finally, the sound of the click and the safe is now open. She sees lots of files, money, some jewelry but there in the right corner was an envelope with 'Portia' scribbled across it. She opens the envelope carefully, and there are the photos. She looks at the negatives, bringing them closer to the light to make sure that was them. She isn't going to leave those behind.

Portia jumps as she hears the front door open. She quickly places the envelope behind her back in her pants and climbs up to the office level. There in the hallway stood George, sweating and panicking. The top of his forehead slightly bleeding. He is going through some files on the computer, looking up something.

Portia is traumatized; she doesn't know what to do. She then remembers Shana's room upstairs. Right outside the window was the tree Shana and she used when they were kids to sneak out and sneak back in. It is safer for her to go up then go out the back then go through the front. Portia hides behind the walls, and while he is distracted on the computer, sneaks up the stairs quietly into Shana's room.

As she enters the bedroom, she hears a loud yell. George must have noticed the carpets. This noise startles Portia, and she accidentally knocks on a photo frame near Shana's old bed. Straight away, she hears George making his way up the stairs. Portia quickly opens the window, jumps on the tree, and falls to the ground scratching her hands and legs. She quickly gets up and runs as fast as she could to the car, not looking back.

George picks up a light cloth to press on his bleeding head and calls the number that he has looked up on the screen.

"Tim, this is Wayne, we have a huge problem, you relocated the girl to the wrong place, you're currently on speaker, and I need you to clarify your location!" He deepens his voice so as not to give away his lie.

"But how is that possible? Didn't you guys notify them to drop us off here?" Tim responds, confused.

"Listen here, I am currently sitting in the room with the Vice President. We thought we were dropping off the two other victims who are now dead because of Shana and this team! You have all messed things up! Detective Grant's family is dead!"

George has his phone connected to the computer waiting for the green light to appear, now that the tracking was in progress.

"Is Karen with you right now?" George ignores Tim's splutters on the other end. He tries to keep him on the phone longer to get a signal to an address.

"Yes, she is."

"You need to get her out of there and to another location."

"Where to exactly?" Tim asks sounding worried. Idiot.

"Anywhere is safer than where she is right now!"

"Hey Tim, Wayne, and Tyler are here, what seems to be the problem?" he hears a woman over the line.

Shit! George only needed just three more seconds.

"I'm on the phone with Wayne!" Tim replies clearly confused.

"No, you're not because I was just speaking to him!" George can hear the woman's confused response.

"Who is this?" The three seconds are achieved successfully, and the location is visible on the computer. He knows exactly where Tim and Karen are, he knows exactly where Shana and Sogoto are heading.

***

Shana is closing in on Sogoto, accelerating at a speed she had never experienced before. Sogoto takes a sharp left, and Shana has to slow down to get in the ally way. He takes a sharp right, and then again, another sharp left. Shana follows straight behind him until she turns another corner and ended up in a maze-like scenario. She is uncertain whether to go left or right, it is as if Sogoto has disappeared.

"Shit! Shit!" Shana mutters: she knows he is heading to Karen. She reverses out of the ally way adjacent to the top of the main road and heads toward the safe house. Just as she hit the main road speeding, she hears a motorbike, looking in front of her she sees nothing. However, as she glances in her review mirror, there is Sogoto.

"You clever son of a bitch!" Shana mutters.

Sogoto fires three shots, one in each back tire, and then straight into the petrol tank. The car is now spinning out of control. Shana's car smashes into oncoming traffic. Her body is thrown around, leaving her head hitting the side of the window before the car comes to a stop. She is slightly squashed in the car and winded, along with multiple bruises, cuts, and aberrations. She tries to get hold of her phone which is squashed under the seat.

She can see it, but the accident had squashed it in far in that it was almost impossible. Her fingertips graze the phone. She can smell smoke, the front of the car was on fire, *'just one more time'* she thinks and shoves her hand down, the metal cutting through her skin. She screams as she pushes it over and over again. Before she can do anything else, she is dragged out of the car by bystanders, right as the car went up in flames. She breathes shakily. She has managed to press the button before they pulled her out that will have locked in her position. She just hopes someone was paying attention.

***

Monica has just gotten off the phone with Louise, having found out that the safe house has been compromised and Sogoto could be on his way. Monica gets in the car as Dr. Marcos jumps into the passenger seat, not wanting to let Sogoto getaway.

"Where do you think you're going?"

"You're not leaving me here!" Dr. Marcos insists. He was as much involved as everyone else.

"Fine," Monica replies quickly, having no time to spare. "Excuse me on my driving!"

"Oh God knows I'm used to it now. Driving with Shana is like a roller coaster ride." The doctor replies, but he can tell Monica isn't listening.

Monica's phone beeps, a green dot comes up on her screen, and a location, it was not far from where she was. Monica quickly makes a sharp U-turn and heads toward the green light.

Monica sees Shana on the side of the road with her car on fire. People are milling around her, but she is pushing them off.

Monica can see the bruises and small cuts on her face from here. The blood dripping off her hand is alarming. She pulls up near Shana and honks.

Shana jumps in the back seat of the car as the car came to a stop.

"What happened?" Monica asks, worrying about all the blood.

"No time to explain, just get to Karen now!" Shana pleads, while she is pulling a small piece of glass out of her hand.

"Why is Dr. Marcos here?" Shana asks in agony as the glass came out. *Finally!*

"Oh please, now you don't need me. I wasn't going to miss this." He cleans his glasses casually with his handkerchief before handing it over to Shana to slow the bleeding.

"This isn't a show or a game Dr. Marcos." Shana snaps, irritated at how calm he was.

"Oh, I am well aware of that," he replies. She knows that he wants to be there right up until the end. She can't blame him – he has been involved since the beginning as well. With that, he leans back to help Shana with her cuts and they both exchange a slight smile. They are closing in on Sogoto, and they both know it.

***

CHAPTER 43

"Can you see that? Look. Can you hear that?
Listen. Most can see, but not all will clearly look.
Most can hear but not all will listen."

Ryan is well looked after at the hospital. He remembers the look of Shana's face as Sogoto divulged the story of her mother's death. He looks up and sees the traffic report and notices Shana's plate number from the burning car. The nurse hands over his antibiotics before exiting the room. Ryan quickly pulls out the drip in his arms, gobbles the antibiotics down, and limps out of the hospital. His leg wound is superficial and only a little painful and won't stop him from getting to her.

Ryan all but ran out to the front of the hospital. He looks around, trying to be quick as possible; no cars with people going either in or out were in sight, all cars appear parked and locked. Until a car pulled in, it was an elderly man driving. He opens the boot of the funeral car and out came several orderlies, placing a body in the back.

Ryan watches, feeling mildly morbid as a plan comes to his mind.

"A 1974 Cadillac miller and meteor traditional hearse, beautiful isn't it?" The old man says, noticing Ryan gaze at his car. The man is throwing the keys up in the air and catching them, back and forth. Ryan's eyes follow the motion of the keys. *Up. Down.*

"Yes, it is," Ryan replies, trying to further avoid any attention as the orderlies head back inside.

"You know it's got 38-year-old interior leather and a new engine in place."

Ryan knows he is going to regret this.

"When is this body going to be buried?" Ryan asks.

"Ah... first thing tomorrow morning." He throws the keys back in the air.

This time Ryan catches them and runs around to the driver's side before jumping in.

"Hey what are you doing? Are you crazy?" the elderly man screams.

"I'll have it back to you before the funeral." and Ryan drives off.

Ryan knows he is driving too fast, already forgetting that there is a dead body in the back.

Ryan hears a *thump,* as he makes a sharp turn on the freeway. The body turns over to reveal an incredibly old lady wearing just a hospital garment, thrown on her side.

"Fuck!" he exclaims, knowing this is officially the point of no return.

Ryan looks around and notices a large jacket on the passenger seat, grabs it, and places it over the dead woman's thighs and buttocks. Every time he looks in the review mirror, he would have seen her saggy backside, he doesn't want the distraction. The jacket does the trick for now.

***

Sogoto pulls up and shields his motorbike in the bushes and by foot, runs a mile straight to the side of the house. He notices one man in uniform running around a government car, and he knows they are planning to get Karen out of there. Sogoto knows what he has to do. He quickly moves behind the vehicle and as the car starts, he makes his way to the driver's side. Just as the man sees Sogoto in his side mirror, it is too late. Sogoto flings the door open and blocks the hand moving toward his gun and stabs the cop straight in his neck. The gurgling sound was annoying Sogoto, to finish him off he simply grabs his head and twists his neck. He takes the body out and places it on the side of the house, just a few meters from the car. He takes the man's glasses off his face and the man's jacket, before getting into the car. *They will come to him.*

***

Monica pulls in, parking the car in front of the house, and Shana quickly notices the blood on the ground and follows the trail to where a man is dumped. She quickly looks at Monica with alarm.

"He is here." Monica nods and walks around the other side, while Shana takes the other side.

Shana sees Wayne's partner on the floor and notices the car was gone. Her worst fear is about to come true.

Dr. Marcos sits in the car, nervously waiting to see what will happen. Then he notices a car speeding in. It is Shana's father.

421

Great! He thinks. He doesn't like him very much and after reading the autopsy report regarding Cherie, he knows all too well what had happened. Liars didn't sit well with him.

George pulls up and sees Dr. Marcos in the car, "Where is Shana?"

"She went that way!" he answers, pointing to the direction Shana was. He may not like the man, but he knows George will protect her. And Shana needs all the help she can get.

George quickly arms his gun and runs toward the side of the house.

Monica has her gun out ready. Then a car pulls up and Wayne opens the door and Karen gets in. Shana quickly realizes Sogoto is driving at the same time Wayne opens the passenger seat to get into the car.

"NO!" Shana screams at the top of her lungs. "Sogoto is driving the car!"

Wayne turns to see Sogoto with a gun pulled at him. He tries to move quickly, but Sogoto is too fast. He shoots twice. Wayne is down, bleeding tediously from the stomach wounds. He is dying. Tim and Louise are on the ground, taking cover, and Shana shoots at the car, before realizing that it is bulletproof.

Monica sees the car coming her way. She too tries to take a few shots, but it is useless.

Sogoto uses this to his advantage, and he turns the car back around.

Monica quickly runs back to her car and pulls the gun on Dr. Marcos and yelling for him to "Get out!" She isn't going to let him get away.

"Monica, you can't do this on your own! Where is Shana?" Dr. Marcos warns, trying to calm her down.

"Get the fuck out, this is not a negotiation! GET OUT!" Dr. Marcos quickly follows her demands and gets out of the car. Not knowing where to go, he stands near the door.

Sogoto is driving toward Shana at full speed, but she isn't budging. Instead, she stands strong and focuses on aiming for the tires, but nothing is happening.

Sogoto opens the window and opens fire at her, George jumps in front of his daughter with a guttural cry. *Bang, bang, bang.* George is hit three times in the chest.

"You're not fucking dying are you Shana?!" Sogoto yells in rage.

He closes his window and turns to Karen who is now kicking and screaming. Keeping one hand on the steering wheel, Sogoto uses the other hand to grab Karen by her hair and pulls her towards him. He lets go of the steering wheel for a quick second to quickly punch her face hard enough to knock her out.

With her head now laying forwards on the hand brake, he pulls out a small box from his pocket. He pulls out a needle from the box, jamming Karen in her neck. He manages to get a small amount of liquid in before the needle breaks with a swerve on the road. He grabs her head, pushing it in the back of the car where the rest of her body was located. "Doesn't matter" thinks Sogoto, "this will keep her unconscious and fucking quiet for a while!"

Monica is right behind him. There is no way she is going to let him get away. *Not this time.* She thinks of hitting the petrol tank, but she can't, knowing that Karen is in there. She doesn't know how to stop the car and doesn't want to hurt her. She is getting close, even though she has no plan. Her only hope is backup!

Shana holds her father's hand. "I'm sorry, I'm sorry for everything!"

Shana sobs. She doesn't know what else to say. As angry as she is with him, she doesn't want him dead.

"Just forgive me, please forgive me!" he whispers.

Shana holds his hand tight and leans over to his ear to whisper, "I forgive you, Daddy."

George smiles and his eyes closed as he leaves this world.

Shana heaves a breath and closes his eyes. Taking a second to compose herself, she quickly runs towards where she parks the car only to see Dr. Marcos there but no car.

"Where is Monica?" Shana is confused.

"She left! She went after him." he points in the direction they took off in.

"Fuck!" she then notices her father's car. As she is running to get in, Tim runs up to her and hands her Wayne's phone.

"What this?" Shana asks in a rush.

"The tracking device on all government cars. This tells you where he is." She looks at it and nods. Tim knows what he has to do - call it in.

***

Shana is making her way out the long driveway and turning on the main road, just missing a car coming her way. It is Ryan!

"Pull over." Ryan is screaming, trying to keep up with her, now driving side-by-side, through oncoming traffic. Ryan swerves to the side, coming to a stop. Shana suddenly stops her car, and Ryan jumps out of the car, limping to the passenger side, before he gets in.

"What are you doing here?" she knows he should be in the hospital. Leg wounds are notorious for causing all kinds of issues.

"Helping you," Ryan replies. "Where is Sogoto?"

"Here." She hands over Wayne's phone.

"He's five miles ahead of us."

"Yes, he has Karen, and Monica is chasing him," Shana confirms placing the car back in drive and moving into the traffic.

"Oh God, this is not looking too good Shana."

"It will be fine, we will get him, we will!" Shana replies, trying to convince herself more so than Ryan.

"Dad's dead" she blurts out a few minutes later, unable to deal with the silence.

"Dead?"

"Yes, he died jumping in front of me. You shouldn't have cut him loose!" Shana swallows back her tears.

"Well, if he died saving you, then I'm glad I cut him loose!" Ryan barks out; Shana's eyes are watering; she doesn't have anything else to say.

"Four miles Shana," Ryan suggests, notifying Shana of Sogoto's directions.

* * *

Karen is slowly opening her eyes. Her head slightly leaning on the door behind Sogoto, was all fuzzy.

The realization of where she was, comes quickly. She knows all too well Sogoto is going to kill her and make her suffer.

Karen places her hand into her pocket and pulls out the pocketknife, sliding the blade out slowly. Just as she finally gets the blade out, Sogoto turns dramatically, overtaking traffic and the knife falls to the ground right near her feet. *Shit!*

"Ah, glad you're awake Karen." His voice sends shivers down her spine. "We are nearly there."

Karen is weak, but she knows she needs to get it together. She can't wait for someone to rescue her and as far as she was concerned, *no one was coming.*

Quite dizzy, she is trying to push the knife forward with what little energy she has in her legs so that she could at least get it close to her hand. She knows that she needs to distract him. Her best bet right now was to use his case against him.

"I know how you watched your father kill your mother. We have that in common you know. You watched someone kill someone you love - I watched you kill my family," Her words are slow and heavy. The drugs are clearly still in her system. Sogoto stays silent.

"I watched how you tied my dad up and cut him open, I heard the screams of my little brother. I heard how you killed my mother all because my father was assigned to an NPA, and they wouldn't let you in."

Sogoto does not respond. It only fuels her growing anger.

"You're the Ten-Ti. The firm believer of The Wise Monkeys. You saw evil and turned a blind eye, you heard evil and didn't say a word, but I'm confused. You are doing evil to those that have done evil. What happened to you?" frustratingly, there is still no response.

She tries to get some sort of reaction. "Ironically, you became exactly like your father!"

"I am nothing like him!" Sogoto yells at her as he is shaking his head in disagreement.

"Do you not kill?" Karen asks rhetorically.

"I kill people who ruined my life, who never gave me a chance. They saw evil when they saw me!"

"That's why you became a leader in The Wise Monkeys, the Holy God! So, you could judge others, but no one could ever judge you?" Karen sneers. "I bet on the sixtieth day you never sleep, because if your soul left your body, then you would have the worst punishment of all."

Sogoto is getting visibly angry. "I am the leader! I am the one in charge, if what I was doing was wrong, then I would have died. It's the universal law, the bad die! A fool is only cured by dying yet I am alive, alive!" he screams.

Karen now has her foot on the pocketknife. Without him noticing, she slides it toward her. Now it is finally in her hand. "You think you are the leader of the Kōshin people; you think you are Shuomen Kongo?"

Karen continues asking questions aiming to aggravate him. She starts a nervous laugh.

"Oh, how I will enjoy cutting you up. I am much stronger than Shuomen Kongo. I am more like the Kami Monkey." Sogoto snarls.

Karen laughs.

"Who? Masaru the Sacred Monkey and protector of the Hie Shrine? The Sacred Monkey that can overcome all obstacles and prevail against all evil? Did you know Masaru is considered a *demon*? He cheated the Kōshin rituals?" She is borderline hysterical now. It has been an incredibly stressful few hour.

"You're calling yourself a Monkey Demon; do you not find that funny?" the knife now at her fingertips. *Come on. A little more.*

"You Americans take a traditional ritual and make of it what you wish, but this has been around before the so-called Jesus God you people worship!"

"America didn't make up the fact that Japan has the largest suicide rate in the world. It's these bullshit beliefs that you have that make people crazy!" Karen can see she is getting to him; he is being challenged. Everything Shana has taught her is being used against him.

"Japan is known for its honorable deaths. You call them suicides, and we call it the true *Seppuku* – since you think you know so much…. did Shana mention how the true swordsman performed the ritual and it's a pure expression of grief!"

"We call it crazy!" Karen laughs, she has the knife in her hand. All she needs is for him to stick his hand out and try and grab her as he did earlier.

"You're going to die Sogoto, whether it's before you kill me or after, you're going to DIE! You won't get the chance of an honorable death." She laughs some more.

Sogoto pulls his hand back to grab her, keeping one hand on the steering wheel. Karen launches the knife into his hand, stabbing him as quickly as possible and then again, before leaning to the other side and stabbing his shoulder. Sogoto has both hands off the steering wheel, not expecting what has just happened. He begins to lose control of the car and there, in front of him, was a truck. He is trying to get back on the correct side of the road, but the car is now out of control. Karen is bouncing back and forth in the back. Knowing that the car is going to crash, she quickly puts her belt on, and hopes for the best. The car hit the front edge of the truck and rolls over repeatedly until it is ten meters away from the road with each bounce. Sogoto is being thrown around the car as Karen holds on for her dear life. The car finally comes to a stop.

***

Monica quickly merges her car to the side, loads her gun ready, and runs to the car. The car is upside down, and the driver's side is now on the opposite side of Monica. She creeps up from behind, holding her gun close to her. *Please God be with me now.*

She turns the corner quickly, pointing her gun to an open driver-side door. She sees Karen in the back, but no sign of Sogoto. Monica looks around but he is nowhere to be seen. She quickly leans into the back and grabs Karen, who shouts in pain. She quickly helps her out of the dismantled vehicle.

Karen is leaning over Monica about to stand on her two feet when she squeals. Monica knows from the look on her face that Sogoto is behind her. She quickly turns her head and there he is, with a gun pointed between her eyes. Monica freezes up. His body is grazed and bruised but it is the crazed look that makes Monica tremble.

"Get on your knees," Monica's eyes now glazed with tears. She knows she was going to die. She falls to the floor on her knees and places her head down. Karen, unable to stand, slid down next to her.

"Sogoto, please I beg you!" Karen weeps, pleading with him.

"Oh, do not worry little girl, I will not shoot you. You will pay your price of evil, as others have done. I will shoot her!"

"Please Sogoto!" Karen cries, not knowing what to do. She knows it has no effect on him. He has no heart.

Monica grabs Karen's hand, putting her at ease. Karen looks up at her, and Monica can feel the tears rolling down her face, "It's ok, I can finally see my Jake."

Sogoto steps closer with the tip of the gun only centimeters away. The sound of a twig breaking came from behind him, and he spins around. Ryan with a gun pulled on him comes into view. Shana comes from the other side also with a gun pointing at him. Monica gasps out in relief, squeezing the shocked Karen's hand tighter.

Sogoto then quickly with his left hand, pulls another gun from under his belt pointing one directly at Ryan and the other at Shana.

"If we die killing you, Sogoto, I'm fine with that!" Ryan smiles satisfied that he was not getting out of this alive. His eyes scan over Sogoto and notices that the car accident took a toll on him.

Karen can hear her mother's screams and her brother's cries. With the memory of her father hitting the floor dead, Karen picks up the gun. She is shaking, but she can't let Sogoto live. Monica notices that Karen has the gun, trying to quietly plead with her, she notices the intense rage in Karen's eyes, the veins in her forehead look as though they would burst.

Karen points the gun, and shoots, ignoring Shana's screams of *"NO"*. The bullet tears through Sogoto in the upper arm, causing him to lose his grip on one of the guns.

Ryan takes the opportunity and distraction to tackle Sogoto to the ground. He places both hands over the hand holding the remaining gun. Sogoto tries to fight him off, but they are both wounded. Shana tries to take a shot but is too afraid of hitting Ryan in the flurry of movement.

"Get the gun off Karen," Ryan yells at Monica. Karen is shaking violently; with the gun pointing clearly at Sogoto. Monica removes the gun from her hand slowly, as the *bang* of Shana's shot echoes. She manages to graze his leg but with the adrenaline pumping, he still won't let go of Ryan. Monica grabs Sogoto's gun and with a furious scowl on her face, she fires.

She misses, but it was enough to scare him and allows Ryan to get free. Monica holds the gun to Sogoto's head, ready to end it.

"Monica, listen to me! Jake wouldn't want you to pull that trigger!" Ryan grimaces in pain as he tries to stand. He can't let her become a killer.

"Let's do things according to plan! Come on, they're expecting us."

Monica then shoots her gun. "That's from Jake."

"No! Monica." They both moved forward, but notice he was still alive; she has only shot him in the arm.

"Shana, this man is not human, I swear he probably has a backup plan." Ryan shakes his head and grabs Shana's gun, hanging loosely in her hands. He shoots Sogoto in the other leg and nods as his wails filled the air. He is alive, but now unable to escape again.

"Can I have a turn?" Karen asks, adrenaline causing her to smile widely. She wants the chance to seek more revenge.

"You had the first shot, Karen, that's enough for now," Ryan instructs, putting away the gun.

They tape his hands and legs and throw him in the trunk of the car before Monica and Karen got in their car to then follow Ryan and Shana.

Shana takes her phone out and wrote a message before taking off *twenty minutes.*

They both smile and drive off.

Ryan gets a call on his phone. "Yes! Ok just hold on."

Even with Sogoto in the boot of the car, they didn't feel safe. *Not yet.*

"Shana, Dr. Marcos is at the airport flying one way to France, but I put him on a watch list, just in case he wanted to get away."

"He got there quick!" she snarks, rolling her eyes.

"What do I tell him?"

"Tell them to let him go, but make sure they search him thoroughly first."

Ryan smirks and sends over the message.

They are now heading into downtown Los Angeles, they turn into North Central Avenue, and there it was in front of them - the final destination. One man is standing outside who guided the two cars into the back hidden from the streets. They arrive at the *JAPANESE AMERICAN NATIONAL MUSEUM*. It is closed to the public now and quite eerie in the dark.

"You sure about this?" Ryan asks, clearly concerned with the outcome.

"What better place than the National Museum? It is full of rich heritage and the cultural identity of Japanese Americans. Patriotic if you ask me." Shana nods.

"Shana, you know they're Yakuza?" Ryan notes.

"Each to their own, I say, my darling! This was our agreement, and to be honest with you I would much rather do what they want, than deal with another organized crime syndicate. Anyway, Yakuza descended from honorable, Robin-Hood-like characters that defended their villages from roving bandits. I have always liked Robin Hood." Shana shrugs.

"Ok, let's do this" Ryan is convinced. Shana gets out of the car; Ryan moves slowly, his limp more pronounced. Monica and Karen walk up to where Shana was. Karen is looking a little confused.

The three men approach Shana and bow. Shana bows back politely as did the rest of the team, following Shana's lead.

They are dressed in *Hakama* traditional Japanese clothing. They wear what seem to be baggy pants that are tied at the waist and fall to the ankles. They are secured by four straps attached on the front of the garment, and two shorter straps attached on the rear. The rear of the garment has a rigid trapezoidal section.

Shana looks closely as she notices the seven deep pleats, two on the back and five on the front. She remembers reading that the pleats are said to represent the seven virtues of *Bushido*, considered essential to the Samurai way. Although they appear balanced, the arrangement of the front pleats is asymmetrical, and as such is an example of asymmetry in Japanese aesthetics.

The *Hakama* was made of stiff, striped silk, all in the color black, they wear them with black *montsuki kimono,* and on their feet is a white tab which was a divided-toe sock.

She knows that what they are wearing was worn on extremely formal occasions and at tea ceremonies, weddings, and funerals. It was one of the most important parts of traditional male formal dress. She remembers her trip to the Nara National Museum many years ago, located in Nara Park in Japan. She loves the permanent collection of Japanese cultural attire and history this museum had.

"We had no doubt!" his silvery voice is calm and pleasant.

"Oh, I'm sure you didn't." Shana pointing to the trunk of the car, eager to finally get this over with.

They open the truck and move to pull him out. Sogoto looks up and sees the man. For the first time ever, Shana notices fear in Sogoto's eyes. It is very satisfying.

As one, they drag him into the museum, Shana and the team follow.

It was a large open space, with many historical Japanese photos distributed all over the walls. Shana sees portraits of Tanaka

Mitsuyoshi. This was said to be one of the first portraits of a Japanese person taken in Japan. Another one is a portrait of Samurai warriors bounded by a strict code of honor and loyalty illustrated in its painting as they all stood leaning in together. They walk up to the second level *West Wing* gallery where Shana notices this section is devoted to archaeological materials. Buddhist and Shinto sculpture, ceramics, lacquer wares, textiles, armor, and cloisonné. They are stunning. The *East Wing* feature paintings, primarily of the Edo period. It is as if one was walking back in time as they climb each step. All around her are artifacts, and stories from the WWII Concentration Camp where the US placed hundreds of thousands of Japanese Americans in. They have even re-created a wooden house that housed families. The entire second floors preservation of replicas really impress Shana.

There, in the open gallery, are men all dressed the same, surrounding a metal table. Sogoto's body is placed on the table, and he tries to fight them away.

Then Sogoto finds his voice and screams. Shana and what was left of her team jump at the sudden noise.

Karen holds Monica's hand, slightly scared of what was happening. Ryan wraps an arm around Shana, leaning on her for strength in more ways than one. A small man move toward Sogoto and place a piece of large yellow tape across his mouth, cutting off the annoying noise. Shana shivers: the sound reminds her of how Grant sounded as he was being cut up.

All the men have Samurai swords on their side. The beautiful *Katan* curved so elegantly with its single-edged blade and long grip especially made to accommodate two hands.

"Thank you." He bows again. "You can go now."

Shana bows. Before she left, turns again, the question burning on the tip of her tongue.

"Can I just ask you one question?" she bows out of respect again.

"Yes."

"Why couldn't you catch him?"

"By Koshen tradition, we are not to go after the Ten-Tin, which has been flawed. We have to wait for him to come to us," he explains.

"What happens if you were to go after him then?" Shana's eyebrows rise, waiting for an answer.

Ryan places his hand on Shana's arm; she is asking too many questions and it is clear that the man is getting irritated.

"It's time for us to go," Ryan tells her quietly. Shana notices his arm and the pain on his face and understood that it truly was time for them to leave. She already has her answers. This is it. It is over.

"Thank you," Shana says one last time before making her way out. They are then ushered out of the building and just like that, the door shuts behind them.

Shana stares at the closed door. Taking a breath, she braces her hand on it. "Burn in Hell" she whispers.

She follows the rest of the crew who was leaning on the car. Driving off just didn't feel right yet. They can still hear the disturbingly loud grunts of Sogoto trying to make their way through the thick tape.

"That's it?" Karen asks, not understanding anything that had just happened.

"That's it!" Shana shrugs as she looks over at Monica for a better response.

"That's it!" Monica confirms as Ryan just nods in agreement.

Karen looks up "Shana, are you sure they're going to kill him?"

Shana grabs her and brings her closer, "just listen."

The four of them lean against the parked cars and listen to the sounds of the torture of the man who has made their lives so hard for so long. It was as if they are listening to Mozart's masterpiece, letting it wash away the past and calming their souls. They can feel the world's harmony settling over them. It somehow had overridden all feelings of despair, fear, and sadness. The waking feeling of genuine emancipation overcame them. It is the perfect sweet closure they all needed.

The End

***